Marcia Willett was born in Somerset, the youngest of five girls. After training to become a ballet dancer, she joined her sister's Dance Academy as ballet mistress. She then became a naval wife and her son was born in 1970. She now lives in Devon with her husband, Rodney, and their Newfoundland, Trubshawe.

Praise for Marcia Willett's novels:

'A genuine voice of our times' *The Times*

'Marcia Willett's particular magic flourishes once again. Her large and growing readership will find *Starting Over* as absorbing, endearing and enjoyable as any of her earlier novels'
Dartmouth Chronicle

'A strong story which explores all the different aspects of love . . . Set in the West Country, I almost felt compelled to get in the car and look for this idyllic place'
Worcester Evening News

'Woven together with plenty of suspense and surprise and quite a few touching moments, it all goes to make a wholly satisfying read' *Kingsbridge Gazette*

'This West Country author has a good ear for dialogue and engaging characters . . . it's a cosy, comfortable read'
South Wales Argus

[illegible] story, sympathetically told, of complex relationships, [illegible] the sort of uncontrollable crises that do happen to real [illegible]
Plymouth Evening Herald

Also by Marcia Willett

Those Who Serve
Thea's Parrot
The Courtyard
The Dipper
Hattie's Mill
Second Time Around
Looking Forward
Holding On

And writing as Willa Marsh

Amy Wingate's Journal
Facing the Music
Sisters Under the Skin
The Quick and the Dead

Starting Over

Marcia Willett

headline

First published in Great Britain in 1997
by HEADLINE BOOK PUBLISHING

First published in paperback in 1997
by HEADLINE BOOK PUBLISHING

2

ISBN 0 7472 5428 1

Typeset by
CBS, Martlesham Heath, Ipswich, Suffolk

Printed and bound in Great Britain by
Mackays of Chatham PLC, Chatham, Kent

HEADLINE BOOK PUBLISHING
A division of Hodder Headline
338 Euston Road
London NW1 3BH

To Cate

Chapter One

The train from Penzance was running late. When the announcement was over, Hugh Ankerton looked at his companion and raised his eyebrows. Lucinda smiled back, shrugging ruefully. During Hugh's first year at Bristol University they'd had plenty of opportunities to become resigned to the vagaries of British Rail.

'You'd better phone your mum,' he suggested, 'and then we'll go and have some coffee.'

He watched her as she went into the telephone box, marvelling as he often did that this pretty, slender, delightful girl should have chosen him from amongst all the men she could have had for the asking. She was tremendously popular with old and young alike. His parents adored her and he knew that his mother would have liked nothing better than to have welcomed Lucinda as her daughter-in-law.

Hugh frowned and turned towards the station buffet. Unfortunately, during Lucinda's week at his parents' farmhouse on Dartmoor there had been a strain in the relationship which his mother had been quick to notice and, he suspected, would mention. As he ordered two coffees and carried them to a corner table, Hugh cursed himself for his inability to control his emotions. It had already led to a sequence of events he would never forget. His guilt seemed to poison his life and he was beginning to despair that he would ever be free of it.

Lucinda slid into the seat opposite and Hugh thrust his thoughts aside, smiling quickly at her.

'Everything OK?'

She nodded and reached for her coffee, her long blonde plait falling forward over her shoulder. Sensitive as always to his moods, she was determined that they should part on a cheerful note.

'I spoke to Mummie. She says she'll check before she comes to meet me. She sends her love to you.'

'That's nice,' said Hugh absently – gave a mental shake and pulled himself together. 'I'm going to miss you. It'll be odd with you so far away.'

'Eastbourne's not that far.' Lucinda sounded encouraging but she looked worried. 'I shall miss you, too, but we can get together most weekends.'

Hugh fought with conflicting emotions. Lucinda, who had been taking a year out during his first year at Bristol, was about to begin a one-year course of home economy at a residential college in Eastbourne. Although he knew that he would miss her terribly, part of him felt almost relieved. Despite her efforts to help him overcome his guilt, he was unable to allow her into his inmost thoughts; a situation which had worsened in the last few months. Yet part of him longed to seize her and never let her go.

Lucinda watched his troubled face and sighed inwardly, recognising the gloom cast by Charlotte's shadow. She sought a way to raise his spirits, hating the thought of leaving him in this distressed mood. She reached out and took his hand and he held it tightly, smiling at her, longing for all to be well between them.

'I'll write as soon as I've settled in,' she said, trying to create an air of intimacy in the noisy little café. 'Let me have your telephone number at your new house as soon as you know it, won't you?'

'Of course I will.' He sounded almost hearty and her heart sank a little.

'Oh Hugh,' she said, and touched her cheek to his hand. 'I *do* love you.'

'Oh Lu.' His grip tightened. 'I know. Me too, you know that. It's just—'

'Yes, yes,' she said quickly, not wanting to go through all the reasons – or excuses – with which Hugh tried to disguise the real problem between them. 'I realise we're young and all that. I just want you to know.'

The Tannoy crackled into speech and Lucinda gathered up her belongings. She and Hugh held each other tight and kissed almost desperately before she climbed on to the waiting train and settled herself by the window. She loved the journey from the West Country but today her attention was only partly held by the view. Her gaze was inward. From the moment that she'd first met Hugh at his sister's engagement party she'd had the odd sensation that they belonged together. That they were both very young made no difference to her. She just knew deep down inside that they should be together.

As the train skirted the embankment and, leaving

Plymouth, headed upcountry, Lucinda grappled with the sensation that she was losing ground with Hugh. If only she'd known the truth about Charlotte Wivenhoe from the very beginning she would have approached the whole thing differently; but how could she have guessed that Charlotte's adolescent passion for Hugh would have such tragic depth? She remembered Charlotte at that party: shy, awkward, embarrassed. After a few attempts at friendliness Lucinda had felt that it was kinder to leave her alone and, later, Hugh had explained that she was a neighbour's daughter with whom he went riding and who had become very fond of him. Even now, despite the trouble Charlotte had made between them, Lucinda smiled to herself, recalling Hugh's diffidence as he explained it to her. He had never once mocked or boasted about Charlotte's infatuation but, rather, had tried to explain the child's crippling shyness and insecurities.

Lucinda had been – still was – touched by his kindness and sensitivity, but was too absorbed in their own developing friendship to give much thought to a fifteen-year-old schoolgirl.

If only I'd realised, she thought, as the train ran along the edge of the moor behind Ivybridge and rattled across the viaduct above the Nethercombe estate. *If only I could do that bit all over again.*

With hindsight she could see exactly where she'd gone wrong. She simply hadn't taken Charlotte seriously and she'd made the mistake of trying to laugh Hugh out of his guilt. Try as she would, she found it impossible to make him take a balanced view. Things had come to a head during her stay with the Ankertons when Hugh had taken her for a walk up by the quarry where Charlotte had died. Once again the familiar questions had been raised. Had Charlotte deliberately ridden out on her pony on such a dangerous path during that stormy night? Had it been accident or suicide? Would the tragedy have happened if Charlotte had not met them both unexpectedly in Bristol? Lucinda, who knew that Hugh blamed her for behaving insensitively on that occasion, had accused him of being morbid. They'd had another row and, although they'd made it up quite quickly, she knew that Frances – Hugh's mother – had sensed the strained atmosphere between them and had been worried.

Lucinda sighed and settled herself more comfortably. Perhaps this separation might be a good thing after all. Hugh might come to terms with himself a little quicker if she were not there quite so much. After all, *absence makes the heart grow fonder.* Lucinda shook her head. It would be quite impossible for her heart to be any fonder of Hugh than it already was.

Whilst the train sped northwards, Frances was hanging the washing on the line strung between two trees in the small orchard beyond the yard and brooding on the relationship between Lucinda and her son. She had been delighted when Lucinda had taken such a liking to Hugh. It had been a tremendous comfort to know that he would start his new life in Bristol with a ready-made friend; and Lucinda was such a darling. Although Frances knew that it was foolish to hope that their love for each other might outlast student life, secretly she prayed that it would. They were so right together. She hated to see them arguing or unhappy and, yesterday, had gone so far as to ask Lucinda what was upsetting them. She had been taken aback when Lucinda – albeit reluctantly – had told her that Hugh was still fretting about Charlotte and that he simply couldn't get over her death.

Frances pegged out the few remaining garments and sat down on the stone wall that divided the orchard from what had once been the farmyard. When she and Stephen had bought the farm ten years ago most of the land had already been sold to neighbouring farmers. The Ankertons had been left with several paddocks, the orchard and a small formal garden behind the house. Their daughter Caroline, then twelve, and two years older than Hugh, had demanded a pony and Frances had taken to herself the chains of Pony Club and gymkhanas along with the burden of Caroline's pony and, not too much later, Hugh's. Both children pulled their weight during the holidays but, with Caroline at Sherborne and Hugh at Blundell's, Frances had been obliged to take the responsibility during term time.

When the Wivenhoes bought The Rectory in the neighbouring village an acquaintance had been formed that never fully ripened into friendship. They were a naval family who had a great many friends already in the area but, more to the point, Frances had never taken to Cass, Charlotte's mother. Now, as she sat on the wall in the late morning sunshine, Frances wondered whether some instinct had, even then, warned her against Cass. It had taken no time at all for Frances to weigh Cass up. Friendly, generous, easy-going she might be but Frances also saw that she was beautiful, flirtatious and unprincipled. Watching Stephen responding to Cass's delightful charm, Frances decided that the relationship should continue on a very casual footing and many of the invitations that issued from The Rectory were refused without Stephen knowing anything about them.

Tom Wivenhoe was a naval commander, away at sea a great deal, and Frances realised that such a neighbour as Cass could be very dangerous. Stephen was a courteous, kindly, simplistic man and Frances – who could be jealous – had a fear of beautiful, elegant, intelligent women. Never once, in twenty-five years of happy marriage, had Stephen strayed but Frances remained cautious. Cass could have eaten him for breakfast. When rumours, eagerly promulgated by mutual friends, told of Cass's affairs she knew she'd been right. She'd longed to refuse when Cass telephoned to ask if Charlotte's pony might be kept with the Ankertons'. Unfortunately, Cass had made the call on a Saturday morning and Stephen had answered the telephone. Frances listened to his laughter and his gallant sallies and knew at once to whom he was speaking.

'Of course!' she heard him exclaim. 'No problem as far as I can see! But it's not really my province and I'm probably speaking out of turn. I'll call Frances, shall I? OK then. Good idea! You do that. Look forward to it.'

When he came into the kitchen she was busy at the sink. 'Who was that?'

'Cass Wivenhoe.' He lounged beside her, watching the potato peelings sliding from the knife. 'They're thinking of buying Charlotte a pony and Cass wondered if she could keep it on our land. Perfectly prepared to pay very generously. Well, why not?'

'I can't look after her pony. I have quite enough on my hands.'

'I don't think there's any question of that.' Stephen sounded uncomfortable. 'Charlotte's very keen apparently – remember, she's not away at school. She can bicycle over and so on. Cass is going to pop in later to discuss it with you.'

Frances thought about it. Of one thing she was very sure: Cass was not the type to look after a pony. She would never carry feed, fill troughs or muck out and Frances felt reasonably confident that, should Charlotte cease to be keen, the pony would go.

Now, five years later, Frances shifted a little on the wall and looked out across the fields to the slopes and crags of Dartmoor. It was a still, warm day and the cry of the skylark high in the blue void above her filled the quiet air. She was remembering Charlotte; brown-haired and brown-eyed like Tom but, unlike either parent, shy and nervous. She had adored her pony, rising early to exercise him and gladly helping Frances in the back-breaking routine which is part of the care of animals. It had been easy to become fond of her. Gradually she lost her shyness and chattered about her smaller brothers and sisters and about Tom – all of whom she obviously adored – but she rarely spoke about Cass.

It was difficult to remember at what point the Ankertons had noticed her crush on Hugh. They had teased him a bit but mainly ignored it. He was very kind to Charlotte; riding out with her in the holidays and pretending not to notice how very often she was to be seen hanging about once she knew he was home. Later, when he knew that she was frightened at the idea of going away to school to do her A levels, he took her to one or two events at Blundell's in an attempt to lessen her fears by introducing her to his friends. This met with amazing success and, although Hugh had left to go on to university when Charlotte started at the school, the fact that she was friends with this popular boy had raised her stock amongst the remaining sixth form and boosted her confidence.

Frances recalled how Hugh had insisted on inviting her to Caroline's engagement party. Dumb with shyness and dressed quite unsuitably, she'd spoiled Hugh's evening by becoming jealous of his attentions to other guests and to Lucinda in particular. That's where the real trouble had started, thought Frances, as she went into the large farmhouse kitchen with its flagged floors and ceiling-high dresser, and pushed the kettle on to the Aga's hotplate. If only Hugh had listened to her! She'd warned him then not to encourage Charlotte any further but Hugh, like his father, was too soft-hearted – too *weak*! – thought Frances, reaching for a mug. It would have been so *easy* for him to have let his friendship with Charlotte fade quite naturally once he went off to university; but no! Frances banged shut the fridge door in her frustration. No, he'd stayed in touch with Charlotte, encouraging her to pester him, until she made a surprise trip to Bristol to visit him and found him with Lucinda.

Frances made tea and wandered back outside into the

yard, perching on the wooden bench against the wall. The garden, like the orchard, looked across the fields to moorland but the farmyard opened into the narrow lane. The family parked their cars here in the open-fronted barn and Frances had made the yard less bleak with tubs of flowers. As she sipped at her tea, she ran through her earlier conversation with Lucinda. It had come as a tremendous shock to hear that Hugh was blaming himself for Charlotte's death. Her deep affection for Lucinda, combined with a very real anxiety for her relationship with Hugh, resulted in a feeling of animosity and resentment against both Charlotte and Cass, and she was still fuming when Hugh arrived. He turned the car in the gateway and she remembered that he would be going off almost at once for the lunchtime session at the pub where he was working for the remaining weeks of his holiday.

Why had she not noticed before how thin he was and how tired he looked? Frances locked her fingers round the mug of tea and studied him as he crossed the yard. From Christmas until Easter she had been almost totally preoccupied with the plans for Caroline's wedding. There had been so much to organise, so many details to check, so much to *do*. It occurred to her that she hadn't given Hugh the attention he deserved. He was such an easy person to have around; fitting in, helping out, unobtrusively supporting her. For most of the year, of course, he'd been away at university, whilst the Easter holidays had been completely overshadowed with the wedding. He'd been off backpacking with a few friends for the earlier part of the summer holidays and this was the first opportunity she'd had to study him for nearly a year; which brought them back to Charlotte's funeral.

'Did you make it on time?' she asked, more for something to say than as a quest for information. It was fairly obvious that Lucinda had caught her train.

'The train was late.' He answered lightly enough but some nuance in his voice caused her to glance at him.

He sat beside her, his arms folded across his breast, his head dropped forward, and she noticed the sharpness of his shoulder blades as well as a kind of desolation in his posture. She wondered whether to probe or to remain tactfully silent but, even as she deliberated, she knew that tactful silence would be beyond her.

'I hope you were able to make up, Hugh. Rows are so horrid, aren't they?'

He shrugged. 'That's life, I suppose.'

'Oh Hugh!' She saw now that there was a bleakness about his expression and began to feel a real anxiety. 'I'm sorry. Was it . . . ?'

He smiled a little as she hesitated. They both knew that he was too kind to tell her to mind her own business. Frances traded on this but only because she cared about him.

'She gets fed up with me sometimes,' he told her. 'And I can't say I really blame her. I haven't been very easy to live with lately.'

'What on earth do you mean?' Frances frowned, maternal prejudice fighting for a brief moment with her love for Lucinda.

Hugh hesitated. 'It's just that we can't see eye to eye about Charlotte,' he said at last.

'About *Charlotte*?' She let him see her surprise.

Hugh sighed and thrust his hands into his pockets. 'You know how I feel about her death, Mum. I told you at the time.'

'But that was then; you were just upset.' She stared at him, frowning, and shook her head. 'You can't seriously still believe that Charlotte's death was anything but an accident? Good heavens, darling, it's nearly a year ago. Surely you're not still brooding over it?'

Hugh looked away from her. 'You sound like Lucinda,' he said. 'How about some coffee before I go to work?'

'Never mind coffee.' Frances felt almost frightened. There was a resigned look to her son's face, a preoccupation which spoke of an internal suffering, and she stretched a hand to him. 'Hugh,' she said pleadingly, 'you *must* believe that Charlotte's death had nothing to do with you.'

'Look.' He took her hand, pressed it briefly and let it go. 'When Charlotte got back from Bristol she was in such a state that she had to be sedated . . . No! Let me finish. If I'd taken your advice and told her that I was seeing a lot of Lucinda it wouldn't have come as such a shock. I couldn't face the idea of upsetting her.'

'Charlotte was neurotic long before you came on the scene,' protested Frances. 'You're overreacting. I remember that there was a tremendous fuss because she wouldn't go away to school despite the fact that her brother and some of her oldest friends were going with her. She was shy and nervous at the best of times and that dreadful car accident she witnessed was enough to push her over the top.'

'If she hadn't seen me with Lucinda in Bristol she

wouldn't have been so upset by the accident,' argued Hugh. 'It was all part of it. That's my point.'

'Hugh!' cried Frances. 'She was *fifteen*, that's all. Fifteen years old. So what if she did see you with Lucinda? She was much too young to think of you as her boyfriend and you gave her no encouragement to . . .' A terrible fear filled her. 'Did you?'

'Of course not,' said Hugh in disgust. 'She was like a little sister. But I knew how she felt about me. Don't you see? I *knew* she was unbalanced, so there's no excuse. For instance, she was always convinced that Cass had lovers by the score and that Tom would find out. She was manic about it.'

'Yes. Well, there she may have had a point,' said Frances. 'But—'

'No,' said Hugh strongly. 'No buts. We knew that Charlotte was . . . well, unbalanced. I should have told her about Lucinda. You were absolutely right. When I went to Bristol I should have dropped her.'

'And you believe that because she saw you and Lucinda together in Bristol she came home and at the first opportunity took her pony out and rode up on to the moor and took a header into the quarry?'

If Frances had hoped to shock Hugh out of his obsession she had miscalculated. He looked at her in horror.

'Yes,' he said. 'That's just what I believe.' He got up. 'I must go. See you later.'

Several hours later, Frances had come to no satisfactory conclusions. It seemed that Hugh had allowed this obsession to develop and she blamed herself for not noticing earlier.

If she hadn't been so preoccupied with the wedding . . . Frances shook her head. There was no point in useless recriminations. Now that she knew, she could help him snap out of it. There was nearly a month of holiday left and she must use it wisely. She had no doubts of her success. Hugh had always been a malleable child, prepared to trust her and ready to take advice.

Frances allowed herself a moment of doubt. Perhaps she'd been a little *too* ready to manage him, and Caroline had been a bossy elder sister; answering for him when grown-ups asked him his name or his age; fastening his buttons and tying his laces; protecting him at school. It was surprising that Hugh had gone off to Blundell's with so little fuss and had managed so well without either of them. Until now . . .

She wondered briefly how Cass had come to terms with her daughter's death. What a terrible thing, to lose a child! She remembered the night of the storm when Charlotte's pony had returned without a rider and she had telephoned The Rectory. None of them had seen Charlotte go out and, to be honest, she'd felt guilty herself for a while although there was no reason for her to expect that Charlotte would take out her pony in such weather. Certainly Cass had never shown the least inclination to blame anyone, although Frances had avoided her even more since the accident and had no idea how she really felt.

Frances glanced at her watch. Stephen, who headed the research and development department of an electronics company, would be working late and she'd half agreed to have supper with a girl friend. Now, she decided, she'd stay in and try to have a talk with Hugh when he came back from the pub. If he was working the lunchtime shift there would be an opportunity later to spend some time with him and to get to the bottom of this obsession.

Chapter Two

'But it's crazy! And I'd no idea he felt like this.' Frances, sorting knives and forks on to the kitchen table, paused to look up at Stephen, nursing his drink.

'Where is he?' Instinctively he kept his voice low.

'He's gone out. Gone to see the Webster twins.'

'Well, nothing to be gained with you getting worked up like this.' Stephen smiled at her, trying to will his sympathy across the spaces of the kitchen.

'But I should have realised that Hugh is destroying himself . . .' she said miserably.

'Oh, come on!' Stephen bit back hasty words and grasped at his temper. A great many late nights spent working in his department and an almost permanent headache threatened to overthrow his patience. Each evening for the last week his return home had been met with the same discussion and whilst he, too, was anxious about Hugh he could see that they were getting nowhere. 'I'm worried about both of you,' he said reasonably. 'I can see that it's quite wrong for Hugh to be brooding over Charlotte's death but it may just work its way out of his system, given time.'

'Time!' Frances ran her fingers through her short dark

hair. 'It's nearly a year, Stephen.'

She picked up her glass and leaned against the sink, watching him. Part of her longed to be soothed by his calm approach, for thus it had been for most of their lives together. She was quick to react, caring, competent but given to being bossy and easily irritated. He was kind, rational, patient but inclined to let things ride and he could be stubborn. At best each complemented the other to create a harmonious balance; at worst they drove each other mad. Frances, having utterly failed to talk Hugh out of his obsession, was really frightened and now she longed for Stephen to take control.

'I just don't see what more we can do,' he said helplessly. 'You've talked it through with him, you tell me. Many times, from what I can gather. I've offered to speak to him but you say that it wouldn't work.'

'I don't want him to know we're discussing him,' she explained. 'If it could come up naturally . . .'

'Well, it won't,' he said flatly, too tired to wrap it up. 'You must see that. What am I supposed to say? "Good grief! Can it be nearly a year that Charlotte Wivenhoe died?" Or should I ask his views on obsessive guilt? Come on, Frances. Be reasonable.'

She looked so miserable that he went to her and slipped an arm about her shoulders. She didn't respond to his embrace but neither did she pull away.

'I spoke to Lucinda today,' she said.

He drew back to stare at her. 'How did you manage that? I thought she'd gone off to Eastbourne.'

'I found her number in Hugh's address book when he

was at the pub.' She met his gaze defiantly. 'I'm really *worried*, Stephen.'

'Yes.' He sighed deeply. 'I see you are. And what did she have to say?'

'She says he doesn't seem to enjoy anything any more. It's as though he doesn't feel he has a right to. She says she's tried everything. Sympathy, rational discussion, angry scenes, laughing at him, but nothing's working. He's going through life on autopilot. Those were her words.'

Stephen closed his eyes and massaged his head with his fingers. 'She had no solution to suggest, then?'

'None. I've tried to make him see that it's Cass's fault but he won't have it.'

'Cass's fault?' Stephen frowned in surprise. 'How so?'

'Well, we all know that Cass played around and that Charlotte knew about it. That's what made her so neurotic and that's why she died. It's got nothing to do with Hugh. If Cass had been a decent mother none of this would have happened.'

'I think that's going a bit far, isn't it?' protested Stephen. 'After all, we don't know—'

'Oh well, I'd expect you to stick up for her,' snapped Frances.

'I'm not sticking up for her,' said Stephen calmly. 'I think it's more likely that it was the culmination of a whole string of incidents. It was a terrible tragic accident, I'm sure of it.'

'Then you'd better try to convince Hugh of it,' said Frances tartly, 'before he decides to throw himself off the Clifton Suspension Bridge.'

'If I thought that there was the least danger of that I certainly wouldn't wait until the subject came up in conversation,' said Stephen angrily. 'Make up your mind. Do you want me to speak to him or not?'

'I don't know,' cried Frances, on the brink of tears. 'I don't know *what* to do! Oh *damn*!'

The telephone's insistent shrill took her out into the hall and Stephen went to refill his glass. He simply did not know how to deal with this crisis. Every time he insisted that he should broach the matter with Hugh, Frances blocked it. At the same time she was making him feel guilty for doing nothing. He guessed that her natural antipathy to Cass was exaggerated by her fear for Hugh and that poor Cass would be made a handy scapegoat. Stephen liked Cass, although he harboured none of the feelings for her that Frances feared, and he felt frustrated. He was sad that, after all their happy years together, she still was insecure enough to have these twinges of jealousy but he seemed powerless to help her.

'Damn and blast,' he muttered and at that moment Hugh himself came in through the back door and smiled at him.

'Hi!' he said casually. 'You're home early for a change. Problem solved?'

'Yes,' said Stephen, taken aback. 'Well, more or less. I haven't seen much of you lately. How's it going?'

'OK.'

Hugh took a glass from the dresser and lifted the bottle with a questioning glance. Stephen nodded, trying to discern the signs of distress on which Frances had remarked. Certainly Hugh was thin but he'd always been a skinny child. His brown hair flopped forward over his eyes, which were hidden behind tortoiseshell-rimmed spectacles, and his wrists, as he wielded the bottle, looked oddly vulnerable. Stephen felt a stab of love for his son and a real sympathy for what he must be suffering.

'What's all this about Charlotte?' he asked before he could stop himself, and Hugh stared at him warily.

'Don't you start, Dad,' he begged. 'Honestly. Just let me deal with it. OK?'

'But you're not dealing with it,' said Stephen. 'Are you? Not if you think you're responsible. You're an intelligent boy . . . man,' he corrected himself hastily. Hugh was twenty, after all. 'Guilt is a very destructive emotion.'

'I know that.' Hugh looked stubbornly unresponsive.

'Nothing happens in isolation,' said Stephen, one ear cocked towards the hall for Frances's return. 'Remember that. Whether it's an action or a word, it has a knock-on effect. A whole chain of events, involving a great number of people, will have led up to Charlotte's death. Your part will have been a very small one and should be kept in perspective.' He heard the telephone receiver click down. 'So how are the twins?' he was asking as Frances came in. 'Are they off to university this term?'

'No, they've got A levels next year.' Hugh sent a grateful glance at Stephen and smiled at his mother. 'So who was on the phone?'

'It was Caroline.' Frances summoned up a smile. 'Catching up with the news. You're just in time for supper, Hugh. Would you like to lay the table while I serve up?'

Hugh drove up the narrow lane that led from the farm on to

the open moor. Sunk in his own preoccupations, he was unaware of the blackberries ripening in the hedgerows or the brightness of the rowan berries. At the top of the lane, with the moor stretching on either side and beyond him to Burrator Reservoir, he paused. Even in his present mood the sight of the great hills with their wooded valleys and high granite tors soothed and moved him. Below, in the valley, the still surface of the reservoir placidly reflected the clear blue sky whilst sheep grazed peacefully on the grassy spaces above. A few ponies clattered past, kicking up their heels in the autumn sunshine, and Hugh let in the clutch and headed for Meavy.

For the past few months he had been living in a kind of despairing resignation, unable to rid his mind of the image of Charlotte, lying in the water at the bottom of the quarry. Had she been killed instantly by the fall? Or had she lain, injured and frightened, unable to move and screaming for help? His imaginings tortured him. If only he could believe – as Lucinda and Frances assured him – that none of it was his fault it might be easier. Even so, the thought of her dying, frightened and alone, was quite sufficient to give him nightmares. He dreamed that he was standing at the top of the small cliff above the quarry, looking down at her. She cried to him, stretching out her arms, but he did nothing to help her. Often Lucinda was in the dream, holding him, drawing him away, as she had in Bristol when Charlotte had come upon them unexpectedly in Park Street. He'd had his arm round Lucinda, kissing her as they looked into a shop window. Once again Hugh remembered the look on Charlotte's face; the shock and dismay, the misery that she had been unable to conceal as Lucinda told her that they were spending a naughty weekend at her brother's flat. He'd allowed Lucinda to take control and made no attempt to soften the blow, unable to conceal his relief when Charlotte said that Cass was with her in Bristol; nevertheless he'd felt guilty almost immediately.

'Why did you say that?' he'd asked Lucinda when they were out of earshot. 'You didn't have to tell her.'

He'd had a sudden desire to run after Charlotte but when he looked back she'd disappeared.

'She'd got to know sometime,' Lucinda was saying reasonably, surprised that Hugh was so upset. 'If she's that serious then it's better to be cruel to be kind. Otherwise you'll keep her hanging on. She needs to make her own friends.'

Hugh, in love and recovering from his first night of lovemaking, was too besotted to argue, but he still felt ashamed of himself. His studies and Lucinda between them postponed his decision as to whether he should write to Charlotte or wait until he saw her again but the problem nagged at the back of his mind. Charlotte had trusted him, depended upon him, and he owed her some kind of explanation and an assurance of on-going friendship.

The news of her death had shocked him into horrified disbelief. Hugh had heard from the Webster twins that she'd returned from Bristol so badly upset that she'd become hysterical and had needed to be sedated. Hugh knew exactly why she was so upset. It was pointless to argue that no one killed themselves for such reasons. The newspapers were full of reports of unbalanced people who killed themselves and others for the most ridiculous reasons. Charlotte wasn't quite normal and he'd known that and taken no precautions.

Now, Hugh parked the car beside the village green where the great oak stood from which the pub took its name, and crossed the road. Inside the Royal Oak it was dark and cool and Hugh went into the public bar with its granite floor and big open fireplace where, on cold winter days, logs burned cheerfully, dispelling gloom. He'd worked for the last few weeks behind the bar, earning money for the term to come, but today he was a customer.

As he took his pint and raised it to his lips he heard Cass Wivenhoe's voice. She was in the passage outside and he dodged back, watching her as she made her way into the other bar. The twins' mother, Kate Webster, was with her and they spent some moments choosing a table and joking with the landlord. Presently Hugh realised that his hands were shaking and he stood his glass down on a table and rubbed them together. What if one of them should come through to the loo? The few locals, having nodded at him, were deep in conversation and Hugh glanced round quickly and slipped out unobserved.

Back in the car he sat still for some moments. The last time he'd seen Cass had been at the funeral. He'd stood at the back, not wishing to be seen, and had mourned alone. How would she react if she were to come face to face with him? Would she accuse him? It was difficult to imagine. Cass had always been so friendly, so easy-going and welcoming, but how could she help but blame him for his part in her daughter's death? The twins – especially Guy – always said that Charlotte was a nutcase, and their mother, on the one occasion that he had been brave enough to raise the subject with her, had said that there were all kinds of circumstances of which the trip to Bristol was merely one and not to be seen out of perspective.

Hugh drove out of Meavy with his heart so full of confusion and misery that he longed to weep. If only he could rid himself of the deadening feeling of betrayal! She had trusted him and he had betrayed her cruelly. If he'd written to her and broken the news of his involvement with Lucinda gently, Charlotte might still be alive. In his worst moments he almost hated Lucinda for her part in his betrayal whilst knowing, in his heart, it was all due to his own weakness. All very well for his mother to protest that it was nothing to do with him and that Charlotte's insecurity was due to Cass's infidelities but how could she be so certain? She and Cass had never been friends, in fact he suspected that she disliked Cass. And now she had enjoined his father in the argument.

Hugh made up his mind. He would return to Bristol earlier than he intended. There was more than a week of the holiday left but he had no intention of staying at home any longer. This term he was to live in a student house and there was no reason at all why he shouldn't join those of his friends who were already there. It would also give him a chance to catch up on some neglected holiday work. He had barely scraped through his end-of-year exams and was dreading the second year of his History course.

He heard his mother's voice as he came into the kitchen. She was talking on the telephone in the hall.

'. . . and I simply don't know what else to say to him,

Annie. He's utterly obsessed . . .'

Hugh made a face and backed out. Soon everybody would know and he would be confronted with sympathetic expressions and tactful conversations about guilt. Deciding to postpone his packing until his mother's call was finished, he crossed the orchard and set out over the fields to the moor beyond.

Chapter Three

Annie Grayshott replaced the telephone receiver and looked wryly at her cup of cold coffee. Poor Frances had been talking for nearly half an hour and Annie felt quite numb with the effort of concentrating. She poured away the coffee and stood for some moments at the high window, gazing out over the rooftops of Ashburton and wondering if the situation with Hugh was really as dire as Francis related. After all, Frances was not the kind of person to dramatise herself.

'I suspect,' she said aloud – the fact that her husband, Perry, had died did not prevent her from continuing to communicate with him – 'that it's wishful thinking to hope she's exaggerating. I simply don't know how to help her and it's making me feel inadequate and useless.'

'She needs to get it out of her system.' Perry's shade was, apparently, hovering near the drinks cupboard. 'I diagnose a sense of humour failure, my darling. You know my prescription for that. You need a drink.'

Annie sighed and decided to take his advice. She poured herself a large whisky and stared speculatively at herself in the glass that hung beside the window. Her jaw-length fair hair had a generous streaking of grey and her tanned skin was especially lined around the eyes but she might have passed for a few years less than the sixty allotted to her. She'd had a successful career as secretary to the managing director of a well-known airline company and when, at thirty-three, she'd married Peregrine Grayshott she'd continued to work for fear that Perry, with his entrepreneurial schemes and brilliant ideas, might not always be in a situation to support them both; for Annie had been trained in a hard school when it came to security. Her father, a profligate, fun-loving man, had died when she was in her mid-teens, leaving her mother penniless. The years of penury had left their mark and Annie's mother was by then a nervous, sickly woman who continued to live in terror of the mounting bills and evictions which had dogged her married life. Annie, who could just remember a gentle, happy, young woman who had adored her little daughter, had vowed that her mother should never know anxiety whilst she, Annie, was able to prevent it. She had worked hard to support her mother and care for her. By the time she met Perry, Annie's love of laughter and her natural warm generosity had been buried beneath her quiet, sensible, practical qualities and, although her mother was now dead, those years of control and responsibility had, in their turn, left a deep impression upon Annie.

Perry, meeting her at a friend's house, had been struck by the thoughtful beauty of her hazel eyes and had seen beyond her reserved responses. He glimpsed the hidden depths of her personality and set himself to draw her out. This was easier than he had dared to hope – simply because

Annie fell in love with him. She was more open with him than with any other person she had ever known. Instinctively she knew that she could trust him absolutely and, although their courtship was a slow, careful discovery, their progress was sure and satisfying. Perry honoured the self-effacing, uncomplaining spirit which had given up so much and he was determined to make her happy or, rather, to help her to discover her own potential for happiness.

Slowly Annie came to see that Perry's love of experimentation and the proving of new ideas was not to be put in the same category as her father's wild-cat schemes. She learned to relax; to enjoy a quality of life which did not necessarily depend on an exaggerated level of material security. With Perry, the spiritual side of her character, so long denied, began to blossom and their contentment was deep and fulfilling. At last, they bought the small cottage in which they planned to spend a blissful and long-anticipated retirement.

Within two years Perry was dead and Annie was left to face the remainder of her life alone. Painfully and very slowly she adjusted to the changes. She missed Perry quite dreadfully. He'd been such a companionable man and a very attractive one: tall, lean, good-looking and full of energy. He was always to be found surrounded by reference books; looking something up, jotting down a note, reading out some fascinating fact. He could scarcely bear to be without his encyclopaedias, his dictionaries, his Pears. Leaves and blooms would be borne home from country walks so as to be identified in his nature books, and insects were studied closely with the aid of his magnifying glass.

The cottage had been so quiet when his voice could no longer be heard, bellowing down the stairs or shouting from the garden, but Annie was grateful that they had been there together long enough for her to be able to imagine him with her still; sitting at the kitchen table with his formidable array of books; hunched over the pond in the garden as he reported on the progress of the tadpoles; lying in bed, spectacles perched on the end of his nose, whilst he read aloud to her. In their twenty-five years together they had shared so much that it seemed impossible that he was not still around somewhere, longing to communicate to her all the exciting new things he was discovering in the afterlife. After a while, she had fallen into the habit of talking to him as though he were still with her and, such had been his influence on her whilst he was alive, she could still imagine what comfort and advice he would be offering her even though she could no longer see him. Without him, the warm, sensitive side of her character seemed in danger of disappearing again beneath the calm, practical qualities which were necessary to help her exist without him.

This frightened her. Should she allow it to happen it would negate their whole life together. She took to talking aloud to him, remembering the particular sayings he had; the words with which he had encouraged her. It seemed impossible that he would abandon her – indeed he had always vowed that nothing could separate them – and she took heart from his promise. Those closest to her had become accustomed to the idea that she was aware of his presence and – such had been Perry's charisma – half believed it themselves.

Annie had turned away from the mirror and was concentrating her mind on Frances. They'd known each other for some years, having been brought together in the first instance by mutual friends. The Grayshotts' move to Devon had cemented the friendship and, after Perry's death, Frances had been the friend to whom Annie had become closest. She'd valued her practical caring and sensitive kindnesses and was very ready now to help Frances if she could. The point was that she couldn't see how it was to be done. This must be the third or fourth conversation they'd had on the subject of Hugh's obsession and, apart from the relief that it brought to Frances to talk about it, Annie had very little comfort to offer.

'Over to you,' she murmured to Perry. 'I'm good at practical problems but it was to you that people came when they needed help emotionally.'

She wandered out into the courtyard. The cottage had been almost completely rebuilt using the original stone and consisted of a very large kitchen, a spacious sitting room, a minute study and, upstairs, two big bedrooms and a good-size bathroom. At first she and Perry had feared that it might be too small but she was glad that they had bought it. Now that she was alone it was more than big enough and she loved the kitchen with its sliding glass doors opening into the high-walled courtyard which, in the summer, was like a natural extension. She could sit in the sun, secure in her privacy, popping in to put the kettle on or to cut a sandwich and, later, she would light her tiny barbecue and sit with a glass of wine in her hand, watching the sunset fade.

After a life run to timetables and heavy schedules, it was

wonderful to be free to pursue those things for which there had been so little time. She read and sketched, listened to music and experimented with cooking but, when Perry died, the savour and novelty disappeared and she still had difficulty in rousing herself from apathy.

Annie sat down in her wicker chair and tried to imagine what Hugh must be thinking and feeling. Perhaps there was something he had not told Frances which might explain his extreme reaction to this girl's death? Before she could develop this theme, however, the telephone rang again and Annie went back into the kitchen to answer it.

'Hi! It's Pippa.' The clear voice of Perry's goddaughter rang in her ear. 'How are you both?'

'We're fine.' Annie knew that Pippa had no difficulty in believing that Perry might be close at Annie's shoulder. She sat down at the kitchen table, wishing that she'd brought her drink in with her. 'How are all of you?'

'We're OK. Well, Robert's busy as usual. You know how he is. But Rowley and I are just fine. Rowley's going to say Hello in a minute. He's working himself up to it.'

Annie smiled to herself as she imagined Rowley staring suspiciously at the telephone. At eighteen months he was very sweet and rather shy; no doubt 'working himself up to it' meant that Pippa was trying to wheedle him into speaking.

'Tell him not to bust a gut,' Annie advised. 'I'll take it as read. So what's new?'

'I was hoping that you were coming up for your visit.' Pippa sounded wistful and Annie had a momentary vision of her, curled up in the chair beside the telephone, her blonde mop on end. 'You usually come in the autumn. We'd love to see you. Or we could come down. Just Rowley and me, of course. Robert's too busy.'

Annie thought quickly. A trip upcountry might kill several birds with one stone; she could visit a few old friends very briefly and finish up with Pippa.

'I've been looking forward to my visit,' she said cheerfully. 'It's just that this lovely weather has made me forget how close the winter is. I'd love to come. Let me get my diary and we'll fix a date.'

Pippa wrote the dates on the calendar that hung on the kitchen wall and beamed at Rowley.

'She's coming,' she said triumphantly. 'Isn't that nice?'

Rowley sat astride his small wooden tricycle and watched her. He was of a cautious disposition and disliked being bounced into sudden reactions. He put his thumb in his mouth and twiddled his hair thoughtfully.

'You remember Annie,' said Pippa encouragingly.

The three of them had paid a visit to her earlier in the summer, on their way down to Cornwall on holiday. They'd stayed overnight, all cramming into the spare bedroom and Robert had vowed that he'd never do it again. Pippa pulled her mouth down at the corners as she remembered his irritation and sighed a little. He seemed to be permanently short-tempered these days; working early and late and with little time for his wife or son. He was an extremely ambitious man, with his eyes fixed permanently on promotion, and Pippa suffered bouts of guilt whenever she fell short of his exacting standards.

This, sadly, happened fairly frequently. Try as she might, Pippa was not naturally domesticated and dinner parties were often culinary disasters. She was at her best with spontaneous entertainments because the longer she had to plan the more nervous she grew. Robert was continually at her shoulder and she would become quite ill with the fear that she would let him down. The agency for which Robert was working was one which prided itself on involving its employees' families and, though he could quite easily have taken his clients out to lunch, tradition made it necessary to be more personal. It was usual, at senior executive level, for clients and their wives to be invited into the homes of those who managed their accounts and Robert was determined that Pippa's inadequacies should not queer his pitch.

To prove that he knew exactly how it should be done he invited his departmental head and the chief accountant, with their wives, to dinner and, by organising most of it himself, put on a pretty good show. Pippa had a migraine for three days following but Robert felt that it was in a good cause and displayed little sympathy. He was a self-made man, hauling himself up from lowly beginnings and terrified that they might show. Being a very bright child he'd won a scholarship to a good school where he studied the actions and speech of the boys who came from privileged middle-class backgrounds and, by the time he left university with a degree in Economics, it would have taken a keen eye and ear to detect his roots.

Soon after he met Pippa at a party he decided that he would marry her. She was pretty, fun and a member of that class to which he aspired. He also realised that she was good-natured and malleable; excellent material for the kind of wife he needed. He was only partly right. Pippa was malleable to the extent that she loved Robert and genuinely wanted him to be happy.

Although she'd been unfashionably set on being a wife and mother she'd allowed herself, on leaving school, to be persuaded into embarking on a secretarial course. Her housemistress, who cherished a secret fondness for Pippa's academic elderly father, had taken the motherless Pippa under her wing and done the best she could for her. She persuaded her that some kind of qualification was sensible and that, despite her inclination towards an early marriage, she might need to earn her own living for a time. After all, she'd pointed out, Pippa should not expect her father to support her indefinitely. As it was, he had lived long enough to disapprove of her marriage to Robert and had died three months after Rowley's birth. Pippa barely missed him. His passion for facts had – unlike his close friend, Perry Grayshott's – been unaccompanied by any desire for human companionship and Pippa sometimes wondered whether her mother had died of loneliness.

She was determined to marry a loving man, have lots of happy children and live in a big rambling house in the country; an ambition which put her out of step with her female contemporaries who were embarking on careers and determined on equality with the opposite sex. She was too inexperienced at twenty either to see through Robert's charm or withstand his determination. It was extremely flattering to have this suave, sexy, good-looking and intelligent man apparently at her feet. He had a witty tongue and his tough early upbringing had given him a maturity which was lacking in her more youthful admirers.

He pursued her with relentless patience and well-simulated passion, privately terrified that her father's dislike of him would carry weight with her. Clever enough to see that her life had been a lonely one and aware of Pippa's own longings, Robert went to great lengths to describe the family life he envisaged for them. His success, however, was due to the simple fact that Pippa had fallen in love with him. To her it was all that really mattered.

Now, confronted by his ruthless ambition, which he made less and less effort to hide, she was anxious to give him the support he needed without allowing their private lives to suffer. Knowing that a certain amount of reshuffling was taking place at the agency and that Robert was pushing for promotion, she was prepared to accept that he was bound to be preoccupied and reminded herself that she was very lucky. Because of her inheritance from her father they were able to live very comfortably in a pretty house in Farnham, and were spared the grim financial struggles of many young couples who were unable to afford to commute.

She told herself that there were bound to be difficult times within any marriage and that once Robert had his promotion he would be his old self. Meanwhile, she had Annie's visit to look forward to and, even more pressing, Rowley's lunch to prepare.

Chapter Four

It was with a mixture of anguish and hope that Frances drove home, having dropped Hugh and his belongings in Bristol. The poor boy was as downcast as ever, she thought, and she worried that her attempts to talk through his guilt only stirred his mind into worse turmoil. Now it was to be hoped that in his second year, and living with a group of his friends, he might be able to pull himself together. Anything, she told herself, having inspected his new accommodation, drunk a mug of coffee made by a jolly young law student and started on her journey home, anything was better than his moping about at home. His friends had been welcoming and full of high spirits and must be more distracting to be with than her and Stephen. She'd been sorry that Lucinda was going to be far away in Eastbourne but, after a little thought, she'd wondered if missing Lucinda might take Hugh's mind off Charlotte.

As she drove, she was suddenly aware of a weariness; a lassitude that was both mental and physical. It was an effort to hold her arms up to grip the wheel. She consoled herself with the thought that this was hardly surprising. The wedding had taken a great deal of her energy and, after all the excitement, she felt exhausted and rather flat, and this anxiety about Hugh was merely exacerbating the condition. Less easy to define were her feelings towards Stephen. She was cross that he had made no effort to talk to Hugh. She knew that it was specious to blame him when she herself had forbidden him to raise the subject. Nevertheless, if Stephen had been prepared to spend time with his son the subject might have arisen. Hugh, given the opportunity, might even have raised it himself.

Stephen, however, had done nothing though, to give him his due, his work was currently unusually demanding. His department was to be moved, lock stock and barrel, to South Wales where it was to be amalgamated with the head office research laboratories; Stephen had been offered overall control. He had told her the news tentatively, dwelling on the promotional aspects of the move, but Frances – feeling touchy about Hugh – said flatly that she had no desire to live in South Wales. Afterwards she felt guilty that she'd shown indifference to the company's acknowledgement of his achievements, which was implicit in the reshuffle, but as yet there had been no opportunity to put this right.

On an impulse, Frances turned off the A38 at Ashburton and drove through the town. Annie's cottage was on the very edge although she was within a ten-minute walk of the shops. The entrance to the garden was along a narrow track which led on to fields. On the east and south ran the high boundary wall of the adjoining property which ensured Annie's privacy. The front garden was just the width of the house, though long, and fields lay beyond to the west and north.

Opposite the gate, across the track, was Annie's garage – formerly a barn – and Frances parked as close as she could to it so as to leave room for any agricultural vehicle which might need access to the fields. Inside the gate, she paused. From this vantage point it would be impossible to guess that she was on the edge of a busy market town. The cottage had turned its back on Ashburton and seemed to doze quietly beneath its thatched roof. The front door, which was off-set beside a deep wide bay window, yawned ajar; above, the curtains stirred sleepily at the open bedroom windows.

She trod up the path between the long stretches of lawn and put her head in at the door.

'Hello! Annie? It's Frances.'

Emerging from the tiny study off the hall, Annie looked delighted to see her.

'Frances! How nice. What brings you to Ashburton?'

'I've been taking Hugh back to Bristol.' Frances felt the need to explain her unannounced visit. 'I would have phoned but I didn't know how long I'd be in Bristol and I simply couldn't drive past without making a quick detour.'

'I should think not.' Annie led the way into the kitchen. 'Just in time for tea. Excellent timing.'

'That would be lovely.' Frances sank into one of the comfortable wicker chairs and glanced around her. 'I do love this kitchen.'

Annie smiled as she pushed her hair behind her ears and fetched the teapot. 'That's because it's hardly a kitchen at all. You notice that we've avoided all the usual things that make the kitchen a workplace.'

This was true. There was none of the usual fitted

cupboards and working surfaces. Instead, built into a central plinth, there was a deep ironstone sink set in a terracotta-tiled area large enough to sit at or work on as required. Above the plinth, around the oaken pillar that it supported, Annie's copper saucepans hung. The Rayburn stood in a deep recess flanked by a working surface on which to stand plates or saucepans. The wall opposite the Rayburn was taken up by the sliding glass doors, to one side of which was a large ancient pine table and various assorted chairs, whilst, on the back wall above an oak cupboard, long shelves held Annie's china. The washing machine and the fridge were housed in a small pantry along with her stocks of food. This left plenty of space for two wicker chairs, judicially placed; one beside the Rayburn and another by the glass doors looking into the courtyard. Spotlights, carefully hidden, illuminated the work areas and lent an intimate glow on dull winter days and at night when the long bright chintz curtains were drawn across the glass doors.

'I'd never really noticed before,' admitted Frances. 'But you're right. It's so comfortable and peaceful. Much nicer than my kitchen!'

'Rubbish!' said Annie. 'Yours is a typical farmhouse kitchen and absolutely right for you. You have a husband to cook for and children and animals to look after.'

'Not any more,' said Frances morosely.

Annie made tea thoughtfully. It had been a tactless remark but it probably gave Frances the opening for which she had been hoping. Mentally she summoned Perry's aid.

'That's true,' she said cheerfully. 'It must be wonderful to have some time to yourself.'

'I was beginning to think so,' said Frances, who welcomed an opportunity to pour out her grievances. 'I was just adjusting to Caroline leaving home when Hugh dropped his bombshell.'

'But it must be a nice change to be free of those wretched horses,' said Annie, determined that Frances should not feel *too* sorry for herself. 'You used to be worn out with all the work.'

Frances was silent. Of course she was delighted to be free, but also she actually rather missed her quiet moments, chatting to the horses with the sun on her back.

'I miss them a bit,' she said eventually.

'Of course you do,' said Annie bracingly. 'But not when it's pouring with rain, I bet! All that mud! How lucky that Caroline has room for them. I was surprised that Hugh was prepared to let his go so easily.'

Even as she spoke she cursed inwardly. What a tactless, stupid thing to say! She passed Frances her tea and sat down, pushing a patchwork cushion into the small of her back.

'Do you know I hadn't thought about it but now I know why.' Frances sat up straight, staring ahead of her as all the facts clicked neatly into place. 'Of course. I'd put it down to his going off to university and growing up. I must admit I was surprised. He lost interest in riding so suddenly but I was so wrapped up with the wedding I didn't really think about it. Oh, I could *murder* that woman!'

'Which woman?' asked Annie, startled.

'Charlotte's mother. It makes me so angry that Hugh is taking all this so much to heart when she's entirely to blame. She was having an affair at the time, you know. Didn't give a damn about the kids. Oh, poor Hugh. And when I think how much he loves riding!'

'It will pass. Nothing lasts for ever.' Annie could hear the futility of her words and tried again. 'It might well be that he *is* growing out of it and not just . . . the other thing. Anyway, it's good for you to have a break from the horses. I know that Perry would be telling you to relax. Do you remember how he used to say that there was nothing more pointless or exhausting than worrying about things that you can't change?'

Frances stirred restlessly. 'No doubt you've been consulting him about me?' she said, half resentfully, half hopefully.

'Naturally,' answered Annie cheerfully. 'And you know his advice as well as I do.'

'What, then?' asked Frances, after a moment.

'"Lift it up and then let it go",' quoted Annie, smiling at her. 'Remember? He believes that worrying about someone simply surrounds them in a miasmic sort of fog. Be positive, that's his motto.'

'He was such a comfort.' Frances's expression softened.

'Still is! And what's all this about a move?'

'Stephen's department's being moved to Wales and he's been offered complete control. It's a step up, of course, but it's such an upheaval.'

'Perhaps it's the best thing at the moment,' suggested Annie thoughtfully. 'A change for all of you. What does Stephen say?'

Frances shrugged. 'He wants to go. He's hinted that he might be made redundant otherwise. Oh, why does everything come at once?' She swallowed some tea.

Annie smiled sympathetically. 'Poor Frances. But don't you think a move might be a good thing? Gives you all something else to think about. If Hugh is as bad as you say he is, it can't be easy for him to be coming back to the scene of the crime, as it were.'

Frances turned her head to stare out through the open door to the courtyard. Annie watched her thinking about it.

'I hadn't thought of that,' she said at last. 'He must be constantly reminded of her wherever he goes.'

'And surely Stephen wouldn't want to take redundancy? He's too young to retire and too old to start again.'

'It's a thought.' Frances began to look happier. 'But Wales . . .'

'Some wonderful places in Wales,' said Annie firmly, aware of Perry egging her on. 'Glorious country. And you'd be just across the bridge from Caroline. Closer than you are now.'

'That's true.' Frances nodded. 'D'you know I think you might have a point.'

'Talk it over with Stephen.' Annie uncurled her long legs and stood up. 'More tea?'

'Mmm, please.' Frances passed her cup, distracted for a moment by Annie's tall elegance, even dressed as she was in old jeans and cotton shirt. How did she managed to stay so slim? Frances always felt the least bit dowdy beside her but she was grateful for her support and correspondingly guilty that she'd been so absorbed in her own problems. 'You must come over. Stephen would love to see you. Come over for lunch on Sunday.'

'I'm off upcountry.' Annie filled the cups and added milk. 'I'm going to visit a few of my neglected friends and stay for a few days with Pippa.'

'How is she?' Frances was fond of Pippa. 'And that darling Rowley. Oh how I'd love a grandchild . . .'

When she'd gone Annie, despite her gaffe, felt satisfied that Frances was thinking more positively. The most important thing was that Stephen and Frances didn't let this problem drive a wedge between them but tried to work it out together, and a move to Wales could prove a well-timed distraction.

'She's such a worrier,' Annie said to Perry as she waved Frances off down the track and then wandered back into the garden.

'Poor old love.' Perry was heading for the pond. 'Too much time on her hands. She needs some distraction.'

'So do I,' declared Annie, exhausted. 'I need a drink!'

To Frances's surprise, Stephen was already home when she arrived back. She was later than she'd realised and he smiled with relief when he saw her.

'I was just beginning to worry,' he said as she dropped her bag on the hall chair. 'Any problems?'

'No.'

To her dismay, she knew at once that she was still feeling cross with him despite her plans on her way home to be positive about the move. Although Frances was capable of being quite outspoken, when Stephen hurt or upset her she had the greatest difficulty in telling him about it. She withdrew into a touchy silence, broken only when he addressed her directly, whilst inwardly raging that he could never recognise his own shortcomings. Stephen, standing silently outside the door or gazing unseeingly from a window, would try hard to recall conversations or actions which might have led to this arctic atmosphere. He tried to show his love by making cups of tea or hurrying to pre-empt her performing other tasks and she would turn away with raised eyebrows or an indifferent shrug, leaving him miserable and frustrated. Frances was frustrated, too, hating herself for being so horrid but unable to forgive him for whatever lapse had occurred.

Now, as he took her jacket and hung it on the peg and said, 'Cup of tea?' she knew that she was going to be unable to be as generous as she'd planned on her homeward journey. How *could* he be so heartless about Hugh?

'I'm not bothered,' she said – and Stephen's heart sank. 'I stopped off and had one with Annie.'

'How is she?' Stephen followed her into the kitchen and stood awkwardly as she busied herself with bringing things out of the deep-freeze. 'We must ask her over.' He was determined to keep the conversation going. 'I haven't seen her for ages.'

'She's off upcountry for a few weeks.' Frances kept her head turned away from him. She suddenly felt rather lonely and longed to fling herself on his chest and bawl loudly. Why did she have these terribly destructive moods? Weariness swept over her again and she paused for a moment, leaning on the sink.

Stephen, sensing a moment of weakness, went to her swiftly. He put his arm round her unyielding shoulders and hugged her gently, prepared for a rebuff.

'I was going to suggest we went out for dinner,' he said. 'You must be exhausted. It's been a trying time for you, what with the wedding and . . . and everything. We could have a long talk about Hugh and . . .' He hesitated, wondering whether it was tactful to mention the move to Wales but she turned within his arms and pushed her forehead into his chest.

'Oh Stephen! I feel so miserable.'

'I know you do, love.' He held her tightly. 'What about it, then? Shall we go out? Put all that stuff back and we'll have it tomorrow.'

She was nodding, relieved to be obliged to give in, comforted by his caring and his reference to Hugh. Perhaps he *did* worry about him after all. She put the saucepans back in the cupboard and went to collect her coat. Delighted and amazed by such an easy victory, Stephen was bundling the frozen packets away and looking for his car keys. If only he could manage to be sensitive and tactful things might work out happily after all.

Chapter Five

It was quite late on a cool misty October afternoon when Annie arrived at Pippa's modern detached house on the new executive estate in the pinewoods of Surrey. Annie parked in the drive and strolled round to the back door. She knocked and went in and stood for a moment, listening. Strains of singing could be heard from the direction of the sitting room. Crossing the hall, she put her head round the door.

Pippa and Rowley, sitting together on the sofa, were watching *Play School* and singing along with the presenter who was dancing various toys, including a large teddy bear and a rag doll, on a table.

'Very nice, too,' she remarked as the song ended.

Two blond heads swung round. Pippa gave a squeak of delight and, leaping up, hugged Annie and then turned to Rowley. 'Look, darling. It's Annie. Aren't you going to say hello?'

Rowley drooped his head very slowly and stared at the hearth-rug. Presently he closed his eyes.

Pippa grinned. 'He thinks that if he can't see us, we can't see him. Take no notice. It's because we've taken him by surprise. He likes to work up to things slowly. We'll leave him for a moment and make some tea. He'll come round later.'

By the time Annie had unpacked and was back downstairs, Pippa had carried the loaded tray into the sitting room and set it down on a low table. Annie sat down, holding a large knobbly parcel on her knee. Rowley was now standing behind the sofa. All that was visible was the top of his head but there were sounds of furious thumb-sucking.

'I had hoped that I was going to see Rowley,' said Annie loudly. 'I've brought something rather special for him.'

'Have you?' asked Pippa, also loudly. 'How lovely. He seems to have vanished. What a shame!'

Annie put the parcel on the carpet by her feet and began to unwrap it with a great rustling of paper. The thumb-sucking noises ceased and an eye appeared cautiously round the end of the sofa. Pushing aside the paper, Annie drew out a bright red wooden steam engine. This was followed by two carriages, painted respectively blue and green, and two open trucks of yellow and red.

'Oh, what fun!' cried Pippa. 'It's really super!'

Annie fitted it together and then produced half a dozen or so jointed figures which she sat in the trucks.

'There,' she said at last. 'I did so hope that Rowley was going to be here to see it. Shall I put it away again?'

Rowley appeared round the corner of the sofa, his eyes fixed on the brightly coloured toy. 'Chain,' he pronounced. 'Chain.'

Annie gave a well-simulated start. 'Good Lord! Can this be Rowley? Surely not! He's much too big.' She beckoned to him and he came reluctantly, one eye still fixed on the train. 'Are you Rowley?' she demanded. 'This is Rowley's train, you see, and I can't let you play with it if you're not Rowley.'

'Am Rowley!' He smacked himself on his chest, fingers spread like starfish. 'Rowley's chain!'

Taking him unawares, she caught him to her and gave him a quick hug.

'There you are then,' she said, setting him down beside the train. 'It's all yours.'

Pippa smiled her thanks and Annie gave her a tiny wink as she accepted a piece of chocolate cake.

'Don't say you've been cooking?' she asked. 'Now did I remember to pack my indigestion tablets?'

Pippa laughed, quite unmoved by insults of her culinary attempts. 'You're quite safe,' she said. 'A friend of mine made it. It's delicious.'

'And how's Robert?' Annie nodded her agreement as she tasted the cake. 'Mmm. Quite delicious.'

'Robert's still busy.' Pippa gave a little sigh and smiled defensively at Annie. 'There's chance of a promotion coming up . . .'

'So you said.' Annie moved her feet carefully as Rowley, muttering to himself, pushed the train past her ankles. 'No news yet, then?'

'Not yet. He's a bit, you know, preoccupied . . .'

Annie smiled reassuringly at her. 'I know. Don't worry. It's you and Rowley I've come to see. I shan't expect to be entertained by Robert.'

When Robert arrived home, however, he was very ready to put himself out to play the host. He was careful never to let any of Pippa's friends or relations see his short temper or hear the sarcastic remarks with which he put her down. He was charming and witty to Annie, though cleverly allowing her to notice Pippa's inefficiencies whilst at the same time pretending that he was perfectly prepared to be patient.

This might – and did – work with many people but it cut no ice with Annie. She and Perry had seen through Robert straight away and – like Pippa's father – had deeply regretted her marrying him. Annie watched him playing with Rowley, who was obviously surprised by this sudden attention, and wondered just *why* Pippa had married him. Well, surely that was obvious! He was one of the most attractive men that Annie had ever seen and she had no doubt that, in Pippa's place, she'd have fallen head over heels in love with him just as quickly. Knowing his faults as she did, Annie was still aware of his magnetism. She sighed for the foolishness of youth. Pippa had been swept off her feet; captivated by his good looks and charm and the fact that he was significantly older than she was. There had been plenty of women attracted to him but he had selected the gauche, inexperienced Pippa.

On several occasions, Annie caught a speculative, almost calculating, expression on his face as he looked at Pippa and, although it was quickly replaced by a good-humoured, affectionate smile when he saw her watching him, Annie felt the stirrings of unease.

Lucinda, who had arrived in Bristol on Friday afternoon, was giving thanks for an elder brother who was not only prepared to lend his flat but who had a girlfriend living in London. It would have been impossible to be alone with Hugh in his student house and it was important that she had the opportunity to see how he was feeling. They'd exchanged a few letters and spoken on the telephone regularly but Lucinda was longing to know whether their separation had made any real difference. She was hoping that he'd missed her enough to take his mind off Charlotte.

Her heart beat fast as she wandered from room to room, longing for the moment when he would arrive. She felt oddly nervous and tried to calm herself by checking that there were enough supplies in the fridge and by making up the bed in the small spare room. Her brother, thank goodness, had never lectured her or questioned her. Apart from saying, 'I hope you're on the Pill, Lu. For God's sake be intelligent about it, won't you?' he had seemed to understand that young though she was, Lucinda had met the right man for her and that was that. From her earliest days, she'd always been fiercely loyal and absolutely single-minded; knowing at once what was right and going for it. Her brother trusted her. It also helped that he liked Hugh very much.

The shrill of the doorbell made Lucinda jump and she ran down the two flights of stairs and threw open the front door. Despite an overwhelming sensation of shyness, she instinctively held out her arms to him and Hugh dropped his bag and hugged her tightly.

'Oh Hugh.' She buried her face for a moment in his jersey and he smoothed the long fair hair, still holding her close. 'It seems such ages.'

'It *is* ages,' he said, as they went up the stairs entwined together. 'But it sounds as if you've been enjoying yourself.'

'It's fun,' she agreed, leading the way into the flat. 'It's helped to have Katie there with me, of course. She sends her love.'

Hugh stared around the large sunny sitting room, silent for a moment, and Lucinda felt a tiny twinge of unease.

'Mummie's invited us for Sunday,' she said rapidly, trying to recapture his attention. 'She's driving over to collect us. It's a pity your old Morris died, isn't it? It was such fun being independent.'

Hugh smiled in recollection. 'I couldn't have afforded to run her,' he said, 'and I can't really justify a car when I live so centrally. Will your mother mind my staying here with you? Or shall I pretend I've come over to meet you both?'

'Mummie's a realist.' Lucinda glanced at him, wondering how far she dare go. Could she say that her mother knew that Hugh was the only man for her daughter and accepted it? Something warned her that this was not the moment for such serious avowals. 'And it helps that she and Frances are third cousins or whatever. You're family so you must be OK.'

He laughed as she hoped he would. 'That's a relief. So.' He looked at her properly and she felt another moment of shyness but she looked at him bravely. 'You're looking very pretty. Very smart.'

'Thanks to French Connection. And I can cook a pretty delicious roulade now.'

'I'm impressed.' Hugh raised his eyebrows. 'Does that mean we're eating in?'

Lucinda made up her mind. She felt that neither of them was ready for too much intimacy yet. They needed a few hours to relax together; to get to know each other again. She was slightly dismayed at the distance between them but she was determined not to rush things.

'Certainly not!' she said, grinning at him. 'I haven't learned *that* much yet. I thought we'd go out. What about that Italian restaurant near Old Market?'

'Well . . .' Hugh hesitated, thinking of his overdraft. The Italian restaurant was very expensive.

'My treat,' said Lucinda swiftly. 'Birthday money. And thank you for my lovely necklace. I know we spoke on the phone but now you can see what it looks like.' She went close to him and held up the charming silver chain which was round her neck. 'Pretty, isn't it?'

'It's not a patch on you,' murmured Hugh, and put his arms around her.

As Christmas approached, Frances became more and more reconciled to the idea of the move to Wales and, after a great deal of heart-searching, agreed that the farmhouse should be sold. The move was scheduled for late spring and Stephen suggested that it might be wise to rent for a while until they really knew where they wanted to live. Neither of them relished the idea of house-hunting in the wet cold winter days so Frances contacted as many house agents with rented property on their books as she could find and sat back to await results.

Caroline, primed by Stephen, was very excited about the move.

'You'll be much closer to us,' she said enthusiastically, during one of her regular telephone calls. 'It'll be fun. I think you could both do with a bit of a change.'

Frances, wandering about the house which seemed so large and empty now with Caroline and Hugh both gone, was inclined to agree with her. She'd written to Hugh to tell him about their new plans and he'd written back to her. There was a time when he would have telephoned but Frances guessed that he was trying to avoid any maternal probings, and felt anxious. The letter was short, though encouraging in his enthusiasm regarding Wales, and told her little. She'd telephoned once or twice at the beginning of term but their conversations were so forced and artificial that she'd decided to leave him to himself for a while. She sent him jokey cards with just a few lines scrawled inside and left it at that.

She had agreed with Stephen that the farmhouse should go up for sale in the New Year; meanwhile she started to plan for Christmas. She was hoping that Caroline and James would come home, knowing that it would be much more fun for Hugh than if it were just the three of them. When Caroline telephoned to say that she and James could come for a whole week, Frances's relief was enormous. She could rely on her daughter to be tactful with Hugh, who was very fond of his sister and got on tremendously well with James.

Frances relaxed and decided that she could look forward to the holiday. It was unfortunate that, as she embarked upon her Christmas shopping, she seemed fated to bump into Cass Wivenhoe. In Creber's buying special chocolates, in the book shop choosing presents, in the Bedford having a restorative cup of coffee: wherever she went it seemed that she was doomed to meet her. Often she managed to avoid her. She became watchful; dodging into doorways, turning aside to stare at window displays. Occasionally, when this was impossible, she kept the conversation as brief as she could. It irritated her that Cass looked unchanged by the tragedy that she had precipitated and which had so changed Hugh: once again Frances felt the old resentment rising against her.

To Stephen's dismay, she began to grow irritable again and, as the holidays drew near, her nervousness at the thought of Hugh's return home made her touchy. Before he had gathered up his courage to probe, it burst from her in a tirade of exasperation.

'That woman!' she cried, one Saturday lunchtime on her return from shopping. 'I can't go into Tavistock without meeting her somewhere!'

'What woman?' asked Stephen apprehensively, although he thought he could make a pretty good guess. 'Whatever's the matter?'

He hurried to put the kettle on whilst Frances banged the shopping on to the table.

'Cass Wivenhoe,' said Frances. 'My God! You'd never believe she'd lost a child!'

She grumbled on behind him whilst he made the tea and desperately tried to think of some formula which would soothe rather than fan the fires of her frustration.

'Look,' he said at last, putting two mugs of tea on the kitchen table, 'you mustn't let it upset you.' He discarded a plea that Cass might be hiding her pain, guessing that Frances would completely misread it as partisanship for Cass, and had a better idea. 'It doesn't matter any more. We'll be gone from here soon and you'll never see her again. Don't let her spoil our last Christmas together in this house. Please, love. We've been so happy here, till just lately, anyway.'

She looked at him quickly and he saw that he'd hit the right note. He pushed her mug closer to her hand and smiled at her.

She smiled back a little unwillingly. 'I hate her,' she said childishly and burst out laughing at herself.

'I know,' he said, encouraged by that laughter. 'Let's not think about it. The kids will be here in a few days' time and we don't want to spoil things for them, do we? It might be the last Christmas we'll have all together.'

'What do you mean?' She looked at him fearfully.

'Just that they're growing older. Caroline and James might have a baby next year and want to stay at home and Hugh might go off skiing or go to friends or something. We'll have to lose them sometime. Let's make it the best Christmas we've ever had.'

'Oh Stephen.' She sounded distressed. 'I'm sorry . . .'

'Forget it,' he said swiftly. 'I understand how you feel. Honestly. Let's just make a pact to be happy.' He reached a hand across the table and she took it. 'And from now on,' he squeezed her hand and let it go, 'we'll do all our shopping in Plymouth.'

Chapter Six

The wind blew from the north-east, driving the towering, bulging mass of pewter-coloured clouds before it and whistling amongst the haphazard piles of granite outcrop. The twisted hawthorn bowed before its freezing breath – the bare black branches rattling and creaking at its passing; the rusty dead bracken shivered at its touch. It swept on across the sheets of thin ice which crusted the flooded bogs and reflected back the occasional gleam of brighter light shafting down between the swiftly rolling clouds.

The frozen ground seemed to echo beneath Hugh's boots as he strode across Haytor Down, hands plunged deep into pockets, his head bent to protect his face from the wind's cutting edge. As he stood on Black Hill, staring across Lustleigh Cleave to the coast, he was certain that he could see white breakers out on the distant sea. He blinked away the stinging tears from his eyes as he cleaned his spectacles on his handkerchief and smiled a little at himself. Surely it was too far to see any such thing! He stood quite still, resisting the wind's thrust, experiencing into the depth of his very soul the glory, the solitude, the indescribable magnificence of the country that lay spread out at his feet.

His introspective mood took pleasure in the bleak, wild day and brought him a kind of comfort.

Christmas was over. Caroline and James had returned to Gloucestershire and now Hugh had too much time on his hands. He had neglected to secure his job at the Royal Oak and another student had beaten him to it, although he'd worked a few days here and there during Christmas and the New Year. Nevertheless, he had decided on an early return to Bristol. Lucinda had gone skiing with her parents and her younger sister but Hugh had declined an invitation to join them. He had pleaded poverty – which was true – although he knew that Stephen would have almost certainly supplied the necessary funds. Hugh, however, had been unable to face a jolly family holiday. He was still confused about his feelings for Lucinda. He loved her, he was sure of that, yet he was unable to pour out his innermost feelings to her. Knowing how she felt about Charlotte's death made it impossible to express himself to her and he'd almost begun to resent her ability to behave as if the tragedy had never happened.

He remembered how they'd gone back to the flat after the scene with Charlotte in Park Street and he'd tried to make love to Lucinda so as to blot out his memory of Charlotte's face and his own feelings of guilt. It had all come flooding back to him during the weekend he'd spent there with Lucinda last term and he'd been unable to shake off his feelings of oppression.

Hugh turned to retrace his steps back to the car park at Haytor Vale. He had deliberately driven some distance from his own corner of the moor in an attempt to avoid the constant reminders of those earlier walks and rides. The move to Wales would bring respite from such reminders but how terribly he would miss Dartmoor! There were other moors, of course, but here, he felt, was his home: the place where he belonged. If only he could conquer his grief and guilt he need not be driven away from it but it was almost a relief that, for the moment at least, matters were being taken out of his hands.

His attention was caught by the sight of a Land Rover being driven along the road below him. It turned on to a track and bumped down towards a collection of barns which were invisible from the road but which Hugh could see clearly from his higher vantage point. A large caravan was parked in a corner and Hugh guessed that the barns were being renovated. He watched a figure swing himself out of the Land Rover, hurry across the yard and go into the caravan. Perhaps, thought Hugh, he was living there whilst he worked on the barns – and he felt a stab of envy for anyone who owned even a tiny part of the moor.

Maxwell Driver closed the caravan door behind him and shivered, glad to be out of the biting wind and back in the shelter of his caravan. Twelve years in the Royal Marines, rising through the ranks to sergeant, had taught him to be neat and clean and the interior of the caravan was intelligently arranged so as to extract the maximum benefit of efficiency and comfort. He switched on the heater, took off his duffel coat – which he hung behind the door – and began to unpack his shopping. He worked methodically, putting each item away in its allotted space and pausing only to pummel himself vigorously against the chill.

He was of no more than average height and his thick jersey disguised his muscular wiriness but he carried with him an air of competence and vitality, and his nickname of 'Slave' Driver had been used only half in jest. The dark hair was a little longer than the Service short back and sides and it was already touched with grey although he was barely thirty.

These seven acres on Trendlebere Down, with the group of barns and the cowman's cottage, were all that remained of his ancestors' farming land on this south-east corner of the moor. His grandfather had had no sons to inherit the farm, and no sons-in-law who were prepared to take it over, so gradually most of it had been sold and the proceeds divided between his three daughters. This small portion was his mother's gift to him and it was all that Max had ever wanted. From a very young man he'd known exactly what he would do with it, should he be lucky enough to inherit it. His twelve years in the Marines had merely been a training for what he thought of as his real career. In his mind's eye, as he walked his few acres and studied the barns, he saw his adventure training school rising before him: this barn for the boys' dormitories; that one for the girls'; a third for recreation rooms. The original small dwelling house was earmarked for his own quarters and offices.

When his father – a chief petty officer in the Royal Navy – died, and his mother announced her intention of giving him the land, he immediately applied for Outline Planning Permission and put in his resignation. He refused a commission and waited patiently for his freedom. In the meantime, he drew plans, worked out his sums and counted up his savings. It was going to be tight; very tight indeed! His bank manager, however, was sympathetic and – luckily for Max – could share his vision. In light of Max's good record with the bank – not to mention his healthy deposit account and good service pension – he was prepared to be helpful in return for a first charge over the property.

So here Max was, ready to go. A gust of wind shook the caravan as he settled himself at the table and drew out the well-thumbed folder. Not this summer but next, perhaps, his dream would become a reality.

Unknown to Pippa, her husband Robert had been carefully pursuing the senior partner's personal assistant, a chic, sophisticated girl who recognised Robert's determination to succeed and was impressed by the senior management's high opinion of him. She'd informed him of this during a lunchtime session at the pub and noted the flash of triumph which he immediately attempted to conceal.

'That's the sort of remark that's guaranteed to buy you a good lunch,' he said, pretending to dismiss it as flattery.

'I can buy my own lunch, thanks,' Louisa said coolly. 'I just thought you ought to know, that's all. It might make up for the embarrassment you had last week.' She watched the dull flush creep into his cheeks and smiled a little.

'Don't remind me,' he said bitterly.

She laughed. 'I shouldn't have mentioned it.' She paused to allow him to experience the maximum discomfort before touching him lightly on the arm. 'Why don't I buy you a drink?' she said. 'You look as if you need one.'

She picked up her bag and went to the bar, leaving Robert

to bite his lip in mortification. So Pippa's débâcle was all over the office! He could guess how, too. The senior partner's wife came from a Colonial Office background and was an old friend of Louisa's father who was in the Foreign Office.

No question how Louisa had got her job, thought Robert spitefully, watching her at the bar and subconsciously admiring her neat bottom in the short black skirt which displayed her well-shaped legs to advantage. He forgot his humiliation for a moment as he appraised her. She was so . . . *economical*, he finally decided; no spare flesh or untidy mane of hair; no drooping clothing or extravagant displays of jewellery. Now if *she* were his wife, the sky would be the limit. Well, why not? The idea caught him in mid-speculation and he swallowed – gulped, in fact – at the sheer enormity of it.

He turned his eyes away from Louisa and thought about the disastrous dinner party. To be fair – did he want to be fair? – Rowley had wakened from his after-lunch sleep with a violent earache. Unable to explain the nature of the pain which made him scream in agony, he had become so uncontrollable that Pippa had abandoned her cooking and fled with him to the surgery. There was a flap on – a boy had nearly severed his finger with a knife – and, by the time Rowley had been attended to and Pippa had dashed off to the late-night chemist, the dinner was beyond hope.

Robert had arrived home to chaos and nothing prepared. Pippa, her hair all over the place and still in her jeans, had protested that she'd been certain that the oven was on when she put the meat into it before rushing off to the surgery.

White with rage, Robert had pushed her aside, made a lightning check of their food stocks and had raced round to the supermarket. The senior partner and his wife had arrived just as he'd been putting the last touches to the table and Pippa was still struggling into her dress.

He'd majored on Rowley's ear infection, of course, attempting to make light of the indifferent food and Pippa's distrait manner, but he didn't deceive Eleanor Spencer. Recalling her polite smile and sharp contemptuous glances, Robert writhed anew. Her raised eyebrows implied that any girl worth her salt would be more than equal to this kind of domestic drama whilst Pippa, one ear cocked lest Rowley should wake and be distressed, was barely capable of conversation and quite unaware of her guests' disapproval.

Robert stirred as Louisa's slim, well-manicured hand appeared at his elbow holding a pint of beer. He pulled himself together and smiled up at her. He made sure that she saw the admiration in his eyes and his smile was a little rueful.

'I simply don't know what to do about Pippa,' he said.

This direct approach silenced her for a moment. She slid into the seat beside him and made a play of depositing her belongings on the edge of the table.

'Do?' she asked quizzically as she raised her glass to him.

He allowed his expression to become faintly tormented. 'We're absolutely wrong for each other. Oh!' He held up his hand and shook his head, as though she might be about to protest. 'It's absolutely my fault. I know that. She was so young and pretty and, to tell the truth, I was flattered by her . . . by her . . . well . . .' He hesitated. He didn't want to sound too conceited.

Louisa sipped her wine thoughtfully. As well as Robert's quite devastating sexiness, his drive and toughness also had a very aphrodisiac effect on her. She knew that he was set for early promotion and even the formidable Eleanor liked him.

'Not quite the top drawer,' she'd said to Louisa privately, 'but with that kind of determination, it really doesn't matter. Personally, I think it gives him a bit of an edge and he certainly knows how to behave himself socially. And, my goodness, what a gorgeous creature he is!' They'd giggled a little together. 'But that wife of his.' Eleanor shook her large handsome head. 'Hopeless. Absolutely hopeless.'

Louisa considered this earlier conversation, turning the wine glass in her fingers. 'She's quite a bit younger than you, isn't she?'

'Mmm?' Robert was pretending to be lost in his own thoughts so as to give her plenty of opportunity to make the next move. 'Yes. Yes, she is. That's part of the trouble.'

They were both silent; Robert wondering if he'd been too precipitate; Louisa deciding whether she should commit herself to a further step towards intimacy. Robert stretched out his long legs, touched her foot accidentally and moved quickly. The physical contact was enough to break the impasse. They exchanged a long, appraising, exciting stare. Robert was the first to look away and Louisa felt a sense of exhilaration.

'I'm having a little drinks party after work on Thursday,' she said casually. 'Why don't you pop in on the way home?'

'I'd like to very much.' He tried not to show his surprise or to sound *too* eager.

'Great.' She paused and their eyes met again. 'I don't know how long it will go on for . . .' She shrugged. 'I might do little eats for a light supper. Play it by ear.'

'Right.' He knew she was warning him not to tell Pippa what time he'd be home. 'Sounds fun.'

'Mmm. Mike and Janet are coming, and Eleanor and John might drop in. And there will be a few of my friends. See how you feel.'

Robert knew exactly how he'd feel. Mike was his boss and it would be an excellent opportunity to be in the company of the senior partner and his wife without having to keep an eye on Pippa. Add to these advantages the possibility of furthering his relationship with Louisa and it became an offer he simply couldn't refuse. He sighed with satisfaction.

'I'll be there,' he said.

Louisa took the opportunity to show how such an evening should be carried off and did it with charm and wit whilst providing excellent food and drink. She made it look so effortless that Robert was genuinely impressed and – since neither of them had a partner – she cunningly deployed him so as to give the impression that they were joint hosts. She made certain that he had the chance to talk privately with John Spencer and cleverly manipulated the conversation so that he shone before Eleanor and Mike. It gave her an exciting sense of power and, when all the guests had gone, their lovemaking was fierce and mutually satisfying.

By February they had been lovers for six months and Robert was even more certain that Pippa was simply a drag on his career and a threat to his prospects. He wished to be free to pursue them – and Louisa – and he was gradually coming to the conclusion that there was no better way than to be brutally honest about it.

Chapter Seven

By the New Year, Frances and Stephen were so far deceived by Hugh's quiet tractable behaviour that they were able to tell themselves that he was on the mend at last. Throughout the Christmas holiday he had been cheerful and so ready to fall in with his family's plans that Caroline roundly told her mother that she'd been making a fuss about nothing. Frances was only too thankful to believe it.

'He was always a sensitive boy,' said Caroline, with the new positive confidence that marriage had added to her natural bossiness. 'Naturally, he'd take something like that harder than most people. You've got to stop worrying about him, Mum. He's probably playing up to you.'

Frances accepted these and other strictures meekly, feeling that their roles were temporarily reversed. She was too relieved to see both her children happy to feel resentful. Caroline's patent satisfaction in the married state was a joy to behold, although Frances couldn't help the occasional anxious glance at James to check that he was not overshadowed by her forceful personality. In fact, he seemed positively to enjoy relaxing back into Caroline's care and control, and Frances could be happy. She wondered from whom Caroline had inherited this dominant streak and decided that it was from her maternal grandmother. One evening, after supper, she said as much to Stephen who smiled a little but remained silent.

'What are you grinning at?' she asked, as she dried the plates he was washing and placing on the draining board. 'Oh, I know what you're thinking! You're thinking she gets it from me!'

Stephen raised his dripping hands. 'I didn't say a word.'

'You didn't need to with that smug look on your face,' she cried indignantly. 'I'm *not* bossy!'

'Perish the thought,' said Stephen, ducking as she swiped at him with the damp tea cloth.

'I only boss people when they need it,' she laughed, and then, more seriously: 'Oh Stephen, Hugh *is* better, isn't he?'

She'd said it a hundred times since Hugh had gone back to Bristol but he answered her as though it were the first.

'Much better. A bit quiet—'

'But Hugh was always quiet, wasn't he?' she broke in anxiously and he cursed himself for his stupidity.

'Oh yes.' He was deliberately casual. 'I only meant that I'd like to see him more lively. But that's Hugh. Nothing to do with . . . the other thing.'

'No.' She wanted to believe that. 'I shall be so relieved to see him settled down. It's a pity Lucinda went off skiing. I'm sure he misses her.'

'Give them a chance.' Stephen swirled the water round the sink and turned to dry his hands on the roller-towel behind the kitchen door. 'He's a bit young to be getting married just yet.'

'I didn't mean quite that.' Frances began to stack the clean plates on to the shelves of the dresser. 'I meant qualified and in a good job. You know.' She sighed as she hung the tea cloth on the Aga's rail. 'But to be honest, I'd be perfectly happy if he and Lucinda wanted to get engaged.'

'No good trying to rush things,' warned Stephen. 'Hugh needs to mature a bit. He's much too young to be tied down yet.'

'Caroline wasn't much older when she met James,' Frances reminded him, pushing the kettle over to boil.

'That's different,' said Stephen, and tried to think why.

Frances, however, made no attempt to take him up on it. She was still musing over Hugh.

'I think you're right about the move,' she said. 'It's a good thing for all of us.' She saw an opportunity to put right her earlier indifference to his achievement. 'Are you excited about it? You must be feeling very proud of yourself. I know I am!'

He smiled then, accepting her gesture and all that it implied.

'It *is* rather exciting,' he admitted cautiously. 'But there are a few snags to be ironed out. We must get on to the house agents. Four months seems a long time but we ought to be getting things going.'

'I'll do it tomorrow,' she promised.

'You do that.' He glanced at his watch. 'Go on. Your nature programme's about to begin. I'll make the coffee.'

As he waited for the kettle to boil, Stephen leaned on the Aga rail and wondered if their optimism regarding Hugh was justified. He had been more cheerful, more ready to join in, but Stephen had noticed that tendency to withdraw manifesting itself again once Caroline and James had gone. The difficulty was that it was impossible now to decide how Hugh might be behaving if Charlotte had not died. He might just as easily be brooding over his pressure of work, or some aspect of his relationship with Lucinda, as anything else.

Stephen straightened up and applied himself to coffee-making. He knew that he was counting on the move as the solution. He was convinced that Hugh was better and that the change of area was all that was needed to complete the healing process. Having come to this conclusion he put all thoughts of Hugh aside and, as he made the coffee, he began to think about his own problems in the department and the complications involved in the move.

The cold winds of the New Year had given way to a mild wet spell and now, with the catkin clusters hanging from the twigs and the pale gold of primroses gleaming from the hedgerows, spring seemed very close. Annie, strolling across the neighbouring field, was undeceived. She knew how swiftly the weather could change; the fragile blooms weighted with snow, the too-daring buds blighted with frost. The bridle path hugged the thorny hedge which soon would be covered with the white blossom of the blackthorn and she paused to lift aside the straggling grasses with the ferrule of her walking stick. A patch of snowdrops sheltered between the roots and she was quite suddenly engulfed in a wave of physical longing for Perry.

How eagerly he had approached the changing seasons – each with some special job to be anticipated – and with what enthusiasm he had invested the quiet pleasures of the daily round! Annie let her stick drop back and leaned on it as the hot tears gushed from her eyes. She might feel the closeness of his spirit but she still yearned for the feel of his arms about her; the consoling warmth of his body. She missed, too, those past days of great excitement, wild uncertainty or glorious success. One never knew with Perry what might be approaching but his great spiritual strength, his ineffable good humour and his overwhelming love for her had more than compensated for the anxieties that had been the inevitable result of the occasional misplacements of trust, which were the occupational hazards of such a generous character.

Annie bent over her stick, one hand clutched against the pain of her loneliness, and wept in despair. How terrible and final was death! Even now she could barely believe that he was gone from her. She caught herself waiting for his voice, calling from the garden or from the landing, or willing herself to think that she could feel his presence.

'Nothing shall part us,' he'd declared when she'd spoken fearfully about death. 'If I go first I shall still be with you if I'm allowed. Though there will be lots of work for a new boy!'

Perry looked upon heaven as a hierarchy. You started at the bottom and worked your way up, unless you had been some great saint on this earth in which case you went straight into the top class. He was looking forward to it, Annie could tell. His natural curiosity rejoiced at there being so much to learn. Yet he would not have wished to go so soon. He had made so many plans for their retirement and, with one of his many gambles having paid off handsomely, he'd resolved to put his entrepreneurial schemes behind him and settle down. He was on his way back from London, after winding up various outstanding commitments, when he had died.

'All done and finished with!' he'd told her jubilantly from the telephone box on Paddington Station. 'Just in time for the train. See you at Newton at about seven o'clock. Drive carefully, my darling. Must go! Out of money. I love you.'

They were his last words to her; shouted as the pips signalled their warning. As he ran for the train the heart attack struck him down and she never saw him alive again. She relived the anguish of that moment as she stood hunched in the corner of the field. How to go forward? How to continue the empty pointless procedure called life? Without Perry it was all dust and ashes. She thanked God that he'd stamped his presence so firmly on the cottage and, dealing with her grief as best she might, settled down to wait for his return to it. If what he believed was true then she must surely feel him near her. However busy he was, 'learning the ropes', he would surely respond to her desperate need and prayers. Gradually, as the months passed she'd begun to feel him near her, aware of his love still shielding and comforting her, but still these terrible moments of grief assailed her, shaking her and disordering her hard-won peace of mind.

Annie left the shelter of the hedge, hesitated, and, turning back, bent to pick up a few of the snowdrops. Holding them against her lips, so as to inhale their delicate fugitive scent, she walked slowly home, along the path and down the track. As she entered the cottage, the telephone began to ring. Laying the snowdrops gently on the terracotta tiles she went to answer it.

'Annie. It's me. Pippa.' The voice burst hysterically out of the handset. 'Oh Annie, something terrible has happened. Robert says he's leaving me.'

'Wait!' commanded Annie, swiftly pushing away her own thoughts as she heard the tears in Pippa's voice. 'Calmly now. Tell me from the beginning.'

When *was* the beginning? Through the days to come, Pippa asked herself that question over and over again. She racked her brain for some sign that she had missed, some portent that would have warned her. There was none.

Robert had told her quite calmly at breakfast-time. He'd chosen it deliberately; Pippa was never at her best early in the morning. She'd tried hard to become accustomed to his early routine, which was always the same. It was she who made the early morning tea, once the tinny wheezings of the alarm clock had roused her, and then there were eighteen minutes in which to get his breakfast before he appeared; showered, shaved and immaculate in his London clothes.

Eighteen minutes is ample time in which to prepare toast, coffee and orange juice – which was all that Robert would touch – so it was perhaps surprising that there were mornings when she was not ready for him. He could never understand how easy it was to forget to buy the new pot of marmalade, to leave the butter in the fridge so that it was as hard and spreadable as a brick or to allow the toast to burn whilst she was dreaming out of the window.

She was pouring his coffee – black – when he came into the kitchen. Robert did not encourage idle chatter at breakfast so Pippa, subsiding into the chair opposite and yawning hugely, was surprised out of her yawn when he spoke.

'I want to talk to you about something before I go,' he said abruptly.

Pippa felt the usual clutch of apprehension and cast her mind over possible bones of contention.

'I've booked the car in for its MOT,' she began – but he frowned impatiently.

'It's much more important than that. I think it's time we had a straight talk.' He was fiddling with the butter knife and wouldn't look at her. 'I suspect that you'd agree with me that our marriage is not all that we hoped it would be. My fault as much as yours, I dare say, but it seems to me that we have very little in common and we're drifting further and further apart. My feeling is that the time has come to bring it to an end and go our separate ways.'

He looked at her at last to see her staring back at him, dumbfounded. He raised his eyebrows, as though inviting her to speak, but she continued to sit in silence whilst she struggled with the blow he had dealt her. He gave a tiny shrug as though marvelling at yet a further instance of their incompatibility. The shrug had the effect of pulling her together and she attempted to speak calmly.

'I imagine you must be serious? You couldn't possibly joke about such a thing? No,' as he shook his head in disgust at the idea, 'no, of course not but . . . I'm sorry, Robert, but

I just can't *believe* what you're saying. How *can* you be serious? I thought you were perfectly happy . . .'

'The fact that you've thought so surely underlines what I've been saying and indicates how little you understand me. You're not interested in my work, you make no attempt to be supportive. You refuse to entertain—'

'That's a lie!' she cried indignantly. 'You refuse to talk about your work and when I ask questions you imply that I'm ignorant and stupid –' he rolled his eyes heavenwards – 'and we used to entertain—'

'Until,' he interrupted smoothly, 'I realized that your haphazard ways and total lack of organisation, coupled with a complete inability to relate to the partners and their wives, were causing more harm than good.'

He stopped, looking away from the shock on her face and the misery in her eyes.

'Robert,' she pleaded. 'Don't be like this. It's . . . it's horrible. You make it sound as if I'm some kind of employee. I'm your wife, not your secretary.'

He bit back the contemptuous retort that leaped to his lips and thought quickly and carefully.

'Look, Pippa,' he said, allowing a tiny touch of patient resignation to tinge the new, kinder inflection. 'I genuinely thought that you felt the same way. I'm sorry that it's come as such a shock. You must agree that we have hardly anything to say to each other . . .'

'That's because you're never here,' she burst out. 'It's nothing but work, work, work. Rowley barely recognises you any more.' She stopped short and looked at him aghast. 'You can't mean it, Robert. You can't leave me and Rowley.

Don't you care about Rowley?'

'Oh, for goodness' sake!' Robert decided that a show of irritation would be the best thing to get him off the hook. 'Of course I care about Rowley. But it would be madness for us to remain together unhappily for the sake of a child.'

'But I love you,' she said. 'I love you, Robert. I haven't changed.' A new frightening thought struck her. 'Is there somebody else?'

'Of course there isn't.' He stood up swiftly. 'Why should there be somebody else? Please try to accept the fact that we're absolutely unsuited, Pippa. It's quite simple. We were in too much of a hurry to get married. Your father was right there. I must go or I shall miss my train. Please give it careful thought and we'll talk again this evening. Only for heaven's sake *think* about it, Pippa.'

She shook her head. 'I simply can't believe this is happening.'

'The sad fact of the matter is,' he said, pausing at the door, 'that you're so wrapped up in yourself and Rowley that you don't notice what's been staring you in the face. I'm sorry, Pippa. It's over. Let's just try to be civilised about it.'

He made his escape, congratulating himself on his clever timing. Pippa sat on. The shock had numbed her and she shook her head several times as though to dispel the words that echoed in her brain. Presently Rowley's shouts pierced her preoccupation and she stood up, almost relieved that the daily round must go on. Perhaps there was some crisis at the office which had pushed Robert over the top and made him act so wildly? She knew that he'd been terribly strung up over the approaching promotion. Perhaps the coveted position had gone to someone else and he was overreacting and taking it out on her? It simply wasn't believable! Rowley's roars increased as Pippa took the stairs two at a time. There must be some explanation and she must be very careful until she knew what it was.

Chapter Eight

Annie had listened sympathetically to Pippa's rendering of events 'from the beginning' and attempted to comfort and support. Afterwards, she put the snowdrops in water, poured herself a drink and carried it into the sitting room. The huge bay window, so odd on a small cottage, allowed the late afternoon light to fill the room. Here, all was peace and tranquillity; the walls, washed in dove grey, were hung with original paintings in gentle, chalky colours; the deep, comfortable chairs were covered in brocades of dusty rose and misty blues. The rugs that lay upon the polished oak floor were of darker subtler shades and the long curtains were a dark rich cherry red.

Annie placed her glass and the tiny lustre jug, which contained the snowdrops, on a low table and went to open the glass doors of the big pot-bellied wood-burning stove which stood on a granite slab in a wide deep recess. She placed several more logs into its cavernous glowing maw and, leaving the doors wide, went to sit in one of the armchairs. This chair had been the one which Perry had favoured. An oak trolley stood beside it which had always been laden with his books and papers and which she had left untouched for nearly a year after his death. Putting away his things had seemed, strangely, more final, more terrible even than his burial. Here he had sat, turning the pages, reading her snippets of information, making notes. Here he had snoozed, head drooping, his book slipping from his grasp; here he had perched, the toasting-fork with its cargo of bread held out to the embers, whilst he propounded his most recent theory.

Gradually Annie had put away some of his belongings and, lately, when the pain of missing him refused to abate, she wondered if she might find comfort from sitting in the chair which he had occupied. It was a bigger chair than she was used to, especially chosen to accommodate the length of his limbs, and she was obliged to pad herself about with cushions. Nevertheless, there seemed some faint comfort from curling into Perry's chair and having his table close at hand. Now, she drew her legs under her and reached for her glass. She sighed a little as she sipped, thinking about Pippa.

When Annie's mother had died Annie's sorrow had been mixed with a tiny quantity of relief. As she grew older, her mother had become more and more demanding and Annie had been allowed no time to develop her own life. She regretted nothing but freedom came late to her and she treasured it. Perhaps it was a fear that she might be drawn back into such servitude that made her wish to hold people at arm's length. Her natural generosity made her feel guilty that occasionally she was cautious of expending time and energy on behalf of others or was sometimes unable to give of herself freely and openly. She had once said as much to Perry.

'I'm not as generous as you are,' she'd cried, ashamed at some small act of withholding.

'Absolute nonsense!' His long arms had enfolded her. 'You were brought up in a hard school, my darling,' he'd said, tenderly. 'You've given of yourself all your life. But we've got so much, Annie. Surely we can spare a little of ourselves? We're so lucky . . .'

Annie swallowed hard as she stared deep into the fire's heart. After all, she had all the time in the world now. Surely some of it could be spared ungrudgingly to Pippa?

'Poor child.' Perry looked in at the door. 'Dreadful man. Always knew it wouldn't work!'

'But what can I *do*?' muttered Annie desperately.

'Time will show,' said Perry confidently. 'Just relax.'

Soothed, she rested her head back against the cushions and sipped slowly. Evening drew on and the room grew darker, lit only by the fire's glow. Clutching the glass against her breast she dozed, dreaming that she and Perry were walking in the field. He was showing her the snowdrops, picking them, delighting with her in their fragile beauty. She smiled at him, wondering why she had imagined that he'd died, and woke to find that her cheeks were wet with tears.

After a great deal of consideration, Robert decided to keep the subject of the breakdown of his marriage very low-key. Never once had Louise intimated that she was looking for a permanent relationship and it occurred to him that she might feel that he was attempting to force her hand. For the first time in his life Robert had met a woman who was at least as tough as he was and it was a novel and exciting experience. As far as he was capable of loving anyone but himself he loved Louisa and he knew that, given the opportunity, they would make a superb team. What Louisa thought was less clear to him but his intuition warned him that she would be extremely displeased if he indicated, however obliquely, that she was the reason that he had decided to seek a separation from his wife. She had managed to distance herself from that whole side of his life and, by behaving as though Pippa and Rowley didn't exist, gave Robert to understand that she wished to have nothing to do with any messy business regarding separation or divorce.

He began his campaign by letting drop remarks which implied that Pippa was just as tired of their marriage as he was and that they had both mistaken a brief infatuation for the authentic fire. Louisa listened, without appearing to, but refused to be drawn. She had no intention of feeling responsible for Robert's mistakes nor of taking the least vestige of guilt to herself. If Robert preferred her to his wife then that was Pippa's problem and she and he must deal with it accordingly without applying to Louisa.

Robert edged his way forward cautiously, trying to gauge Louisa's true feelings for him whilst coldly and brutally severing the bonds that bound him to Pippa and Rowley. He planned his strategy well in advance; anticipating her reactions, prepared for her unhappy protests. He was impregnable. She battered uselessly at the well-fortified wall of his indifference to her sufferings; pleaded in vain with his fully armoured and ruthless determination. Presently she began to give up hope.

* * *

The snow fell lightly. It floated, twirling prettily in the wind, and settling gently on the cold dry earth. The light dusting of white did not worry Frances, who was setting out to have tea with Annie. Stephen had gone to Wales for a few days and Frances, suddenly restless, had decided that Annie needed cheering up. She telephoned and suggested that she should drive over after lunch and Annie had sounded pleased at the idea. Frances looked at the idly falling flakes and refused to be deterred. There had been several wintry showers in the last few days, none of which had amounted to anything. Nevertheless, she put her gumboots and her long waterproof coat into the back of the car before she set off up the lane. As she turned on to the Princetown road she knew a moment of anxiety. Perhaps it was foolish to be going out on such an afternoon – but her flash of good sense was swamped by an uprush of rebellion. She was tired of sitting at home, waiting for people to come to view the house, or brooding over the wisdom of selling up and moving. Endlessly she weighed the pros and cons. Would it not be wiser to rent out the farmhouse, in case they wanted to come back?

'But there won't be a job for me here,' Stephen had pointed out, reasonably enough, when she voiced this suggestion. 'You'll be OK when we get an offer. This is always the worst time. Life is easier when your decisions are made for you.'

As she drove through Princetown, Frances wondered whether this were true. She wasn't at all sure that she liked having decisions taken out of her hands. At the sight of the prison, standing bleak and forbidding in the whitening fields, she gave a little shiver. Having your decisions made for you was in some sense like being a prisoner: your own will subdued to the requirements of those about you. Instinctively she thought of Hugh. He had spent his young life continually having decisions made on his behalf. Poor Hugh! But, she argued with herself, it's always so with children. How can they decide what is best for them?

As she branched left on to the road to Moretonhampstead she remembered that the small Caroline had often made decisions for herself; what she would wear, what should be read to her, what she wanted to eat. But then, thought Frances, Caroline always knew exactly what she wanted. Hugh never did. Brooding on the difference in temperament between her two offspring, Frances hardly noticed that the snow was falling more heavily now, nor that the wind was increasing in its gusty fitfulness. She was absorbed by a new idea. Had Hugh's fondness for Charlotte been based on the fact that she was even more indecisive and unsure of herself than he was? It must have been rather a nice change for Hugh to be looked up to and deferred to; to be the one who boosted her confidence and encouraged her.

Not that Hugh is unconfident, Frances told herself, changing down in readiness to negotiate the Cherrybrook Bridge. The road was becoming a little more slippery and she drove cautiously but her mind was still on Hugh. She caught her breath abruptly as she breasted the hill beyond the Warren House Inn and the car was buffeted by a gust of wind which blew the snow hither and thither upon the road and caused her to grip the wheel more tightly. Jerked out of her musings she gazed round her. It had been snowing here for some time and the vast spaces of the moor, across to Fernworthy Reservoir to the west and over to Hookney Tor and King Tor to the east, were blotted out by a blanket of snow.

So wrapped up in her thoughts had she been that Frances suddenly realised that she had taken her usual route to Exeter instead of the road to Ashburton. Cursing silently, she turned right at Beetor Cross, now beginning to feel seriously nervous, realising that it was some time since she'd seen another vehicle. What a fool she'd been to set out so blithely without checking a weather forecast or, at least, making a hot drink in the flask! She drove slowly, praying that she met no on-coming vehicle in the narrow lane.

As she reached the junction at Harefoot Cross it was snowing in earnest and now she felt the full force of the wind which was blowing from the north-east; she could barely see beyond the windscreen. The winter afternoon was dark with whirling snow and her arms ached from gripping the wheel so tightly. She turned left, the car's back wheel sliding precariously, and gave a tiny scream as a vehicle lurched out of the snow directly in her path. She swung the wheel violently to the left and felt the car sliding out of control. Quickly she turned the wheel back but she was too late, the car described a graceful semi-circle and came to rest at an angle which told her that she was off the road. She could hear the wheels spinning as she revved the engine and, determined not to panic, she sat quite still, trying to decide what to do.

She had read somewhere that, under these circumstances, it was always best to sit in a car and wait for help rather than to set off alone; but supposing no help came? Frances felt a chill that had nothing to do with the weather conditions. These roads were all but deserted in the depths of winter and, in such conditions, very few people would be likely to be setting out to drive across the moor. She shivered. At least in the car she would be warm. The heater . . . Frances paused, mid-thought. Supposing the exhaust were to fill up with snow? She might die of carbon monoxide poisoning! She would feel drowsy first, of course . . . Convinced that she was already feeling drowsy, Frances abruptly switched off the engine.

The silence was absolute. Staring out at the blinding snow, which was now covering the windscreen, Frances knew real fear. She felt trapped and vulnerable and the idea of spending the night alone on the moor in a snow-covered car filled her with dread. Resolutely she marshalled her courage and her wits. It was barely four o'clock and still daylight and Widecombe was less than a mile or two away. She had but to follow the road down into the village and ask for shelter at the pub; better surely than freezing to death in the car! Frances pushed back the seat, so as to have the room to exchange her shoes for boots, and dragged her coat on with difficulty in the cramped space. Hanging her shoulder bag round her neck, she climbed from the car and peered into the snowy landscape. Surely there would be a landmark that would indicate the road; a signpost, perhaps, or some telephone poles? She knew a sudden reluctance to leave the safety of the car and hesitated, the keys in her hand, wondering whether to get back in and wait to be found. A glance at the rounded mound, disappearing beneath the ineluctably falling snow, made her shudder. Turning her back on the car she struck out bravely in the direction of Widecombe.

Max, coaxing the Land Rover up the hill out of Widecombe, cursed as a woman appeared suddenly out of the snowy wastes of the moor. She ran into the road towards him, waving her arms, and Max cursed again as he gingerly turned the wheel so as to avoid running her down. As he came level with her he leaned across, struggling to open the passenger door whilst keeping the Land Rover moving at an infinitesimal speed.

'I can't stop,' he shouted. 'Get in if you can.'

He stretched a hand as the figure scrabbled frantically at the swinging door, seized his wrist with a cold wet hand and was hauled head first on to the bench seat.

'Thank God you came along!' grasped Frances, half sobbing with gratitude, as she scrambled into a sitting position. 'I lost my bearings and wandered off the road. The relief when I saw your headlights! I was afraid you weren't going to stop.'

'I didn't,' Max pointed out. 'It would have been madness in this weather. Where did you spring from?'

'I got pushed off the road, just along here.' Frances peered from the window, her teeth chattering. 'I didn't know whether to stay in the car or start walking.'

'You should've stayed in the car,' said Max. 'It's always safest.'

'I might have frozen to death.' Frances stared at his stern profile, put out – despite her gratitude – by the unfeeling certainty of his reply. 'I could have been there for weeks.'

'I doubt it.' Max smiled a little at the indignation in her voice. 'Where were you headed for?'

'I was going to tea with a friend of mine in Ashburton,' she answered and was embarrassed by his silence, imagining that he was criticising such irresponsible behaviour. 'It was barely snowing when I set out,' she said defensively, peering again from the window. 'Where are we going?'

'Home,' said Max briefly. 'You'll have to come along, I'm afraid. I'm not risking tea parties in this weather.'

'Oh dear,' said Frances anxiously. 'Annie will worry if I don't turn up. May I telephone from your place?'

'I don't have a telephone.' He sounded unconcerned by her plight. 'Your friend will have to wait till it stops snowing. It won't amount to much.'

'How do you know it won't?' she asked, somewhat sharply. 'It can be terrible up here on the moor.'

'I know that,' said Max calmly. 'My family have farmed up here for the last century or more. As for the snow, I listened to the weather forecast at lunchtime.'

'Oh.' Frances subsided back on to the seat, feeling rather foolish. 'Then I'm surprised you ventured out in it,' she observed waspishly, after a moment.

'It's worse than I allowed for,' agreed Max placidly. 'But the Land Rover's a good old girl. She'll get your car out of the ditch, I dare say, when it lets up a bit.'

'Thank you,' said Frances, slightly surprised at the offer and now rather ashamed of herself. 'That's very kind.'

'Nearly home.' They were bumping over some kind of track. 'We'll make some tea and get ourselves warm and then we'll decide what we're going to do about your car and your friend. Here we are.'

Frances climbed obediently down from the Land Rover and followed the confident young man across a yard. She felt that she'd met her match in organisation and she was too tired and too relieved to resent it. Annie and the car must wait. Nothing, at this precise moment, could be more important than shelter from the snow and a cup of hot tea.

Chapter Nine

It was one of Robert's colleagues who eventually told Pippa the truth. Whilst Terry Cooper was in strong competition with Robert and had his own axe to grind in discrediting him, he also had rather a soft spot for Pippa who had been extraordinarily kind to his wife, Mary, when she miscarried with their first child. When he had proved to his own satisfaction that Robert and Louisa were having an affair, he talked it over with Mary and then went to see Pippa.

She was very surprised to see him, standing on the doorstep one wild wet afternoon in March, and brought him inside quickly with offers of tea.

'Thanks.' Terry brushed the drops of rain from his sleeves and followed her through to the kitchen. 'How are you?'

It was an unnecessary question. He could see quite clearly that she'd lost a great deal of weight along with the sparkle that had been one of her chief attractions. There was a set look about her lips and she failed to hide the misery in her eyes as she asked after Mary with a brave attempt at cheerful interest. Terry's heart hardened towards Robert but also sank a little as he contemplated the task he had set himself.

'How's Rowley?' he asked, sitting down at the kitchen table.

Her smile grew a little warmer. 'Asleep,' she said. 'He's been promoted from a cot to a bed and he's in and out all night long. He's exhausting us all, himself included.'

'That can't be very helpful at the moment.' Terry took the bull by the horns. 'I've been hearing rumours about you and Robert splitting up.'

Pippa stared at him, her hands clutching a little more tightly to the teapot. 'But who has . . .?' She swallowed and put the teapot gently on the table. 'I see.'

'Robert has dropped one or two hints,' said Terry, determined that she should know all of the truth, however painful. 'Apparently you're both regretting marrying in haste and are now repenting at leisure.'

The tears which seemed, these days, to be her constant companions overflowed and streamed down her cheeks.

'*He* is repenting,' she said, almost fiercely. '*I'm* not. I love him. I don't know what's happened to us.'

'Well, I can tell you what's happened to *him*.' Terry clung to his resolve though he shrank from the pain he was about to inflict. 'Louisa Beaumont has happened to him.'

Pippa frowned a little as she wiped the tears away. 'Do you mean John Spencer's assistant?' For a moment she was too busy identifying Louisa to assimilate the full meaning of his words. As she did so the colour washed into her cheeks and her face grew grim. 'Ahhh!'

It was a long drawn-out breath which allowed everything to fall into place.

Terry watched her, feeling ashamed and relieved in equal

parts and hanging on to Mary's advice. 'She has a right to know,' she'd said angrily. 'She can't fight with her hands tied.' Terry, man-like, had hesitated. 'She might know already,' he'd said diffidently. 'Then you won't need to tell her,' Mary had said briskly. 'But don't give me this crap about Pippa wishing they'd never married! She adores the creep!' Once again Terry tried to be fair. 'He's ambitious,' he began but Mary snorted contemptuously. 'He's a liar and a cheat,' she told him. 'Look, lots of relationships break up for all sorts of reasons but people should have the decency to do it honestly. If she's holding him back or he's tired of her, let him say so!' Terry strove to be reasonable, against his instinctive dislike and mistrust. 'We don't know what he's said to her,' he pointed out. 'We only know what he's saying at the office. He might even be trying to protect her.' 'Whilst having an affair with Louisa Beaumont?' Mary arched her brows and Terry sighed. 'I know! I know! But I only discovered that by chance. No one else suspects anything.' 'OK!' Mary spread her hands placatingly. 'Drop in and see her. You'll see how the land lies. And if she doesn't know and you won't tell her then I will! She's been a good friend to me.'

Remembering this conversation, Terry watched Pippa gain a little control and begin to make the tea. 'I'm sorry,' he said helplessly. 'Mary – we thought that you should know.'

Pippa, her back turned to him, nodded and he knew that she was weeping.

'Oh hell!' he said frustratedly. 'I – we just didn't know what to do, Pippa. It's a hell of a situation. You don't know whether to stand back or join in.'

'No, honestly.' She was shaking her head quite decidedly. 'I'm glad you told me. It explains things. I asked him if there was someone else but he absolutely denied it. It just seemed so odd, coming out of the blue . . .' She couldn't contain a small sob and reached for some kitchen roll. 'Sorry.'

'For heaven's sake,' Terry gestured helplessly, 'it's I who should be sorry. But Mary said – we both felt . . .'

'You were absolutely right.' Pippa blew her nose resolutely and began to pour the tea. 'I'd much rather know the truth – if you're absolutely sure . . .?'

'I'm quite sure, love,' said Terry gently. 'There's no way I'd make that kind of accusation if I wasn't certain.'

He didn't tell her of the indiscreet note on Robert's desk which he'd read upside down whilst Robert talked on the telephone; a long kiss he'd witnessed on a pavement outside a quiet restaurant before Robert hailed a taxi which carried Louisa away; the expression of triumphant happiness with which Robert had stared after her. And once he'd known . . .! Well, there were a thousand tiny signs which, cautious though Robert and Louisa were, could not be entirely hidden.

'Well then.' Pippa passed him his tea, aware of his discomfort but too utterly unhappy to be able to do much about it. 'I'm . . . grateful.' She almost laughed. 'What a silly word. I'd rather know, Terry. Honestly I would. Now things make a bit more sense. And it must have been awful for you. It's one of the most difficult decisions a friend ever has to take.'

'Mary's worried about you. Says she hasn't seen you for a bit. She sends her love and says she's going to phone you later this afternoon. Just to . . . you know . . . well, in case you need to . . . well, talk or anything.'

'I've been feeling a bit low,' admitted Pippa. 'I haven't felt like talking to anyone, not even Mary. But now I know where I stand it'll be good to talk to her.'

She sensed that having said what he'd come to say Terry longed to be away and, when he'd gulped his tea and stood up, she made no attempt to detain him. After he'd gone, she stood in the hall and knew that, until now, she'd never been really unhappy. It was bad enough that Robert had ceased to love her but with the knowledge of him betraying her with Louisa and humiliating her in the eyes of all who might know, she experienced a new depth to the despair and misery which she'd been attempting to contain. As she stood, locked in her own private hell, she heard the sound of thumping on the stairs.

Rowley appeared, taking one step at a time. Under his arm he clutched his book of the moment; in his other hand he held his shoes.

'Get up!' he announced, beaming at her with more than a touch of bravado. 'Rowley get up.'

She'd told him that he must always wait in bed until she came to fetch him but now she went to him quickly and gathered his warm body into her arms. At least she had Rowley. No fear, she thought bitterly, that Robert would want Rowley! She kissed him, burying her face for a moment in his neck and then sat him on the last but one stair.

'What have you got there?' she asked him. Her heart felt like a weighty suffocating stone in her body and she marvelled that she could speak so easily and naturally.

'*Mrs Tittlemouse*,' he cried triumphantly and beat her gently on the head with the little book as she bent to tie his shoes. '"Tiddly, widdly, widdly, Mrs Tittlemouse,"' he shouted triumphantly. 'Mummy read.'

But as she sat with him pressed against her – his head bent eagerly over the pictures, his thumb in his mouth – her mind was far from Babbitty Bumble and Mr Jackson. Instead she saw visions of Robert entwined with Louisa's slim strong body, and her pain was so sharp she feared she might die of it.

Hugh pushed aside the books that crowded the small table in the corner of his bedroom and leaned back on the uncomfortable wooden chair to stretch his cramped arms. He removed his spectacles and rubbed at his eyes, yawning cavernously. He felt permanently tired; incapable of any sustained effort, yet he was barely keeping abreast of his work which he was finding dull. He stood up and wandered across the untidy room, kicking aside discarded clothes and shoes, to collapse on to the narrow bed. Lacing his fingers behind his head he stared up at the blotchy ceiling and tried to analyse his depression.

He had imagined that his three years at university would probably be the most care-free that he would ever know – halfway between the restrictions of childhood and the responsibilities of adult life – and they had certainly started happily enough. He thought about Lucinda, remembering what fun he'd had with her in those early weeks of his first term at Bristol. If only he'd had the sense to be firm with Charlotte then . . . Hugh took his hands from behind his head and covered his face with them. Was there to be no end to his remorse? Would he ever be allowed to climb down from this wearying treadmill?

He missed Lucinda but their most recent weekend together had been a disaster. She'd talked of her skiing holiday and some friends she'd met out there. Hugh, surprisingly and unreasonably jealous at the repeated mention of one young man's name, had unfairly accused her of being obsessed with him. Lucinda had gently pointed out that this was exactly how she felt about Charlotte – and there had been another row. They'd patched it up before Lucinda had gone back to Eastbourne but Hugh was beginning to fear that he was incapable of having a normal relationship with anyone ever again. He was just wondering whether he should go downstairs and telephone her, when one of his fellow students hammered on the door to say that they were going to the pub. Hugh sat up and shouted that he would be right down.

Just as they were leaving, someone remembered that there had been a telephone call for him earlier. The message had been written down on a scrap of paper which was now passed across as they all stood jostling together in the small hall, pulling on coats. Hugh took it and read the illegible scrawl with difficulty. Lucinda had telephoned and asked him to call her back.

Hugh hesitated, fighting with his conscience. He decided that he didn't have what it took to cope with an emotional situation on the end of the telephone line. He needed a mindless jolly evening with these cheery young undergraduates who were still able to regard life as a bit of a lark.

'I'll give her a call when we get back,' he said half-heartedly, knowing perfectly well that they'd probably be back far too late to be making telephone calls. 'Let's go.'

His friends cheered loudly, buffeting him on the back, and the whole crowd rushed out of the door and headed for the pub.

Mrs Driver beat a tattoo on the caravan door and stared round at the site whilst she waited for her son to let her in. Nothing escaped her sharp gaze and she was filled with pride at his achievements. Max opened the door.

'You don't have to stand out there in the cold, Mother,' he told her impatiently, drawing her in to the warm interior. 'Why don't you just walk in?'

Mrs Driver gave a characteristic sniff. Her lively brown eyes peered hither and thither, checking to see that Max wasn't letting himself go.

'Wouldn't want to interrupt anything,' she said primly.

'What sort of thing did you have in mind?' asked Max sardonically. 'D'you think I drag a few village maidens in and have a quick orgy before lunch? I should be so lucky!'

Mrs Driver ignored this provocative statement and perched herself at the table. She stared at him keenly, saw that he looked fit and contented, and nodded at him, satisfied.

'Passed the test, have I?' he asked drily. 'Don't worry. I'm eating well enough.'

'And drinking, too, no doubt,' she responded tartly. 'Down the pub most nights, I dare say.'

'Now and then.' Max was unmoved by her accusation. He grinned at her. 'So what's the news from the big city?'

She made a little face and he knew a moment's concern although he didn't show it. The deep love between them was rarely visible to the naked eye; neither was given to displays of emotion.

'Cuppa?' He lit the gas beneath the kettle and primed the little pump over the sink.

She settled herself more comfortably, patting her surprisingly dark, tightly curled hair. Like her son, Mrs Driver had begun to go grey very young and had been dyeing her hair ever since. It was her one vanity. It lent her lined face an oddly youthful aspect and it was still possible to see the pretty girl she'd been once. She slipped her old tweed coat from her shoulders, glanced at the papers on the table and felt another enormous, if well-concealed, surge of pride for her son. Like Max she loved the moor and she was delighted that there was still someone here, where her family had farmed for generations.

'Coming on, is it? See you've started roofing.'

'I'll show you the new kitchen in a minute.'

He smiled to himself at the surprise he had in store for her. She hadn't been up for a week or so and great strides had been made in the small dwelling house. She saw his private grin and gave another sniff.

'Hope you're going to get a cook to go with it.'

'Oh, don't go on!' He put the mug beside her. 'Kids don't need cordon bleu. Sausages and chips and beefburgers. That's what they like.'

'Be lucky to get that, with you in charge of a saucepan. Burnt offerings, more like. Finish that stew up, did you?'

'It was delicious.' He glanced at her. 'If you're that worried you'd better apply for the job.'

She narrowed her eyes at him. 'I've got better things to do with my time than looking after you and a lot of kids.' They were both far too wise to imagine that they could live and work together. 'You need a nice young girl . . .'

'Well, now you're talking, Mother!' cried Max. 'Haven't I been saying the same thing for the last few months?'

'Get on with you.' She'd disliked Stella from the beginning but had been determined not to interfere. Even when she knew that Max was unhappy and Stella was playing the field in his absence, she'd said nothing but, privately, she'd been delighted to see the marriage finish – though she would never have dreamed of mentioning it to him.

'So how's life amongst the nobs?' Max sat down opposite. 'Bit quiet yet, isn't it?'

Mrs Driver worked at a smart country house hotel on the outskirts of Plymouth. She liked to regale Max with sharply observed tales of her fellow employees and guests alike but, today, she frowned a little. Max braced himself but his impassive expression remained unchanged.

'It's that puppy,' she said at last. 'He's been round the back again. He's been dumped, I'm sure of it.'

'You shouldn't have fed it.' Max refused to be moved

by the unwanted puppy's plight. 'What d'you expect if you give it titbits? Bound to come back.'

'He was in a terrible state.' Her distress was obvious – she loved animals – but Max hardened his heart.

'Call the RSPCA,' he said ruthlessly. 'They'll look after it.'

'Put him in a cage with all the other waifs and strays,' she said indignantly. 'Poor little thing.'

Max sighed. 'You can't cope with a dog, Mother,' he said firmly. 'Not with your job . . .'

'I know that,' she said impatiently. She hesitated, eyes on the table, her brain busy. 'But I was thinking, Max—'

'No,' said Max strongly. 'Absolutely not! I don't need a dog.'

'He's such a dear little thing,' she said wistfully. 'Hair all over its face . . .'

'Dogs usually have,' said Max sarcastically. 'All over their bodies, too. It's one of their characteristics.'

'You gurt fool.' She laughed unwillingly. 'I mean he's got this fringe. He's a real mutt. You remember Mutt, Max?'

'I remember Mutt, Mother,' said Max with daunting finality.

'Remember how he used to guard your things?' Her tone was frankly reminiscent. 'The dear of him! Hated it when you went off to school. Waiting at the gate with your shoe or some such when you came back each afternoon . . .'

'Very touching, Mother, and the answer's still "No!"'

'He'd look after the place when you go down the pub . . .'

'I rarely go to the pub,' said Max crossly. 'Forget it! Now

drink your tea and I'll show you the kitchen.'

Mrs Driver sipped her tea thoughtfully, not displeased with her work. Max eyed her uneasily across the table and she smiled sweetly at him.

'Perhaps you're right,' she said. 'That was a nice cup of tea, son. Good and strong. Just how I like it. Now, what about this kitchen . . .?'

Chapter Ten

It was the third couple to view the farmhouse who put in an offer for it. Stephen, anxious to give Frances no more grounds for dithering, insisted that they should accept it. Frances could only agree – it was a very reasonable offer – and immediately felt a great sense of relief. The decision was made. Now she must simply get on with the packing up. It was fortunate that Caroline's leaving home had precipitated a frenzy of clearing up and sorting out. Since the young couple had very little with which to furnish their new home, Frances had spent weeks ransacking cupboards and attics so that, when the time came, odd pieces of furniture, piles of linen and any number of boxes containing useful odds and ends had gone off in a small hired van to Gloucestershire.

It now became vital to find accommodation for themselves. Frances and Stephen had already begun to explore a little and had made several trips up the Wye Valley, having carefully studied the details of the rented houses available. Having found a buyer for the farmhouse, however, they were tempted to think of buying at once although Frances still held back a little.

'It would be so easy to get carried away,' she said, after she and Stephen had been rather bowled over by a delightful, but tiny, cottage for sale within the radius they had set themselves. 'We must be sensible. There's no way we could all fit into that little place.'

'But we don't want anything too big,' cautioned Stephen. 'After all, Caroline's gone and Hugh won't be with us for too much longer . . .'

'But they must be able to come home!' protested Frances. 'We shall want to see our grandchildren. If there's no room they won't come.'

Stephen debated as to whether he should point out that they could visit the children in their own homes but decided against it. He had no wish to rock any boats. Frances seemed to be accepting the move and had even stopped worrying quite so much about Hugh.

'Fair enough,' he said peaceably. 'Let's stick to renting for a bit. Anyway, it's always easier to buy when the money's safely in the bank. Much less complicated. It's silly to tempt ourselves.'

It was James's mother who finally answered the problem. A newly widowed friend of hers was planning to go to New Zealand to see her daughter and her young family. She would be gone for at least six months – probably twelve – and would be delighted to rent to the Ankertons. Although it was on the very boundary of their radius, it was too good to refuse. Since they had already prepared themselves for the tiresome business of putting their furniture into store, it came as a very pleasant surprise to find that their future landlord was prepared to put away as many of her own things as could be stored into the attic in order that they might have some of their own belongings around them.

Frances was delighted and, whilst Stephen was at the new office, spent many hours with this kindly woman who missed her daughter and new grandson so much and shared Frances's own views on the importance of holding the family together. The two of them pottered happily in the roomy comfortable house, deciding what pieces could be put away to make room for those items which Frances hoped to bring with her. The garden was thoroughly explored and Frances promised to care for especially tender plants and to be very sensitive when it came to pruning.

By the time Easter arrived she was positively looking forward to the move. They were ready for a change, she told herself, convinced now that it was the right thing for the whole family. So the weeks slipped past. The conveyancing proceeded slowly and Frances methodically began her packing.

Towards the end of the Easter term, Lucinda came to a difficult and very painful decision. Unwavering as she was in her love for Hugh, she realised that she was getting nowhere with him. In fact, she felt that during the last month their relationship had deteriorated. Unable to help him, she decided that a complete break might be the answer. Since she was unable to penetrate the wall which Hugh had erected between them, then he must be given space and time to come to terms with his problems in his own way. For the time being, she must be absolutely unavailable to him.

She cried bitterly for a while and then telephoned Hugh. She had already realised that a meeting face to face could be inconclusive. Apart from anything else, she wasn't sure that she could deal him – and herself – such a blow in the flesh, as it were. She told him that she had been offered a job in Geneva at the end of the summer term and would be flying straight out from college then. She was to be an au pair to an English family for nine months.

Hugh had been shocked into silence and then had pleaded with her to reconsider.

'It's no good, Hugh,' she'd said gently, although the tears were pouring down her cheeks. 'We've just been getting on each other's nerves lately, haven't we?'

Hugh, who had been thinking this very thing, began to panic. 'I know I've been behaving badly,' he began, 'but please, Lu—'

'I still love you, Hugh,' she said, praying that she wouldn't weaken, 'but we've got to have a break or we'll destroy each other. We'll give it a year and then see how we feel. I'll write from Geneva but don't feel tied or anything. I'm sure it's for the best. I'm working with this family through the Easter holidays so as to get used to the children and I'll be off at the end of June.'

'Lucinda!' cried Hugh. 'Please don't do this. Look . . .'

When Lucinda could bear it no longer, she hung up on him and went to cry her heart out, feeling like a murderess. White-faced, Hugh went upstairs and shut himself in his room.

Frances took one look at her thin, unhappy son and her heart sank. She had allowed herself – encouraged by Caroline – to believe that he'd been much better at Christmas and that all was well with him, so the shock was doubly great. He was quiet and withdrawn although he listened politely to her descriptions of their new home and smiled obligingly when she made jokes. It was rather like living with a well-mannered stranger and Frances felt that her heart must break. During the final weeks of term he had developed a hard, persistent little cough. She lay awake listening to it at night and heard it echoing through the house during the day. He was lethargic and had no appetite and, one morning, woke with a sore throat and a raging fever. Frances called her GP, who diagnosed glandular fever. Thankful to have something positive to work on, Frances administered antibiotics and insisted on bed rest but, when she came upon Hugh weeping silently into his pillow, she became really frightened.

She stood over him and demanded to know what was worrying him. Hugh, too weak to resist, told her that Lucinda had decided that they must have a complete break, related the history of their rows over Charlotte, and finally dropped into an exhausted sleep.

Much later, when Hugh was in bed watching the portable television, Frances related it all to Stephen.

'It's Cass's fault!' she cried for the hundredth time and, glancing quickly at the door, lowered her voice. 'How can we make him see that it was because of *her* that Charlotte died? This is what it always comes back to in the end. Oh, poor Lucinda. She tried so hard with him.'

Stephen shook his head. He knew that Frances loved Lucinda too much to blame her in any way and that, once again, Cass was a handy scapegoat. Nevertheless, he was deeply distressed and quite at a loss.

'Poor Hugh,' he said. 'Poor boy.'

'He's so thin,' mourned Frances. 'And he's just so listless. Of course the antibiotics don't help but even so . . . Oh God, Stephen. What are we going to *do*?'

'I'll talk to him,' began Stephen, but Frances shook her head. 'Why not?' he asked almost irritably. 'You always do this! You ask my advice but won't let me help. He's my son, too. Why shouldn't I speak to him?'

Frances was silent. She knew that she'd always instinctively regarded Hugh as *her* property. *She* understood him. Stephen was too tough, too severe with him. Part of her knew that this was foolish and that Hugh might have been less sensitive had Stephen been allowed more of a say in his upbringing; however it was rather too late to worry about that now. Moreover, she didn't want to start a row. She prevaricated.

'I only meant,' she said mendaciously, 'that you should wait until he's a little better, that's all. *Then* speak to him by all means. He's just very woolly at the moment. Sort of weak and tearful and not really capable of concentrating. It's pointless attempting any serious discussion with him.'

Stephen looked slightly mollified and Frances rammed home her advantage.

'You really should have a chat with him,' she said. 'I've failed completely. He only broke down and told me about Lucinda because he's high on these antibiotics and absolutely exhausted.'

She smiled at him, seeing that he was quite taken in by her calmly judicious tone, and felt a twinge of conscience. It was wrong of her to be so certain that she was the best one to deal with Hugh – nevertheless she couldn't help feeling that it was probably true! She went to sit beside Stephen on the sofa and slipped her hand into his. It was important that he felt included but that she remained in control. Stephen returned the pressure of her hand absently.

'I wish I could think of some positive way of breaking through this guilt,' he murmured.

'I'm sure you will in time,' said Frances guilefully, certain that he would be far too busy to give it any lasting attention. On reflection it really was best left in her own capable hands. 'Are you all ready to go at the office?'

'Yes. Yes, we are.' Stephen switched his thoughts back to the new amalgamation. 'Of course, old Chris is none too happy at being made redundant . . .'

Frances encouraged him to talk, so steering the conversation away from Hugh whilst allowing her thoughts to run on privately. Left to himself, Stephen would be fully occupied with office politics and his promotion. Meanwhile, Hugh should be given the chance to recover undisturbed until she deemed it wise to attempt to reason with him.

Stephen, setting off to the office the next morning, was by no means so preoccupied as to forget about Hugh's problems. He had been deeply shocked and saddened by

Lucinda's break with Hugh. Something positive must be done to persuade Hugh that he was not responsible for Charlotte's death. Stephen spared a thought for Charlotte. He remembered the love she had lavished on her pony, her brief smiles, her shyness; remembered, too, how they had teased Hugh about her infatuation for him.

Stephen shook his head. Gentle, kindly Hugh had been too naïve to see what effect his friendship might have on this troubled child. No doubt she had weaved whole fantasies about him until they were more real than life itself. Hugh had taken her to his sixth-form socials so as to break her in gently but how had *she* seen it? He had no doubt that, once she had started at Blundell's, she had boasted of her relationship with Hugh, who was by then in Bristol. Had her classmates known of that trip to Bristol? What shame she would have suffered if she'd had to tell them he had another girlfriend! How then could she have kept up the fiction that was so necessary to maintain her confidence?

There was no doubt that Charlotte had suspected her mother of having affairs and, thought Stephen, it wasn't too far-fetched a suspicion. It was a pity that Frances had always had such an antipathy to Cass. Stephen sighed but he could understand why Frances feared her. Cass was a very beautiful woman and a very friendly one. Even Hugh had been slightly bewitched by her . . .

Stephen paused overlong at the junction as an idea occurred to him. His heart began to thump a little faster as he thought of Hugh, lying ill and unhappy. Might it work? He considered sounding out his idea with Frances but rejected it at once, knowing her reaction. No. Better that Frances shouldn't know just yet . . .

Stephen let in the clutch but, instead of turning right towards Yelverton, he turned left towards the village where the Wivenhoes lived in their Georgian rectory.

Hugh recovered slowly. His cough ceased to shake his thin frame but the listlessness persisted and Frances's GP made it clear that it would take time before he was fully restored, and advised against his return to Bristol at the beginning of term. Student life, with its late nights, inadequate food and hours of study, was quite the wrong thing for him at the moment. He recommended good fresh air, nourishing food, a certain amount of physical labour and plenty of sleep. Frances touched briefly on Hugh's depression and was encouraged to believe that the foregoing regime would do much to restore his mental health. Having had a private word with his tutor, who agreed that a certain amount of work could be done at home, Frances gave herself up to restoring Hugh to full strength.

She hoped that the move would distract him a little but she wished that there were more to keep him occupied. He accepted the fact that he might have to go back late to Bristol and docilely agreed to study at home. Frances refused to let him work in the smoky atmosphere of the pub and racked her brains trying to think of some light physical work amongst congenial companions which would keep him employed.

It was whilst she was returning from lunch with Annie that she remembered Max Driver. She felt a tiny stab of amusement as she recalled her adventures on that snowy afternoon. She'd been rather impressed with his caravan and with his plans for his adventure training school. And how efficiently and cheerfully he'd hauled her car back on to the road later that evening, when the snow had ceased to fall and a full bright moon shone down on the magically transformed landscape! He had insisted on driving behind her to Annie's cottage lest she became stuck again with no one to help her. Frances, remembering, felt a warm little glow and recalled, too, how Stephen had refused to be amused by her adventures. He'd asked, rather crossly, why on earth she'd taken the long road over the moor – given that she was silly enough to go out on such a day! – instead of going down through Poundsgate or, better still, through Yelverton and along the A38. She'd replied that she'd been driving on the moor now for ten years and in all weathers and had taken the road she always took to Exeter without really thinking about it. When she'd enthused about Max, and how wonderful he'd been, Stephen had merely shrugged and Frances wondered secretly, and with a certain satisfaction, whether he were a tiny bit jealous.

Frances paused at the junction at Hemsworthy Gate as an idea occurred to her. She wondered briefly if she should first discuss her idea with Stephen but rejected this almost immediately. She suspected that Stephen would put a damper on it. No. There was no need for him to know anything just yet . . .

Frances let in the clutch but, instead of turning left on to the Widecombe road, she turned right for Trendlebere Down where Max Driver lived in his caravan whilst his barns were being renovated.

Chapter Eleven

It was several days before Pippa was able to confront Robert with her new knowledge. This was partly due to the fact that he was careful to give her little opportunity for any kind of communication. He had told her that he wanted a separation and now, it seemed, it was merely a question of working out the mechanics; selling the house, finding new homes. During the long days, she wondered how they could have come to this point so speedily; horrified at how quickly a relationship disintegrates once one of the partners has decided it should end! He left for the office early each morning, arrived home very late and slept in the spare bedroom. When he was in the house for any length of time, he shut himself in the study. On the occasions when Pippa had gone to him and pleaded with him to give their marriage another chance, to *talk* to her, he repulsed her with a barely concealed impatience which implied amazement at the pointlessness of such a request.

It was difficult, bogged down as she was in such hurting misery, not to take these implications to herself; to believe that only someone as inefficient and woolly-headed as herself would believe that he could possibly put up with her. It was almost impossible to sustain any kind of self-esteem under this implacable despising and, once she knew about his affair with Louisa, her confidence reached a new low level. She tried to console herself with the truth – that it was because of Louisa and not because of her deficiencies that Robert wanted a separation – but this was cold comfort. The thought of them together made her physically sick; a condition made worse by the fact that she still wanted him. In some dreadful way, the thought of him with Louisa heightened her own desire and she hated herself for it.

It was her conviction that it was because of Louisa that Robert had changed which made Pippa decide to make one last try. She managed to contain herself until the weekend, only to discover at the last moment that Robert was going north to see his mother. He had kept his family very much in the background until he'd swept Pippa into the registry office and married her in the breathless haste so disapproved of by her father. Later he'd introduced her to his mother and sister, both tough, working-class women, who disliked Pippa on sight and found her affected. She'd hidden her own shock – Robert had carefully implied a very different background – and tried to befriend them but with little success. Even the arrival of Rowley hadn't thawed the ice.

As Pippa waited for Robert's return she was certain that his family would make no attempt to heal the breach. They would be on his side. She was just as certain that he would say nothing to them about Louisa. Despite their obvious pride in him, they wished him to marry one of his own kind and Louisa would be just as unacceptable as she, Pippa, had been. He arrived home in the early hours of Monday morning by which time Pippa was already in bed, although not asleep. As she lay, tensely listening to him creeping up the stairs and quietly closing the spare room door, she rejected the idea of a confrontation at so late an hour. She continued to lay awake – rehearsing her lines, anticipating his responses – fell into a heavy sleep just before dawn and woke abruptly, fearing that she had overslept.

Pippa rolled across the lonely expanse of sheet and peered at the clock. It was still early. She lay back with a tiny sigh of relief but her heart began to jump and hurry as she thought about the coming interview. Determined not to appear at a disadvantage, she rose and went to shower in the small bathroom off the bedroom. As she brushed her hair she gazed out beyond the looking-glass at the April morning. The sky was clear and blue and beneath the boundary hedge the massed daffodils spread a golden pool of sunshine on the lawn. She remembered with what happiness she and Robert had first seen the house, their delight when they knew they could just afford it, and felt the sobs rising in her throat. How *could* he toss it all so lightly aside? How forget so soon their hopes and plans? He'd been so thrilled when she'd become pregnant – although he insisted now that it had been an unwelcome mistake, a trick on her part – so proud when she'd presented him with a son!

And now, thought Pippa, as she buttoned her shirt and swallowed back the tears, he hardly speaks to Rowley.

She slipped out of the bedroom and went quietly downstairs. It was with a shock that she realised that Robert was there before her. He made a point of being out of the house early these days but, even so, she had imagined she would be first in the kitchen. His casual, indifferent raising of his eyebrows at her – as though she were an acquaintance to be but distantly acknowledged – had the effect of stiffening her spine.

'Did you have a good trip?' she asked, noticing that he'd already made his coffee. She took down a mug and went to the cupboard. 'How is your mother? And Susan?'

'Fine, thanks.' He stood by the toaster, waiting for the slices to spring out, and stared into the garden.

'I want to talk to you.' She made her own coffee and sat down at the table opposite the place that he'd set for himself.

'Have you come to a decision as to what you want to do about this house?' he asked coldly, taking his toast and turning to look at her at last as he put it in the toast rack.

'No,' she answered steadily, holding the mug tightly in her shaking hands. 'I want to ask you about your affair with Louisa Beaumont.'

She saw the quick flicker of his eyelids, the tightening of the lips, before he gave an impatient half-sigh, half-snort and rolled his eyes heavenwards as though praying for patience.

'I've already told you—'

'Yes, but I know the truth now, you see,' she cut in quickly, feeling sick with nerves but still maintaining her exterior calm. 'Why did you pretend about it, Robert? Why say all those hurtful things about my inefficiency and stupidity and not loving me—'

'Because they're true,' he interrupted curtly. He made no move to sit down or to eat his breakfast. 'This has got nothing to do with Louisa. I've been seeing her a bit on business, that's all. Why can't you accept the fact that we got it wrong, Pippa, and that it's *over*?'

Once again he'd thrust her back into uncertainty and, seeing her hesitate, he attacked her. 'Why must you continue to seek these humiliations? I don't *enjoy* saying these things but you won't seem to accept the truth. It's over! We don't love each other any more!'

'That's your truth, Robert, not mine.' She stared up at him pleadingly as he bent across the table, his hands gripping the back of his chair. 'I still love you, even though you seem to have changed out of all recognition.'

'Look.' He paused, biting his lip. 'You make me say these things, Pippa. The truth is, the person you married isn't the real me. You've met my family. You must be able to see that I've had to struggle to get on. I wanted to marry well and I was prepared to put on an act to succeed. Well, I did. But I can't keep it up any longer.'

She was still staring at him but her face was white and shocked. 'Do you mean that it was *all* an act? That you never loved me at all? That . . . Oh, no. I *can't* believe it . . .'

'Whether you believe it or not, it's the truth,' he said brutally. 'And it's not worth the effort any more.'

He jammed his chair under the table, seized his mug and drank his coffee in one long swallow. 'I'm going.'

'Wait.' Trembling, she got to her feet. 'On what grounds are you seeking this separation?'

'Irrevocable breakdown of the marriage,' he said at once. 'Incompatibility, lack of support.' He shrugged. 'It's not important at the moment, is it? I intend to continue supporting you and Rowley but not in this house. I can't afford it. If you find something smaller we can sell this and divide the proceeds.'

'And what if I start divorce proceedings on the grounds of your adultery?'

He laughed then and his laughter was like a blow in the face. '"Hell has no fury, like a woman scorn'd", eh, Pippa?' The amusement fled from his eyes and he looked cruel. 'Try it and see where it gets you.' He picked up his briefcase and looked back at her, shaking his head pityingly. 'You know you really shouldn't listen to arseholes like Terry Cooper. Did he also tell you that I've been promoted over his head and that he'd do anything to bring me down?' He watched her face and smiled. 'Of course he didn't. Him and that ghastly feminist wife of his! Forget it, Pippa. You'd be wasting your money.'

He opened the door and hesitated, his head bent in thought, and even then her love for him weakened her.

'Oh Robert . . .' she cried. 'Oh please . . .'

She stretched out a hand to him but he shook his head.

'No more,' he said. 'I've had enough. I'll be home tonight to pack some things and I shall move into temporary accommodation till you've sorted yourself out.'

The door closed behind him and Pippa was seized with a convulsion of pain, humiliation and anger.

'Bastard!' she cried. 'Bastard!' And she snatched his mug from the table and hurled it at the closed door.

The gesture merely underlined her impotence and she burst into tears, sinking back into her chair, her fingers digging into her scalp . . . Some sixth sense warned her that Rowley was approaching. Quick as light she was on her feet and hurrying to the sink where she splashed cold water on her face. She was drying it on some kitchen towel when he pushed the door open. His pyjamas sagged at the seat and his blond hair stood on end. Under his arm were the inevitable books.

'Daddy all gone,' he said contentedly, and then saw the broken pieces of china lying on the floor. 'Broke,' he said, staring at in distress. 'Got broke.'

He bent down to look at it, stretching out his hand, and she cried out quickly, 'Don't touch it! You'll cut yourself!'

He drew his fingers back hastily and looked at her, trying to gauge the extent of her distress; sensing that something was amiss. She smiled at him as cheerfully as she could and he felt relieved.

'Mummy mend,' he said with the nonchalant confidence he reserved for his own misdemeanours.

Not this time, thought Pippa, lifting him into his highchair. It is beyond my power now.

She prepared his breakfast and all the time she was forcing herself to make the final decision. There would be no more pleading, no more begging. She would put the house on the market today and she and Rowley would find another home; but where should they go and how could she live without Robert?

•

The April sunshine warmed the deep stone ledge that ran along the wall of Annie's courtyard and shone on the velvety bronze and gold of the wallflowers in their stone trough. Annie, sitting on the ledge, raised her face to the sun and breathed in their heavy rich scent. Beyond the cottage, in the upland fields, she could hear the high thin bleating of the new lambs; closer at hand, a wren chattered shrilly at an intruder venturing too near her nest on the other side of the wall. Ivy-leaved toadflax and pennywort grew in the crevices of the ancient granite and a honeysuckle climbed a small pergola, fixed in the corner to create shade.

Annie was thinking of Perry; of his love of the minutiae; his delight in the tiny creatures that scurried about in the cracks of the stone and under the leaves.

'Come and look at this little chap,' he'd cry, poring with delight over a tiny beetle, magnifying glass extended. 'See his wings? Incredible detail. What colours!'

She'd found herself learning to study creatures from which formerly she'd have drawn away in fear or – worse – crushed with her hasty shoe. Now she was loath to kill any living thing. She opened the windows to aid the escape of the bees and butterflies; caught spiders with pieces of card and a tumbler and released them into the garden; fished waterlogged beetles out of saucers and set them to dry on stones. Even the snails that she found on her wall she was unable to crush but hurled them into the wild garden beyond the high walls.

The house martins were back. They perched on what remained of their mud nest under the eaves and chattered volubly to one another.

'Making plans,' murmured Annie aloud, lest Perry should have missed them. She shielded her eyes with her hand as she watched them. 'Perhaps they're deciding how to improve on last year's design.'

The arrival of the house martins had been a cause for

jubilation; the prospect of summer close at hand.

'There will be so much to look forward to,' Perry had promised. 'The wonderful thing about the country is that there is always change. New things to be watching for. We'll learn them all in time. The first primroses. The arrival of the house martins. Each plant will have its turn and the baby birds will learn to fly. And then when the martins migrate we'll know its time to be stocking up with logs and finding where the best holly grows ready for Christmas.'

He'd had the knack of making each small event special, so that every day was exciting, but could she maintain that interest all alone? She sighed a little, her heart heavy with unrequired love for him.

'Only one thing to do with love!' Perry's voice was so real that, instinctively, she glanced around for him. 'Give it away. There's no other use for it. Give it away! You get it back one hundredfold.'

'But to whom shall I give it?' wondered Annie sadly.

'Pippa?' hazarded Perry gently. 'She needs love. And a home.'

'A home?' Annie experienced a twinge of anxiety. Her old instincts to preserve her own freedom momentarily assailed her.

'Poor child. How frightened and unhappy she must be.' Perry seemed to be pottering in the shadowy kitchen. 'And with a child, too. No nest for Pippa to return to.'

Annie stared up at the martins. Pippa had telephoned several days before, to tell her that the house had sold. It had been snapped up by a company moving one of their employees into the area and who wanted to push the sale through as quickly as possible. They'd been asked to be ready to move out within two weeks. Pippa was desperately searching for somewhere to live. Mary and Terry Cooper had offered her temporary accommodation but Pippa had refused. Mary had, at last, been delivered of a healthy baby and Pippa felt that it was unfair to squash in to their little house at a time when Terry and Mary needed to be alone with their long-awaited child. Moreover, she told Annie, she had no desire to remain in a neighbourhood which held such unhappy memories. At this point in the conversation, Pippa's doorbell had rung and she'd been obliged to hurry away.

Now, Annie shifted restlessly on her ledge as she imagined the small cottage filled with Pippa and Rowley and their belongings . . .

'Courage!' whispered Perry, close behind her. 'Remember Isaiah? "But they that wait upon the Lord shall renew their strength; they shall mount up with wings as eagles; they shall run, and not be weary; and they shall walk, and not faint." Have faith, my darling.'

The telephone rang.

'I don't know where to go, Annie.' Pippa was close to tears. 'Robert's found a flat in London and he's moving a lot of furniture into it. He doesn't care where Rowley and I go. He says to take what we want but how can I? I've nowhere to put it. I've just realised, Annie. I don't belong anywhere.'

'Of course you do,' said Annie comfortingly. 'You just don't know where it is yet.'

'But how shall I start finding it?' Pippa sounded exhausted.

There was the sound of wailing in the background and Annie heard whispering as Pippa and Rowley conferred together. As she listened, she heard Perry's voice, superimposed over the whispering.

'The only thing to do with love,' he was saying, 'is to give it away . . .'

Annie clutched the receiver as Pippa spoke in her ear.

'Sorry, Annie. Rowley thought I meant that we couldn't keep his books and that train you gave him. I'm just trying to explain to him.'

Her voice had a forced brightness now that she knew Rowley was in earshot and Annie's heart went out to her.

'Pippa,' she said aloud, 'you must both come here. Just till you get yourselves sorted out.'

'To *you*?' Pippa sounded amazed. 'Oh, we couldn't! You'd hate it. All your lovely peace and quiet. Oh Annie . . .'

'No arguments,' said Annie firmly. 'I shall love to have you. After all,' she added, as though this clinched it, 'you *are* my goddaughter-in-law.'

'Can you have goddaughters-in-law?' asked Pippa waveringly, but her voice held a hopeful note.

'*I* can!' said Annie. 'You'll have to put your furniture into store, I'm afraid. I've no room for that. But bring your treasures and Rowley's. We'll manage somehow, you'll see.'

Chapter Twelve

Despite Max's willingness to meet Hugh, with the view to employing him for a few hours' work doing odd jobs, Frances hesitated. There were several reasons for this and she felt confused, beset with an odd kind of lassitude which was most unlike her usual decisiveness. To begin with, she tried to analyse the pleasure she had experienced in seeing Max again. He'd been outside in the yard when she pulled in through the gateway at the bottom of the track and he'd frowned at the car, puzzled for a moment, before his face cleared and he raised a hand to her. He was dressed casually in jeans and a ribbed military jersey and looked very much the part – dynamic, forceful, alert – as he gesticulated to one of his workforce. The smaller of the barns and the dwelling house were newly roofed and two men were working on the roof of the second barn. It was to one of these two men that Max had been talking, but now he came over to Frances and nodded to her as she climbed out.

'Didn't recognise you for a moment.' He smiled a little as he remembered the snowy afternoon. 'Been to any good tea parties lately?'

She laughed, warming to his friendliness, relieved that

he seemed to think it quite natural that she should drop by.

'You're getting on!' she exclaimed, indicating the new roofs. 'It's beginning to come together, isn't it?'

He nodded, looking round at his little empire with satisfaction. 'It is. I've started on the inside of the house now but, my goodness, there's plenty to do. I'm just going to put the kettle on.' He tipped his head towards the roofers. 'It's chilly work up there today. Cuppa?'

'Oh!' She hadn't expected such ready hospitality but was delighted at the opportunity to have a talk with him. 'That would be lovely.'

She followed him across the yard, avoiding stacks of slates and a pile of sand, and into the small square stone house.

'So what d'you think?'

He stood aside and let her pass before him into the kitchen. Her cry of delight pleased him and he grinned in spite of himself.

'Bit opulent, isn't it? Just for one chap. But this is where we'll all eat, you see. I knocked several of the small rooms into one to make this big one.'

'It's terrific,' said Frances, taking in the pine units, the huge refectory table and the four-oven Aga across the back wall. 'I can just see you in here after a day out on the moor, pony-trekking or canoeing or whatever. All those hungry children . . . I hope you can cook?'

He grimaced. 'If I have to. But I expect to have someone to take over the domestic side.' He plugged in the kettle and switched it on. 'I've moved in here now I've got one of the bedrooms and the bathroom straight but I haven't got the Aga set up and running yet. It's a bit extravagant while I'm on my own. Come and see the next project on the list while the kettle boils.'

They crossed the hall and he opened the door to the sitting room; bare, except for a set of kitchen steps, a trestle table and various pots of paint.

'Will you all be able to cram in here?' asked Frances, trying to imagine a dozen armchairs packed into the average-sized room. 'Won't it be a bit of a squash?'

'I hope we shan't have to pack whole groups in here. I doubt I'll have many takers in the depths of winter and there's the recreation room over in the big barn. This is mainly for me and the staff.'

'It'll be very cosy on winter evenings,' said Frances, nodding towards the large stone fireplace. 'You could get a whole tree in there.'

He laughed. 'I'm thinking about having a wood-burning stove. More economical.' He shook his head, suddenly serious. 'There's still so much to be done.'

'I was just thinking,' said Frances casually, following him back to the kitchen. 'Hugh's at home at the moment. He's looking for some part-time work, just until we move. I suppose you couldn't use a helping hand?'

Max, manipulating tea-bags into four mugs, bent his disconcerting gaze upon her.

'Hugh? That's your son, isn't it? Didn't you tell me that he was at university?'

'That's right.' Frances tried to maintain her casual tone, wondering what else Max remembered. The warmth and intimacy of the caravan, during that snowy afternoon, had encouraged confidences over the hot, reviving tea. 'He's had glandular fever and the doctor says he needs more time at home. He's better but he needs feeding up and fresh air and so on. I just thought that some physical exercise – just a few hours here or there – would probably be good for him.'

Max prodded at the tea-bags thoughtfully. 'I could do with another pair of hands,' he admitted. 'If he's up to it. I don't want anyone full time . . .'

'We're moving soon,' said Frances quickly. 'I'm sure I told you? We're going to Wales.' She remembered Max had been a sergeant in the Marines and wondered if she'd made Hugh sound rather feeble. 'You know these young chaps,' she said lightly. 'He's bored with nothing to do. It would be good for him to be busy.'

'I couldn't pay much.' Max took a spoon from the sink, dried it on a tea cloth and passed it to Frances with the sugar and a mug of tea.

'He wouldn't want much,' said Frances. 'It's just to stop him . . .' She paused, rejecting the word 'brooding' and trying to think of something more manly.

'He's bound to be bored,' said Max. 'Stuck at home with nothing to do. I expect he wants to get back to his mates.'

'Of course he does,' agreed Frances readily, although she was faintly put out that Max considered her own company to be of little value to Hugh. 'But my doctor thinks that student life is not what he needs at the moment.'

Max was silent and Frances wondered whether he was considering that if Hugh wasn't fit for student life he mightn't be much help as a fellow-labourer.

'Send him over,' he said at last. 'We'll have a chat.'

* * *

So why was she hesitating? she asked herself as she stood ironing in the spare bedroom that doubled as a laundry room. Perhaps it was because she didn't quite know how to start; how to bring it up, as it were, with Hugh. She was afraid to appear too managing and didn't want to make it sound as if she'd deliberately visited Max so as to wangle a job for her son. Hugh might resent such interference. Remembering Stephen's reaction to her description of Max she felt that she couldn't take *him* into her confidence either. He might not be very pleased at the thought of her going to see Max and having cups of tea with him.

Frances smiled, remembering. It had been fun to see him again, to hear how his plans were maturing. She wondered if he might not be a little lonely, stuck out there on his own, and was surprised that he had no wife or girlfriend. He was good-looking and friendly, although she could imagine that he might be stubborn. Her instinctive reaction to him – an unusual fluttering of the heart and a desire to flirt a little – whilst held in check had rather taken her aback.

She fitted one of Stephen's shirts on a hanger and made a face at herself as she passed before the dressing table on the way to the wardrobe, unwilling to accept the unwelcome thought that insinuated that he was young enough to be her son.

Hardly! she thought defiantly. He's past thirty and I'm only forty-four . . .

Frances paused, bending to examine herself more closely in the glass. She pushed her chin out; studying her jawline, peering for wrinkles, pushing her short hair back from her brow which was so often creased with an anxious frown.

I worry too much, she thought abruptly, straightening up. All this trouble with Hugh. And Stephen's no help . . .

She hung the shirt on the outside of the wardrobe door with its neatly ironed fellows and thought about Stephen. Just lately, he'd been rather more preoccupied than usual. Frances spread her cord skirt inside out across the ironing board, unable to define Stephen's present mood. It was probably simply that he was looking forward to taking up his new position.

She heard Hugh's bedroom door open and his footsteps heading for the bathroom and glanced at her watch: nearly midday. No doubt this sleeping late was good for him but she suddenly felt that he was ready for more than resting and reading and watching television. Was he sleeping? Or was he just lying in his bedroom, miserable and depressed? She stood the iron down and went to the door.

'So there you are,' she said as Hugh emerged, tousled and yawning, from the bathroom. 'Come on downstairs and we'll have an early lunch. Ironing has given me an appetite.'

'OK.' He smiled at her, looking vulnerable and somehow younger without his spectacles. 'I'll get some clothes on.'

'You do that,' she said. 'I've just had rather a good idea. Come on down when you're ready and we'll talk it over.'

Stephen, meanwhile, was pursuing his own idea. Cass had been delighted to see him but private speech with her had been impossible. With three children home for the holidays there was the constant danger of interruption and Stephen had no desire for his plans to be made public. Cass, intrigued by his need for secrecy and silence, readily agreed to meet him. This was a little more difficult to organise. He didn't want their meeting to take place where their numerous friends might witness it and carry tales back to Frances. Although there was no doubt that Charlotte's death had taught Cass such a severe lesson that her days of dalliance were past, nevertheless she was a beautiful and desirable woman and people loved to gossip.

Several times he wondered whether he should explain his thought processes to Frances but he knew that it would be almost impossible to explain what he hoped to achieve without raising her suspicions. He was convinced that old jealousies and resentments would surface and she would refuse to allow Cass to have any part in Hugh's healing. It was a very sensitive area for all of them and he spent a great deal of time wondering how to explain Hugh's problem without hurting Cass. It was going to mean reopening the painful past and he wondered whether he had the courage to do it; or the right.

They decided to meet at a pub in Plymouth, near the Law Courts. It was to appear as though their meeting was quite accidental and they agreed that Cass should arrive first, twenty minutes or so before Stephen turned up for a lunchtime beer and a sandwich. Cass, with many years of experience behind her, played up beautifully; hailing Stephen with surprise as he approached the bar and insisting that he join her at her relatively private table.

'Phew!' He glanced around quickly before smiling at her. 'I'm not used to this sort of thing.'

She laughed. 'I can see that. Don't look so nervous. You

have nothing to fear. I'm a reformed character now, you know.'

Stephen looked embarrassed. 'Oh, I realise that. I didn't mean . . .' He hesitated.

'For heaven's sake!' She put a hand on his arm and shook it. 'Don't be silly. It's so nice to see you but I have to say that I'm dying of curiosity.'

Stephen was serious at once. 'I've been over this so many times,' he told her. 'I've practised a hundred different ways of saying it but . . .' He spread his hands and shook his head.

'Sounds terrifying.' Cass watched him closely. 'Supposing you just tell me straight out. Try not to worry about what it sounds like or anything like that. Just say it. I expect I can bear it.'

'Oh Cass.' He wondered how deeply she must still be suffering, began to lose his nerve and deliberately thought of Hugh. 'OK, then . . .'

She continued to watch him just as closely through his stumbling narrative and he was aware of her compassion for Hugh's plight as well as her own grief. When he reached the end of his recital he saw that there were tears in her eyes.

'Poor, poor Hugh,' she said. 'Oh poor boy. How terrible. I had no idea . . .'

'Of course not,' he said quickly, and covered her hand with his own. 'Why should you? You had your own grief to contend with. Oh Cass, I'm so sorry to drag all this up again. It's just . . .' He swallowed, squeezed her hand and released it. 'I'm at my wits' end. And now this break-up with his girlfriend . . .'

'Of course I understand. Of course I do. It's dreadful that he should be suffering so much when he was so good to her. Poor little Charlotte. How she adored him!'

'You see, I wondered if there was anything we could do.' Stephen took a draught of beer. How to come to the point? He could hardly ask her outright to abase herself to Hugh, taking all the blame for her daughter's death!

'Would he talk to me?' wondered Cass. 'Let me explain that it was nothing to do with him?'

'It would be incredibly kind of you,' said Stephen at once. 'But it's got to be right, hasn't it? He carries some responsibility – just a little. I can see that . . .'

'He was *much* too young to understand what he was getting into!' cried Cass. 'The blame lies with me and Tom. Absolutely! It's shocking that Hugh is carrying this burden. I'll do whatever I can to relieve him of it.'

'That's amazingly generous of you,' he said gratefully. 'It's unforgivable of me to rake it all up.'

'I wish you'd come to me before,' she said thoughtfully. 'But how can we do it? What does Frances say?'

'She doesn't know,' mumbled Stephen, hating the idea of sounding disloyal to Frances. 'I thought I'd sound you out first, just in case. Didn't want to raise false hopes.' He finished his beer quickly.

'I know that Frances doesn't like me,' she said sadly.

'Nonsense. It's simply . . . She just . . .' Stephen floundered to a halt.

'Poor Stephen. I see. This makes it even more difficult.'

'I planned to tell her,' cried Stephen defensively. 'Once we'd spoken . . .'

'Perhaps it's better not to,' said Cass reflectively. 'Let's not rock any boats. Hugh is the important one here, after all.'

'That's what I thought.' Stephen stood up. 'Shall we have another drink? And what about a sandwich?'

'Good idea.' Cass smiled at him. 'Bring back a menu. We've got to try and think this one through.'

Stephen went up to the bar, his heart light with relief, confident that with her help Hugh would be restored to normality. Cass sat on at the table, trying to think of what she would say to Hugh if she could manage to see him alone. Both were so taken up with their thoughts that neither saw a black-haired woman on the first floor who watched them from her table at the top of the stairs.

Felicity Mainwaring pursed her thin lips. So Cass was up to her old tricks again! And with Stephen Ankerton! So much for all that rubbish about turning over a new leaf with Charlotte's death.

Not, thought Felicity vindictively, that I've ever believed a word of it! Leopards don't change their spots! I wonder if poor old Frances knows?

And, as the girlfriend with whom she was lunching returned from the loo, Felicity bent forward eagerly, ready to spread the word.

Chapter Thirteen

Much to her relief, Frances had no difficulty in persuading Hugh to consider working with Max Driver. Her real anxiety, which was to present the idea without appearing managing or contriving, proved to be groundless. This was because Hugh was too apathetic to care how she'd met Max in the first place or in what circumstances she'd bumped into him again. She told him about the possibility of some part-time work and explained Max's project.

At the sound of the Outward Bound school Hugh became a little more animated and Frances, quick to see that his interest was roused, elaborated on Max's hope and plans. When she described the location, Hugh frowned a little as a memory stirred.

'I know Trendlebere,' he said. 'I've seen the place. And probably Max, too. He was getting out of his Land Rover.' He remembered standing on Black Hill in the biting wind and envying the unknown figure his small piece of Dartmoor. He felt the prickings of curiosity. 'I'll go and see him.'

'I thought we could both go,' said Frances, surprised at Hugh's readiness to agree to her suggestion. 'Perhaps I could help to break the ice . . . you know?' She watched him anxiously.

Hugh felt the helpless frustration he'd known for most of his life. From his earliest moments there had been someone at hand; doing up his shoes, deciding whether he needed his jersey, stepping in to smooth his path. Because he was of a gentle disposition, which hated to hurt and was reluctant to assert itself, he'd allowed his mother and sister to pilot him through life. It had been a tremendous relief to get away to school; to be expected to make his own decisions; to take responsibility for himself. Of course, it had been a painful process. He was so used to being dependent that he was often slow and cautious but gradually he had emerged from the shelter of that crushing care and at last breathed deep the heady air of independence.

Now, Hugh fiddled with his food and wondered how he could achieve his own ends without hurting his mother's feelings. He knew that she was worried about him – more than that, frightened for him – and felt ashamed that he was unable to pull himself together and grateful that his parents had been so patient. Nevertheless, some instinct told him that he should go alone to meet Max Driver; that it was important that he shouldn't turn up under his mother's aegis. How to tell her?

'It might be better if I went on my own,' he said at last.

'Oh!' Frances could not contain an exclamation of disappointment.

'I think it would be best,' said Hugh rapidly. 'Don't you think so? I might even stay on a bit if he's got things that need doing.'

'I might want the car,' said Frances, secretly dismayed at how much she'd been looking forward to seeing Max again but refusing to heed the internal warnings of her conscience. 'We'll have to sort the times out sensibly so I can drop you off and pick you up. It's rather different than being five minutes away at the Royal Oak.'

'Yes, of course.' Hugh sighed inwardly. 'Are you going out this afternoon? Do you need the car?'

'Well no. But— Blast!'

Frances got up to answer the telephone and Hugh pushed away his plate. He hated being taken and fetched like a child going to a party. If only he could be truly independent! An idea slipped into his mind and he sat up a little straighter. Frances returned looking rather anxious.

'That was the solicitor,' she said. 'There's a bit of a panic, apparently. Our buyer's buyer has got a problem. These damned chains! He had to take an important incoming call but he's phoning back in a minute.'

Hugh could see that, for the present, the problem of getting over to Max Driver had been pushed to the back of her mind and, when the telephone rang again and she rushed out to answer it, Hugh was ready to act. He grabbed an old envelope, wrote a message on the back, took the spare car keys from the hook on the dresser and let himself out quietly.

The glory of the still-warm afternoon penetrated even Hugh's unhappiness. He drove slowly, noticing the hawthorn was in blossom and the gorse bushes were bright with yellow flowers. The new bracken, springing from the black peaty earth like so many tiny trees, covered the slopes with a tender hazing of green and, in the overarching blue sky, cushiony white clouds drifted idly before the gentle breeze. Hugh paused to watch the shining water leaping down from the hills, gushing out from issues, splashing down to the rivers in the wooded valleys. He smiled to see the lambs hurrying to press close to their mothers' flanks or nuzzling greedily to feed, their stumpy tails wagging furiously. A herd of ponies galloped across the further slopes, manes streaming out, hooves clattering, sure-footed, amongst the scree.

The familiar beloved scene soothed his tired mind and eased his anguish. In these great majestic spaces, his problems seemed to dwindle into proportion and become containable, even solvable. Thus it had been, at least, until Charlotte's death. After that, the magic had only partially worked. Hugh drove on, his spirits rising as the journey progressed, his melancholy receding, his burden of guilt made lighter by the beauty all around him. He made no effort to hurry but, as he drew near to Trendlebere, anxiety began to edge out his temporary measure of peace.

Max's Land Rover was in the yard but there was no one about. Hugh looked around him. He could imagine exactly how it would be; children bustling about, carrying rucksacks, climbing into a mini-bus which would have canoes strapped to the roof; all the paraphernalia of maps and compasses and water-bottles. Hugh was back for a moment at CCF camp with some burly instructor ordering them about . . .

'Can I help you?'

Hung swung round and the picture was complete. He stared in amazement at the man who had just emerged from the house and who was watching him with interest. Hugh began to laugh and then controlled himself.

'Sorry. It's just . . . I know you. You're Sergeant Driver. "Slave" Driver . . .' He shook his head. 'I don't believe it.'

Max regarded Hugh thoughtfully. 'Are you Hugh Ankerton, by any chance?'

'I am. And you were one of the instructors on my CCF camp in Shropshire. You nearly killed me trying to show me how to capsize a canoe and come up smiling.'

Max's eyes crinkled a little at the corners. 'I can't say I remember.'

'I can!' said Hugh with feeling. 'You were always telling us that pain is free. I still have nightmares about it.'

'Well, for God's sake don't tell your mum,' said Max. 'She likes me.' He studied Hugh, trying to remember him. 'It must have been years ago.'

'Seems like yesterday,' said Hugh firmly. 'And I certainly shan't tell my mother. She'd never let me work for you!' He felt a pang of anxiety, wondering if he'd overstepped the mark with his silly joke. 'Sorry. It's just that I could imagine it all so clearly. You know? The kids milling about and the canoes on the mini-bus and suddenly, there you were. I think it's a brilliant idea,' he said seriously, and then felt rather shy.

'Thanks.' Max was non-committal. 'You think that the kids will enjoy it then? You know, capsizing canoes and so on?'

'Well,' said Hugh, with engaging naïveté, his shyness forgotten. 'It'll be a bit different, won't it? You were trying to lick us into shape, weren't you? Training us up for military careers. These children will be paying, won't they? I imagine they'll be expecting to *enjoy* themselves.'

Max laughed then. 'You think we shouldn't tell them that pain is free?' he suggested, and Hugh turned scarlet.

'I didn't mean . . .' he began awkwardly and then laughed too. 'You've got to admit it was hell,' he said.

'Of course it was,' said Max. 'We had to do something to put all you little bastards off the idea of joining up. Now this will be different. Come on. I'll show you around.'

Later, drinking tea with Max in the big kitchen, Hugh was nearly as excited as Max was. He could see, in his mind's eye, the dormitories, the recreation room, the bustle and activity.

He sighed with pure envy. 'You *are* lucky,' he said. 'It's a terrific project.'

Max leaned against the sink, watching him. He recalled quite clearly all that Frances had told him during that snowy winter afternoon. He saw the shadows beneath Hugh's eyes behind his spectacles and noticed how the fingers of his left hand plucked at the knuckles of his right. He was visited by the faint memory of a boy, unable to right his canoe, being dragged up gasping and spluttering; the drowned frightened face.

'Not your scene though?' he asked casually. 'The summer camp doesn't seem to be one of your happiest memories.'

'I've never been very good at water sports,' admitted Hugh. 'I can't see properly without my specs. But I love hill-walking and hiking. And I love Dartmoor.'

'And you can ride.'

It was a statement and Hugh coloured slightly.

'Yes, I can ride. I don't do much at the moment . . .' His

voice tailed off, and Max turned away as the kettle boiled. 'Mum said you might be able to give me a bit of part-time work. I'm quite good with a paint brush. I helped my sister decorate her cottage and I've done quite a bit with Dad around the house.'

He fell silent, thinking that his experience sounded pretty limited and wondering if he'd dare to suggest his idea to Max. He looked at him as he made tea and felt the power of the older man; experienced, independent, sure of himself. Despite his nickname, he'd been one of the nicer NCOs at the camp, more approachable than the others and with a dry humour that delighted Hugh. He remembered that Max's face had been the first thing he'd seen as he was dragged choking from the water and he'd gasped 'Sorry, Sar'n't' to him from between chattering teeth.

'You drown yourself while you're in my charge, boy,' Max had muttered, his arms strong and safe about Hugh's limp form, 'and I'll kill you.' And Hugh, even in his pitiable state, had given a little chuckle.

This memory gave him courage in the face of Max's confidence and strength and he made another push at selling himself.

'I don't mind what I do,' he said, as Max gave him his mug of tea.

Max looked down at him. 'I need a bit of help,' he said. 'I'm not getting on quite as quick as I hoped. The trouble is, I'm working on a strict budget and I can't afford much.'

'I had an idea,' said Hugh rapidly. 'I don't need the money so much but I'd like to be busy, you know? I wondered if I could stay here. Work in exchange for bed and board. I could sleep in the caravan.'

Max was staring at him in surprise. He saw the eagerness in Hugh's face and guessed that it must be difficult for him, stuck at home, not really ill but forbidden to return to his work and friends. Frances had told him enough about Hugh for Max to guess that he was oversensitive and much too biddable, and he'd already summed Frances up as an overprotective mother.

'Would your parents object to that?' he asked.

'Mum will fuss a bit,' said Hugh honestly. 'She's a worrier. But it will make life easier for her in the long run. I have to borrow her car, you see. She'd have to drop me off and pick me up.'

'Well . . .' Max hesitated. 'If your parents agree, I don't see why not. If that's what you want. Bed, board and beer money. How does that suit you?'

'Sounds great!' Hugh grinned at him. 'I'll start tomorrow, shall I?'

'As long as your parents are happy,' warned Max.

'Don't worry,' said Hugh confidently. 'They will be.'

As he drove home he felt happier than he had for months and months. Why he should feel so excited at the thought of living in an ancient caravan and painting the walls of an old barn he couldn't quite analyse. It seemed to represent freedom: a job, his own place to live, a share in Max's project. He thought of coming out of the caravan and looking across Lustleigh Cleave and away to the sea and his heart thrilled with pleasure. He'd had enough of living at home or with students and with being weighed down with a sense of futility and guilt. Perhaps, working for Max, he'd have no time to tread the circular path of remorse. Hugh thought about Lucinda and how much he missed her, and shook his head fiercely. He would *not* drift down that path of despair. Somehow, being with Max he'd felt different; as if he could be in control of his life rather than allowing himself to be a victim.

He put the car away, hanging on to this determination which tended to diminish a little as he went into the kitchen and saw his mother's anxious face.

'Sorry,' he said automatically. 'Sorry about the car.' Guilt returned and settled round him like a mantle. 'I didn't know how long you might be so I thought I'd just dash over and see if I could get something sorted out.'

'That's OK.' Frances had had time to come to terms with her disappointment and besides, she'd been more than preoccupied with the problems regarding the sale of the house. 'I've been a bit tied up on the telephone.'

'How is it?' asked Hugh, anxious to show concern. 'Got it sorted out?'

'I don't know.' She looked rather harassed. 'Our buyer's buyer has got a bit of a problem but they're trying to put it right.'

'I'm sure it'll be OK,' said Hugh comfortingly. 'Now don't start panicking.'

'I'll try not to.' She made herself smile at him, trying not to think what would happen if the sale fell through. 'How did you get on with Max?'

'Very well indeed. He was one of the instructors on that CCF I went to in Shropshire. Amazing, isn't it?' Hugh decided not to go into details. 'He's offered to put me up to save you driving to and fro.'

'But . . . how d'you mean? Put you up?'

'I'm going to sleep in the caravan. It'll be great, Mum. I'm really looking forward to it. It's like a sort of a holiday.'

Seeing the happiness on his face, Frances tried to hold back her instinctive reactions against such an idea. He looked better than she'd seen him look for months – bright and excited – and she pushed down her disappointment at being deprived of those daily visits which she'd been anticipating. His wellbeing was more important than a mild flirtation with Max and, anyway, she was far too worried about the house sale to feel in the mood for such light-hearted foolishness.

'As long as the caravan isn't damp,' she began but Hugh, amazed at her capitulation, put his arm around her and gave her a hug.

'Come on, Mum,' he said. 'It's practically summer and Max has been sleeping there all winter. It's very cosy. Let's have a drink, shall we? To celebrate.'

Frances let him bustle about and tried not to feel hurt at his evident unconcern at the idea of leaving her. It would do him good to be with Max and, after all, they'd be off to Wales in a few weeks. He could hardly come to harm in that time. Assuming, of course, that the sale went through. Frances groaned with irritation and frustration and wondered if it had been wise to sign the lease to rent the house in Wales. As Stephen had pointed out, he had to live somewhere and the farmhouse would sell sooner or later, but still . . .

She realised that Hugh was talking to her and made an effort to concentrate. He was looking so much happier that her spirits rose again. This, after all, was the most important thing: that Hugh should come through this terrible depression. She realised that she would have to take him over to Trendlebere with his belongings tomorrow and her spirits rose higher still. She would see Max and have a little chat with him, perhaps a cup of coffee . . .

Relieved at such an easy victory, Hugh went to pack his things.

Chapter Fourteen

Annie's optimistic determination that she could cope with Pippa and Rowley was reinforced when she saw Pippa's bravely suppressed misery. She was waiting for them in the front garden and hurried out to hug Pippa and help her unload the car.

'I've tried to bring the minimum we could manage with,' Pippa said anxiously. 'If only we knew how long we'd be here!'

'Don't worry,' said Annie cheerfully. 'We'll squash in. I've cleared the study so that Rowley can have his toys and books in there.'

'Oh Annie . . .' The tears sparkled in her eyes and she bent quickly to pull out another case.

Annie glanced at Rowley, who stood watching the proceedings, a knitted golliwog in a red jacket clutched to his chest. He went to stand beside Pippa, hugging her leg, as she reached into the car.

'Here.' She emerged looking flushed. 'You carry your case, Rowley. Isn't it smart? It's his own special overnight case.'

It occurred to Annie that it must be quite dreadful to be

continually hiding one's feelings, trying to remain cheerful, for the benefit of another person. How often must Pippa long to break down, weep, scream, and how often must she have to restrain herself because of Rowley's presence? Annie remembered how readily, after Perry's death, she had dissolved into tears, how impossible she would have found it to hold a conversation or pretend at cheerfulness.

'It's a lovely case,' she said, admiring the bright plaid bag, which Rowley now held with a kind of ostentatious casualness in an attempt to disguise his pride. 'Shall we start carrying some of these things inside?'

'Mummy coming?' asked Rowley cautiously, softened by the admiration of the case, but still not quite ready to capitulate.

They went together up the long path, the two women weighed down by bags, and slowly the luggage was stowed away into the spare bedroom and the study and in the cupboard under the stairs. Rowley was established in the courtyard with his toy cars and, whilst Annie made tea, Pippa recounted the latest details of her marriage, one eye on Rowley playing happily beyond the window. Annie guessed that it was to be the first of many such conversations and feared that she lacked the suitable qualifications required by a confidante or advisor.

As the days passed, however, she realised that her role was to be mainly as listener. Pippa needed someone to whom she could pour out her hurts and who would lend a sympathetic ear. Relieved that she was not to be called upon to tender too much advice Annie gladly complied, allowing her to go over and over Robert's betrayals.

When advice *was* required Annie called upon Perry's fund of wisdom and Pippa, who knew that Annie coped with her loss by involving him in every aspect of her life, had no difficulty at all in believing that he was still near at hand, ready to help her, too. Like Annie, she could easily imagine that his own deep spiritual strength continued to be available and found great comfort in it. He had been a wonderful, if unconventional, godfather, and Pippa missed him terribly. It had always saddened her that he had never trusted Robert. Now, it seemed that he was to be proved right. She admitted to Annie that she had been too easy-going for Robert's ambitious nature but was still quite certain that the real rupture had been caused by his affair with Louisa.

'If only I could stop loving him,' she'd cry. 'How can I love a man who's been so cruel?'

Unfortunately there was no satisfactory answer to this age-old question and Annie wisely made no attempt to offer one. She tried to distract her from her pain with trips to the coast and the moor, which were also intended to give Pippa a feel of the countryside. After all, she and Rowley had to settle down somewhere. Why not here?

Pippa gazed at the moor and the sea, at modern bungalows and stone cottages, and could think of no good reason why not but was unable to feel any enthusiasm either. She seemed to be stuck in a fog of lassitude and misery and any decision seemed utterly beyond her. Nevertheless, Annie was right: she and Rowley had to live somewhere. She struggled to be more constructive and merely found herself weeping again. She wanted to be with Robert; the three of them happily together in the house in Farnham. What had she to do with cottages in Devon? She felt as though she had suffered a terrible accident and that she was torn and bleeding from some invisible wound, growing steadily weaker rather than stronger.

Although she always tried to be brave and cheerful with Rowley, left to herself it seemed that her unhappiness would never abate and Annie began to be seriously worried about her. Finally, after a great deal of careful consideration, she enlisted Frances's help.

Mrs Driver drove carefully down the track and paused to peer anxiously from the car window. Now that she was here, her courage was beginning to desert her. To her surprise a young man appeared at the caravan door and advanced to meet her. She climbed out and stood for a moment, waiting. The young man raised a hand in greeting and smiled at her.

'Hello. Can I help you at all? Are you looking for Max?'

'I'm his mother,' she said cautiously. He sounded too well-spoken to be a casual labourer yet he appeared to belong.

'I'm Hugh Ankerton.' He held out his hand. 'I'm helping out. Decorating and things. Max has moved into the house now, so I'm in the caravan. He's popped into Ashburton but he'll be back soon. Have you got time to wait?'

Mrs Driver shook his hand and eyed him speculatively. A cunning idea was forming at the back of her busy mind.

'I've brought him something,' she said.

'Oh?' Hugh raised his eyebrows.

Mrs Driver decided to trust her instincts. 'He's in here,' she said, and opened the back door of the car. Curled up on an old blanket was something that looked like a grey and white sheepskin rug. As Hugh looked closer, the rug raised its head and two bright brown eyes appeared through a tangled fringe of hair.

'Good heavens!' he exclaimed involuntarily and the rug's stumpy tail began to beat rhythmically. 'Hello, old chap,' said Hugh softly. He reached a hand to it and the rug licked it and sat up expectantly.

'He was being ill-treated,' Mrs Driver was explaining, delighted with Hugh's reaction. 'He's a stray, see? Barely more than a puppy. He kept coming round the dustbins and the manager said he'd drown him if he saw him again.'

'How awful.' Hugh crouched beside the car and began to stroke the rug who responded gratefully.

'So I thought,' continued Mrs Driver, somewhat speciously, 'What about Max? I thought. Always loved dogs, Max has. And I thought, Just the job up there at Trendlebere. He needs a guard dog up there on his own. And he'll be company, too. I didn't know you were here with him.'

'I think it's a brilliant idea.' Hugh, crouching by the car, was enticing the rug from the seat. 'He's lovely, isn't he? What breed is he, would you say?'

Mrs Driver bit back the obvious retort and smiled down benignly upon Hugh's innocent head. 'He's a Mutt,' she said serenely. 'We had one when Max was just a tacker. Good dogs, they are. Faithful. And brave, too!'

Hugh watched the Mutt sniffing cautiously at the cement mixer and jumping back nervously as he displaced a slate from a nearby pile.

'He's young yet,' said Mrs Driver defensively, as though

Hugh had questioned the Mutt's bravery.

Hugh grinned. 'He's great,' he said. 'What's his name?'

'I've called him Mutt, just like the other one. Mutt by name, Mutt by nature. He knows his name.' Mrs Driver crossed her fingers behind her back. 'Go on, try him.'

'Here, Mutt. Good boy, then.' Hugh laughed as the Mutt careered towards him, tail waving, and Mrs Driver gave a silent sigh of relief, feeling an overwhelming surge of affection for the obliging animal. 'It would be lovely to have him here,' he admitted. 'But what will Max say?'

'Ah,' said Max's mother thoughtfully. 'Any chance of a cuppa?'

'Of course,' said Hugh, distracted as she'd hoped he would be by her suggestion. 'Sorry. I should have thought of it myself. Have you seen the new kitchen?'

'I have.' She followed him inside, keeping a wary eye on the Mutt. 'Very posh for someone who can't cook. So you're managing in the caravan?'

'I've had glandular fever,' admitted Hugh. 'I'm not fit enough to go back to university yet so I'm giving a hand here. I can't believe my luck! It's all very exciting, don't you think?'

She nodded, smiling a little at his enthusiasm, and was visited by another idea. Perhaps discretion, in this case, would be the better part of valour and Hugh was proving himself – albeit unconsciously – a most useful ally.

'I brought some tins of food along,' she said casually. 'What say I just leave the Mutt with you? I've got to be off soon or I'll be late. Think you could cope with him?'

'I should think so.' Hugh looked a little anxious as he

disposed of the tea-bags and passed her a mug. 'If you think it'll be OK with Max . . .?'

'We've talked about it already.' Mrs Driver sounded admirably confident. 'If he's changed his mind I'll take him away. *I* can't keep him, you see. I've only got a small flat and I'm out working. Wouldn't be right.'

The Mutt, having explored the kitchen, sat down and stared up at Hugh. His tail moved slightly and Hugh could see the bright eyes regarding him steadily through the fringe of hair.

'I can see that,' he agreed. 'But . . .'

'The dear of him,' said Mrs Driver, regarding the Mutt fondly and surreptitiously adding more cold milk to her tea. 'He's taken to you already, I can see that. That loyal he'll be, given the chance. I can't bear the thought of him being put down. If you could've seen him, scavenging around the dustbins . . .'

'Poor old chap,' said the gullible Hugh. 'Well, if Max knows about it . . .'

'I've got his bed in the car and a week's supply of food,' she said quickly, determined to strike while the iron was hot and hoping to get away now before Max returned. 'All on the back seat, it is. You get it in while I finish this tea and then I'll be off.'

Frances was only too ready to be enlisted by Annie. She found Pippa's problems a welcome distraction from her fear for Hugh and her anxiety about the sale of the house. Somewhere along the chain one of the links was at straining point and Frances roamed to and fro, willing the danger to be past. Stephen tried to reassure her but he seemed oddly distracted and she had the feeling that he wasn't really concentrating on her. She put it down to pressure at the office and turned with relief to Pippa's woes.

She'd met Pippa several times before and adored Rowley, who had taken to Frances from his earliest meeting with her, showing none of the shyness he exhibited with others. He ran to show her his newest toy or clambered on to her lap with a book and Frances hugged him and kissed him and he never protested.

'I'm the granny he never knew,' she said, flattered by his affection, whilst Pippa, delighted to be relieved of her duties for an hour or so, was only too happy to agree.

When Frances telephoned one morning with the news that the house sale had fallen through, Annie was sympathetic.

'Whatever will you do?' she asked. 'And you've got the house all lined up in Wales. Oh, Frances! I'm so sorry.'

Frances sounded very flat. 'Stephen's going anyway,' she said. 'As he says, he's got to have somewhere to live. I'm just going to have to try to find another buyer. The agent's advertising it again this week but it'll be like starting all over from the beginning. Another six weeks at least even if we find another buyer straight away. It's just that I hate being on my own. It feels so empty with half the stuff packed away and I get a bit nervous without Stephen.'

'Poor Frances! You'll have to borrow Pippa and Rowley,' said Annie lightly.

'Oh!' Frances sounded suddenly animated. 'What a brilliant idea. D'you think they'd come? There's so much more room for them here and I'd love to have them.'

'Well.' Rather taken aback by Frances's quick response to her joke, Annie thought about it. 'I'll speak to Pippa,' she said. 'She's shopping in Ashburton. I don't want to make it seem as though I don't want her here.'

'No, no, I see that. But it would be an answer to all our problems,' said Frances eagerly. 'You're terribly squashed there.'

'Yes, we are.' Annie thought of quiet moments and the study to herself again, but had no intention of trying to influence Pippa. 'I'll speak to her,' she promised.

Rowley, sitting in the supermarket trolley, stretched out his legs and gazed with rapture at his new shiny blue sandals. The crepe soles were brightly white and the buckles glittered satisfyingly. Max Driver pushed the trolley gently aside so that he could reach the tins of soup and Rowley, too excited by his new acquisitions to feel his usual suspicion of strangers, beamed at him.

'Sangals,' he enunciated carefully, and stretched out his foot so that the stranger should share in his great moment. 'New sangals.'

'Ah,' said Max, rather taken aback by this uninhibited approach and unused to the ways of the extremely young. 'Very nice.'

Rowley detected a lack of fervour in this response and frowned a little. 'Sangals!' he shouted and rocked the trolley.

'Steady on!' Max put out a restraining hand just as Pippa hurried back with various items.

'I'm so sorry,' she said, putting the things into the trolley and passing Rowley his golliwog. 'He's a bit above himself. We've just been buying his summer sandals and he insisted on wearing them out of the shop.'

Rowley held out the golliwog. 'Woglet,' he said willingly, and offered him to Max.

'Oh dear,' said Pippa, embarrassed. 'The shoes have gone to his head. He's usually very shy and silly with strangers.'

'I'm flattered.' Max smiled reassuringly at her. 'It's a very nice change. My experience with children so far has been quite different.' He hesitated, shook Woglet formally by his knitted hand and turned away.

Outside on the pavement they met again. Pippa was buckling Rowley into his pushchair when Max came out with a box full of shopping. He smiled at Rowley, who immediately arched his back, thrusting himself against his harness, and shouted, 'Daddy!'

Pippa turned with such a naked expression of hope in her face that Max was shocked. She recovered herself quickly but he saw the disappointment in her eyes before he climbed into his Land Rover, parked at the kerb, and drove quickly away.

Swallowing back her tears, Pippa pushed Rowley back to the car park. It was one of her private fantasies that Robert should come after them, restored to his former self, and with some acceptable reason for his behaviour of the past six months. But what reason could there be? In the long lonely nights, Pippa spent hours thinking of such reasons; enacting scenes of remorse and forgiveness; longing for the clock to be turned back.

She strapped Rowley into his car seat, loaded the

shopping in beside him and climbed into the driver's seat. As she started up the ignition Rowley flung Woglet into the front seat. Pippa jumped, stalling the engine, and knew a sudden desire to scream loudly; to tear Woglet limb from woolly limb. She clenched her hands tightly on the wheel, realising that unless she took some very positive action she might go quite mad with despair. It was time to make a decision about her future and to give serious thought as to where she and Rowley should go. The cramped conditions in Annie's cottage were no good for any of them. It had been a refuge, a haven from the storm, but the storm was passing. Pippa took a deep breath, picked Woglet up and restarted the engine.

'Woglet!' demanded Rowley, stretching out his hand and leaning forward as far as he could. 'Woglet!'

'No,' said Pippa firmly, driving slowly through the car park. 'You shouldn't throw him about like that. How would you like it? He's got a headache now and needs to sit quietly.'

There was a silence from the back whilst Rowley digested this information. She glanced across her shoulder at him as he sat in his little chair – head drooped, staring at his feet – and she felt a pang of remorse. She wondered how much he missed Robert and how this upheaval would affect his life. Before she could repent and pass Woglet back, however, Rowley stirred.

'Sangals,' he murmured with quiet contentment, Woglet's injuries forgotten in the contemplation of the blue shiny shoes, and, putting his thumb in his mouth, he gave himself up to happiness.

By the time she arrived back at the cottage he was nearly asleep, exhausted by the excesses of his day. She carried him in and laid him to sleep on the truckle bed in the spare bedroom which they shared. She dropped her bag on to her own bed, tucked Woglet in beside him and went downstairs and out into the courtyard where Annie was reading.

'I've been thinking, Annie,' she said without preamble, afraid that she might lose her nerve, 'it's time we found a place of our own. I've thought about it carefully. I don't want to buy anything just yet and anyway the money hasn't been sorted out but I'm going to look for somewhere to rent.'

'Well,' said Annie, putting down her book. 'How odd that you should bring this up. Frances telephoned earlier. Their sale has fallen through and she's looking for a lodger.'

'A lodger?' Pippa wrinkled her brow as she curled up in the wicker chair. 'Why should she want a lodger?'

'Stephen's off to Wales next week and she's got to start all over again to sell the house.' Annie shrugged. 'It could take at least six weeks, probably much longer. She's very nervous at being stuck out there all alone. And now Stephen will have to go on paying the mortgage as well as the rent on their new place. Does the idea appeal?'

'Yes, it does,' said Pippa, who rather dreaded being alone herself. 'And she's so super with Rowley. But I wonder if I should? Shouldn't I be thinking of being more independent?'

'I don't see why.' Annie frowned thoughtfully, massaging her brow with her fingers and pushing her hair behind her ears. 'I think it's good for you to have some company. You're more than welcome to stay here . . .'

'I know,' said Pippa quickly. 'I know that. It's just that I think we've cramped you for long enough and we need more space, too.'

'Well, you'll have it with Frances,' said Annie. 'Some of their furniture has gone on to Wales and she's packed masses of stuff already. There will be plenty of room and she'll be delighted to have you. Why not try it for a few weeks? You can be watching out for something of your own to rent.'

'So I can.' Pippa looked more cheerful. 'That's a good idea, Annie. It's another step forward. Only a tiny one, I admit . . .'

'It's not a contest, Pippa,' said Annie gently. 'Take as long as you need. I've loved having you both and you can always come back if it doesn't work out.'

'Bless you.' Pippa stood up and bent to give Annie a swift kiss. 'You've saved my life. D'you mind if I phone Frances? I'd like to sort it out straight away.'

'You do that.'

Annie relaxed back in her chair and breathed deeply. It seemed that, after all, not too much had been demanded of her and she'd managed to meet Pippa's needs despite her own fears of inadequacy. Ridiculously, she could almost *feel* Perry's warm approval and she smiled. She thought of having the cottage to herself again, quiet breakfasts, afternoons naps in the courtyard. Her eyes closed . . .

'Sangals,' said a voice clearly in her ear. 'Annie do.'

She opened her eyes upon Rowley's seraphic smile, gasping as his weight fell upon her chest. He wriggled up beside her and, patting the blue sandals with a possessive pride delightful to behold, held out his chubby foot in its bright red sock.

Chapter Fifteen

When Stephen left for Wales, he and Cass still had not formed any definite plan although she had declared herself willing to talk to Hugh, taking the responsibility of Charlotte's death to herself and reminding him of Charlotte's own character.

'However wonderful life might have been,' she told Stephen during one of their pub meetings, 'maybe sooner or later her happiness would have been destroyed by her lack of confidence or her . . .' she gesticulated as though trying to draw down a word out of the air, 'her . . .'

'Negative approach?' suggested Stephen. 'Natural pessimism?' He shook his head. 'I didn't know her well enough to make a judgement. She was just a little girl who was mad about horses.'

Cass frowned as she tried to put her thoughts into words. 'I agree with you. These problems seem ridiculous when applied to a child of fifteen. Charlotte was happiest in her own tiny circle. Outside it she lost her confidence.'

Stephen remembered Caroline's engagement party, when Charlotte's shyness had taken the form of rudeness, and her hostility to Lucinda had been embarrassing for everyone.

'I know what you mean,' he said.

'She could have known great happiness in very specialised situations,' said Cass sadly. 'She adored the little ones and loved being at Meavy School where the classes are tiny and she knew everyone. She was Head Girl there, you know. It was the greatest moment of her life.'

Cass's eyes filled with tears and she bent her head.

Stephen watched in horror and tentatively slipped his arm around her shoulder.

'Forgive me, Cass,' he said. 'I have no right to put you through this.'

'Yes you have.' She tried to smile at him but her mouth went awry and she shook her head, swallowing hard.

Stephen moved so that his broad shoulders hid her from the view of other people in the bar. It was almost shocking to see the light-hearted Cass in tears and he felt helpless and anxious.

'Look,' he said, 'let's forget this whole business, shall we? Hugh's straightening himself out, you know. He's got a job with this chap . . .'

'Oh please,' begged Cass, wiping her eyes. 'You don't know what a *relief* it is to talk about Charlotte. You see, Tom and I feel so guilty. We were both playing around, you know.'

Stephen said nothing and she smiled at his tactful silence, more in control of herself now.

'Of course you know. Everyone knows.' She stretched her long legs under the table and leaned her head back so that it rested on his arm. Her face, as she stared across the room, was sombre with memories. 'Tom was . . . was with someone else that weekend, too, and we both know that if we hadn't been committing adultery Charlotte might still be alive.'

Stephen, unable to offer consolation, tightened his grip on her shoulder. She nodded at him as though grateful for his gesture but her face was strained and unhappy.

'We can't talk about it, you see. We're kind and loving to one another but it gets too emotional if we try to discuss it. We both know how we feel and we know how much we've lost. We just wanted to put it behind us and make our marriage work. We came very near to losing that, too. By dying Charlotte made us face that fact. She saved our marriage, which was what she was trying to do all along.'

'She seemed to be quite unlike either of you.'

'Tom always said she was like his mother,' said Cass. 'She was another mixed-up unhappy soul, apparently. I never knew her; she died quite young. Charlotte looked like Tom and she adored him. He'll never forgive himself for letting her down. I know how he feels. It was quite lucky that he was plunged into the Falklands War just afterwards. It kept him busy but he feels it still. We've learned a very hard lesson. But talking to you like this is such a tremendous relief.'

'I'm very glad,' said Stephen. 'If it helps . . .'

'Oh, it does.' She smiled at his expression. 'It must seem odd to you but, you see, all my mourning's been done alone. I can't share it. We've tacitly agreed never to mention her. The children do, thank God, but I long to *remember* her. All the little touching things that made up the sum of her life. It's my punishment. I am not allowed to talk about my dead child because I killed her.'

'Come on, Cass . . .' Stephen shook her gently.

'But I did,' said Cass sadly. 'I didn't care how my playing about affected her or how frightened she was that Tom and I might split up. And at the end I was completely obsessed with . . . with this other man. He threw me over just before she died.'

Her lips shook and she covered her mouth with her hand. Stephen drew her closer and held her whilst she wept. He was shocked at what grief his good intentions had unearthed and he felt inadequate to deal with it.

'I'm so sorry.' He murmured it over and over again, as if it were an incantation.

Presently she straightened up and felt for her handkerchief. 'Forgive me,' she said, drying her cheeks. 'It's such a luxury. Generally I feel too much of a hypocrite, you see. Weeping and wailing when it was because of me she died. Even with Kate or Mrs Hampton, who knew Charlotte all her life, I feel this terrible guilt.'

'You didn't push her into the quarry, Cass,' said Stephen. 'I still think it was an accident.'

'That awful car smash,' said Cass. She finished her drink with a long swallow, her eyes on the past. 'I expect you heard the rumours. Jane had been having an affair with Philip while Alan was at sea. Alan had been posted to Chatham and I was helping Jane to get away before Alan found out about the affair or Philip found out they were leaving. Charlotte stumbled on our little plot, thinking that I was meeting my lover. In an attempt to expose me she let the secret out to the one person we were keeping it from.

Philip rushed off and there was that awful car accident. Blood and glass everywhere. Charlotte and I were first on the scene. I was so angry with her. I screamed at her.' Cass's voice trembled. 'Oh God. I told her it was all her fault. I actually said that. It was enough to unbalance anybody, let alone Charlotte.'

'It was the accident that upset her,' said Stephen comfortingly.

Cass shook her head. 'You can't isolate things like that,' she said. 'It was all part of the same pattern. We were all of us guilty and Charlotte paid the price.' She drew a deep breath. 'Oh, it's so good to *talk*, Stephen. I know you won't breathe a word about the accident, although I should think most people guessed. But it's been so much on my conscience. Wherever I look there's guilt. It's a relief to speak about it.'

'I'm happy to have been of any help to you,' he said sincerely. 'I just wish I wasn't going off to Wales so soon.'

'So do I!' Her tone was heartfelt. 'I shall miss you. And we haven't got Hugh sorted out yet. We mustn't let him feel like this, Stephen. It's so terribly unfair.'

'There's still time.' He removed his arm and picked up their glasses. 'I'm trying to think of a way of getting you together with him so that he doesn't suspect. Look, let's have another drink. I think we both deserve one.'

She smiled warmly at him and he went up to the bar. A man, who had been watching them from the corner of the bar, turned away at his approach and gazed thoughtfully into his beer but Stephen was thinking about Frances, and wishing the whole thing could be sorted out and done with, and didn't notice him.

When Frances arrived at Trendlebere one morning with the news that the house sale had fallen through, Hugh found it very difficult to pretend disappointment. He felt genuinely sorry for his parents but his first feeling was pleasure that he could continue to work with Max. He was enjoying himself for the first time in eighteen months and, although he had by no means been able to put his guilt behind him or to forget Lucinda, his periods of depression were far fewer.

The buildings were taking shape. Max had been surprised at how hard Hugh could work. He looked so thin and his spectacles lent him an academic air which belied the practical nature he had inherited from Frances.

'You're looking better,' she said as they stood together in the yard. 'You'll be able to go back to university soon. No chance of you coming home, I suppose?'

Hugh was spared the effort of thinking of a sensible answer by the appearance of Max. Frances turned her attention to him and Hugh was left making an attempt to sort out his feelings. He was startled by the strong reaction he felt against going back to university. As for returning home . . . He strolled along behind Max and Frances, only half listening to their conversation and feeling a wave of rebellion building up inside him. He didn't want to go back to Bristol. He wanted to stay here, watching the adventure training school taking shape, seeing the buildings being transformed. He wanted to be here when the mini-bus was purchased and the canoes were stacked in the open-fronted barn which adjoined the recreation room. He wanted to be waiting here in the yard when the first children arrived; to take them walking or pony-trekking over his beloved moor. He *belonged* here now.

Hugh stuck his hands in his pockets and watched a buzzard circling up above Yarner Woods. The old frustration washed over him. What was he thinking of? It was Max's place, Max's dream, Max's school. But surely Max would need someone to help him? He couldn't run it single-handed. As Hugh watched the buzzard, soaring higher as the thermals bore him upward, he realised that, during the past few weeks, it had become his dream, too. He longed to be part of it as he had never longed for anything before in his life.

He turned, hearing his name, and arranged his face in an easy open expression. He must go carefully, sounding out Max and putting his hopes to him before he confronted his parents. His father, he suspected, might just be on his side. His mother . . . Hugh guessed how she would react if he told her that he didn't want to finish his degree and he shuddered inwardly. He simply must get Max on his side.

He went towards them thinking that, despite her disappointment about the house, his mother was looking quite cheerful.

'I see you've acquired a dog,' she said.

The Mutt had appeared from a sortie down in the paddocks and was gambolling ecstatically around Max as if they had been separated for several years. Hugh glanced at Max and smothered a smile.

'He was sort of wished on us,' he said tactfully and Max gave a derisive snort.

Frances bent down to pat the Mutt who gave her a muddy paw to hold and then rolled on to his back, all four legs extended in the air.

'Daft animal,' muttered Max. 'No pride at all.'

'He's sweet,' protested Frances. 'The children will love him.'

Hugh, remembering the scene when Max had returned from Ashburton to find the Mutt ensconced in the kitchen on his blanket gnawing happily on one of Max's gumboots, grinned. Max's observations on his mother's cunning had been pithy and to the point but, when she reappeared at Trendlebere several days later, he'd been admirably restrained. Mrs Driver had cleverly omitted to bring the subject up at all. She talked of many things, avoiding Max's sardonic expression, and only at the last moment as she went out had she paid any attention to the Mutt who was busy working his way through Max's second gumboot.

'The dear of him,' she murmured, pausing by his blanket. 'Good boy, then.'

The Mutt wagged his tail, one eye on Max, but continued with his gnawing. Hugh had held his breath, waiting for the blow to fall, but Max, who knew when he was beaten but who had no intention of giving his mother any satisfaction by admitting it, merely opened the kitchen door for her with a dangerous gleam in his eye.

Now, conscious of Max's reservations on the Mutt, Hugh changed the subject. 'How d'you think it's looking?' he asked.

'You've got on so fast,' Frances said. 'Max says he hopes to be ready by next Easter. What a pity we'll be in Wales.

You could have come over and lent a hand.'

'Bad luck about the house,' said Hugh, trying to sound as if he meant it.

'Oh, it's infuriating,' but she managed a smile. 'I hate being alone at night, too. We're rather isolated. Still, there's nothing we can do about it. Stephen's off this weekend.'

'Does that mean you want this young man back?' asked Max and Hugh's heart stood still with terror.

'Well, it occurred to me, I must admit,' said Frances. 'But he'll be off to Bristol soon. No, I've had another idea.' She looked at Hugh. 'D'you remember I told you that Pippa's staying with Annie? Well, it's a terrible squash there so I've suggested that she comes over to me for a bit. There's so much more room and she's a bit low at present. What d'you think?'

'I think it's a brilliant idea,' said Hugh with so much feeling that Max gave him a quick glance. 'Just the thing.'

'That's OK then. And I was wondering,' she looked a little shy, 'perhaps you'd both like to come for lunch sometime? Come and have a good old Sunday roast and meet Pippa and Rowley, once they've settled in.'

Hugh looked at Max. 'Would you . . .? Could we . . .?'

'That's a very kind offer,' said Max, and Frances and Hugh both breathed private sighs of relief. 'Thank you. Now, I'll leave Hugh to show you his handiwork. See you.'

Frances watched him go and then turned to Hugh. She was so delighted to see him looking happy and fit, so pleased that she'd persuaded Max to come to lunch that, for the moment, her frustration at the vagaries of house-selling was temporarily forgotten. Hugh spent a little time with her, made her some coffee and saw her on her way to have lunch with Annie. After she'd gone he found it difficult to settle and presently wandered away up to the road and over on to the slopes of Black Hill.

Max watched him go. He had begun to guess what was on Hugh's mind and he, too, needed time to think about it. With Hugh's help he was forging ahead and a few telephone calls – a telephone had been installed at last! – had elicited a keen interest from some of the local schools. Max felt that the reality of his long-held dream was nearly within his grasp and he realised that, once his school opened its doors, he was not going to be able to manage it all on his own.

There was no doubt in Max's mind that Hugh would be an ideal member of staff. He was keen, strong and very excited about the future of the school. Added to this he was an experienced walker and rider and he knew the moor very well indeed. Max knew that he would be prepared to turn his hand to anything that arose and his ready humour would be invaluable when dealing with children.

Max cursed softly under his breath and turned back into the house, the Mutt at his heels. If only Hugh had finished at university he would have offered him a job without more ado. However, he knew, just as well as Hugh, what Frances's reaction would be if Hugh refused to return to university. His parents, very naturally, would insist that he qualify before making up his mind and, even then, they would probably prefer to see him following one of the professions. Could he encourage Hugh to go against the wishes of his family? Obviously not. Of course, Hugh might want to join him once he'd qualified but could Max wait that long before taking on the staff he needed? Already he was receiving enquiries for next Easter holidays. There was still so much to be done, so much organisation . . .

Max shook his head. He was tempted to offer Hugh a full-time job and weather the storm with his parents. His instinct told him that Hugh was in the right place, that he was coming to terms with himself, and that it would be quite wrong – even dangerous – to push him back into his old pattern of life.

Chapter Sixteen

Pippa's removal to the farmhouse proved to be a tremendous success. Once she knew that Hugh would not be moving back whilst he could be at Trendlebere, Frances set to with a will. She prepared Caroline's room for Pippa, made up a bunk bed for Rowley in the small bedroom next door, and wished that she had not been quite so efficient in her packing up. The house – except for the sitting room and the kitchen – had a bare, bleak look to it but she did her best to make the two bedrooms as welcoming as she could.

Pippa was ready for the change. Annie had given her a bolt hole and had listened readily to her griefs but she – and Perry – felt that Pippa needed time to recover and were reluctant to pressure her. Frances went much further. She positively encouraged Pippa to talk, entering into the subject of Robert's betrayal with an energy and interest which enabled Pippa to be even more forthcoming.

With Frances she could discuss her feelings and Frances had no hesitation in presenting her own views. Although she was clearly on Pippa's side, she was able to be rational and Pippa began to be less emotional and more positive. Naturally this did not happen all at once. From the very beginning, however, the two women got on well together. Frances was motherly, though keeping in check that bossiness which would have crept into her dealings with her own children; Pippa found it a luxury to relinquish some of her responsibilities and be looked after as though she were a child again. Frances was only too ready to play with Rowley, read to him, feed him, and Pippa, who had never known the blessing a willing, happy grandmother can be to a tired mother, gladly allowed Frances to take charge.

Encouraged by Frances, she went for long walks or drives across the moor, explored Tavistock and Chagford and began to relax a little. In the evening, with Rowley tucked up in bed, the two women talked endlessly into the night. Frances was fascinated by Robert's behaviour but her genuine desire for Pippa's wellbeing robbed her curiosity of any suggestion of inquisitive ghoulishness. She cared about Pippa and Rowley but her instincts were to mend rather than to widen the rift. Because of this, she encouraged Pippa in her belief that Robert was suffering from one of those mad moments that can happen in even the most secure of marriages. Frances genuinely had no idea how damaging her advice might be to someone as impressionable as Pippa and, unlike Perry and Annie, had no hesitation in speaking her mind.

Pippa – who was one of the 'absence makes the heart grow fonder' school rather than the 'out of sight out of mind' adherents – began to feel more hopeful.

'You should never have moved out,' said Frances, one evening as they sat at the kitchen table for supper. 'It was your home. And Rowley's. You should have stayed put.

Robert would probably be back with you now if you had.'

'D'you think so?' Pippa looked stricken at the thought.

'You made it too easy for him to behave foolishly.' Frances poured some wine into Pippa's half-empty glass. 'It would be easier for him to come back if you were still there.'

'Oh Frances,' sighed Pippa. She put both elbows on the table and propped her chin in her hands. 'You sound so certain that he'll come back.'

'I *am* certain,' said Frances, topping up her own glass. 'It was all too quick, too sudden. It's a flash in the pan. Have you thought of writing to him?'

'No,' said Pippa, instinctively shrinking from the possible rebuff such a communication might bring. 'We do everything through our solicitors.'

'That's what I mean,' said Frances impatiently. 'You've been far too easily swayed. Why shouldn't you write to him? Surely he wants to know about Rowley? Even if you divorced, he'd still want to see Rowley.'

'It was so difficult,' said Pippa helplessly. 'I couldn't get *hold* of him, if you know what I mean. We're supposed to be having a . . . a "temporary sabbatical" from each other to straighten out our ideas.'

'"Sabbatical"!' snorted Frances contemptuously. 'I've never heard so much rubbish in all my life! This is all that Louisa's doing, I have no doubt whatever about that. You're just playing into her hands.'

'But if he loves her what can I do?' asked Pippa miserably.

'You shouldn't have let him bully you into things,'

scolded Frances – but her voice was kindly. 'You should have stood firm.'

'I tried that,' protested Pippa. 'He just came home later and left earlier and slept in the spare bedroom. By standing firm I just made him more and more determined and cross.'

'Mmm.' Frances drank some wine thoughtfully. 'You may have a point, actually. Better to be restrained and dignified than screaming like a fishwife. When he comes to his senses that will probably impress him.'

Pippa smiled a little and then sighed. 'Would I ever be able to trust him again, though? It wouldn't be easy, Frances. I can't pretend nothing's happened.'

'Of course it won't be easy,' agreed Frances bracingly. 'You'll have to be amazingly generous. But you still love him and he's Rowley's father.'

'We make it sound like his coming back is an accomplished fact,' said Pippa bitterly.

Frances stood up to put the kettle on and patted Pippa's shoulder consolingly. 'I have a feeling in my water,' she told her confidently.

Pippa shook her head, pushed back her chair and wandered over to the open door. There had been rain earlier and the scents of the damp earth and newly mown grass drifted towards her on the evening air. The grey clouds were shot through with crimson and gold, splashed with the sunset's glow. Long shadows lay across the lawn and a cool breeze rustled lazily amongst the rhododendron leaves. A bat swooped suddenly from the eaves above her and Pippa shivered and folded her arms, rubbing at them in the chill air. She felt a sudden irritation at her inactivity and with it came a spurt of rebellious anger. Why *should* she wait passively for Robert to return to her? Why shouldn't *she* make a move? Offer him an ultimatum?

She wriggled impatiently at such a foolish idea. What ultimatum did she have to offer? And if he did come back of his own free will, *would* she be capable of the kind of generosity that Frances was recommending? Her much-battered pride stirred a little. Staring out into the dusk, Pippa imagined Robert on his knees whilst she told him what he could do with himself. This brought only a very temporary satisfaction. She knew that if the flesh and blood Robert stood before her she would still want to fling her arms around him.

'How pathetic can you get?' she muttered, and turned back into the warmth of the kitchen, comforted by the aroma of fresh coffee and the sight of Frances's matronly figure bustling about. 'You spoil me,' she said, and gave her a quick hug.

'You deserve a bit of spoiling.' Frances returned the hug and put some chocolates on the table. 'But you mustn't give way. A marriage is always worth fighting for. People give up too easily these days. They're too self-indulgent.'

If there was an edge of complacency in her voice, Pippa was too young and inexperienced to comment on it. Certainly everything that Frances propounded sounded right – in theory. Putting such high ideals into practice might be rather more difficult.

'Chance would be a fine thing,' sighed Pippa to herself as she helped herself to a coffee cream.

Frances closed the back door and switched on the lamp. The room sprang into warm intimate life. The china on the old dresser twinkled softly; the rich grainy wood of the old oak table gleamed. Beneath the window, the sagging sofa with its differently coloured cushions made a bright pool of colour. Looking around her, Pippa saw the result of years of family living and felt a lump in her throat. The tattered cushions had been made by Frances in the first months of her marriage; a small framed tapestry hanging beside the dresser was Caroline's childhood effort; an unevenly shaped vase containing dried flowers had been Hugh's very early attempt at pottery. On the window sill stood a photograph of a young Stephen holding Caroline by the hand whilst Hugh gazed out at the world from the safety of his father's arm.

Pippa knew a sharp envy. How lucky Frances was to have such a lovely home and a devoted husband! She wondered where she and Rowley would be twenty years from now and if Robert would be with them. How *could* he have destroyed everything they'd had together? Surely Frances was right in saying that anything was worth sacrificing if they could only start again?

Pippa put sugar in her coffee and stirred thoughtfully, brooding on the merits of communicating with Robert by letter . . .

When Hugh had thought through his idea, rehearsed how he would present it and finally brought himself to the point, Max was ready for him.

'OK, Hugh,' he said, after he'd listened to Hugh getting

thoroughly confused in a one-sided argument against the usefulness of a university degree. 'I know what you're trying to say. You want to jack in your degree course and come in with me.'

Hugh stared open-mouthed at this succinct précis of his lengthy dissertation. 'Yes,' he said, gulping a little at such a direct approach. 'That's exactly it.'

Max shuffled some papers into a pile and pushed them aside. He was in the small room, designated as the office, sitting at his desk whilst Hugh perched on the edge, watching him anxiously.

'I've thought about it, too,' said Max, who disliked beating about the bush. 'I have to say that if you'd finished at Bristol I'd offer you a job now. Hang on,' as Hugh burst into speech, 'hear me out. I don't give a damn whether you've got a degree or not but it will upset your parents if you don't go back to university and it would be wrong of me to encourage you to go against them. It's a good rule, anyway, to finish what you start.'

'But I don't *need* a degree,' cried Hugh, thumping the desk to emphasise his point. He pushed back his hair with agitated fingers. 'I want to be here with you. I can do all sorts of things. I can take the kids out . . .'

'Look, Hugh.' Max held up both hands, palms out. 'You don't have to sell yourself to me. You're exactly right for what I need. I know that.' He smiled a little at the gratified expression on Hugh's face. 'It's a bit more complicated, unfortunately.'

'But it doesn't have to be,' said Hugh. 'Why can't it be kept simple? I want to work here. You want to offer me a job.' At the thought of it his eyes shone despite his frustration. 'Why need it be difficult?'

Max pushed back his chair and folded his arms across his chest. 'I'll tell you the way your parents will think,' he said. 'No. Listen. It's good sense. For a start, we don't know whether my venture will work. We may not get enough children to make it pay. It's untried. You could waste a year here with me and have nothing at the end of it. You'd be out of a job, still unqualified and another year older. Your parents will tell you that it's safer to qualify and look for a sensible job.'

'I don't want a sensible job,' said Hugh mutinously. 'And we know it'll work.' He stared at Max pleadingly. 'Please, Max . . .'

'It's not up to me, boy!' said Max impatiently. 'I've wondered if I could cope on my own until you finish next summer but it's not just a question of the children's activities, it's a question of administration and so on. I can only afford one member of staff to begin with and I need that person almost immediately. I can hardly take someone on and then give them the push when you're ready to join me.'

'It's *my* job,' said Hugh stubbornly. 'It's exactly right for me. All of it.'

Max got to his feet and, pushing Hugh ahead of him, went outside, stepping over a recumbent Mutt, who lay stretched across the doorway. It was a hot early June morning. A heat haze glimmered over the soft chalky blue of the distant hills and dazzled from the stony tors. Below, the inky-dark depths of the wooded valley looked cool and mysterious. Sheep filed sedately across the narrow dusty tracks in the heather beyond the dry-stone wall, disturbing a skylark who rose up and up, his song spilling out joyously into the quiet air.

Hugh caught his breath and Max's fingers tightened on his shoulder.

'OK,' he murmured, as though Hugh had spoken. 'I'll speak to your mum. I'll do what I can. I promise nothing,' he said harshly as Hugh's face, turned up to him, blazed into hope. 'Don't count on it. But I'll do my best.'

He turned away and went back to his paperwork but Hugh stayed on for a moment, his heart high with hope. Gingerly he tested himself. He thought about Charlotte, picturing her lying in the bottom of the quarry. The usual surge of horror filled his heart but it was not so fierce, nor yet so annihilating as he had known in the past. He could imagine her lonely death, grieve for her, but there was now a tiny part of him which could – simultaneously with his grief – believe in a future for himself. That old familiar horror no longer had the power to blot out all other sensations. Hugh seized on this tiny part gladly, concentrating on it. It held out a promise to him, refusing to allow itself to be submerged by his instinctive habit of guilt. He must not allow this fatal tendency to edge its way into this precious part in which his own survival lay. For a brief moment he allowed himself to think of Lucinda, remembering her love and her longing that he should be healed and whole again. Perhaps, when she returned . . .

Taking a deep breath Hugh flung out his arms, as though he would embrace the scene before him, rejected an urge to go tramping off over the hills and went gladly back to his work.

Chapter Seventeen

Annie gave the terracotta tiles a final wipe, wrung out the cloth and hung it over the tap to dry. The sharp lemon smell of the cleaning fluid struggled briefly but unsuccessfully with the heady voluptuous scent of the roses that stood in a cut-glass jug on the plinth beside a new magazine and the unopened post. Both these were treats, being saved for her morning break, but Annie paused to sniff luxuriously at the roses which she'd picked from the masses of blooms that climbed the high wall in the front garden. She had no idea what 'make' they were. She chuckled aloud as the word slid into her mind. It was Perry's word.

'What make are they?' he would demand of dog-owners and rose-growers alike, ignoring their reproachful hints of 'breed' and 'species'.

She glanced with pleasure round the newly cleaned room, revelling in the peace and quiet, rediscovered since the departure of Pippa and Rowley.

'But I'm very fond of them,' she murmured, almost defensively, as though she had been accused of the contrary.

Nevertheless, it had been good to restore the cottage to its former tidiness and to fall back into her own routines.

'The thing is,' she told herself, as she put the Hoover in its cupboard and tidied away the polish, 'I'm simply not the maternal type. It's just as well we didn't have children. They'd never have survived infancy.'

Perry, she decided, would have been a kindly, jolly sort of father, provided that he'd been able to concentrate for long enough on his offspring. Annie had visions of an infant choking on leaves innocently stuffed into its mouth whilst Perry watched a caterpillar feeding; or quietly drowning in a pond whilst its father examined the breeding habits of a water beetle. She shook her head, only partly distressed by these deficiencies in both their characters. Neither of them had ever felt the lack of children.

Of course, some women were naturally maternal or was it, wondered Annie – struck by a new idea – simply a glorified desire to dominate and control? She dismissed this ungenerous thought as an unworthy, if natural, urge to be dismissive about qualities she didn't have and immediately found herself thinking about Frances. Annie still felt guilty at the readiness with which she had encouraged Pippa's removal to the farmhouse. It was always difficult to be clear-sighted and impartial about decisions which directly concerned one's own wellbeing but she was quite certain that Pippa would be more comfortable with Frances. They would chat endlessly and make much of Rowley . . . but what would Pippa do when Frances found another buyer and went off to Wales?

Annie stood for a moment, as though waiting for some divine revelation on this point; willing to receive an order or instruction. When none was vouchsafed her she sighed with relief, pushed the whole problem to the back of her mind and settled down to read her letters.

The mist rolled softly in from the west, blanketing the moor in its damp grey folds, touching the trees with its glittering moisture. It slid into the valleys, hanging above the river like white smoke, and curled with chilly breath amongst the rocky outcrops. Here, a fist of stone thrust through the low cloud, upwards into the sunshine above; there, a shaft of sunlight penetrated the gloom, piercing earthwards to gleam briefly upon the wet shining surface of the black road.

Max drove carefully, brooding on his approaching interview with Frances. To his relief, it was she who had suggested that he should come to the farmhouse. He had no desire to put his case with Hugh lurking just beyond the door. He wondered if she'd guessed why he wanted to talk to her. She'd sounded surprised, but pleasurably so, and very readily invited him over. Max swore a little under his breath. He knew that Frances regarded him in a faintly romantic light and it made him feel uncomfortable. It was flattering, no doubt, but he had neither the time nor inclination for that kind of thing. There was work to be done and he had no energy for distractions. Women, in his experience, were nothing but trouble.

Instinctively he thought of Stella. He could do so now with indifference. It was ten years since they'd married – young, passionate, full of ideals – and five since she'd left him for his oldest friend whilst he, Max, was on his tour of Northern Ireland. It hadn't come as a surprise. She hated Service life; miserable at the endless separations, bored without him to take her out and keep her cheerful. She whined at him when he telephoned, cataloguing endless disasters which he, as her husband, should be on hand to put right. Their precious leaves and weekends together had been ruined by her sullen anticipation of their imminent parting.

He had done his best; writing regularly, getting home whenever he could, but it was not enough. When he suggested that they should start a family, she retorted that she had no intention of bringing up children single-handed; he had no right to ask it of her. He pointed out – unwisely – that other women managed and she told him that she wasn't 'other women'. She was different, special. He lost his temper and observed that things might be better if she were rather less special and rather more ready to shoulder the responsibilities of a serviceman's wife. She never forgave him for it.

Max raised his eyebrows in a mental shrug. It was over, water under the bridge, and he'd managed well enough. He deliberately brought his mind to bear on the arguments which he hoped would carry Hugh's case with Frances but he was not particularly sanguine. As he left Princetown and headed towards Yelverton the mist thinned a little, diffused now with a faint golden light, but he drove slowly through the plantations that edged Burrator Reservoir and was relieved to find the turning to the farmhouse.

He left the Land Rover in the lane and stood for a moment studying the old granite house which was not unlike his own, or indeed, any of the other moorland farmhouses. This was bigger than his and had been made couth with its freshly painted door and window frames and by the tubs of flowers in the newly paved farmyard. It could not be mistaken now for a working farm. A wooden tricycle stood forlornly by the open-fronted barn and a small sodden knitted garment lay neglected by one of the tubs.

Hesitating to use the front door, Max followed the path round to the back door and knocked. He could hear the sounds of two voices upraised in song; one high and sweet; the other tuneless and growly. Taking a deep breath, he opened the door and put his head inside. Before he could speak he was visited with a sense of *déjà vu*. A small boy sat in a highchair at the kitchen table. Facing him, with her back towards Max, a girl was coaxing him to eat between snatches of nursery rhyme.

'Daddy!' shouted Rowley, knocking the laden spoon aside and, once again, Max saw the flash of hope turn to disappointment as Pippa spun round.

They stared at each other in silence and then both spoke at once . . .

'I'm sorry. I *did* knock . . .'

'I'm sorry. He calls everyone Daddy . . .'

. . . and apologised together. Pippa laughed and Max bowed, indicating that she should speak first.

'You must be Max,' she said. 'Frances is expecting you. We've met, of course. I'm Pippa and this Rowley.'

'How do you do?' said Max gravely to Rowley.

Rowley's underlip began to protrude, his head drooped and he stared fixedly at his blue sandals, which were not nearly so new or shiny as when Max had first been invited to admire them.

'Oh dear,' said Pippa. 'We're having a bad day. Woglet's gone AWOL and we've got the sulks. Take no notice.'

Max chuckled a little at the outrage on Rowley's face as he heard his woes so summarily dismissed.

'I'm sorry to hear that,' he said. 'I have the feeling I was introduced to the person involved at our last meeting. A coloured woolly gentleman, I think?'

Pippa laughed at this description. 'Quite correct,' she said. 'He's dropped him somewhere . . .'

'Hang on,' said Max suddenly as a memory stirred.

He went back outside and round to the yard. The sodden heap beside the tub proved to be the golliwog and Max bore it back triumphantly. Pippa gave a cry of delight but Rowley peered cautiously, head averted, unprepared to express unqualified delight or gratitude just yet.

'He'll do splendidly,' said Pippa, squeezing Woglet out and putting him to dry on the Aga. 'What d'you say, Rowley?'

'Burn,' said Rowley sulkily. 'Woglet burn.' He'd been warned against touching the Aga.

'He'll be fine just there on the rail,' said Pippa. 'Are you going to thank Max for rescuing him? Ah.' She broke off, relieved. 'Here she is!'

Frances, who had seen the Land Rover from her bedroom window, smiled at Max. She'd gone up to change and, halfway out of her jeans, decided that it was silly. Despite the fact that it was June, it was a chilly day and she would look foolish in a cotton dress. She pulled her jeans back on, cross with herself for feeling fluttery, and went back downstairs.

'He's found Woglet,' Pippa was telling her. 'Rowley must have had him outside earlier, before the mist came down.'

'Well done,' said Frances brightly. 'Now perhaps he'll eat his lunch. We'll leave you to it. Come on through, Max.'

He followed her into the sitting room, too preoccupied with the coming ordeal to do more than glance around the comfortable room.

'You'll have guessed that it's about Hugh,' he said at once, lest there should be any misunderstanding.

'I thought it probably was . . .' Frances gestured to him to sit down and he chose an armchair beside the big open fireplace. She sat at the end of the sofa nearest to him. 'He hasn't been . . . well, depressed again, has he?'

He seized the opening, delighted with her choice of words. 'Quite the contrary,' he said positively. 'Obviously I remembered what you told me about him and then he told me that his girlfriend packed him in . . .'

Frances grimaced. 'It's a great pity. She's such a sweet girl. I have to admit that I'm hoping that things may come right with him and Lucinda.'

'Well, all I can say is that he's very happy. He's cheerful, he works hard and he's on the ball. He doesn't brood and he's full of bright ideas. I don't think you need to worry any more.'

'Oh Max.' She smiled at him gratefully. 'How sweet of you to come all this way to put my mind at rest. I've been so worried. It's really a huge relief.'

'I didn't come just for that,' he told her.

'Oh?'

'No.' He leaned forward, his forearms on his knees, his

hands joined. 'Look, Frances. Hugh doesn't want to go back to university. He wants to stay on with me and I'm very happy to offer him a job . . .'

She was protesting long before he'd finished and he stopped so as to hear her out.

'I knew we'd have trouble with him.' She implied that Max and she were adults, of one mind, and Hugh merely a fractious child. 'He ought to have gone back halfway through this term, really, only I felt he needed a complete break and he seems to have done the work his tutor has sent him. He's a very understanding man. I've had a quiet word with him . . .'

I bet you have, thought Max. 'Hang on a minute,' he said. 'I don't think he ought to go back.'

Frances stared at him, puzzled. 'Not go back?'

'No.' Max spoke sharply, his eyes fixed on hers. 'Look. He's happy, Frances. He's doing what he wants to do. I can offer him a full-time job . . .'

'Painting and decorating?'

'Of course not!' he said impatiently. 'I'm opening a school. I need instructors and administrators. Hugh would be good at both those things. He loves riding and walking and he's brilliant at organising. And he wants to do it, Frances!'

'But, Max, he's got to finish his degree course. Perhaps then he could join you.'

'It'll be too late.' He dared not offer her that option. 'I need someone now. It's taken off quicker than I thought. I've got schools phoning up wanting to book children in. I've got to be ready.'

'But surely Hugh wouldn't want to do it as a career?' She sounded confused.

'Why not?' he challenged her. 'I do!'

'That's different,' she said at once and he raised his eyebrows at her. 'Oh, yes it is. It's your school, your project, your property. There's a difference in being the owner and in being simply one of the supervisors. And what happens when he gets older? You can't keep at that sort of job when you get creaky. What then?'

'Oh, Frances.' Max laughed a little. 'You can't legislate for everything in life. We might have a war. Anything could happen. The point is that Hugh is happy. His mind is taken up with this project, he's busy, excited. Isn't that important? What happens when he goes back to university and starts brooding again?'

'I think he ought to graduate,' she said stubbornly. 'He can join you then.'

'It'll be too late,' he said flatly. 'I need someone now. I can't sack whoever I took on instead when Hugh graduates. It wouldn't be fair.'

'You could have Hugh as well,' she said almost pleadingly but he smiled and shook his head.

'I couldn't afford it. I shall have to employ a cook-matron as well as my assistant, and I have to pay them through the winter, don't forget, when I may have no courses. My budget's very tight.'

They stared at each other.

'I don't know what to say,' she said anxiously. 'I'll have to speak to Stephen.' She shook her head. 'I know what he'll say.'

Max spoke gently. 'Hugh's happy,' he said. 'Really happy. He feels part of it all. He *is* part of it all, dammit. How will you feel if you force him to go back and he goes downhill again?'

'I think that's most unlikely,' said Frances sharply. 'If he's better, he's better. Why should he go downhill again?'

'Because he's going to be very upset if he has to go back. He's not a child, Frances. He's a man. He knows what he wants. Don't make him fight for it. Worse, don't send him back where he's come from, back to that old boredom and unhappiness and guilt.'

She jerked her chin up at him, resenting his advice, and he cursed under his breath.

'I'll have to speak to Stephen,' she repeated, and her eyes were hostile.

'Fine.' He stood up. 'You do that. Thanks.'

She got up uncertainly but, before she could stop him, he went swiftly out, crossed the hall and let himself out at the front door. By the time she reached the yard he was gone.

Chapter Eighteen

It was several weeks after Stephen had moved to Wales that rumours of his 'infidelity' began to filter through to Frances. At first she was inclined to discount them – although she experienced a twinge of fear; a tightening at the pit of her stomach. It was Felicity Mainwaring who was the first to spread the gossip and it was a mutual friend who thoughtfully passed it on to Frances, on a Friday morning in the Bedford Hotel.

Frances and Pippa had driven into Tavistock together, parked the car in the Bedford's car park and separated to do their shopping, agreeing to meet for coffee later. Frances arrived back first. She loaded her shopping into Pippa's car, climbed the iron staircase that led from the car park into the hotel and went into the bar. There was no sign of Pippa but she was ready for her coffee and decided not to wait. Nodding to one or two familiar faces she went to order and then sat at the table in the corner.

Immersed in thoughts of Hugh and Max's proposals for his future, she was only half aware that the group at the table by the far window was breaking up.

'Miles away, I see!' Pat's voice made her jump. 'You're

looking very serious. Problems?'

'No, no.' Frances made a quick disclaimer. 'Just this house business. The sale fell through and Stephen's had to go on ahead to Wales.'

'Oh.' Pat looked serious. 'Probably just as well, isn't it?' She raised her eyebrows, nodding with an insufferable air of complicity. 'You know? Under the circumstances?'

Frances frowned a little. 'What circumstances?'

'Oh Lord! Don't say I'm talking out of turn? I imagined you knew.' Pat grimaced with exaggerated embarrassment.

'Knew what?' Frances was losing her patience but she felt uneasy. 'Sorry, Pat. I haven't a clue what you're talking about.'

Her brusque tone nettled the other woman who shrugged a little. 'Oh, well. It's simply that Stephen's been seen around with Cass Wivenhoe lately. Knowing her reputation I assumed that you must be glad that he's out of reach.'

The bright greedy eyes scanned Frances's startled face ('My dear! She hadn't a clue! I could have *died*!') – and Pat stepped quickly aside as the coffee arrived. 'I must be off.' She bent forward a little, lowering her voice. 'Hope I haven't let any cats out of the bag. See you.'

Frances swallowed, smiled quickly at the waitress and pretended to search for something in her handbag. Out of the corner of her eye she saw Pat go out with her friends and relaxed, making an effort to calm herself. It was gossip, of course; malicious gossip, nothing more. He'd probably run into Cass somewhere . . . Frances frowned. If that was so, why hadn't he mentioned it to her? It was the kind of detail that Stephen usually passed on, although her antipathy to Cass might have made him oversensitive.

With another tiny lurch of the stomach, she remembered the New Year's drinks party at which Cass had been another guest. It had been impossible for Frances to be polite to this woman whose past immoral actions were having such an effect on her son's life and she had snubbed her. Frances's hand clenched at the handle of her cup as she recalled how swiftly and smoothly Stephen had moved in; talking to Cass, joking with her, covering up the awkward moment with great social ease. Frances had been deeply hurt. He had taken Cass's part, publicly sided with her, and it had been like a slap in the face.

Even now, nearly six months later, she felt a surge of humiliation as she imagined Cass's private triumph. How *could* Stephen behave so disloyally? It seemed that he was more concerned about Cass's feelings than he was about her own, or Hugh's . . . And now she had this new anxiety about Hugh. Familiar voices caught her attention and she waved with relief to Pippa and Rowley, standing in the doorway looking for her. Nevertheless, even with the distraction of ordering more coffee and orange squash for Rowley, and having to admire his new T-shirt, Pat's remark remained firmly lodged at the back of her mind.

Robert sat in the pub waiting for Louisa, a nearly empty pint glass on the table before him. Although their affair was progressing, she was still playing it very cool and he was beginning to grow impatient. He'd imagined that, with Pippa and Rowley off the scene, she would have been prepared to let him more openly into her life. Three months on, however, they were still keeping up the fiction at the office that they were just good friends. Out of office hours things were rather different but she was still very cautious. She obviously had no intention of being cited co-respondent in a divorce suit and Robert, who had hoped that he might move into her comfortable flat, had been very firmly put in his place.

On top of these irritants, John Spencer had been taken ill rather suddenly and was not expected to return to the office. There were murmurs of a takeover by an American company and an edgy, expectant atmosphere prevailed. Robert, finishing his beer, wondered how this might effect him and glanced again at his watch. As he stood up to buy himself another drink, Louisa arrived. His heart gave a little tick at the sight of her but she avoided his attempted embrace and slid into the seat opposite his.

He smiled at her, wishing that he had the courage to seize her roughly or bully her a little. He knew that he was a little scared of her and wondered why it lent an edge to the relationship.

'Drink?' He looked down on the smooth cap of brown shining hair, the neat nose and small determined jaw and had a vision of her in more intimate surroundings, not cool then but insistent and demanding, and he felt excitement rise in him.

She was watching him, reading his thoughts and she laughed a little. 'Not tonight, ducky. I'm going to be busy. A meeting's been set up at John's. I'm driving down to Sussex this afternoon.'

His disappointment was swamped by a keen interest.

'Oh? Something moving, is it? It's true then, this story about a takeover?'

She shrugged a little, allowing him to see that she was in the know but sworn to secrecy. 'Can't say anything just yet.'

'Oh come on, darling.' He bent over her, instinctively lowering his voice. 'Surely you can tell me?'

She leaned back from him, a fleeting expression of distaste showing in her face, and he drew away, humiliated. She saw his petulant look and touched his arm, letting her fingers linger on his wrist.

'No sulking!' she said but her voice was more intimate and he smiled unwillingly.

'You make things bloody difficult!' he muttered, but she laughed at him.

'You like it,' she said provocatively. 'What about that drink? Orange juice, I think, in view of my drive. And a ham sandwich.'

He went to the bar, looking back at her as he queued. She was staring absent-mindedly at the table; probably thinking about the forthcoming meeting. A pleasurable anticipation stirred within his breast. This takeover might give him a much-needed break, especially with Louisa in on the ground floor this early in the negotiations. She and Eleanor Spencer were close, very close, and more than capable, between them, of influencing John. What was good for Louisa was good for Robert and vice versa. There was no question, in his mind, that their futures lay together and he knew that Louisa would do her best for both of them.

He thought of the rather silly letter he'd received from Pippa, via his solicitor, only that morning. She'd suggested that he might like to visit them, to see how Rowley was coming on. He could say lots more words now, etc., etc. She'd put the address very clearly; some remote farmhouse in the wilds of Dartmoor.

Robert shrugged his indifference. He'd been lucky there, very lucky. She'd behaved beautifully, moving out without a murmur, and playing his game by his rules. Poor old Pippa! He shook his head, caught Louisa's eye and gave her a tiny wink. She raised her eyebrows and smiled, a knowing, intimate smile, and his heart speeded a little. No. Pippa and Rowley must be kept right out of the picture. His future was with Louisa and he had no intention of muddling the issue with letters and visits.

Stephen replaced the telephone receiver and sat still for a moment, thinking. Frances had seemed rather odd; almost as if she were in one of her moods. But why? Of course, there was this long rigmarole about Hugh refusing to go back to university, wanting to stay on and join Max Driver in his adventure training school. Beset with problems at his new office, Stephen tried to concentrate on Hugh.

'How is he?' he'd asked Frances.

'He's better,' she'd admitted, almost reluctantly he felt. 'He's much better. But his head's full of this nonsense. You'll have to speak to him, Stephen.'

'I can't get away at the moment,' he'd said at once. 'There's too much to do here. On top of the work aspect of things there's been some rather high-handedness regarding staff being made redundant and so on. There's a lot of ill-feeling and tempers to be soothed. Why don't you bring him over for the weekend with you?'

'I can't come,' she'd said, almost triumphantly.

'Oh, why not?' he'd cried, disappointed. 'Oh Frances . . .'

'I've got two lots of people coming to view the house,' she'd told him. 'I can't put them off.'

'But can't Pippa cope? I thought that this was going to be one of the advantages of having her there . . .'

'I can't expect her to show people round,' said Frances impatiently. 'It's one thing having someone here house-sitting but she can't sell the house like I can. She doesn't know it well enough. I can't risk losing a sale.'

Stephen had agreed, reluctantly, but now, as he wandered into the garden in the dusk and sipped gratefully at his glass of whisky, he tried to analyse the quality of her mood. He knew Frances of old and he knew that those clipped tones, implying that he should have grasped some point or been more on the ball, generally led up to one of her arctic silences. It must be Hugh's latest bombshell that was worrying her and he hadn't shown enough anxiety to satisfy her maternal instincts. Stephen sat down on the garden seat and wondered how disastrous it would be if Hugh were to have his own way. Of course, this school, and his prospects within it, needed to be investigated but, if it were truly what he wanted and if it had stopped that dreadful brooding and was making him happy, it shouldn't be discounted out of hand.

Stephen breathed deeply and allowed the whisky to soothe him. After all, the whole summer lay ahead and no decision need be taken just yet. As soon as he had things running smoothly at the office he'd go back for a weekend and see this Max Driver and talk to Hugh. Stephen took another sip and thought about Cass. He was glad that she'd had that opportunity to unburden herself, to mourn for Charlotte. There had been no self-pity, no dramatics and Stephen knew that he'd genuinely helped her. Nevertheless, he was glad that the meetings were over. The risk had been so great. He hated the idea of being disloyal to Frances, or hurting her, but he had decided that, this once, Hugh must come first. When Cass had suggested that she should write to Hugh, Stephen had told her to write to Hugh care of Max Driver and had given her the address.

Now, Stephen blew out his lips, amazed suddenly that he'd dared to take such a risk and thankful that no one had been hurt. Cass, indeed, was the better for the meetings and perhaps Hugh might yet benefit. It was over.

Stephen finished his whisky and stood up. He must organise some supper and then he had work to do. He went back inside, disappointed that Frances would not be coming for the weekend. He had been looking forward to it but she had a point. She was more likely to bring off a sale than someone who had been staying in the house for just a few weeks. He made himself a sandwich and settled down to work.

Chapter Nineteen

When Pippa received no reply to her letter it was almost as if she had to live through the pain of Robert's betrayal all over again. Although she had told herself repeatedly that there would be no answer, promised herself that she expected no letter in return from Robert, when she was obliged to give up hope she realised just how much she had been counting on it. Her talks with Frances had almost persuaded her that, should he return, she would be able to make a great effort to put the past behind her. Such was Frances's confidence in his return coming to pass that Pippa had dared to allow herself to hope. Now, the pain and misery struck at her anew and one afternoon, whilst Frances was in Plymouth, she put Rowley in his seat in the back of the car and drove over to see Annie.

On the way she suddenly decided to drop in on Hugh and Max. They had come over to the farmhouse for Sunday lunch and, despite a certain tension, things had gone rather well. Frances had behaved with a strange, almost defiant gaiety, Max – who now knew of Pippa's situation – had risen to the occasion and entertained them with amusing tales of Service life and Hugh looked happier, fitter and utterly relaxed. Pippa had noticed these things but as though she were in some way isolated from them. Her own unhappiness prevented her from being able to enter fully into the proceedings.

Now, however, she felt that a return visit would not be out of place and she was interested to see the place which Hugh had described so minutely and with such enthusiasm. She drove down the track and sat for a moment looking at the little group of buildings. They were all reroofed now, the stone repointed, windows and doors renewed. As she looked, Max came out of the house – the Mutt prancing before him – and raised his eyebrows in surprise as he saw her sitting there.

'Hi.' She opened the door and went to meet him. 'Sorry to turn up unannounced but I couldn't resist coming to have a little look. Hugh made it sound so fascinating.'

'That boy should be my publicity agent,' said Max. 'I shall be very happy to show you round. Hugh's off somewhere at the moment. He received a letter this morning and when he'd read it he came over all peculiar and asked for the morning off.'

'Heavens!' Pippa stared at him in surprise, fending off the Mutt's exuberant greeting. 'Whatever could it be?'

Max shrugged. 'He didn't say and I didn't ask.'

Pippa coloured a little, assuming that he was obliquely accusing her of nosiness, but further embarrassment was prevented by shouts from Rowley. He was entranced by the sight of the Mutt and was fearing that he might have been forgotten. Max bent to look into the car.

'Get out!' commanded Rowley. 'Dog! Rowley see dog!'

He struggled with his harness.

'Do you mind?' Pippa looked anxiously at Max. 'I only meant to stop for a second. And if Hugh's not here . . .'

'Oh, you must see it all now you're here,' said Max, who liked to show off his achievements although he wouldn't have admitted as much. 'Get him out. Would you like some coffee?'

'Oh no,' she answered at once, going to release Rowley. She had a terrible fear that he was simply being polite. 'We don't want to keep you. I know you're awfully busy but I would love a little peek.'

She stood Rowley down, he shrieking delightedly as the Mutt lavishly washed his face for him, and Max laughed with her as Rowley flung his arms round the Mutt's neck and child and dog toppled over together – a mass of waving legs and feathery tail. They all went round together, Rowley and the Mutt pattering in the rear, and finished up in the main house. Pippa gasped when she saw the kitchen.

'It's terrific,' she said simply.

'*Aut optimum, aut nullum,*' said Max carefully and with a certain amount of self-consciousness – and laughed. 'That wretched boy! He's got me at it now!'

'What is it?' asked Pippa, amused. 'I'm hopeless at languages.'

'He's got a passion for Latin quotations,' said Max. 'That one, loosely translated, means "nothing but the best".'

'Well, he's right.' Pippa nodded as she looked around her. 'It's all absolutely fantastic, Max. You must be thrilled.'

'I am,' he admitted, warmed by her praise. 'I've waited a long time for this.'

'I can understand Hugh's longing to be part of it,' said Pippa, as they went back outside. 'It's so exciting being in on something like this from the beginning. Oh, I *do* hope he can persuade Frances and Stephen round to his point of view.'

'So do I.' Max was taken aback at her unexpected partisanship. 'But I dare not say any more. It's right that they should think it over carefully. If this doesn't work for me then Hugh would come down with me.'

Pippa made a face, dismissing his fears. 'Well, for a start I'm sure that it *will* work but, even if it didn't, Hugh could take his degree as a mature student. It wouldn't be the end of the world. Or at any rate,' she glanced at Max, 'not for him.'

He smiled at her perception. 'But it would be for me,' he agreed. He looked round at his little empire. 'It's got to work.'

'It will.' She smiled at him. 'And when he's old enough, I'll send Rowley along.'

Max grinned. 'God forbid!' he said with feeling.

They both laughed, looking at Rowley who was sitting in the remains of some builder's sand and crooning to the Mutt who was licking his face enthusiastically. When Rowley saw them looking at him he was overcome with a fit of shyness and threw himself flat on his back, his arms over his face. Pippa bent down and scooped him up.

'Come on you,' she said. 'Have you shown Max your nice new T-shirt?'

Rowley peered down at himself and pulled out the T-shirt by its hem.

'Efflunt,' he said carefully, showing it proudly to Max. 'Efflunt.'

'So it is,' agreed Max, admiring the cartoon elephant displayed on Rowley's chest. 'Very smart. Sure you wouldn't like a cup of something?'

Although Pippa wasn't his type – Max preferred dark, more voluptuous women – he'd enjoyed showing her round and felt oddly disappointed now that she was preparing to leave.

'Absolutely sure. Thanks all the same.' Pippa strapped Rowley into his seat. 'Annie's expecting us. Thanks for the guided tour. I think it's wonderful. I'm really impressed.'

'You and Frances must come over,' said Max, surprising himself. 'Hugh and I will make you dinner. That'll really impress you!'

'Sounds lovely,' said Pippa, who had also been warmed and cheered by the visit. 'Give Hugh my love.'

She drove away and Max stood waving after them. The Mutt, disappointed at losing his playmate, brought a stone and deposited it at Max's feet. He stood, tense and expectant, staring fixedly at the stone.

'Daft animal,' muttered Max. The Mutt's tail moved slightly but his gaze remained on the stone, every muscle willing his master to pick it up. Max moved the stone infinitesimally with his toe and the Mutt's head dropped even lower, his nose centimetres from Max's shoe.

Max sighed. 'You have given the word "dogged" a whole new meaning,' he told him and, picking up the stone, he threw it across the yard, the Mutt in hot pursuit.

When this exercise had been repeated several times, to

the Mutt's intense enjoyment, Max went back to the office and sat for a while, thinking about Pippa and what an idiot the unknown Robert must be. When he saw that he'd been sitting doing nothing for ten minutes he threw down his pencil and went to make himself some coffee. Presently he realised he was worrying about Hugh; wondering where he was and what his letter had contained. Max cursed under his breath. He wasn't used to letting people get under his skin. He took his coffee back to the study, pulled his papers towards him and immersed himself in figures.

The Mutt pottered for a bit and then sat, ears cocked, watching the sheep on the hillside. His instinct to herd them together had been instantly and severely checked by an irate Max and the Mutt, who was by no means unintelligent, had learned that if he wished to live on the moor he must become indifferent to the other animals with whom he shared it. The Mutt yawned widely as if to indicate his indifference, lay down with his head on his paws and feigned sleep.

Hugh had climbed Black Hill and headed for Hound Tor. Cass's letter crackled in his pocket and every so often he put his hand over it, feeling its shape and the crispness of the paper. A first quick reading had set his brain reeling and filled him with a desire to get right away so as to concentrate on it in solitude. As he walked, his thoughts and impressions were too jumbled, too confused, to bring any real release but a great hope was welling in him. It surged in his breast, causing tiny spurts of laughter – or were they sobs? – to escape occasionally from his gasping mouth. He walked fast, his eyes fixed on the milky blue sky above him, unaware of his surroundings.

In the shelter of Greator Rocks, he sank down on the sheep-nibbled turf and pulled the letter from his pocket. Cass had not spared herself but she had done her best to protect Stephen. Hugh's eyes leaped greedily over the words.

My dear Hugh,

I bumped into your father recently and was deeply distressed to hear that you feel guilty and responsible for Charlotte's death. I was shocked to think that you could imagine yourself responsible and, after a great deal of thought, I've decided that you should know the whole truth.

I was never a good mother, Hugh. I was irresponsible and too fond of having a good time. Charlotte suffered most of all my children. Her insecurity was, I think, part of her make-up but I'm afraid that far from trying to build up her confidence I simply destroyed it. From the beginning, she hated change, meeting new people, going to new schools. As a naval child it was hell for her. Added to this I liked to play the field and, as she got older, Charlotte was always afraid that one day I would go too far and Tom might find out. Once she came home early from school and surprised me with a lover, and as time went on she became more and more suspicious.

I ignored her unhappiness and was delighted when you took her under your wing and persuaded her to go to Blundell's. It is wicked that you who were so kind and patient with her should bear any blame in what happened. The showdown had been building up all her life. I'd fallen in love with someone, Hugh. I was quite mad at that time, obsessed. And Tom was playing around too. I think Charlotte guessed this, which would have really been the last straw. She adored her father and always considered him perfect. We were both with our lovers when she came to Bristol that weekend and neither of us was to be found when she returned.

Yes, she was upset about finding you with your girlfriend. She'd built up a fantasy about you as young girls do. But that had nothing to do with what happened. She became frightened when she found that I was away, spent that night alone at home, and when Hammy and Kate arrived the next day she was hysterical. If I had been there, Hugh, instead of with my lover, Charlotte would be alive today.

Whilst Charlotte was recovering, my lover decided to give me the push and I was desperate, phoning him and meeting him, still not caring about Charlotte, and her suspicions of me became beyond what was normal.

At this time I was involved in a plot with someone else – not my secret so I can't tell you – and she was trying to leave the village without a third person knowing. Suspecting that I was meeting my lover, Charlotte blurted out this secret before the third person. In his rage he crashed his car, killing himself and damaging two other people. Charlotte and I were first on the scene, seconds after it happened. Because I was furious with her and miserable because I had been jilted I screamed at her, telling her what she had done, saying that this accident was all her fault. I used those words to her, Hugh, and the last sight I had of my daughter was her shocked desperate face covered with tears and horror as she stared at the results of her indiscretion and suspicions.

She ran into the village to get help and then went straight to your place and fetched her pony. I try to think it was an accident, that she didn't deliberately kill herself, but in my more honest moments, I know that I may as well have pushed her over the edge. Charlotte died because of MY selfishness, MY irresponsibility, Hugh. It had nothing – NOTHING – to do with you. If I or Tom had been at home – and we both should have been, Tom's boat was alongside that weekend – instead of gratifying our own selfish desires she would be alive now.

My dear Hugh, that you, who brought her some of the little happiness she knew, should be destroying your own life out of misplaced guilt is too awful to contemplate. Please believe me and put it all away from you, except for remembering the happy times you had with her. They were precious and I bless you for giving them to her. If she had been going to kill herself because of you she would have done it on her return from Bristol. She was alone that night, remember, she had plenty of opportunity.

No, Hugh. You must believe me. At the end she

hated me and I think it turned her brain. The car accident and her part in it was the last straw. Oh Hugh, I saw the guilt and terror on her face and did nothing. She thought in that last terrible moment, you see, that she had been wrong. That I was innocent and because of her misplaced jealousy she had not only misjudged me but been responsible for this carnage. I saw her thinking it, Hugh, as she stood by those crashed cars with people screaming and the blood pumping out and all the glass and I did NOTHING. Yes, I did do something, Hugh. I rejected her, I let her feel ashamed, I let her believe in her own guilt, and it was far too much for her.

Forgive me, Hugh, for this shocking letter. I've tried to be dispassionate and I don't want to harrow you. You've suffered quite enough already. Don't hold it against your father for telling me your secrets. He loves you and he is frightened for you and can't bear to stand by and see you suffering. He has allowed me to unburden my grief to him and given me the chance to mourn. I have selfishly used his kindness and his anxiety for you and I feel so grateful to him. This letter is partly selfish, too. It's a relief to pour out my guilt but it's also because I can't bear to have you on my conscience, Hugh. I have quite enough already. Please believe me. It would be so wonderful if I could think that at least one person can remember Charlotte with happy memories. Don't spoil them with unnecessary guilt.

Bless you, Hugh, for all that you did for her. I think

of you with such gratitude. I would be grateful if you would destroy this letter when you've finished with it. I know that I can trust you to keep my shameful secrets.

With love,

Cass.

He read it three times. Horror, sympathy, gratitude, freedom, all visited him in turn and at last, still clutching the letter, he rolled over and lay face down in the turf. It was not his fault! He had not caused Charlotte to take her own life! He had hurt her, yes, but he had not killed her. He remembered Charlotte; riding with her, talking to her, comforting her, encouraging her. He remembered her shy smile cast swiftly upwards at him and her small hand, with its bitten nails, lying trustfully in his.

Oh Charlotte! he cried silently. We *were* happy, weren't we? and tears sprang to his tightly closed eyes.

One day his memories would be without pain, he could believe that now, but it was still too soon. He thought of her as Cass described her at the scene of the accident and he writhed in the agony of it. It was too much to bear.

He leaped up and turned back towards Haytor. Poor, poor Cass! How did she live with such anguish in her soul? Hugh squeezed the letter. He would destroy it – but not yet; not quite yet. He needed to read it several times; to let the truth sink deep into his heart so that he could truly believe it. Yet already he knew that it was true. The poison was drawn out of his system and he drew several deep breaths of warm summer air down into his lungs. He swung his arms, hugging himself, bringing the letter against his face, pressing it to his eyes as though he might weep, and with a cry of pure release he began to run, leaping and springing across the moor; back to Trendlebere, back to Max.

Chapter Twenty

After Pippa had gone, Annie went upstairs to her bedroom. The sun had all but disappeared behind a high thin cloud and she felt chilly. The bedroom, which was over the sitting room, was a good size with hanging cupboards built into two deep recesses. The bed stood against the back wall and Annie could see beyond the garden to the fields whilst she drank her early morning tea. Because the front garden was so long it was possible to see the end of the lawn from the bed and Perry had erected a large bird table at the furthest point so that she could watch the birds feeding. He had even supplied her with a pair of field glasses.

Annie pulled an old cardigan from the chest and, slipping it about her shoulders, sat down on the window seat, perching sideways with one leg curled beneath her. She had been brooding over Pippa and the unhappiness she was suffering but, as so often, her thoughts were distracted and drawn back to Perry. How tidy the room looked without his paraphernalia lying about! She crossed her arms over the pain in her heart and visualised it as it had been once; with books in a pile beside the bed, threatening to topple the lamp on to the floor. A notebook would be near at hand with his out-of-date copy of Pears – his newest one was kept downstairs – and several pencils. Odd sheets of paper with scribbled notes would lie on the chest or on the window seat with his spare pair of spectacles. He'd used the second bedroom as a dressing room so the only garment likely to be flung across the bed or on the armchair by the window would be his dressing gown, with his flat leather slippers kicked off anyhow so that a hue and cry would be raised each morning to locate them.

Annie leaned back against the window wondering if she would ever come to terms with her loss. She could see him quite clearly with her mind's eye; sitting on the edge of the bed, reaching for the field glasses with one hand, dragging on his dressing gown with the other, whilst a toe probed helplessly under the bed for his slippers.

'Did you see him?' he'd cry excitedly. 'Great big green chap! I wonder if it was a woodpecker! Now which one would it be, I wonder? Where's the blasted bird book? No, no! Don't move, my darling. I'll make some tea while I'm looking him up . . .'

And when he returned with the tea, he'd have all the information ready for her, telling her its habitat, breeding habits and distinctive markings whilst she sat propped about with pillows, sipping her tea, and he ranged to and fro by the window, peering out in the hope of seeing the woodpecker again.

How much easier life had been, supported by his love, his generosity of spirit, his instinctive gentleness! There had rarely been a person that Perry had really disliked . . .

Annie huddled her cardigan about her and turned to stare

out of the window. The one person whom Perry had never liked was Robert. He had refused to be taken in by his charm or been impressed by his apparent devotion to Pippa.

'Can't like the fella,' he'd mutter. 'Something about him. Poor little Pippa! She's making a terrible mistake.'

Annie had agreed with Perry but there was nothing to be done about it; not then, anyway. Now . . . Annie sighed. It worried her that Frances was encouraging Pippa to hope for Robert's return; to by-pass lawyers and communicate with Robert direct. It was clear that Pippa still loved him but surely, now that he had shown his colours so clearly, it would be emotional suicide to consider taking him back? Pippa had talked about forgiving and forgetting but Annie had remained silent. She was of the firm opinion that certain things should be neither forgiven nor forgotten. When Pippa told her that she'd written to Robert, asking him to come down to Devon, she'd felt a terrible misgiving, followed by grief when Pippa told her miserably that he hadn't bothered to reply.

As usual, when confronted by the need to advise, Annie had sent a hasty prayer into the ether, begging for help. Denied any useful message – no doubt Perry was off somewhere 'learning the ropes', thought Annie – she'd found herself gently leading the conversation towards Hugh and asking whether he was coming to terms with his problems. Surprisingly this had quite an animating effect on Pippa, who described the little site at Trendlebere with enthusiasm and spoke warmly of Max. Annie mentally raised her eyebrows. Frances, too, had spoken warmly about Max. The prospects for his adventure training school and the pros and cons of Hugh's putative full-time job within it had occupied the next half-hour and then it was time for Pippa to get back.

It had been a breathing space, giving Annie time to decide on her position. If Pippa were to ask outright whether she should make a real attempt to get back to Robert she must know how to answer.

'Can't like the fella!' She heard Perry's voice coming from a distance; clearly but with an intimate undertone, as if he might in some celestial bar, foot on the rail, chatting confidentially to a fellow spirit. 'Don't trust him for a second.' It was a warning.

The words seemed to echo in her head and she shivered, as though some premonition had touched her. She sat quite still, listening intently, but there was nothing more to be heard and, after a moment, clutching her cardigan tightly across her breast, she stood up and went quickly downstairs.

Robert was feeling frustrated and impatient. Louisa hadn't been as forthcoming as he had expected about the changes at the office and, just lately, she had been avoiding him. She pleaded pressure of work – there was a great deal to be done with the takeover going through – but she remained obstinately silent when he asked her to confirm the rumour that they were being bought out by the American company with whom they had liaised for years, or when he quizzed her about new policies. At last Robert could bear it no longer. Except at the office, he hadn't seen her for nearly two weeks and her telephone rang unanswered.

He decided to risk her displeasure and turn up

unannounced at her flat. He knew she hated this but he was beginning to feel quite desperate. He pressed the bell, spoke into her intercom, and climbed the flight of steps to the first floor where she stood waiting for him. There was a quizzical coolness about her and his heart sank. She was the only person – apart from his superiors – who had ever had the power to put him on the defensive.

'Sorry to burst in unexpectedly,' he said, following her into the flat. 'You seem so elusive these days.'

'Well, it's probably a good thing that you've turned up,' she said, moving away from him as he attempted an embrace. 'Drink?'

He shrugged, thrusting his hands into his pockets. 'Why not?'

He was beginning to be angry now which, although he had no idea of it, stiffened her resolution. Louisa had been playing for time, which had now run out, and his uncouth attitude strengthened her decision. When Robert was sullen or cross, his origins were not so easily disguised and he was at his least attractive to her. It had been exciting to manipulate him but the novelty was wearing thin, especially in light of the new challenge which she had been offered. She passed him his drink and raised her glass.

'To the future?' she suggested.

'Have we got one?' he asked rudely.

She smiled a little secret smile that infuriated him. '*I* have,' she answered. '*You* might have a problem.'

He put his tumbler of whisky down with a sharp click on a small table. 'What's that supposed to mean?'

Louisa sat in the armchair by the fireplace. 'Sit down,

Robert,' she said calmly. 'I'm glad you've come. It's time. I know I've been driving you mad but everything had to be kept under wraps until final decisions were made.'

Robert sank on to the deep comfortable sofa. 'I think you might have trusted me.'

Louisa nodded. 'I might have done,' she agreed, 'but there was rather a lot at stake.'

Robert's heart beat faster. He began to suspect that she was simply leading him on, teasing him a little, so as to make the news more exciting. Could she have pulled off something really big for him? He tried to smile and picked up his drink again, deciding to play along with her game.

'I've missed you,' he said, looking at her in a way which once had made her shiver with pleasure. 'Don't think I'm not interested in my future but I'm more concerned with us.'

Louisa shrugged a little and pursed her lips thoughtfully. 'That's rather a pity,' she said. 'It's your future I really wanted to discuss with you.'

Robert pressed his lips together, refusing to allow himself to be rattled.

'OK,' he said lightly. 'Let's do it your way. Let's talk about my future.' He swallowed some whisky and stood the glass on the table. 'Where shall we start?'

'With Harrison Pawley,' she replied instantly. 'Remember him?'

'He's the head of Pawley and Straker,' replied Robert with a faint lifting of his brows. The excitement was back, thudding in his breast. 'So they've bought us out. It's not a surprise.'

'But do you remember him?' persisted Louisa. 'Remember meeting him at John's, the summer before last?'

Robert frowned a little. 'Of course I do. Big chap with a very serious wife. Quaker stock, aren't they?'

Louisa smiled, rather as if he had said something very clever. 'Right,' she said. 'He's a great family man. Remember how John encouraged you all to bring wives and children and how sweet Hannah Pawley was with Rowley?'

'Pippa brought him along in his carry-cot,' recalled Robert. 'She was terrified he was going to cry. So what?'

'So Harrison Pawley is your new boss and he is very keen on the family and disapproves strongly of divorce, egged on by Hannah who is one very powerful lady. He remembered Pippa. Asked after her and Rowley when John was talking about your position in the company. A very exciting position, I may say. Pippa obviously made an impression.'

There was a silence. Robert sat very still.

'What did John say?' he asked at last.

'John has been very vague of late,' said Louisa. 'He's on strong medication. I stepped in quite quickly and said that Pippa hadn't been too well and was recuperating with friends down in the West Country.'

'Hang on a minute.' Robert's usually keen brain felt fuddled and slow. 'Harrison's going to have to know sometime. No good kidding him along. I can tell him that she ran out on me. Left me in the lurch. I can't be held to blame for that, can I? Or,' his face changed, 'or do you think that bastards like Terry Cooper will drop me in it?'

Louisa spread her hands. 'Who can tell? All I'm saying

is that I think you'll do better as a married man in our new organisation.'

'So do I!' Robert grinned at her. 'Haven't I been telling you so all along? So we give Pippa time to fade out, meanwhile spreading the tale of how she abandoned me – surely you and Eleanor can help me there? – and then, when the time is right we get married. So come on!' His sullenness had evaporated like mist before the sun. 'What's this very exciting position? Put me out of my misery.'

'Head of Sales.' She watched him, eyes narrowed, a tiny smile on her lips. 'Harrison is deeply impressed by your file.'

'Wow!' Robert exhaled mightily, slapped his hands down on the chair and pushed himself up in one quick movement. 'I don't *believe* it.' He paced across the room. 'Head of Sales! God! They'll all be sick as dogs! I can just see Paul's face. And Martin's. Not to mention Terry bloody Cooper's!' He slammed his right fist into his left palm. 'My *God*!' He paused by her chair and bent to kiss her. 'Don't think I don't know how much of this is due to you. Christ!' He picked up his drink and downed it in one quick gulp. 'I just can't take it in.'

The quality of her silence penetrated his excitement and he turned to look at her.

'You haven't got it quite right,' she said, and he frowned at her.

'But you just said—'

'Oh, yes.' She nodded. 'Head of Sales. That bit's right. Not the rest. I've been offered a job in the New York office and I've accepted it. I fly out next month.'

He felt as though he had been punched in the midriff. 'You . . . *what*?'

'Mmm.' She nodded. 'It's a fantastic opportunity with an unbelievable salary. PA to one of the partners.' She felt sorry for him now that the worst was over. 'Sorry, love. I decided that marriage wasn't quite my thing. I'm more ambitious than I realised.'

He stared at her. 'I thought you loved me.'

She knew that she'd have to be brutal. 'Uh-uh.' She shook her head. 'A severe case of lust, but it was nice while it lasted.'

'You put it in the past tense, I note.' His hands were balled deep in his pockets, his face grim.

'That's right. That's where it belongs. I'm sorry, Robert.'

'You bloody cow.' It sounded as if he might burst into tears. 'I left Pippa for you.'

She laughed then, unmoved by his self-pity. 'Ah no, Robert. Let's be honest. You left Pippa because you wanted promotion and thought she might hold you back.'

'I love you,' he protested. 'For Christ's sake . . .'

'Too bad.' She held up her hands, palms out, rejecting him. 'I never said I loved you and I never said I'd marry you. It was your decision to leave Pippa. Nothing to do with me.' She gave a short laugh and he stared at her, shocked and disbelieving at these revelations. 'Funny, isn't it? You left her because you thought she'd hold you back and now you need her to make certain you achieve your ambition.'

'What do you mean?' His voice was stifled with frustration.

Louisa stood up and went to pour herself another drink.

'Make no mistake, Robert. They'll be out for your blood. You're going to be promoted right over their heads and they won't hesitate to throw the shit at the fan once they find out. If Harrison – not to mention Hannah – finds out that you've abandoned Pippa and Rowley you can forget it.'

'But . . .' Robert was shaken with fear. 'How do you mean? He's hardly likely to demote me if he finds out.'

Louisa gave a sigh which expressed a desire for patience and poured him some more whisky. 'Look,' she said, 'it'll be at least three months before the positions are confirmed and it's only a matter of time before everyone knows. Paul and Martin, and especially Terry, are going to make certain that Harrison knows the truth. Once he does, I think changes will be made before anything becomes official.'

'But what can I do?' He looked ashen and his hand vibrated a little as he took his glass. 'Please, Louisa. Please reconsider. Together we could brazen it out . . .'

'Forget it, Robert! Nothing doing.' She went back to her chair. 'You've got one chance and it's a faint one.'

He grasped at her suggestion that there might be a ray of hope. 'What? What chance?'

'You must get Pippa back.' He gaped at her and she nodded at him coolly. 'You must go and see her. Eat humble pie, abase yourself. Whatever it takes. Beg her to come back to you.'

'Are you mad?' He almost laughed. 'Do you honestly believe that she'd—'

'Yes, I do.' She sipped her whisky calmly, watching him over the glass. 'She was always potty about you. She'd be wanting to believe that it was all a terrible mistake. As long as you make up a good enough lie.'

'But what could I say?'

She stared at him contemptuously. So much for his undying love! He was already scheming, thinking furiously, his passion for her abandoned to his ambition. Well, she'd asked for it. It was what had turned her on in the first place. She felt a pang of pity for Pippa – but only a pang. If you were stupid enough to love blindly you could hardly blame anyone else if you fell into a pit. Louisa shrugged.

'For God's sake, sit down,' she said impatiently. 'Let's be calm and think about this. You'll need a very sound plan . . .'

Robert sat down obediently, his head reeling. The shock of losing Louisa's affection was passing and his disappointment was being submerged by the waves of determination. Head of Sales. Nothing must be allowed to stand in the way of this glittering prize! Robert gulped at his whisky and tried to concentrate on Louisa's level voice outlining her plan.

Chapter Twenty-one

Frances was back from shopping by the time Pippa arrived home but it wasn't until Rowley had been bathed, given his supper and put to bed that she had the opportunity to see that there was something amiss. To begin with, Pippa assumed that Frances was merely tired, but there was something withdrawn about her silence, a shocked inward-looking expression on her face, which made Pippa study her carefully.

'I think we need a drink,' she said in an attempt to lighten the atmosphere a little. 'We're not used to all this rushing about, are we? We've got lazy. Too much sitting in the sun.'

She went to pour Frances some of her favourite Chardonnay, puzzled by her apathy. It was with difficulty that she'd persuaded Frances to take even a barely sensible sum towards their keep and Pippa liked to bring treats home, such as the wine or chocolates. Robert paid a generous amount into Pippa's account and, as she pointed out, it was only right that she and Rowley paid their way. Frances took her glass listlessly and Pippa touched her arm.

'Are you OK?' she asked.

Frances nodded, swallowed, then shook her head. To her

horror, Pippa saw that she was near to tears and she set her own glass down swiftly and sat beside her on the sofa. Frances glanced at her and made an attempt at a smile.

'Sorry,' she said. 'It's . . . I've had a bit of a shock.'

'Would you . . .? Do you want to talk about it?' asked Pippa diffidently.

'I don't know,' said Frances slowly. 'I can't believe it's true.'

She sat for some moments staring straight ahead of her. Pippa sipped at her drink, feeling anxious. Despite how close their friendship had become, she was aware of the age gap between them. Frances was such a motherly figure that Pippa felt unequal to approaching her quite as she might a woman of her own age. Frances had been the one to give advice and encourage Pippa to tell her troubles and it was unsettling to see her so upset. Just as she was about to make another attempt at communication, the telephone bell shrilled. Both women jumped violently. Frances's untouched wine spilled over her hand and she swore and then glanced at her watch.

'You take it!' she said to Pippa urgently. 'It'll be Stephen. I don't want to speak to him. Tell him I'm out . . . Gone to see a friend. Anything.'

Too amazed to resist, Pippa got to her feet and hurried out into the hall.

'Hello there!' Stephen's voice sounded cheerfully in her ear. 'I thought you must be outside or something. Have I dragged you away from bath-time?'

'No, no,' said Pippa hastily. 'No. I was just . . . bringing in the washing. Frances isn't here, I'm afraid. She's . . . gone to have supper with a friend.'

'Oh.' Stephen sounded disappointed but resigned. 'I'm sorry I missed her. I got held up at the office. Well, would you tell her that I'm looking forward to the weekend? I'll give her a buzz tomorrow, just to confirm times and things. I hope nobody else wants to view?'

'I don't really know,' said Pippa slowly. 'I've been over with Annie all day and only just got in.'

'Oh, well. I shall hope for the best. How are you? And Rowley?'

'We're fine. Just fine,' she said, trying to sound as normal as possible. 'I'll tell Frances you called.'

'You do that. Give her my love. Bye.'

Pippa replaced the receiver thoughtfully and went back to the sitting room. Frances watched her sit down and pick up her glass.

'It was him?'

Pippa nodded. 'He sent his love. And says he's looking forward to seeing you at the weekend.'

'I'm not going!' said Frances violently, and Pippa gazed at her in amazement as she finished her wine with a gulp and rubbed her hand across her face.

Pippa leaped up and took her glass to refill it. 'What's up?' she asked worriedly. 'What's wrong, Frances? *Please* tell me.'

Frances took the glass automatically without looking at her and took several deep breaths. It was as if she were trying to decide whether she could bring herself to speak. 'I met a friend of Stephen's in Plymouth today.' Her voice was flat. 'We chatted and I said that Stephen had gone to Wales. He must have thought that I meant that Stephen had left me and he said, "So it was that serious, was it? Well, I did wonder." And I asked him what he meant and he told me he'd seen Stephen in a pub with another woman.'

'Well, so what?' said Pippa, when the silence lengthened and Frances seemed to have finished. 'Why shouldn't he be in a pub with a woman? It was probably a colleague or an old friend.'

'It was Cass Wivenhoe,' said Frances dully. She lifted the glass to her lips and swallowed back some wine.

'Who?' Pippa frowned. 'Well, if you know her . . .'

'I guessed from the description. And someone else told me that they'd seen them together. In a different pub, on a different occasion,' she added as Pippa opened her mouth to make the obvious remark.

'But, Frances,' protested Pippa. 'Come on. You can't condemn him unheard because he's had a drink with someone you both know. Even if it *was* twice. They might have met accidentally.'

'No.' Frances shook her head. 'Mark said he had his arm round her, kissing her. He said he was so absorbed in her he didn't even notice Mark up at the bar although he stood beside him to order their drinks.'

Pippa was silenced. She drank a little wine and tried to think of something to say.

'He's always had a thing about Cass.' Frances's tone was almost conversational but Pippa recognised the brittle quality of it. 'Always. Even though it was because of her that Hugh is in this foolish state. How *could* he? Her of all people! He knows how I feel about her. I hate her!'

'Oh Frances,' said Pippa helplessly, 'I'm so sorry. Only

don't you think you should speak to him? Confront him?'

'No!' said Frances fiercely. 'He'll just laugh it off. Tell me it's a load of lies. He's always played up to her, flirted with her. It's humiliating.'

'But how will you sort it out?' asked Pippa, aghast at this hitherto unseen side of the practical organising Frances. 'What will you say to him?'

'I shan't say anything to him,' snapped Frances. 'I shan't speak to him at all!'

Pippa finished her drink quickly and went to pour another. She hesitated for a moment and then refilled Frances's glass. She'd never seen her drink so fast. She remembered Frances's advice to her about forgiving and forgetting and the sanctity of the marriage bond and realised that this was an opportunity for Frances to practise what she preached. Glancing at her flushed cheeks and angry eyes, she decided that this wasn't the moment to mention it and sat down beside her again.

'What will you say? About the weekend?'

'I've told you,' said Frances, taking her third glass of wine. 'I shan't say anything. You can tell him that we've got people to view again.' She looked at Pippa swiftly, pleadingly. 'You will, won't you? You'll do that for me? I just couldn't bear to speak to him!'

'Yes, of course I will,' said Pippa soothingly, her heart beating fast with anxiety, and the realisation that she had become embroiled in doing Frances's dirty work. 'But you'll have to speak to him sometime, won't you? I mean, he'll think it a bit odd, won't he? If you're always out or something?'

'I don't care what he thinks.' Frances looked as though she might burst into tears and Pippa's heart sank. 'He knows I'm upset at the moment because he won't come home and talk to Hugh. Says he's too busy. He'll think it's that.'

'What if he *does* come home?' suggested Pippa nervously. 'Supposing he gets worried and comes rushing home?'

Frances shrugged. 'Then I'll tell him what I think of him!'

Her indifference didn't fool Pippa and she slipped an arm about Frances's shoulders, unable to think of any comforting words. Frances made a pathetic effort at a smile, as though acknowledging the gesture, but her lips shook and she set down her glass.

'I'm going upstairs for a bit,' she said. 'Don't wait supper for me. I'm not hungry.'

Pippa watched her go. She didn't feel particularly hungry either but sat on, as the dusk deepened, sipping at her wine and feeling more and more depressed.

Upstairs, Frances wandered aimlessly about the bedroom, pausing to stare out of the window at the high shoulders of the moor, still faintly flushed by the sunset's dying glow. She was desolate. Mark's unbiased report had convinced her where Pat's had not. His own shock at Stephen's behaviour was so genuine that it left no room for doubt.

She remembered now his suppressed excitement which she had assumed was related to his new appointment and felt both rage and misery in equal parts. Somehow, the fact that he had chosen to be unfaithful with Cass made the whole affair far, far worse. It was doubly insulting and hurtful. Frances sat down on the edge of the bed and stared at the floor. But what to do about it? How should she deal with it? She felt that she could never bear to see him again. If he were to appear at this moment she would want to rend him and spit on him. He had destroyed her trust and love for a brief foolish moment of passion.

Frances felt quite certain that whatever had been between Cass and Stephen was over. It would be almost impossible for them to continue their liaison at such a distance and given their commitments. Nor would Stephen be so anxious for her, Frances's, company at weekends. Her lip curled. He felt guilty, no doubt. At the thought of him and Cass together her heart was wrenched with pain and she buried her face in her hands. Never, never would she be able to be with him intimately again. Her rage and humiliation was swamped with desolation as she thought of all that she would miss; the comforting hugs, the quiet times, shared jokes, the casual intimacy of twenty-five years of marriage.

'How could he?' she moaned, as the tears rushed into her eyes. 'Oh, how could he?'

She stiffened, hunched over her knees, as she heard a whimper and then a louder cry. Rowley! She listened, her maternal instincts active even in her misery. Sometimes he had bad dreams and needed comforting, sometimes he went back to sleep. There was a second, louder cry. Even as she tensed, preparing to rise, she heard feet on the stairs and Rowley's door open. Presently Pippa's voice could be heard, gentle, soothing, and Rowley's childish treble raised in tearful explanation.

As Frances sat, listening to the monotone of Pippa's

reading voice, she recalled all the things that she had said to Pippa on the subject of infidelity and divorce. A slow hot shame engulfed her and her hands clenched a little. How swift she'd been to advise and pontificate from her position of smug ignorance! How ready to tell Pippa that she must forgive and forget; that she must seek a reconciliation with the man who had betrayed and humiliated her! Frances squeezed her eyes shut in self-disgust. She heard her complacent voice telling Pippa that the marriage and Rowley were more important and should be put above Pippa's own private feelings.

Sitting there alone, Frances wondered whether it might be possible to die of shame. Whatever must Pippa have thought of those earlier declarations that she would never speak to Stephen again? Frances massaged her forehead with her fingers. So now what? Did she admit to Pippa that she'd had no right to lay down the law upon a subject on which she'd had no experience? Retract everything she'd said? Or should she make an attempt to follow her own advice?

She dropped her head back into her hands. How could she? Could it be remotely possible that, knowing what she knew, she could behave as if nothing had happened?

'No,' she said aloud. 'No! Oh God . . .'

She began to weep, silently and hopelessly. Her life had been shivered into pieces and it could never be mended. Once again she thought of Pippa, remembering things she'd said during those long evening talks. How easy it had been to find solutions for her, to recommend codes of behaviour; and how patiently Pippa had listened, even agreeing that Frances was right!

Frances groaned aloud in her agony, feeling just as humiliated by her smug ignorance as she was by Stephen's infidelity. She remembered Pippa's cry: 'How can I go on loving a man who's such a bastard?' and her heart contracted with a kind of fear. Did she still love Stephen? Would it be possible simply to cast him out of her life? She sat still, staring straight ahead of her into the gathering twilight, and thought about him; his patience with her moods; his humour that prevented her from taking herself too seriously; the endless gestures of love.

She put her hands to her cheeks and began to cry in earnest, rocking to and fro on the edge of the bed, so bereft in her loss that she didn't hear the door open or Pippa come into the room.

'Oh Frances.' Pippa slipped an arm about her. 'Don't be alone. Come downstairs and let me make you some tea. Don't sit here in the dark. You've been so wonderful to me, now let me help you.'

Feeling her humiliation complete, Frances gave a long low wail and turned her wet face to Pippa's breast, and Pippa held her tightly, murmuring comforting nothings to her, as she had held Rowley and soothed him only minutes before.

[illegible]

[illegible] This was where [illegible]

[illegible] the length of his [illegible], he'd arrived.

Chapter Twenty-two

Hugh was sitting at the table in the caravan. This was where Max had sat during the long cold months of the previous winter, working on his plans for the adventure training school, and Hugh liked to sit here now, in his own private quarters, thinking about how those plans were becoming solid reality. In the last few weeks he'd been spending less and less time at this table. It was becoming increasingly necessary to be in the office; making telephone calls, working out timetables, planning the brochure.

Hugh grinned to himself as he recalled those heady moments when he challenged Max's ideas and put forward his own, arguing them through, carrying his point. Some of them were good ideas. The horses, for instance . . . He rocked himself back on the little chair, stretching the length of his arms, hands gripping the table. It was sensible, he'd argued, to have their own ponies; four ponies for the younger children; four horses for the bigger ones. No riding stable would lend their livestock in the middle of the season and, if they wanted to include pony-trekking on the itinerary, then they must have horses available rather than putting the children in the charge of other people.

Max had rubbed his jaw thoughtfully, taking Hugh's point. It would be difficult and expensive taking the children to other stables.

'I haven't costed horses in,' he began.

'I have,' said Hugh cheerfully. 'When we worked out that new set of figures I included them. They'll pay for themselves in two years. I'll get my own horse back from Caroline.'

'Hang on a minute,' said Max. 'I haven't got enough land. They're picky feeders, horses. My fields would be overrun with nettles and dock in no time. They have to be run with sheep or they ruin the pasture.'

'I know that,' said Hugh thoughtfully. 'Of course we could simply open the gates and let the sheep come off the moor to graze. Are you a Commoner?'

'I've got grazing rights on the moor, yes,' said Max, 'but that doesn't help. We can't let horses go wandering off. It would be a day's work just rounding them up each time we need them. It's not on.'

'No,' agreed Hugh regretfully. 'No, you're right. We could do up the old stable block and perhaps we could persuade some of the local farmers to let us some grazing. You must know enough of them.'

'Yes, I do,' agreed Max slowly.

'Well, then.' Hugh watched him eagerly. 'We *need* our own horses. I know there's the white water canoeing and orienteering and hill-walking and climbing. But the riding will give us an edge. They're not expensive to buy. Honestly, it would be cheaper in the long run . . .'

Max burst out laughing. 'You sound like my ex-wife

setting off for the sales,' he said, and became serious again.

Hugh had remained silent. He had no wish to trespass on this delicate ground, which Max rarely mentioned, nor did he wish to be sidetracked. He was very serious about his horses.

'OK,' said Max, after a moment. 'I'll make a few phone calls.'

'Think how good it will look on the brochures,' said Hugh exultantly. 'We need a photograph of them grazing. We can put a couple in your fields and take the photograph so we include one of the barns. It'll be great!'

Max shook his head at this enthusiasm. 'We haven't got them yet,' he said blightingly. 'And I shall want to go through those figures carefully before I do anything else. Feeding horses costs money and they'll need shelter. I'm a farmer's son, don't forget. You won't be able to fool me.'

'I don't have to fool you,' said Hugh cheerfully. 'It's all above board. *Magna est veritas et praevalebit*.'

'What does that mean?' asked Max suspiciously.

'"Truth is great and will prevail",' translated Hugh. 'I wouldn't lie to you.' He grinned at him. 'You can trust me.'

'I believe you,' said Max grimly, aware that he was being managed. 'But I'll see them just the same!'

Now, the next morning, Hugh laughed as he remembered how they'd worked through the figures . . . Max was telephoning a few of his farmer friends even now! He sobered as he remembered Max's latest suggestion and his heart beat with thick hard strokes. When they'd finished the figures Max had looked at him.

'OK,' he said. 'I'll go along with it. But only if you're

going to be here. I shan't have the time to cope with horses as well as everything else and I can't guarantee finding anyone who will be as mad about the beasts as you are. They'll be your responsibility. You'd better have a talk with your father before I commit myself.'

'I don't need to talk to him.' Hugh looked very grave. 'I've made up my mind. I'm twenty-one. I don't have to ask permission to live my life how I want to.'

'That's fighting talk, boy,' said Max, after a moment. 'I don't want to cause trouble with your family.'

'You won't,' said Hugh. 'Honestly. It's only Mum. I'm sure Dad will see it my way and then he'll talk her round. They just want to make sure I'm not being rash but Dad will see that it's going to be great.'

Max sat silent, biting his lip. 'I've had a thought,' he said at last. 'You can't go on living in that caravan. You could move in here with me, of course, there's plenty of room for us both, but I know you like your own quarters. I'd decided to make the top floors of the dormitories into self-contained flats, as you know. Being built into the hill, they can have their own entrance on that level without any egress into the dormitory. We can afford to convert one of them. Perhaps the one over the boys' dormitory would be the best one for you. It's just a huge cave at present. What d'you say?'

Hugh stared at him, his eyes round. 'But we agreed that it would have to be for our cook-cum-matron-cum-secretary,' he said.

'Yes,' said Max irritably. 'Well, you can see how far we're getting with *that*. No takers so far. No female wants to live in the wilds of Dartmoor, keeping unsocial hours and looking after a load of children. We're going to have to hope we find a local who's prepared to come in daily. Several different people, perhaps, on a rota. What we really need is a retired steward. Ex-navy. That would be perfect.'

Hugh, however, was too surprised at Max's offer to concentrate on this very real problem. Max smiled at his expression.

'Think it over,' he advised. 'You're welcome here. You can have the spare bedroom as your own private sitting room. But your parents may be a little more impressed if you can show them your own little flat.'

'It would be terrific!' said Hugh. He shook his head in disbelief. 'Gosh! You're sure we can afford to do it up?'

'It's been costed in.' Max shrugged. 'I assumed we'd have a live-in helper and he or she had to go somewhere. I imagined that my assistant would share the cottage. Or he might have been a local and come in daily. It's not working out quite as I saw it. Anyway. Think about it.'

Now, Hugh pushed back his chair and stood up. Several times since the conversation he'd been to look at the big space above the dormitory, his mind full of plans and visions. Max had a point. It would certainly help his case with his parents if they thought that such an apartment was to be put at his disposal. He took a deep breath and paced the few feet allowed in the cramped caravan. He wasn't quite so confident as he'd made it sound but he was determined to carry his point. He was right; he knew he was. His parents must be persuaded to his way of thinking. There should be no arguing or tears, just an acceptance on all sides, but he must be tactful and careful in his approach to them.

'*Festina lente*,' muttered Hugh, and then laughed aloud.

He'd never been so happy; and since Cass's letter . . . He glanced instinctively, guiltily, at the drawer where it reposed. He couldn't destroy it yet. He needed to know it by heart so that no doubt could ever assail him again and no guilt could eat away at his confidence.

He thought about Lucinda, wondering how she was and whether she regretted her decision that they should part. He knew now that she'd been right, that he'd needed time and space, but he longed to see her again, to ask her forgiveness for his boorish behaviour of those last few months. She'd sent a postcard which had found its way from Geneva to the farmhouse but it had been merely a brief 'hope all is well' message which had told him nothing about herself. Nevertheless, she had written. He had no idea how to contact her and was reluctant to telephone her mother. He'd decided that he must wait, get on with the job in hand, and hope that, one day, she'd come back to him.

He sat down at the rickety table, stretched mightily and bent once more to his work.

Hearing the sound of the car bumping along the track, Annie put the secateurs into the basket and went to meet Frances at the gate. She had been astounded at the latest drama, related by Frances during an earlier telephone call, and quite unable to believe that Stephen was a philanderer. She'd been so sceptical that Frances had become cross which – later – made Annie smile. It was as if Frances *wanted* Stephen to be guilty and was indignant that her friend refused to see him in such a light. As she dead-headed the roses, waiting for Frances to arrive, Annie brooded on the difficulties which beset human relationships. There were so many pitfalls. Frances was not pleased that Annie considered Stephen incapable of committing adultery; she felt that Annie was being unsympathetic, siding with him. If Stephen were to be found innocent, however, Frances might well resent any criticism Annie had made of him in her effort to be supportive.

Annie snipped thoughtfully, the August sunshine hot on her back. The scent of the roses was heavy all about her and butterflies sunned themselves on the purple buddleia that grew in the corner of the wall beside the cottage. Foliage had the faded dusty look that heralds the end of the summer and Annie was trying to be positive about the hints of autumn which were already beginning to appear: blackberries ripening in the lane; the first faint flush on the rowan berry.

Perry, no doubt, would have seen all kinds of signs and portents to rejoice in but Annie merely felt the usual keen sense of loss and knew how long the winter would seem without him. She tried to concentrate on Frances. Since Perry had died, she had been embroiled in other people's disasters: first Frances's worries about Hugh, then Pippa's problems with Robert and now Frances and Stephen.

'If only I were better at it,' she muttered, pricking her finger and swearing under her breath. 'I just haven't got what it takes.' She sucked her finger, imagining how wonderful it would be if Perry were to come strolling out of the cottage, ready to deal with Frances. He would hug her, listen to her, sympathise, whilst being spine-stiffening and positive all at the same time. He'd never taken sides but always seen things impartially, yet had never been resented for it.

'You're a fraud,' she'd told him often enough. 'You fool *all* the people *all* the time!'

'It's a gift,' he'd answered, unabashed. 'Don't give me away!'

'It's all very well for *you*,' she'd grumbled. '*I* can't win. If I'm nice to people I sound sycophantic and if I'm honest with them, I sound brutal.'

He'd laughed. 'It's quite simple,' he'd told her. 'People need to feel good. The truth's all very well, if they're strong enough to take it. Generally they aren't. Anyway, they want to feel that you're on their side because it's the right place to be, not because you're humouring them. The only way to play it is to be reasonable but supportive.'

Remembering, Annie gave a derisive snort. 'Simple!' she said aloud and, hearing the car coming along the track, hurried to the gate.

Frances parked the car, crossed the track whose muddy ruts were iron hard, and paused for a hug from Annie, which she returned rather listlessly.

'This *heat*!' she said, as they went up the path together. 'I'm exhausted just driving over in it.'

'A long cold drink,' diagnosed Annie, glad to have something positive to be doing. 'The sitting room's the coolest place to be. Go on in and I'll bring us something cold and refreshing.' She pushed Frances gently through the door and went on into the kitchen.

Frances was standing by the window when Annie came

in with the tray, staring out into the garden. Her shoulders drooped and her face was drawn. She looked her age and Annie's heart went out to her as she took in the untidy dark hair which needed attention and the limp cotton frock which was just the wrong length: too long to be chic, too short to be stylish. She tried to imagine the glamorous blonde – with whom Stephen was misbehaving and whom Frances had described with miserable envy – and found it quite impossible to take it all seriously. Frances turned back into the room with a sigh as Annie put the tray down.

'I stopped off to see Hugh,' she said, wandering over and perching on the edge of an armchair, 'but there was nobody about. Oh, it's all too much!'

Annie glanced at her anxiously and gave her a glass full of freshly pressed orange juice.

'I'm so sorry,' she began lamely, sitting down. 'It's ghastly for you.'

Frances sipped gratefully at the cold liquid. 'It's too much,' she repeated. 'All the forms for Hugh's grant should have been filled in and signed. They ought to be sent back or he won't get it in time.'

'He's going back, is he?' asked Annie, assuming that this decision had now been taken by Hugh.

'Of course he's going back!' said Frances impatiently. 'He's just got a bee in his bonnet about this job. I really can't see why Max can't cope until next summer and take him on then, if Hugh still wants it.'

Annie considered and rejected several comments. The whole subject was fraught with danger. She remembered Perry's advice: she must be reasonable but supportive.

'It must be infuriating for you,' she said warmly. 'Children are such a worry. But would it be the end of the world if he didn't go back? It sounds a wonderful job for him. After all, Hugh's not your run-of-the-mill young man, is he?'

Frances, who had drawn breath at the beginning of this observation, hesitated. 'How do you mean?'

'Well.' Annie frowned thoughtfully. 'I just can't see him settling to a nine-to-five type job in some city office. He loves being out and about, doesn't he? I must admit it sounds perfect for him. This Max Whatsit would probably take him in as a partner and then he'd be all set. Why should he have to be just like everybody else? He's obviously got special qualities. This Max has spotted his potential by the sounds of it. An ex-Royal Marine must be very difficult to please. I think I'd be rather proud of Hugh if he were my son.'

She sat back in her chair and drank her orange, exhausted by her effort; definitely reasonable but was it supportive? Frances was staring into her glass.

'I suppose you have a point. But he ought to have a degree. He ought to qualify.'

'Why?' asked Annie, rallying. 'It's just a middle-class conception. Like buying your own house or sending your children to private schools. It's something that your peer group does. You must have the courage to be different. You owe it to Hugh. It could ruin his life if he missed this opportunity. It's what happened to Perry, you know.'

'What did?' Frances stared at her, faintly alarmed.

'Perry wanted to join the Forestry Commission,' Annie told her. 'He always had a thing about trees and wildlife.

But his parents thought it was far too manual a career, not proper for a boy of his class, and insisted that he became an accountant. As soon as he could he struck out for himself but it was too late and he never found his right niche. He was like Hugh, just not cut out for the nine-to-five routine, and I think if he could have done what he wanted to do in the beginning he would have been much happier.'

'But Perry was a very happy person,' protested Frances. 'He was one of the jolliest men I've ever met.'

'Perry always made the best of everything,' agreed Annie, 'and he loved life. But he would have been more content and more fulfilled if he'd been allowed to follow his own heart. It was a great sadness to him and he never quite forgave his parents although he could sympathise with their outlook. You have to be very special to be able to be different.'

'I'm not saying that Hugh can't do this job,' began Frances slowly. 'All I'm saying is that he ought to qualify first.'

'But by then it could be too late.' Annie pressed home her advantage. 'Max might have found someone else and Hugh will do jobs that he doesn't want to do and flit aimlessly about for the rest of his life, searching for something special. Just like Perry did. These opportunities only come once.'

Frances was silent. Annie finished her drink and stood up to refill the glass from the jug on the tray. Her heart was hammering and she cursed Perry's shade, terrified that she'd taken too much to herself. She raised the jug and Frances nodded.

'Yes please,' she said. 'It's delicious. Oh, why is life so *difficult*?'

'It's hell,' agreed Annie, deciding that she'd said quite enough about Hugh. 'Now tell me all about this business with Stephen . . .'

Chapter Twenty-three

Because he was used to Frances retreating into silence when she was cross with him, it was several days before Stephen began to feel seriously worried. When she cancelled a second weekend, however, and she was regularly unavailable when he attempted to speak to her on the telephone, he decided that he must take steps to resolve the matter. He was still certain that it was Hugh's refusal to return to university which was upsetting her and suspected that she was annoyed because he hadn't come home to deal with it. Now that things were settling down in the department, Stephen decided to do just that but first he telephoned Hugh to see exactly what the situation was.

Hugh felt an anticipatory thrill of anxiety when he heard his father's voice but he was determined to be positive.

'How are you?' he asked cheerfully, as though a telephone call from his father was a perfectly normal everyday event. 'Getting sorted out?'

'Slowly, but yes, I think I am.' Stephen sounded much as usual and Hugh relaxed a little. 'I'm hoping to get home next weekend but I decided to have a chat with you first and see how things are. Mum's being a bit elusive and I think she's cross with me because I've been somewhat preoccupied. Have you seen her lately?'

'Not very lately,' answered Hugh, rather surprised by this approach. He decided to take the bull by the horns. 'She's cross with *me* because I've decided to take up Max's offer of a job but I don't see why she should be upset with *you*.'

'Ah, well.' Stephen still sounded friendly, even amused. 'She thinks I should have rushed over and given you a piece of my mind.'

Hugh risked a chuckle. 'It wouldn't have done any good. I don't want to be difficult, Dad, I really don't. I hate to upset you or Mum but I just know this is right for me. I love it here. And after all, what sort of job am I going to get with a History degree? It doesn't lead on to anything, like Engineering or teaching qualifications.'

Stephen was silent for a moment. Hugh sounded happier and more confident than he could ever remember and what he said made good sense.

'Look,' he said at last, 'between you and me I'm not against the idea. I'd like to speak to Max and get a few things straight but otherwise I'm inclined to say go for it.'

'Oh great, Dad! Thanks!' Hugh could hardly believe it.

'Hang on,' warned Stephen. 'That doesn't mean that the war is over. Your mother is going to be very unhappy about the fact that I'm siding with you.'

'You can handle Mum,' said Hugh with complete confidence. 'You can talk her round. Make her see that it's a good idea.'

'Thanks,' said Stephen drily. 'Chance would be a fine thing. At the moment she won't speak to me at all!'

'That's just Mum,' said Hugh comfortingly. 'Can you really get home? I'd love you to see what we're doing here. It's brilliant.'

'I shall certainly come over to see you,' said Stephen. He hesitated a little. 'You sound very happy, Hugh. Much more like your old self. I'm delighted to hear it.'

'I feel terrific,' admitted Hugh and remembered Cass's letter. 'I had a letter from Cass Wivenhoe.'

'Oh, she wrote, did she?' Stephen's voice was warm but almost immediately he was overcome with embarrassment, wondering how Cass had broached the subject. 'I hope you didn't mind my mentioning your feelings to her?'

'Not a bit.' Hugh felt odd, reassuring his father. 'It was nice of you to worry. She said . . . well, she said all sorts of things that made me see it differently. It's been such a relief. It was really kind of her. It can't have been easy.'

'I'm sure it wasn't,' agreed Stephen, remembering Cass's grief. 'But in some ways I think it did her good to talk it all out with me.' He paused. 'Oh, by the way . . . no need to tell your mother about that. She's never cared for Cass and I don't want her to get the wrong idea. You know what I mean?'

'Absolutely,' said Hugh at once – this was being a quite amazing conversation – 'I shan't say a word. But I wrote back to Cass and thanked her.'

'I'm glad. See you soon, then. I'll give you a buzz when I know I'm coming over. Take care. 'Bye.'

Stephen replaced the receiver, wondering if he were being disloyal to Frances. It was almost impossible to play it straight down the middle without upsetting anybody. He decided that this time Hugh must come first. It was wonderful to hear him so cheerful and so purposeful; and he had a point about a History degree. It wouldn't necessarily lead on to employment and he was obviously very excited about his role in the adventure training school.

As for the letter from Cass . . . It seemed to have done the trick with Hugh. Stephen wondered if he, too, should write to Cass; to thank her for her generosity to his son. On reflection he decided that it was best to leave well alone. As it stood it could be explained, if necessary, without any guilt on his side. Anything else would certainly be disloyal to Frances. He sighed as he thought of the approaching battle. It would not be easy to talk her round to Hugh's point of view whatever Hugh might believe. First, though, he must see Max Driver and discuss it thoroughly with him. He needed all the ammunition he could get if he were to be able to persuade her.

Mrs Driver heard Hugh talking to his father, listened unashamedly for a moment, and then, nodding with satisfaction, wandered back out into the yard. She was delighted that Hugh was making a stand and intended to throw his lot in with Max; they would make a good team. Apart from the fact that she'd worried about Max being too solitary, she approved of Hugh's enthusiasm and good humour. She'd already had several chats with him, during which she had learned much more about him than Hugh could possibly have guessed. She looked around the yard, conjuring up memories of the past, and, hearing a voice down in the paddock, strolled to the gate. The Mutt was skittering about, quartering the grass, whilst Max, his back towards her, urged him on.

'Nowhere near it, you useless hound. Miles out. Go on. Find! *Find*, you hairy idiot!'

The Mutt, yards of tongue hanging out as he panted with exertion, raced to and fro like one demented until, finally, he seized upon a ball which he bore triumphantly back to drop at Max's feet.

'About time,' said that unappreciative task master. 'Right. Now *watch*, this time. Ready?'

Off went the ball with the Mutt after it and Max swung round, smiling to himself, and came face to face with his mother, leaning on the gate. She beamed at him.

'Enjoying yourselves?' she asked unnecessarily.

Max fought with himself for a moment and then sighed. 'OK, Mother,' he said. 'You win. Game, set *and* match.'

It was hot; too hot. Pippa, lying on a sunbed in the orchard, was glad of the shade provided by the old bent apple trees. She lay on her back, hands behind her head, and gazed through the twisted branches and dense foliage to the sky beyond. Rowley, lying on another chair, was deeply asleep. The shadow of the leaves, shot through with fingers of sunshine, dappled his bare brown legs.

Pippa was thinking about Frances. Ever since the evening when she had cried in Pippa's arms their relationship had moved on to a different level. The mother-daughter friendship had changed and their affection for each other had deepened. Watching Frances attempting to deal with her new knowledge, Pippa felt an overwhelming compassion for her. She saw that the older woman was trying to practise what she had been preaching and knew that Frances was feeling ashamed of her earlier readily given strictures.

The trouble was that Frances was not winning. Whatever good resolutions she might form, when Stephen telephoned she simply could not bring herself to speak to him. Although Pippa could understand Frances's emotions, she had been slightly shocked when Frances refused to go to Wales. Pippa had been obliged to tell Stephen that there were more people coming to view the house, which luckily had proved to be the case, and had invented a sick friend to explain Frances's unavailability. She felt unhappy about lying to Stephen and yet, knowing what Frances was suffering, she felt that her loyalty must be to her. Imperceptibly they drew closer together and the age gap seemed to dwindle.

The odd thing was that Stephen seemed to have no idea that he'd been found out. Although he was disappointed that Frances was not going to Wales he seemed to be resigned, even faintly amused.

'I expect she's waiting for me to speak to Hugh,' he'd said to Pippa one evening, as though he realised that Pippa knew that something was up and needed reassuring. 'Tell her he's next on my list.'

At no time did he sound guilty or cross, nor was there any defensive note in his voice; simply patience. It was rather puzzling. Surely he must have guessed by now why Frances was behaving so strangely?

Pippa sat up to check on Rowley. His feet were no longer in the shade and she picked up the soft cotton shirt she'd been wearing earlier over her T-shirt and dropped it lightly across his legs lest they should burn. Gentle though she was the movement disturbed him and he stretched, blinking his eyes sleepily. Glancing at her watch, Pippa saw that it was past four o'clock; nearly tea-time and he'd had a good long sleep. She smiled at him, wrapping the long Indian cotton skirt – borrowed from Frances – round her bare legs. It was so hot that even the air seemed to burn the skin.

'Hi,' she said and, bending forward, kissed his warm cheek.

He put his thumb in his mouth and stared up drowsily at the leaves above his head. His small body was absolutely relaxed and Pippa wondered whether he might doze again. She'd just decided that he would – if she kept very quiet – when he spoke.

'Cake,' he said thoughtfully, round his thumb. 'Choclick cake.'

Pippa chuckled. He had helped Frances to make the cake that morning before she'd gone off to see Annie. He sat up and beamed at her and she kneeled on the grass and hugged him, trying to hide the sudden pain in her heart. Frances's misery had somehow underlined her own and confused her. If Frances, despite her age and wisdom, was so shattered by Stephen's infidelity, how could Pippa hope to rise above her own anguish? Rowley hugged her in return, placing his pursed lips against her cheeks and murmuring, 'Kiss, kiss, kiss.' She blinked away her tears and sat back on her heels, picking up his sandals.

She had buckled the first one when he stiffened to stare above her head. 'Daddy!' he cried and Pippa sighed.

'Hello, Max,' she called, not bothering to turn round.

'This is getting to be a habit, isn't it?'

'I do hope not!' Robert's voice was amused but there was a great deal of concern in it, too.

Pippa spun round, her hand at her throat, and stared up at him. He smiled down at her but his smile was wary, his hands bunched into his pockets.

'Hello, Pippa,' he said.

She turned quickly away to fasten Rowley's second sandal and then stood up swiftly. Her heart hammered against her side and her throat was so dry, she was obliged to swallow several times before she could speak.

'What do you want?' she asked hoarsely, too shocked for natural politeness. 'Why are you here?'

'You invited me,' he reminded her gently. 'You wrote to me and asked me to visit you.'

'That was weeks ago,' she said, and swung Rowley into her arms, holding him as a shield between them.

'Hello, old chap.' Robert touched Rowley's hand awkwardly. 'How are you? You've grown.'

'Choclick cake,' said Rowley, refusing to be sidetracked and apparently unmoved by the sudden appearance of his father. He dug his knees into Pippa's side as though urging her towards the house. 'Go in.'

'Would . . . would you like a cup of tea?' asked Pippa, hardly knowing what she was saying. Inside her head her thoughts raced wildly. Why had he come? Had he finished with Louisa? Could he be regretting his behaviour? Although she had longed for him, missed him, thought about him almost constantly since their separation, his unheralded appearance in the flesh completely disorientated her. She could think of nothing to say to him and briefly understood Frances's reluctance to speak to Stephen.

'I should love one,' he was saying, as they moved together across the orchard. 'It's been a long hot drive down from London.' He looked directly at her as he opened the gate for them to pass through. 'I'm sorry I startled you.'

She avoided the intimacy in his eyes, reminded all over again how very good-looking he was; how desirable. He followed her into the kitchen and watched her put Rowley into his highchair. The silence was electric. Hands trembling, Pippa cut the cake, gave some to Rowley and then made the tea. Robert watched her.

'Pippa,' he said at last, when the silence had become unbearable. 'I don't know what to say to you. I knew it would be difficult and I rehearsed all the way down in the car but . . . Oh hell!' he said violently. 'I've been such a *fool*! A *bloody* fool!'

'Bloody fool,' murmured Rowley stickily. 'Bloody fool,' and he hurled Woglet across the kitchen.

They both moved instinctively to pick up the toy and, as their hands touched, Pippa leaped back. He caught at her and she twisted away from him.

'No,' she said breathlessly. 'No.'

'Why should you want to have anything to do with me?' he asked bitterly. 'After my unforgivable behaviour.' He laid Woglet on the tray beside Rowley's plate but his eyes were on Pippa. 'How on earth can I begin to explain? I've been mad. Quite mad.' He shook his head, as if amazed at himself. 'It's been like an illness, a terrible virus. And when I think of all those things I said to you . . . Oh God!' He held out his hands to her. 'What can I say to you?'

Pippa stared back at him speechlessly and he laughed mirthlessly, thrusting his hands back into his pockets. She poured the tea and pushed a mug towards him across the table. He ignored it.

'Please,' he pleaded. 'Could we just talk? Please let me try to explain. I don't deserve it . . . but please?'

'Not here,' she said at once. 'Not now.'

'But . . . OK. But where?'

She swallowed nervously, trying to be calm.

'We could meet later,' she said at last. 'At a pub or something. Where are you staying?'

'I haven't booked in yet,' he said. 'I came straight here.' He looked at her hopefully but she had no intention of inviting him to stay. 'I expect I'll find somewhere.'

'More cake?' asked Rowley winningly, beaming hopefully at his parents.

It occurred to Pippa that she might possibly faint. She felt weak and sick and, despite the fact that she could hardly bear to look at Robert, yet she didn't want him to go; at least, not too far. She needed time.

'Could I look at your Yellow Pages?' he suggested, hoping to spin out more time with her, make himself more at home. 'Just to see . . .?'

'No. No.' She shook her head. He simply must leave before she broke down completely. The shock was too great. 'Just go, Robert. Please go,' she said rapidly. 'I need time. Phone me later when you're sorted out. You've got the number? It was on the letter, wasn't it? Sorry but I just need time . . .'

'Very well.' He looked grim. 'But you'll meet me, won't you? You won't change your mind? Promise?'

'I promise. Just . . . let me think. Please.'

'I'll phone,' he said and went out through the open door.

Pippa sat down suddenly at the table whilst Rowley watched her, puzzled.

'Daddy gone,' he told her in an effort to cheer her and was even more alarmed when she buried her face in her hands. 'Rowley get down,' he commanded anxiously.

He struggled to free himself and the chair rocked. Pippa pulled herself together and went to him.

'It's OK,' she said. 'Everything's OK,' and he looked relieved as she smiled at him. 'Come on. We'll see if *Play School*'s still on.'

They went together into the sitting room and she settled him on the sofa. Whilst he watched the television she sat silently beside him, her mind leaping dizzily over the scene in the kitchen. Robert had come back to her!

He's come back! she told herself and her heart thumped with excitement . . . and terror.

She hugged Rowley tightly, trying to take it in, but it was all too much. She remembered the look of desperation in Robert's eyes, the look of pleading, and her excitement grew. It was true: her private fantasy that Robert should return to her had become reality, yet a small part of her remained angry and resentful. Did he expect her to be ready to take him back the minute he asked her? Pride stirred in her breast but love was too powerful for it and, when the telephone rang, she ran eagerly to answer it.

Chapter Twenty-four

Robert unpacked his overnight case, glanced round the small bedroom and, pocketing the key, let himself out. He had lied when he told Pippa that he had nowhere to stay. The first thing he and Louisa had done – once the plan had been refined down to the last detail – was to find accommodation for him. They studied a map of Dartmoor, saw that Tavistock was the nearest large town to the farmhouse and had looked up the biggest hotel. Although it was the middle of the tourist season the Bedford had a single room free and Robert had booked it. He was chagrined by Pippa's refusal to offer him a bed – preferably hers – but remembered Louisa's advice to take it slowly.

'Don't expect her to fall into your arms at once,' she'd warned him. 'Apart from anything else – she has her pride. You must make allowances for it.'

At that point Robert had made another attempt to change her mind. He tried to convince her that they could bluff their way out of this new situation, so winning his promotion and staying together, but she'd proved adamant and at last he'd given up and concentrated on the plot to convince Pippa that he loved her. Now, as he descended the stairs, his expression was sullen. He hated the idea of eating humble pie, of crawling to Pippa and telling ludicrous lies. Remembering the passage at the farmhouse an ugly light came into his eyes and he dealt the banister a blow with his clenched fist. Secretly he had believed that she would be so delighted to see him there would be no room for pride. Her letter had implied as much.

The arrow of pain that lanced his arm calmed him a little. He simply had to take the long view. A short burst of humiliation would enable him to fulfil his ambitions and, after all, Harrison wouldn't hold out for ever.

'Once you've made it' – he could almost hear Louisa's voice in his ear – 'they'll hardly give you the boot if your marriage should happen to break up. It's just a short-term necessity . . . a means to an end.'

Robert put his head into the dining room and surveyed it dispassionately. He could not imagine himself and Pippa sitting here this evening; he needed a much more intimate setting. Sighing heavily he went along the passage to the bar and ordered a brandy and soda. A few people sat at tables, others were drifting in from a day spent on the beach or the moor and Robert stared in distaste at sunburned arms and shiny faces. A sense of frustration welled in him. How on earth could he be expected to woo Pippa under these unromantic conditions?

He turned back and, leaning his elbows on the bar, stared into his drink. It was necessary to be alone with her. He thought about her as he had seen her that afternoon; hair tousled, some appallingly shapeless garment draped round her, her face bare of any adornment. He compared her unfavourably with Louisa's chic attractions and sighed heavily and self-pityingly. They'd been so good together . . . Suddenly it occurred to him that – once he'd attained the positions promised to him – Louisa might come back to him. He straightened at the thought, her words taking on new meanings. 'A short-term necessity . . . a means to an end.' His heart jumped and hurried in his breast. Perhaps, once he'd achieved and he was doing too well to be replaced, perhaps then . . .

Robert swallowed his drink and a new determination settled in his soul. He'd been a fool not to guess it before and Louisa was far too proud to tell him in words of one syllable. The job in New York was merely a fill-in; a way of getting out of his hair and stilling the gossiping tongues. Meanwhile . . . He glanced at his watch. Pippa would be here soon and he still had no plan as to where he should take her so that he could act out his part with conviction. He had hoped that, by taking her unawares, he might break down her defences at once. After all, her letter had been very revealing. He felt quickly in the inside pocket of his blazer . . . yes, it was still there; a necessary part of the plot. He was convinced, however, that she had not been unmoved by his pleas. If he could get her alone he would break down her resistance, especially now that he'd realised that not only his own career but also his future with Louisa was riding on it.

He took a deep breath, smiled at the girl behind the bar and was smitten by a brilliant idea. He leaned forward with a conspiratorial look and instinctively she bent her head to his.

'D'you think it might be possible for me to have a

picnic packed up for this evening?'

She looked at him in surprise. 'For this evening? Well, I don't know. We do picnics for lunch but . . .'

'Please?' he said, using all his charm. 'It's terribly important.'

'Well,' she hesitated. 'It's not usual in the evening, you see. Dinner's served in the dining room.'

'I know.' He held on to his patience and lowered his voice a little. 'The thing is . . . look, I'll be absolutely honest with you. My wife ran out on me and I've come down to try to persuade her to come back. There's my little boy, you see . . .' He allowed an anguished look to hover on his face and shrugged his shoulders helplessly.

She looked distressed. 'Oh, I *am* sorry. Oh dear.'

'Well, you see what I mean?' He gestured behind him at the other guests. 'I can hardly talk to her privately here and I don't know the area. I thought that we could take a picnic out on the moor somewhere. More romantic.' He smiled at her. 'I need all the help I can get.'

'It's just that they'll be busy in the kitchen . . .' She took in his woebegone expression and made up her mind. 'Hang on a sec.'

She let herself out of the bar and hurried down the passage to the kitchen. Robert smiled to himself. Really, it was almost *too* easy. When she returned he looked at her hopefully and she smiled at him and gave him a little wink.

'It'll be simple food, mind,' she whispered, hurrying to serve a waiting customer, 'nothing special. And don't let on to anyone.'

He winked back at her and glanced again at his watch.

By the time Pippa arrived the hamper was stowed away in his car and he'd had a chance to study the map.

She paused in the doorway, looking for him, and he had time to assess her and gauge her mood before she saw him. His first feeling was relief that she'd changed her clothes. She wore a white broderie anglaise shirt with a long navy-blue and white skirt that fitted over her hips and swirled around her ankles. On her bare feet she wore flat leather sandals. Her expression was a mixture of expectation and fear and it was with confidence – well hidden – that Robert went forward to meet her.

'Thank you for coming,' he said, looking deep into her eyes. 'Would you like a drink?'

Pippa glanced round the now-crowded bar and felt the safety afforded by its numbers. 'Yes.' Her voice was husky with nerves and she cleared her throat. 'Perhaps a glass of wine. Thank you.'

There were no tables free and Robert was obliged to leave her standing alone whilst he went back to the bar. He made a little grimace at the girl who grinned at him encouragingly. She'd already decided that his wife must be mad. He paid for the drinks and carried them back to Pippa who was overcome with shyness. She took the glass and sipped at it quickly for something to do. She couldn't look at him. Robert was pleased by these signs. At least she wasn't indifferent.

'I hope you won't be disappointed,' he began, 'but I've organised a picnic.'

She glanced up at him quickly and, as quickly, looked away. 'A picnic?'

'I didn't know where to take you so that we could talk properly,' he explained. His voice was gentle, caressing. 'I *must* talk to you, Pippa. Could we drive out on to the moor somewhere?'

He watched her closely, her hands were trembling a little and her colour was high. Again he felt a surge of confidence . . . but he mustn't rush her. He must be patient, grateful for the least gesture of conciliation.

'Well, I suppose . . .' Her heart was thumping so hard that she could barely speak.

'The hamper's in the car, ready.' He took control for the moment. 'Drink up and we'll get out of this crowd.'

She drank obediently, though she was stiff with terror, and, at last, he took her empty glass, placed it with his own on the bar and, with a last wink at his helpful accomplice, led the way out.

'You bought yourself a car, then?' she asked in a high, unnatural voice as he started the engine.

'It's hired,' he told her as he drove out of the car park. 'I haven't needed one until now. I'm hoping that you can direct me to somewhere fairly secluded.'

The thought of being secluded with him was so daunting that she was unable to answer him and it was he who pulled off the Princetown road on to a track that he'd found on the map whilst he'd been waiting for her. He backed the car into a long-abandoned small quarry and switched off the engine. They sat for a moment gazing out over the moor and away into Cornwall where the high peaks of Bodmin Moor dominated the distant horizon. The west was blazing with the approaching sunset and their eyes were dazzled although neither was aware of the beauty before them. He turned to her, staring at her profile until she coloured under his steady gaze.

'This is the most difficult thing I have had to do,' he said softly. 'How can I possibly make you believe me? I feel as if I have been living through a kind of nightmare and I've suddenly woken up. It's been like a sickness. An obsession.'

'So it *was* Louisa,' said Pippa slowly, still staring ahead.

'Oh yes,' said Robert indifferently, almost dismissively. They'd agreed that this must be admitted. 'Of course it was. She made a set at me and for some reason I was just bowled over by her. I'm sorry,' he added quickly as Pippa made a convulsive movement. 'I'm really sorry. I lied and cheated and behaved appallingly.' He put a hand to his head as though bemused. 'I can't explain it. Not even to myself. I was mad. Bewitched. And then I woke up.'

'Have you been living with her?' asked Pippa. She needed to know the facts before she could take in what he was telling her.

'Good heavens, no!' he said at once. 'I wasn't quite *that* possessed. And anyway, it wasn't like that. I never thought of her in terms of marriage or a serious relationship. It was as if the world had turned inside out. You and Rowley became unreal to me. How can I explain it?' He shook his head desperately. 'I can't. You can't explain madness.'

Pippa was silent and he wondered what she was thinking. Had he been convincing? He cursed inwardly and touched her lightly on the arm. She leaped away from him as though he'd bitten her and he gritted his teeth in irritation.

'Sorry,' she said, and folded her arms across her breast. 'It's just . . . too quick. I mean . . . it's so,' she hunched her shoulders, 'so unbelievable. Isn't it?'

He thought quickly. 'Of course it is. Didn't I just say so? But what more can I say? I know exactly what the word "bewitched" means now and I feel angry.'

'Angry?' She looked at him at last, frowning.

'Of course I do!' he cried and slapped the steering wheel. It was time for a touch of frustrated violence. 'How d'you imagine I feel? It's as if I've been cheated out of ten months of life. As if I've been in a coma or something. I come out from some kind of spell and find I've lost my wife and child! How d'you *think* I feel?'

He stared out over the steering wheel which he'd grasped in both hands, arms stretched to the full. He'd made his expression deliberately grim, his voice deliberately loud, and Pippa huddled back in her corner. Her body, weak and betraying, longed for his touch, but her pride stiffened her spine and held her away from him.

'When did you . . . change?' she asked at last.

He sighed deeply, as though his suffering was so great he could hardly be expected to think clearly. His answer, however, was exact.

'When your letter came,' he told her. It was Louisa who had decided that the letter should be the turning point. 'It seemed to arrive out of the blue like a . . . well, some sort of talisman. And when I read it everything just dropped back into place. It seemed to break the spell. From that moment the affair was over.'

'But I sent that letter weeks ago,' she protested, although

she was moved by what he'd told her.

'Oh my darling.' He shook his head. 'It's taken me this long to get up the courage to see you. When I realised just what a bloody fool I'd been I was too ashamed to bring myself to speak to you.' He gave a mirthless chuckle. 'I walked up and down, raging to myself. It was your letter that gave me hope.' He felt casually inside his jacket. 'Yes, here it is. I've carried it with me ever since it arrived. It's a wonder it's not in pieces I've read it so often.'

He tossed it on to her lap and she sat staring at it. It was folded into a small square, the edges slightly torn, the paper grubby. Robert looked at it from the corner of his eye, remembering Louisa's slender fingers, folding and refolding, smoothing it out, crumpling it a little, making it look well read. After a moment, Pippa picked it up and opened it out.

'You could have telephoned,' she pointed out, recalling how she'd written down the number, hoping. She'd been unbearably moved by the endearment he'd used to her and was touched by the state of the letter.

'I was afraid,' he answered at once, thanking God for Louisa's foresight. She'd thought of everything that Pippa might throw at him. 'It's so easy to misunderstand things on the telephone. I wanted to *see* your face, your reaction. Pippa?' He risked touching her again but this time she stayed perfectly still. 'Your letter gave me hope. Is there still a chance?'

'You said such dreadful things . . .'

Robert bowed his head, outwardly distraught, inwardly furious. Did she want him to crawl on his knees? Probably . . . 'Give her anything she asks,' whispered Louisa's voice.

'It's *worth* it.' He thought quickly, assessing what he knew of Pippa, fairly certain that it was only her pride that was standing between them. He put his head in his hands. Stealing a glance at him, Pippa saw the clenched jaw, saw him swallow. Could he be *crying*? She clasped her hands tightly and tried to decide what she should do.

'It's just . . .' she began in a small voice. 'It's just it might happen again. I mean, how would I know . . .?'

She got no further. Robert dropped his hands and put both arms swiftly round her, pulling her close.

'Oh my darling,' he breathed, 'can you honestly believe I'd be so crazy? Never again! My God! If you *knew* what I've been through.'

At the feel of his arms round her she shuddered violently, desire clouding her judgement and confusing her thoughts.

'I love you,' he murmured, turning her chin up. 'Christ! I've missed you.' He began to kiss her, confidently, passionately and, after an anxious moment, she responded. Keeping his triumph firmly hidden, he held her closely, kissing her, talking to her, until the real danger was past and he knew that the situation was finally under his control.

Chapter Twenty-five

It came as rather a shock to Robert to learn that Pippa was not renting the farmhouse but living there as a paying guest. It made his siege a little more difficult. After her capitulation, early on that first evening, he had fully expected to be asked to bring his things from the hotel and stay with her and Rowley but she made no mention of such a move. At the end of the evening – when they were picking at the contents of the hamper – he suggested that, since he had only a few days' holiday, he spend as much time with them as was possible but at this point Pippa backed off a little. She felt as though she'd been swept off her feet and she needed a little space to think things through. Robert knew exactly what she was thinking and was determined not to give her the chance to strengthen herself against him.

It was at this point that she told him about Frances. Robert thought quickly. Whether he could get *her* on his side rather depended on what type of woman Frances was and how much she had been told. He couldn't risk a scene. He decided that, until his position was more solid, it would be unwise to risk a confrontation. He wanted to follow up his first meeting with Pippa very quickly, however, and Louisa's advice rang constantly in his ears.

'Get her into bed as quickly as you can,' she'd told him, and laughed at his expression. 'You look as if you don't know whether to be shocked or gratified,' she said. 'It's no time for the finer feelings. Of course, if you could get her pregnant . . .'

At the time he *had* been shocked at Louisa's directness, flattered by her insinuation that his prowess in bed would turn the tide in his favour, hurt that she seemed quite unmoved at losing him. Later, he'd convinced himself that this was because she was planning to come back to him, although he was concerned about Pippa becoming pregnant. Surely that was a rather drastic step if he intended to leave her again once his object had been achieved? On the other hand, Pippa loved children and he was prepared to support them . . . He'd kicked his conscience into submission and concentrated on the job in hand.

Pippa, ashamed at having been so easily overwhelmed by Robert's closeness and his explanations, drove home and poured out the whole evening's happenings to Frances who was waiting up for her. The shock of Robert's return had temporarily pushed Frances's preoccupation with Stephen's affair with Cass to the back of her mind. Despite the fact that she had repeatedly assured Pippa that Robert would come back to her, she was unsure of her ground here.

Earlier, whilst she pottered about, listening out for Rowley and wondering what Robert might be saying to Pippa, she tried to put herself in Pippa's position. Overwhelmed with her own misery and anger she knew now that her advice had been simplistic to say the least. All very well to tell Pippa that she should forgive and forget when she had been treated so cruelly but would *she* be able to be as generous? Each time she thought about Stephen and Cass together she felt sick, knowing now exactly how Pippa must have felt about Robert and Louisa.

Frances writhed when she remembered how readily, how smugly, she had given advice. How easy it had been to theorise about Pippa's situation; how simple to urge a generosity that she, herself, was very far from feeling now. Although she longed to know what excuses Robert might be offering, she almost dreaded Pippa's return. She knew that Pippa had been surprised at her reaction to Stephen's infidelity. So definite had Frances been, so ready to give her opinions, that Pippa had been naturally shocked to discover that Frances had no intention of practising what she preached. It had been an embarrassment for both of them.

When Pippa had at last appeared, everything was exactly as Frances had feared. She was confused, excited, defiant and fearful in turns and Frances, for once, was at a loss for words. Pippa required support – but for what was not quite clear. Frances watched her struggles sympathetically and anxiously. Part of Pippa wished to believe Robert absolutely; part wished to punish him. Part of her wanted to accept him back unconditionally and with relief; part of her was too proud to be able to do so. What *ought* she to do?

At last the question was asked outright and Frances stared across the table at her; too afraid to answer. She no longer felt qualified to pontificate upon the problems of other people. Her old confidence – that she 'knew best' – had been shaken and she looked into Pippa's pleading eyes and was silent. Pippa struggled on a little longer; asking questions, answering them herself and punctuating them with cries of indignation. At this safe distance from his charm she could despise herself for the weakness of the flesh.

'Do you . . . do you still love him?' asked Frances at length, almost fearfully.

'I think so.' Pippa stared back at her tragically. 'Oh, what shall I *do*?'

'Don't be rushed,' suggested Frances cautiously. 'You need time to think it over . . . Or . . . Or don't you? Perhaps you feel . . . well, that you can trust him?'

Her timidity was almost comical but Pippa was in no mood to be amused.

'He was quite distraught,' she said, remembering. 'He was in tears at one point. D'you think it's possible to be, well, what he said? You know? Bewitched?'

Frances thought about Cass; her beauty, her charm, her ability to draw men – and women – to her . . .

'Yes,' she said grimly. 'Yes, I *do* believe that there are women who have that power.'

Pippa knew exactly what Frances was thinking. They looked at one another for a long moment.

'Well, then,' said Pippa, at last. 'Well, then . . .'

'It's late,' said Frances, straining her hair back from her worried brow with both hands. 'Let's sleep on it, shall we? Shall you be able to sleep?'

'I don't know,' said Pippa. She shook her head and tried

to smile. 'Silly, isn't it? I've spent all these weeks longing to have him back and now he is I'm playing hard to get.'

'You've got to be certain.' Frances gave her a good-night hug. 'It's one thing to imagine something. It's a bit different when it becomes reality.'

'I'm taking Rowley to see him tomorrow. I'll see how we get on as a family again.'

Pippa wandered out into the hall and Frances watched her climb the stairs before she went back into the kitchen to tidy up.

Frances's confidence received a further blow the following morning when Annie telephoned. Pippa and Rowley had just left so Frances was able to tell Annie the whole story of Robert's return. Her reaction was startling.

'Oh no!' she cried. 'She's not thinking of going back to him, is she?'

When Frances gave a faithful report of the previous evening's happenings Annie gave another wail of despair.

'For heaven's sake!' cried Frances, her nerves worn thin by worry. 'Do you know something we don't know? You were never like this before when we talked about it.'

'I never thought he'd come back!' retorted Annie. 'I never liked him and neither did Perry. I just know it would be disastrous. What's he up to, anyway?'

'What d'you mean – "up to"? He says that he was bewitched by this woman and now he's seen sense and, if you ask me—'

'I've never heard such nonsense,' said Annie roundly, her anxiety for Pippa making her more outspoken than usual.

'"Bewitched" indeed! Of course, it's a good excuse if Pippa's daft enough to believe it!'

'Just a minute,' said Frances, who'd been clinging desperately to Robert's explanation, hoping that something similar might be the reason for Stephen's behaviour, 'I don't see why we should totally discount it.'

'Oh, honestly! Well, be careful, Frances, that's all. I know you've been preaching love and forgiveness to her and all I can say is, I hope you're prepared to behave with the same mindless generosity to Stephen. I haven't noticed quite such sweetness and light on *your* part.'

She put down the receiver with a determined click, leaving Frances both hurt and cross.

'Well!' she said, and sat down with a bump. 'Honestly!' she cried . . . and burst into tears.

Presently, having had a good weep into some kitchen towel, she pulled herself together a little and stared around the deserted kitchen. She simply couldn't sit here brooding – but what could she do? Where could she go? Suddenly she thought of Hugh. With all these dramas, his problems had been pushed to one side and she felt an overwhelming desire to see him. He, at least, would be kind to her.

Hugh, immersed in more calculations and wondering if they might be eligible for a grant to help with the stable block, viewed his mother's arrival with a certain amount of alarm. Max was shopping in Ashburton and Hugh went out to greet her with an air of bravado. Since his father's telephone call he no longer had any fears for his future; nevertheless he would have preferred not to have to confront his mother until everything was finally settled.

He saw that she was looking weary and drawn and he felt a concern for her which outweighed his nervousness.

'How are you?' he asked, kissing her. 'You look a bit tired. Is Rowley keeping you awake at nights?'

'If only it were as simple as that,' she said, trying to smile but her lips shook a little. Driving over, she'd allowed her misery to get out of hand; imagining Stephen with Cass and convinced that their own marriage was finished. 'Oh Hugh, I feel so miserable,' she said childishly.

Hugh looked at her anxiously, half fearful that this was some new ploy to bring him to heel, but she looked so unhappy that he took her arm.

'What's up?' he asked. 'Come on in and let me make you some coffee. I'm working in the caravan this morning.'

She followed him up the steps and watched him light the gas and put the kettle to boil. The caravan was nearly as tidy as when Max had been using it. The bunk was made up and things tucked away neatly in their proper places.

'Now then.'

He sat down opposite, bundling his paperwork to one side across the rickety table, and smiled at her. She felt her resolve that he should not be involved weaken and she stretched a hand to him, needing comfort.

'Your father's having an affair,' she told him, and saw him stiffen with shock and rejection at the idea. Immediately she was filled with horror at herself, wishing the words unsaid. 'With Cass Wivenhoe,' she cried, as though that justified her telling him, frightening him.

'With *Cass*!' exclaimed Hugh, and shook his head. 'I don't believe it.'

He was so positive that Frances was silenced for a moment. The kettle began to sing and Hugh stood up and collected two mugs. She stared at him, mesmerised by his steady movements.

'But he was seen,' she said at last, determined that now he knew he should be convinced. 'By two separate lots of people, in two separate pubs. They were meeting secretly.'

'I know,' said Hugh calmly as he put a mug down on the table in front of her. 'But they weren't having an affair.'

She shut her eyes for a moment. Suddenly she felt terribly tired, quite unequal to telling him about Stephen's silly infatuation with Cass. Best, perhaps, that he should not believe it. She felt exhausted and alone and unhappy.

'The thing is,' Hugh was saying slowly, 'they were meeting to talk about me.'

Frances's eyes flew open and she stared at him. 'About *you*?'

Hugh nodded. He looked so calm, so *sure*, that she was puzzled. 'Dad was worried about me when Lucinda left and I was ill. He couldn't think of anything else to do so he spoke to Cass. They were trying to find a way of telling me the truth.'

'The truth?'

Hugh nodded. 'The real truth. About Charlotte but mainly about Cass herself.'

'But what . . .?' Frances shook her head, dismissing this fiction. 'Someone saw them,' she said. 'Kissing. And . . . and things.'

Hugh frowned. He sat for some moments staring at the table and then he nodded. 'I can imagine how it might have looked,' he said. 'But it wasn't like that. Once they started talking about Charlotte, Cass got upset. She was . . . was crying, I think, and Dad was trying to comfort her. It might have looked as if they were . . . well, kissing.'

'And how do you know all this?' asked Frances indignantly. 'Your father's always had a thing about Cass. He's always taken her side. Meeting to talk about you was just a wonderful excuse . . .' She gave a little sob and picked up her coffee mug in an attempt to control herself.

Hugh sat for some time in silence, debating with himself. He knew now why some instinct had prevented him from destroying the letter but still he hesitated, thinking about Cass. He glanced at his mother's face and, without further ado, stood up and went to the locker beside his bunk. He took the letter from its envelope and put it beside her on the table.

'Read it,' he said, 'but you must promise never to mention it to anyone.'

Curiously she unfolded the sheets, frowning over them, turning to the signature at the end and then reading it from the beginning. Hugh sat drinking his coffee in silence until she'd finished. When she looked at him there were tears in her eyes and Hugh nodded, as if in answer to her horror. Frances swallowed and began to refold the sheets but Hugh reached out and took them from her.

'I should have destroyed it,' he said, 'as she asked. But I couldn't bring myself to do it. This letter took away all my guilt. I'm cured now and I feel so grateful to her. It must have been so awful to write all those things down. To expose herself like that so that I shouldn't go on suffering.'

Frances sat quite still, immobilised with shame. She saw the pain that Cass had been hiding and guessed how difficult it must have been to write such a letter.

'Dad phoned.' Hugh was watching her. 'He said you weren't speaking to him but he thought it was because of me. He's really worried.'

'I know.' Frances tried to smile. 'I'd heard these rumours, you see . . .'

'Poor Mum. You got your wires crossed. I can see how it would look. Will you tell him?'

Frances shook her head. 'Not yet, anyway. Perhaps when I feel stronger, when we can laugh about it. So I have Cass to thank for your recovery?'

'Yes. Mainly her, partly all this.' His gesture embraced the caravan, the site and the moor in general. He looked at her. 'Dad says I don't have to go back. He sees my point of view. I wish you could, too. I'd feel so much happier about it.'

Frances turned the coffee mug in her hands. She thought of Cass and of poor dead Charlotte; remembered how desperate Hugh had been, how thin and ill. She thought of how she had misjudged Stephen, how readily she had advised Pippa from a position of utter ignorance, and realised that she might also be wrong about Hugh.

'OK,' she said at last, too tired and confused to hold out any longer. 'Have it your way. I only want what's best for you, you know. It's all I've ever wanted for you.'

'I know.' His eyes were shining. 'It's going to be great. I

just know it.' Instinctively they reached out to each other and hugged awkwardly across the little table. He looked at her affectionately. 'Mum?'

She smiled at him. He looked ridiculously happy and her heart lifted as the shock of Cass's revelations subsided a little. 'What is it?'

'Why don't you phone Dad? Now. I've got his office number and he'd be so relieved to hear from you. Why don't you?'

'Why don't I?' echoed Frances, and a great joy began to well within her, driving out the pain and hurt.

She saw Hugh's relief as he scrabbled amongst his papers for his address book and together they went out into the sunshine, across the yard to Max's office and the telephone.

Chapter Twenty-six

As soon as she had slammed the receiver back on its rest, Annie was seized with a terrible compunction.

'Damn and blast!' she muttered to herself, going to pour herself a large Scotch, despite the fact that it was barely midday.

She wandered with it out into the courtyard, sat down and stared morosely at nothing whilst she sipped. The sensation of guilt was becoming familiar to her and it was this as much as anything which had been responsible for her outburst to Frances. She knew now that, instead of sitting by passively, she should have *talked* to Pippa, encouraged her, been positive about Robert's going. She should have reminded Pippa of her father's dislike of him and his fear that, sooner or later, she would regret marrying him; told her of Perry's reservations and her own mistrust of Robert.

But no! Annie thumped her hand on the arm of the wicker chair and gave an exclamation of pain. No, she had to be her usual aloof self; distancing herself from other people's problems, holding back lest something should be demanded of her. And now she had probably upset Frances as well! It had been an unforgivable thing to say to her in her present state of unhappiness. Nearly weeping with frustration and fury, Annie leaped to her feet and hurried to the telephone. At least she could apologise to Frances. She listened to the bell ringing out and, having given Frances time enough to come from the furthermost point of her establishment, she gave up and went back to her drink.

Surely, she thought, sitting down and drawing up her legs beneath her, surely Pippa wouldn't be stupid enough to go back to Robert?

She thought back over the endless conversations – well, monologues – during which Pippa had poured out her feelings. The sad fact of the matter was that she still loved the bastard! Annie groaned aloud.

'It's your fault,' muttered Annie to Perry's shade. Concern for Pippa made her dissatisfied with herself and she needed a scapegoat. 'I asked for help when I invited her. *You* made me invite her and now see what's happened. Where were you when I needed you?'

She finished her drink and wondered if she might be going out of her mind; screaming at Frances, talking to the dead. She sat quite still, aware of a formless fear in her heart, and remembered Perry's warning. 'Don't trust him for a second.' Once again she shivered, as though at a premonition. But what could she do? She racked her brains, trying to think of what she might say should Pippa tell her that she was returning to Robert. Suddenly she felt cross. Here she was, longing to help, ready to take responsibilities that once she would have rejected, and her mentor was playing hooky! If Perry chose to encourage her from beyond the veil he might at least play fair and give her some ammunition with which to fight these ongoing battles.

'Help!' she commanded. 'Help me, d'you hear, wherever you are?'

She climbed out of her chair and went into the kitchen to refill her glass. Perry, it seemed, was with her after all. He was occupying a favourite spot; leaning against the Rayburn, ankles crossed, head bent in thought.

'I'm frightened,' she told him. 'I've got this awful premonition.'

Perry continued to meditate and Annie rolled her eyes in exasperation, splashing another measure into her glass. Nevertheless she felt strangely comforted; less alone. Suddenly she remembered that, after Perry's death, she'd come across his Bible, bristling with pieces of paper stuck in different pages. There were references to every kind of need; where to look if one was depressed, in danger, in doubt, worried, discouraged, afraid, lonely. Annie had turned the pages slowly, reading passages here and there, and comfort had begun to steal into her heart. She had no doubt that they had been put there lest one day she might need them. Perry knew his Bible far too well to need such references. Often and often had she turned to them for comfort. Perhaps that's what she needed now . . .

'Good idea,' said Perry, disappearing into the hall. 'Of course you're never alone. You know that. "If I take the wings of the morning, and dwell in the uttermost part of the sea; Even there shall thy hand lead me, and thy right hand shall hold me." Take heart, my darling.'

There was silence; presently Annie picked up her glass and went into the sitting room to look up Psalm 139.

* * *

Robert lay on his bed, hands laced behind his head, staring at the ceiling. He couldn't remember when he'd last felt so exhausted. He'd forgotten how tiring it was to be a family man. Making up to Pippa was bad enough; lying to her, fawning over her, playing the part of the erring husband. On top of all this he'd been obliged to play with Rowley, carry him, amuse him, pretend to be enchanted by his observations and distortions of speech. Too late he'd realised that he was not cut out for fatherhood. It hadn't mattered too much previously. He had left home before Rowley was up and about and had taken care to arrive back late enough to avoid the bath-time routine. It had worked well enough.

On his return to the hotel, though, after the long day with both of them he'd had serious misgivings. He missed Louisa, feeling miserable at the thought of a future without her, and was now suffering a severe loss of confidence. His conviction that she would return to him in due course no longer seemed so probable. Suppose she met someone else – someone without a wife and child to support – out in New York? He covered his eyes with his forearm and lay perfectly still.

He simply must not lose sight of the ball. He forced himself to think the whole thing through again very thoroughly. To obtain the coveted position, to fulfil his ambitions, Pippa must be wooed back. He and Louisa had gone over it a thousand times. He dared not take the risk of trying to bluff it out; pretending that Pippa had done the dirty on him. She had too many friends at court who, once the rumours got about, would be only too ready to defend her reputation. That damned Terry Cooper, for one!

Before Robert left London for the West Country he'd had a brief interview with Harrison, during which the great man had actually asked after Pippa and Rowley. Robert had maintained the fiction that she wasn't too well and was staying with a friend in the country, saying that he was going down almost immediately for a few days and hoped to bring her back with him. At which point Harrison had told him that Hannah was coming over shortly and suggested that they all got together for a meal.

Robert shifted on the bed, stretching nervously, his heart beating fast now, as it had beaten then, in terror. It was no use having second thoughts. Whether Louisa returned to him or not, it was essential to his career that Pippa be brought back into the fold. There were ways and means of keeping his input into family life to the minimum. He was beginning to see that a small flat in London would be essential. His increase in salary would help towards paying for it and for the freedom he would require. He would settle Pippa and Rowley in a small house out in the country somewhere. He would find a cottage to charm her – cheaper than the executive house they had bought in Farnham – and encourage her to become involved in village life. Another idea occurred to him. Why shouldn't he gradually reduce his travelling so that he finished up weekending? Pippa had always respected the work ethic, been ready to put his job first, and this new position would be very demanding. There would be social events, of course; enough to show her that he wasn't playing about and to indicate to Hannah and Harrison that they were a happy couple. They could even invite them down to the cottage occasionally . . .

Feeling a great deal happier Robert relaxed, staring once more at the ceiling, improving on his plan. Perhaps Louisa had a point. He'd arrived back at the hotel quite determined that there should be no more children but, given this newly thought out scenario, the more children there were, tying Pippa to her country cottage, the better. He smiled a little. The day had gone very well; very well indeed. He'd hinted that perhaps this Frances woman might be prepared to look after Rowley whilst he and Pippa had some time alone. They could find a little hotel, off the beaten track, and then . . .

Robert's smile grew wider, he breathed more deeply, and soon he was fast asleep.

He had good reason for his complacency. His loving behaviour, his attention to Rowley, his apparent rage at his own inexplicable behaviour, all these were working to soften Pippa's already malleable heart. Pride forced her to be a little distant, not *too* ready to succumb, but her fatal weakness was – had always been – that she loved him. She was too honest, too naïve, to imagine that he could be playing a part.

Whilst Robert lay prone upon his bed plotting their future, Pippa argued it all out with Frances. She told her that, once he was under this spell, Robert had changed completely. She counted it a virtue in him that, having thought that he had stopped loving her, he was unable to make love to her, behave as a husband to her, even be polite to her. It had been beyond him. It proved that Robert was unable to dissemble and must, therefore, now be sincere. The spell had shattered: he was his old self.

Frances, still trying to take in Cass's letter and her own misinterpretation of Stephen's behaviour, remained silent. She no longer felt qualified to judge or advise, although her own private grief and happiness was inclined to bring her down in favour of a reconciliation. After all, it was what she'd always recommended. Whilst Pippa talked on – convincing herself, exonerating Robert – Frances recalled her conversation with Stephen. Her heart glowed with pleasure as she heard his voice again, inside her head, full of delight and relief, telling her how he had missed her, how worried he'd been, how he'd telephoned Hugh in an effort to sort things out . . . Clutching the telephone receiver, Frances had felt weak with love and longing for him. Hugh had disappeared tactfully outside and Frances had been open in her pleasure at the suggestion that he should come home at the weekend. Afterwards she had wished that they could be alone together and laughed at herself, embarrassed at such feelings at her advanced age.

She pulled herself together and found Pippa watching her curiously.

'Are you OK?' she asked. 'I'm sorry. I've been droning on, haven't I?'

'Of course you haven't,' said Frances at once. 'I just wish I could help. I don't know what to say. To tell you the truth, I'm feeling a bit of an idiot.'

'Why? What's been happening?' Pippa took in the brightness in Frances's eyes, her smiling countenance. 'Come on. Spill the beans.'

'I've been such a fool.' Frances shook her head,

reproaching herself. 'I went over to see Hugh after . . .' she hesitated but decided against reporting Annie's observations, 'after you'd gone and he told me that Stephen had been seeing Cass in an attempt to sort out this problem about Hugh feeling responsible.'

'So that was it.' Pippa sounded almost as relieved as Frances had been. 'Oh Frances, you must be so happy.'

'I feel very ashamed,' admitted Frances. 'I've always believed that Stephen had a soft spot for Cass and I'm shocked with myself for being so ready to believe ill of him. And her.' She paused, wondering whether to explain how she'd misjudged Cass, refusing to believe her capable of grief, but remembered Hugh's repeated injunctions for absolute secrecy on certain portions of the letter and resisted. 'She's written to Hugh taking the blame to herself and freeing him of all guilt. It was a very generous letter. She talks of meeting Stephen and I can see now how the rumours got about.'

Pippa wrinkled her brow. 'But why didn't he tell you?' she asked. 'It was risky, wasn't it, doing it so secretly?'

'I've myself to blame for that,' sighed Frances, determined to make reparation where possible. 'I've always been jealous of Cass. She's one of those women. You know? Always looks wonderful. Sexy without trying. Friendly, easy-going.' She shrugged. 'From the beginning I was afraid of her, I suppose. She always made me feel inadequate and dowdy.'

'Sounds like Louisa,' mused Pippa. 'She always made me feel a frump. And she's so intelligent. I can see why Robert fell for her.'

'But she couldn't hold him,' pointed out Frances comfortingly. 'He's come back to you, hasn't he?'

Pippa nodded but she looked anxious. 'I can't decide if I'd ever feel quite safe with him again,' she said sadly. 'That's the trouble. But I'm so pleased for you, Frances, I really am. I must admit I found it almost impossible to believe.'

'He's coming for the weekend,' said Frances happily. 'I spoke to him from Trendlebere. We sort of made it up on the phone but I can't wait to see him. I'm really looking forward to it, silly old fool that I am.'

'Then Rowley and I must get out of your hair,' said Pippa decidedly. 'We'll make ourselves scarce for the weekend. Perhaps Annie will have us.'

'Don't be silly,' said Frances at once, although her heart jumped a little at the thought of being alone with Stephen. 'I wouldn't dream of it.'

'Actually,' Pippa's cheeks were flushed, 'Robert suggested that we might have a couple of days on our own. Although I have the feeling that he meant just the two of us. He was wonderful with Rowley,' she added defensively, lest Frances should jump to conclusions. 'It's just that . . . Well, you know . . .' Her voice trailed off and her flush deepened.

'Well, of course I understand,' said Frances quickly. 'It's perfectly natural that he should want you to himself. It's just . . . I mean I was wondering how *you* felt about it. Whether you felt ready . . .' She floundered to a halt, each now as embarrassed as the other.

'I think I would,' said Pippa in a small voice, staring at

the tablecloth. 'I love him, you see. I can't seem to help it, but I feel so awful. So ashamed.'

'Why should you feel ashamed?' demanded Frances, her heart going out to her. 'He *is* your husband. Why shouldn't you feel all the natural things a woman feels for her husband? Just because he's had a silly five minutes . . .'

She stopped, remembering Annie's words, her own feelings when she thought Stephen had been unfaithful and, lastly, her newly made vows never to interfere again. Pippa, however, was staring at her with bright eyes, her breath a little uneven, her hands locked tightly together.

'Oh Frances, do you think I should? Just to see how I feel. It would help me make up my mind, wouldn't it?'

'Yes,' said Frances baldly, throwing caution to the wind at the sight of the happiness on Pippa's face. 'We'll have Rowley. No, no protests. He'll be fine with us and he won't be in our way at all. Stephen and I will have plenty of time on our own. I insist!'

Before Pippa could protest the telephone rang. Frances went to answer it and presently returned. 'It's Annie,' she said. 'Would you like a few words?'

She smiled to herself as Pippa hurried out into the hall. Annie had been apologetic about her earlier outburst and Frances had been careful to say nothing about Pippa. She'd told Annie the glad news about Stephen and been very ready to pass her over to Pippa. If Annie had any views about that situation it was best that she told them to Pippa herself. When Pippa came back into the kitchen, however, she looked just as radiant as when she'd left it.

'Everything OK?' asked Frances.

'Mmm.' Pippa nodded, then frowned. 'She was a bit odd, actually. Sort of . . . tongue-tied, if you know what I mean. Not like Annie, really. Anyway,' she shrugged the problem aside, 'shall we have a drink?'

'Good idea,' said Frances readily. 'Are you seeing Robert this evening?'

'No.' Pippa was fetching the glasses. 'We had a good day and I decided an evening apart was probably sensible. I feel I'm being a bit rushed. I don't want to look too eager. I have my pride. What's left of it.'

Chapter Twenty-seven

The morning after Frances's visit to Hugh, a smart-looking estate car edged its way down the track and came to rest beside Max's Land Rover. Max and Hugh, who were out in the yard, stared at it and glanced at one another questioningly. It was Hugh who hurried forward when he realised who their visitor was.

'It's Cass,' he cried over his shoulder. 'Cass Wivenhoe.'

Max, who had heard about Cass – first from Frances, then from Hugh – stood his ground. He watched the tall woman hug Hugh; noticed how the thick fair hair was caught back from her face, saw the slim long legs and the voluptuous breasts, and realised he was holding his breath. Annoyed with himself, he half turned towards the house – after all, he had work to do – but Hugh was calling to him, leading Cass forward to be introduced. Max looked into her dark blue eyes and had the horrid feeling that she knew exactly what he was thinking as he held out his hand.

'This is Max Driver,' Hugh was saying enthusiastically. 'I told you about him in my letter.'

'The devil you did!' exclaimed Max, caught off guard. 'I deny everything,' he said to Cass and she laughed.

'*Nulli secundus*,' murmured Hugh provocatively. 'That's how I described you to her.'

Max looked at Cass, torn between showing his ignorance or bluffing it out.

'Shall I embarrass you,' she asked, still laughing, 'by telling you that he praised you to the skies?'

'"Second to none",' translated Hugh, grinning. 'That's what I said.'

'Well, now that I feel a right fool,' said Max grimly, 'I'll leave you to talk. I've got work to do.'

'No, no. Please don't go,' said Cass, serious now. 'I've got a proposition to make to you and I'm feeling very nervous about it. I didn't mean to upset you.'

'You haven't upset me,' said Max, feeling churlish and wondering what on earth she could have to say to him. 'Shall we go inside? Hugh can make some coffee.'

He cast a quelling glance at the still-grinning Hugh and ushered Cass into the kitchen. The Mutt, exhausted by an earlier – and unsanctioned – rabbiting expedition, staggered to his feet and came to greet her.

She bent to stroke him and then stood looking about her. 'You know,' she said, 'Hugh described it all so minutely in his letter that I feel that I've been here before. It's wonderful. All of it. A brilliant idea.'

She smiled at Max who felt ridiculously elated by her approval and, to prevent himself from grinning foolishly back at her, ordered the Mutt back to his bed by the Aga.

'I hope it is.' He indicated a chair and she sat down at the table. 'The bookings are coming in but we can't find a cook-housekeeper. You don't know anyone, I suppose?'

'Not offhand,' said Cass thoughtfully, 'but I'll think about it. I suppose it's seasonal work?'

'It is a bit.' Max sat down opposite. 'Although it looks as if we'll be doing weekend courses through the winter. That's the problem, really. We can't tell how it will go and not many people are prepared to just try it for size.'

'Hugh says that you were going to build a flat for whoever took the position?'

'That's right. There's an area above each of the dormitories. I'd budgeted for one of them but since we've no takers I've offered it to Hugh. It looks as if we'll have to make do with local people. On shift, perhaps.'

'I'd love to look around after we've had our coffee,' said Cass, smiling her thanks to Hugh as he passed her a mug and put the sugar bowl beside her. 'But the thing that interested me most was the stable block.'

Max frowned, puzzled at this statement. 'How so?'

'Well, as soon as I read Hugh's letter I had an idea.' Cass stirred sugar into her coffee and looked from one to the other of them. 'Has Hugh told you that my daughter died in a riding accident?'

'Yes,' said Max, caught off guard. 'That's to say—'

'Good,' said Cass. 'So I don't have to go into details. Well, my proposition is quite simple. Tom and I would like to donate a sum of money towards the stable block, in memory of Charlotte.'

The two men stared at her speechlessly. She glanced at them and then looked down into her gently swirling coffee. 'Charlotte loved horses,' she said quietly, reminiscently. 'She adored riding, and she loved Dartmoor, and this struck me as a wonderful way of remembering her. I do hope you'll consider it.'

She looked directly at Max who, for some reason, felt almost resentful. Taken aback by her offer, moved by her suggestion, he thrashed about trying to analyse his antagonism.

'I know what you're thinking.' She was watching him, her eyes sympathetic. 'You feel I'm muscling in on your project, don't you? If you accept this money it won't be *your* thing any more, *your* achievement. I knew you'd feel like that.'

'It's exactly how I feel,' he answered, astonished at her for understanding and at himself for admitting it. 'Silly, isn't it?'

'Not at all.' She shook her head. 'You must have dreamed about this for years. It'll be very hard to share it.'

Max looked at Hugh, who had remained silent. 'I don't mind *him*,' he said, attempting a lighter tone. 'He's muscled in and almost taken the whole bloody thing over. Daren't do a thing without consulting him. The stables were his idea.'

'He didn't tell me that,' said Cass. 'And don't get the wrong idea. This isn't a conspiracy. Hugh is as taken aback as you are.'

Max began to laugh. He wasn't used to people who spoke his thoughts before he'd barely thought them. 'I'm glad to hear it,' he said.

'I certainly am,' declared Hugh, drawing a deep breath. 'Honestly, Cass. It's . . . it's an amazing idea.'

'And a very generous one,' said Max. 'But really . . .'

'Oh, please,' begged Cass. 'Don't turn me down out of hand. At least consider it. You can't think what it would mean to us. It would be such a wonderful memorial. All those children, riding out over the moor, as she used to do . . .'

She broke off, swallowing hard and drank some coffee. The two men stared at her in horror and she smiled at their expressions.

'Don't worry,' she told them, 'I don't intend trying to blackmail you by bursting into tears. It's just . . .' She shook her head and then leaned forward. 'You know what it's like,' she said directly to Max. 'The idea came in a flash and I've fallen in love with it. I can't bear to let it go. No one need know but ourselves.'

Max scraped at his jaw with his fingers and tried to stop feeling dog-in-the-mangerish. It was a wonderful offer.

'I have to admit that it would be a godsend,' he said frankly. 'There's always more expense than you think there's going to be in this sort of venture and every little helps. What sum . . .?' He hesitated a little. 'What sum did you have in mind?'

Cass named an amount and both men drew in their respective breaths.

'Golly!' murmured Hugh, biting his lip to stop himself from beaming.

'That's a very generous amount,' began Max.

'The thing is,' said Cass eagerly, sensing that he was weakening, 'my old pa left a sum in trust for each of my children. They each get the same amount. We've been wondering what we should do with Charlotte's, which becomes available in November. She would have been eighteen years old.' She paused and then shook her head. 'It's all too late for her, of course, but it would mean so much to us.'

'It's more than we need,' said Max gently, moved by her sadness.

'Does that matter?' she asked pleadingly. 'Couldn't you use it for other things as well? You've got to buy horses, haven't you? Or it could go towards building the two little flats, in case you get someone applying for the post? Or you could just invest it against later costs?'

'I don't know what to say,' said Max, at last, and glanced at Hugh who, at the mention of Charlotte's eighteenth birthday, had lost any desire to smile. 'What do you think?'

'I think it's a wonderful idea,' he answered soberly. 'It would be a great help to us financially, there's no point in denying that, and I think it would be a lovely thing to do. This whole idea is about children and for children and I think that a memorial is exactly right. Charlotte would have been absolutely thrilled to think that she was being remembered in such a way.'

Cass smiled into her coffee but Max caught the flash of tears in her eyes. 'Poor Max,' she murmured. 'It's not as if you even knew her.'

'But I agree with Hugh,' he said, and was rewarded by the expression on her face as she looked swiftly up at him.

'Does that mean that you accept?' she asked.

'I accept,' he said, holding out his hand to her.

She took it in her own and held it tightly. 'Bless you,' she said, and dropping his hand, covered her face with both of her own. 'Sorry,' she said, muffled. 'I'm just so happy.'

Hugh and Max exchanged glances and Max jerked his head towards the kettle. Hugh leaped up with alacrity and began to fill it from the tap whilst Max spoke at random about the stable block and where they hoped to build.

'There's some old sheds there already,' he said, his gaze fixed firmly on the wall above Cass's head. 'So there's no problem with planning permission. We'll have some more coffee and then we'll show you round. You ought to know what is going to happen to your money.'

'No,' said Cass, blowing her nose, and swallowing hard. 'That's just what I don't want. The money is yours to do what you want with. You don't have to explain or to account for it. As long as it's going towards giving children a happy time on the moor I don't want to know.'

'But you'll come and see us?' asked Hugh anxiously, taking her mug and refilling it. 'You'll come and see how it all looks when we've finished?'

'Of course you must,' said Max, blessing Hugh silently. 'If we promise not to consult you, you must promise to come and see the results. You and Tom.'

'We should love to come,' said Cass, laughing now. 'Thank you. As long as you . . .' She hesitated and Max raised his eyebrows.

'As long as I . . .?' he prompted.

'There must be no feeling of obligation,' she said to him. 'Remember that you're doing us a very great favour.'

He knew that she didn't want him to feel differently about his project; that she would have hated it if their bequest spoiled his own feelings of achievement.

'It's a deal,' he promised. He lifted his mug as if to toast their pact but in reality to hide his expression. 'To the stable block,' he said.

'Anyway,' said Hugh behind him. 'You'll have to come again to sort out the details. Gosh! This is really exciting!'

'Drink up,' said Max, who had regained his composure. 'We'll show you round and you can be thinking of some nice girl who'd like to join us.'

'I should have thought,' observed Cass, with a return of her old provocative manner, 'that any single girl would jump at it.'

'So did we,' said Max regretfully. 'Obviously Hugh and I don't have what it takes.'

'Don't you believe it,' said Cass. 'The fact is that the modern girl has no sense of adventure. Now what you should be looking for is a woman of my age . . .'

'You're on,' said Max instantly, and all three burst out laughing. 'Come on. Let's be having that guided tour.'

They showed her round, revelling in her admiration, and persuaded her to stay to lunch. When she finally drove away they watched her go with a feeling of deflation. Max sighed and Hugh glanced at him mischievously.

'Nice, isn't she?' he asked provocatively.

'Nice?' repeated Max. '*Nice*? Can't you think of a better word than that with all your fancy education? Nice!'

'*Nulli secundus*?' suggested Hugh slyly, ducking out of reach as Max aimed a blow at his head.

'It'll make one hell of a difference,' he said thoughtfully, as Hugh bobbed back again beside him. 'It's odd though, isn't it? I should have divided it amongst the rest of my kids if I'd been her.'

'I think it's a lovely idea,' said Hugh evasively, unwilling to betray Cass's terrible remorse. 'Oh Max! We'll have to do our sums all over again. We'll be able to do the flat. Probably both of them if we're careful.'

'She's obviously very grateful to you for looking after Charlotte,' remarked Max. 'I think she's trying to thank you too, if you get my meaning.'

Hugh blushed. 'She's done enough for me already,' he muttered.

Max laughed. 'I've never felt so happy about losing half a day's work. Come on. Let's do some costings so that we can see exactly where we are.'

Chapter Twenty-eight

Annie's telephone conversation with Pippa left her feeling even more uneasy. First Frances had talked, full of joy to find that she'd completely misread the situation with Stephen, tactfully ignoring Annie's earlier outburst; then Pippa had spoken to her . . . Now, on Sunday, with lunch over, Annie – roaming the house, staring out of windows, fiddling with ornaments and plumping cushions – tried to dispel the weight that was pressing on her heart.

'But what could I have said?' she cried desperately, as though she had been accused.

Pippa's voice had been light, breathless, excited; she and Rowley had just spent a wonderful day with Robert: he was terribly miserable and ashamed of his behaviour; yes, she promised not to come to any sudden decision . . . Annie took a deep breath and, going into the sitting room, curled up in Perry's chair.

'What could I have done?' she asked him for the hundredth time. 'How could I tell her that I felt that you were warning me against Robert? On what grounds could I have forbidden her to go back to him? Perhaps he *is* sorry. How can I take the responsibility of deciding?'

Silence. Annie sighed deeply, almost self-pityingly. The whole thing was quite ridiculous: Pippa was a grown woman and capable of making her own decisions but somehow this fact was not as comforting as it should have been. Unable to bear inaction any longer, Annie got to her feet, collected her bag, changed her shoes and went to fetch the car.

As she drove out of Ashburton and up towards the moor, it suddenly occurred to her that she would visit Hugh: see this adventure training school that Frances had talked about and meet Max Driver, who had saved her from the snow. As Annie turned right at Welstor Cross and drove up on to the open moor, she caught her breath. A great sea of purple heather blazed in the early September sunshine; the yellow flowers of the gorse burned brightly. It was almost gaudy, thought Annie, gazing about her in delight. The earthy colours of peat and granite, the bleached grasses of late summer, all seemed to have been submerged beneath this wash of colour. White cushiony clouds, gold tinged, bowled gaily before the westerly breeze and the rowan's berry was vivid against the pale blue of the sky. The clouds cast indigo shadows which, fleeing across the rocky outcrops, made a startling contrast with the gay patchwork of gorse and heather.

Imperceptibly, Annie's heart lifted and she turned towards Trendlebere with a feeling of expectation. Leaving the car on the track, she stared out over the woods of Lustleigh Cleave and the small quiet fields, where the stubble glowed in the sunshine, and turned to see the sea, sparkling on the far horizon.

'What a place,' she said to the man who had materialised beside her. 'What a wonderful, wonderful place!'

'So glad you like it,' said Max drily. He was becoming accustomed to women driving down his track: Frances, Pippa, Cass – and now this tall, lean woman, dressed in old jeans, with her greying hair tied back beneath a spotted handkerchief. 'I don't think we've met?'

Annie turned to him quickly. 'I'm so sorry. I was completely carried away. You must be Max. I'm Annie Grayshott. I've come to see Hugh.'

'He has a great many friends,' said Max politely.

Annie looked at him sharply. 'Are we all driving you mad?' she asked. 'Coming over and nosing about? I'm sure Frances and Pippa have been. Frances especially.'

'She's been concerned about Hugh,' replied Max evasively, knowing that these two women were friends, 'but I suppose she approves of me at last.'

Annie chuckled. 'She always approved of *you*,' she said meaningfully – and rather disloyally.

'Hugh's not here,' said Max, not too sure of his ground. 'He's gone off for a walk. The weather was too much for him to resist and, after all, it is Sunday. He can't work all the time.'

'When you love what you're doing it ceases to feel like work,' said Annie, her eyes on the view. 'Don't you agree?'

'I certainly do,' said Max, hesitating a little. 'Shall I show you round in his absence?'

'I should love to see it all,' said Annie, 'but I don't want to distract you from the job in hand. To tell you the truth . . .' She paused and he watched her rather anxiously. Did she, too, have some ulterior motive for her visit? Was he about to be offered another bequest? He felt an hysterical urge to laugh wildly. 'I'm very worried,' said Annie, almost crossly, and stared out again towards the sea.

'Ah,' said Max, somewhat helplessly, losing all desire to laugh and cursing Hugh silently. 'Would you like to come in and wait for Hugh? I've no idea how long he might be. Perhaps you'd like a cup of tea?'

If Annie noticed the slight reluctance in his manner she gave no sign of it. 'Thank you,' she said. 'A cup of tea would be lovely.'

Max turned towards the house, wondering if it would have been more sensible to open a restaurant. There seemed to be a constant procession of people passing through his home, all in need of refreshment. Annie made the usual noises of appreciation at the sight of the kitchen and then stood beside the table, lost in thought. Max made the tea without attempting conversation and presently she looked at him.

'Have you ever felt that something's wrong?' she asked. 'Really wrong. You know? Here.' She thumped her breast. 'So that your heart feels heavy and you feel weighed down by care?'

Max sighed inwardly. What had happened to his quiet bachelor existence? First Hugh had come, getting under his guard and taking up residence, and bringing with him, as it were, a whole string of women with their attendant problems. He thought of Frances with her anxious frown and her fears for Hugh; then Pippa with her vulnerable face and lack of confidence, both of which had wakened previously dormant protective instincts. Cass had moved him with her beauty and her generosity and her sadness for her dead daughter; and now . . .

Annie was watching him hopefully. 'Do you know what I mean?'

'I think I do.' He prodded at the tea-bags, praying for inspiration and wondering why women were so complicated. 'Is it . . .? Is it about Hugh?'

'Oh no!' said Annie at once, and he felt a wave of relief. 'No, it's about Pippa.'

'Pippa,' said Max thoughtfully – and took the tea-bags from the mugs and dropped them in the waste bin.

Annie watched, distressed. She preferred Earl Grey in the afternoon, made in a pot with real tea and drunk from a bone china cup with an accompanying saucer. The sight of Max pounding a tea-bag to death in a pottery mug was an alarming sight but she smiled at him hastily, as he turned. After all, she had burst in on him unceremoniously, distracting him from his work with her problems, and she must be grateful.

'Yes. Pippa.' Annie took the mug and glanced at the contents fearfully. 'Do you know about her situation?'

'Yes,' said Max reluctantly, having no wish to discuss it. 'But . . .'

'My dead husband couldn't stand Robert, you know.' Annie sipped the tea cautiously and blinked once or twice, rapidly. 'Did you know that the wretched man is back on the scene?'

For one bizarre moment Max wasn't sure to which man she referred. 'He's trying to wheedle her back to him,' said Annie, making it clear. 'God knows what lies he's telling her but I know it'll be disastrous if she goes back to him.'

'I see.' Max stirred his tea.

'But what can I *do*?'

'I don't see that you can do anything,' he said unhelpfully. 'I don't think you should interfere in other people's lives.' He remembered the look on Pippa's face on the two occasions that Rowley had called him 'Daddy'. 'After all, she still loves him, doesn't she?'

Annie looked at him in surprise. 'She thinks she does,' she said at last, grudgingly.

Max laughed. 'It's always dangerous, judging other people's marriages.'

'I know that,' she said impatiently.

'So what's your problem?'

'It's Perry,' she told him. 'He keeps telling me that it's wrong. Warning me.'

'Who's Perry?' asked Max, at a loss.

'My husband,' said Annie, and sighed deeply.

'I thought you said he was dead,' said Max sharply.

'He is,' said Annie. 'But he still tells me things, if you know what I mean. I hear his voice quite plainly sometimes. It's very real.'

Max shut his eyes for a moment and breathed deeply. This was all he needed: a nutter who talked to a dead husband . . . Hugh burst into the kitchen with the Mutt at his heels.

'Annie!' he said. 'How nice to see you. Has Max been showing you round? Great, isn't it?'

'I haven't seen anything yet,' admitted Annie, returning his hug. 'I've been boring poor Max to death with my worries about Pippa.'

'Pippa?' Hugh dragged a chair up to the table and sat down whilst the Mutt drunk deeply at his water bowl. 'What's wrong with Pippa?'

'Robert is back,' said Annie succinctly.

'Oh no,' said Hugh. 'She's not going back to him, is she?'

Max stared at him. 'What do you know about it?' he asked.

'Oh, I've talked to her a bit and Mum told me what he did. He's an absolute bastard, isn't he, Annie?'

'A shit of the first water,' said Annie gloomily and Max opened his eyes at her. 'He's come to get her back. And I keep getting this warning from Perry that she mustn't go back to him. I don't know what to do.'

'Oh hell,' said Hugh, duly impressed. Like Pippa, he had no difficulty in believing in Perry's continuing presence. 'What does Perry say?'

Max covered his face with his hands and swallowed down an urge to burst into hysterics. Were they quite mad? . . . Or perhaps it was he who was the crazy one?

'It's this heavy feeling,' Annie was explaining. 'I just know it's wrong. But what can I do?'

'What d'you think, Max?' Hugh turned to him eagerly and Max took another deep breath.

'I've already told Annie,' he said carefully, 'that there's nothing anyone can do. It's Pippa's life and . . . she loves him.'

Annie and Hugh stared at him in silence and then looked at each other. Hugh drew down the corners of his mouth, as if disputing Max's reasoning, and Annie raised her eyebrows.

'But if she's getting these warnings—' began Hugh.

'Hugh!' cried Max. 'Perry is dead. I'm sorry,' he said to Annie, who nodded her understanding of his inability to accept the concept of messages from beyond the grave. 'But honestly . . .'

'All the more reason to take notice of him,' declared Hugh. 'He can see what's going on.'

Suppressing an oath, Max slapped his hands down on the table top and pushed back his chair. 'OK,' he said, with ominous calm. 'OK. Let us accept that Annie is being warned – although I should have thought it would be better if Perry warned Pippa – ' there, he thought, I'm at it now! 'but what is she supposed to do? Have you told Pippa how . . . how Perry feels?' he asked her.

Annie shook her head. 'I telephoned,' she said, 'but somehow I couldn't bring myself to . . . well, say it. It sounds rather amazing if you're not used to it,' she admitted with a certain naïveté.

'Oh, surely not!' said Max with heavy sarcasm – and pulled himself together. 'So what next?'

'Well, I was trying to work it out for myself,' said Annie, bravely swallowing her tea as quickly as she could so as to get it over and done with. 'If there *is* something wrong, perhaps I could get to the root of it and expose him, as it were.'

'Sounds reasonable.' Max was making more tea, resigned to this Mad Hatter's tea party.

'Where shall we start?' asked Hugh.

There was a silence. 'If you won't accept that he has returned simply because he's realised his mistake and genuinely wants her back . . .' Max paused, hoping to make his point but the other two gazed at him eagerly, waiting, 'then we must ask ourselves *why* he wants her back?'

He plunged a tea-bag into his mug, raising his eyebrows questioningly at Annie.

'No!' said Annie quickly. 'Oh, no. Thank you so much. That was . . . delicious but one is enough. You think he has an ulterior motive?'

'If you don't accept the first premise,' he said pointedly, 'then there must be another reason. Otherwise, why is he here?'

'Perhaps this other woman has given him the push and he's feeling lonely,' suggested Hugh. 'And then another woman will come along and he'll be off again.'

Max shrugged. 'Your guess is as good as mine. Is there anyone at his office who could throw some light on it?'

Annie looked thoughtful. 'There was the chap who told Pippa about the affair in the first place.' She wrinkled her brow. 'What was his name?' She began to look excited. 'You know, I think you've got a point.'

Max bowed ironically. 'Good. Well if you don't want any more tea, why don't you get Hugh to show you round? The name's more likely to come back to you if you're not thinking about it.'

'That's right,' said Hugh, getting up. 'You'll think of it at three o'clock in the morning. Be sure to write it down before you forget it again.'

'I'll do that,' said Annie, standing up and holding out a hand to Max. 'I'm very grateful to you. For the tea and for listening. And,' she smiled, 'for not mocking about Perry.'

Max flushed. 'It's a pleasure,' he mumbled, and felt a fool, realising that she'd known exactly how he'd felt.

Annie followed Hugh into the sunshine and did the tour of the little empire. He told her about Cass's offer – which Max had no intention of keeping secret – and showed her the site of the new stable block; but, all the while, part of her mind was replaying those early conversations she'd had with Pippa and she was cudgelling her brain for the name of the man who had caught Robert out and shown him up for what he was.

Chapter Twenty-nine

After a great deal of careful consideration Robert decided on absolute luxury for his seduction scene. The school holidays were over and he was able to book a double room with a view across Salcombe harbour and out to sea. He realised that the intimacy of a small place was not needed here. What he required was impersonal service and absolute privacy; he would supply the intimacy. The other advantage to his choice was that the drive would give them time together. After all, what else would they do? It was hardly likely, after the months of unhappiness, followed by months of separation, that they could behave like a happily married couple. He couldn't see them lying on a beach together or browsing round shops. No. Something that isolated them from the rest of the world and gave him the opportunity to talk to her would give him his best chance with her. What better than a long gentle car ride amidst wonderful scenery? He planned to pick her up late enough so that it would be lunchtime by the time they reached the hotel. After that . . .

He had brooded a great deal on what happened after that. He knew that Pippa couldn't carry her drink very well and became relaxed and giggly very quickly. He'd wondered whether he should arrange to have dinner in their room but suspected that it would look too obvious; too much like the big seduction scene. They would have their after-dinner coffee in their room – with a brandy or two – looking out over the harbour and, by that stage, she would be just in the right mood for a bit of gentle persuasion. She was still wavering a little and it was time for him to take complete charge of the situation. He smiled a little contemptuously; it had never been difficult to get Pippa into bed. Louisa now . . . He shook his head, clenching his fists in his pockets. The temptation to telephone her was overwhelming but she'd been firm.

'You never know who might be listening,' she'd said. 'It's too risky.'

'I don't have to phone from the hotel,' he pleaded. 'I can go out and find a box.'

'No.' She'd been adamant. 'Drop me a card when the citadel's been stormed.'

Robert glanced at his watch. They'd agreed that Pippa should meet him at the Bedford, lest Rowley should get worked up when he saw them going off together, and she should be here by now. He turned to pick up his overnight bag, let himself out and ran lightly down the stairs. He left his key at the desk and went out by the back entrance. As he opened the door on to the iron steps he saw Pippa reversing her car into a space at the far end of the car park. He went to meet her, taking her case, slipping an arm around her shoulders.

'I can't tell you how much I'm looking forward to this,'

he muttered in her ear and she shivered a little as he led her over to his car and bundled the cases into the back.

He took the longest route across the moor; up through Princetown, left at Two Bridges and on through Postbridge; turning right at Challacombe Cross, cutting across to Southcombe and dropping down into Widecombe. He'd driven the whole route across to Salcombe the day before, when Pippa had insisted on a day apart from him so as to put her thoughts in order, and had examined the hotel room thoroughly, checked the menu and explored the town. It had been a kind of dress rehearsal.

Pippa sat beside him feeling shy. It seemed so odd to be with him like this. The old ease of familiarity had vanished months before and she felt as she had when she'd first met him. She remembered how she'd felt weak when he looked at her with that sombre, unsmiling stare, her very bones dissolving with longing for him: how her eyes had strayed to his hands, his mouth, his long legs negligently crossed and her heart had raced and her mouth had been dry.

Now, in the car, she felt some of those sensations and she needed to know, beyond any doubt, that he loved her. Sensing her reactions he put out his hand and touched her knee with his finger.

'OK?' he asked gently.

'Mmm.' She nodded, not trusting herself to speak.

'Shall we stop for coffee?'

She shook her head, afraid that her legs wouldn't hold her up. He nodded and drove on through Widecombe and headed for Ashburton. Although Robert made appreciative murmurs of the countryside and the glorious weather and

Pippa assented, neither of them was truly aware of the beauty through which they passed. Both of them had one thought in mind. What would happen later on, after dinner?

Robert was feeling fairly confident and his confidence was increasing as the day wore on. There was no mistaking Pippa's sidelong glances, her shyness, the tremor when he touched her. He was too experienced to misread the signs. The danger lay in the hours in between. Nothing must be allowed to dispel this building up of desire. As for himself, he knew that he could perform quite adequately given the chance; she was certainly pretty enough and desirable enough for that.

Pippa was racked with terror. Knowing that she was to be compared with Louisa, she'd driven into Tavistock in an attempt to find something to wear in the evening. Expecting to see Robert at every turn, she'd fled from shop to shop only to find that the end-of-season sales had nothing to offer her.

Frances had soothed her with the consolation that at least it wouldn't look as if she was dressing up for him. They went through Pippa's clothes together and decided on a long apple-green skirt in delicate lawn. It had a matching crossover top with a low-cut neck and loose sleeves to the elbow. It was a charming outfit and Frances, having washed and ironed it for her, told her she looked perfect in it.

Pippa stared out of the car window, her hands clenched between her knees, and hoped that Frances was right. Today she had worn her jeans and a striped shirt in butcher-blue cotton, which made her eyes look even bluer and set off her tan. If only she could think of something to say: some intelligent conversation. How dull he must find her, after Louisa!

Robert allowed the tension to build, knowing it to be to his advantage. By the time they arrived at the hotel he was enjoying himself. It was flattering to know that Pippa was feeling as she did, despite everything, and he had no qualms now about the future. He wondered if she were still on the Pill but suspected that she'd stopped taking it. She'd always complained that she hated it: that it made her feel sick, made her put weight on. She'd lost weight, no doubt of that, but that could simply be due to her pining for him. He smiled as he followed her into their suite and saw her expression as she took in the size of the room and the view from the window. He'd be sending Louisa that postcard tomorrow, he was certain of it.

After a late lunch, they wandered out into the delightful little town and Robert led the way down the steps to the passenger ferry that plied between Salcombe and East Portlemouth. Pippa was enchanted. On the far side of the river they disembarked and walked along the sandy beach, looking out between the two headlands to the open sea. It was perfect. Presently, Robert took her hand, and in the shelter of some rocks, he cupped her face in both his hands and kissed her long and deep. He laughed with inward exultation at her trembling, and led her tenderly back to the ferry. This was just an aperitif, as it were, to keep her on the boil. He didn't touch her again.

They had tea on the terrace, reading papers and magazines, until it was time to dress for dinner. Pippa, who had been unable to concentrate on a single article or story, was relieved when Robert knocked on the bathroom door and said that he was going down for a drink and that she must take her time and come down when she was ready. He'd showered quickly and, whilst she was running her bath, had dressed swiftly in a pale grey lightweight wool suit. He had no intention of being involved in a scene which might pre-empt the later show. A situation with himself, half-dressed, and Pippa, in a bath towel, might get out of hand.

Pippa heard him go, her feelings a mixture of disappointment and relief. She wanted him so much that she could barely stand up, the longing was so strong. She tried to calm herself as she lay in the bath, taking deep breaths, her eyes closed. There was no doubt that he felt just as she did. He was so tender but beneath the gentle exterior was a will of iron. She remembered it and shivered. Climbing out of the hot, scented water, she wrapped herself in a large fluffy towel and wandered back into the bedroom. The setting sun sent long red fingers to dye the water, its refracted light shivering into a thousand glittering particles. The boats rocked at anchor and the sea birds swooped, crying – such an evocative sound! – as they followed a fishing boat up to its mooring. Glancing down, she saw that Robert had come out on to the terrace, a drink in his hand. He swung round and looked up at their window and, seeing her, raised his glass. She stared down at him and he gazed back, with that long unsmiling look, until she turned back into the room and began feverishly to dress.

Robert made certain that the dinner lasted as long as possible, beginning with sherry for Pippa, continuing with as much wine as he could persuade her to drink and finishing, as he intended, with coffee and brandy up in their bedroom. The food had been excellent and, though neither of them was particularly hungry, they had taken each course so slowly that they had managed to make a good showing. Robert was pleased with his performance. He'd kept the talk away from the office or from Rowley, keeping up the pretence that they were on the brink of an exciting new relationship and that he was absolutely enchanted with her. He had eyes for nobody else, alive to her every wish and whim. Pippa, drugged by desire, and alcohol, abandoned all ideas of further explanations, promises for the future, or their on-going *modus vivendi* and gave herself up to pleasure. As the wine loosened her tongue and relaxed her, she became more talkative, ready to laugh at his jokes and, by the time they went upstairs, he knew the battle was as good as over.

Still he spun it out as long as he could; taking time over the coffee and then lingering over the brandy. Pippa went to the bathroom and, when she returned, he was waiting for her, knowing that the moment was now right and that to delay it any longer could ruin everything. As she moved to gaze out of the window at the water, black now in the moonless night, he put out his arm and drew her towards him. She hesitated for a brief second but he knew now that force would be welcomed; it must be seen to be him making the running so as to ease her pride. He pulled her into his arms, pushing up her chin, kissing her this time with passionate desire. She gasped and he dragged her closer and felt for the ribbons which tied her little shirt. She strained towards him and, as he fumbled, the shirt fell clear of her breasts. He unzipped the skirt and then eased her towards the bed, holding her in one arm, whilst he divested himself of his shirt and trousers.

In a swift practised movement, he swung her on to the bed, pausing to drag off his socks – he'd removed his shoes whilst she'd been in the bathroom – and rolled back across her, pinning her to the sheets with the weight of his body.

He made it last as long as he could, enjoying his reacquaintance with her body whilst she clung to him, all pretence long gone. When it was over, he held her for a while, feeling her tears wet on his cheek and, when he adjudged the moment right, he rolled her on to her back and began to make love to her all over again.

Much later, when she lay deeply asleep, Robert shifted quietly across the bed and padded into the bathroom. Dragging on the shirt and cords he'd worn earlier in the day, he picked up his jacket, slipped on his shoes and let himself quietly out of the room. In the dimly lighted lounge, he sat down at one of the writing tables and took a postcard out of his jacket pocket. On the front was a picture of the hotel and Robert studied it for a moment, made a mark with his pen, turned it over and began to write on the back. When he'd finished he strolled over to the reception desk where the night porter sat.

'Can I help you, sir?' He showed no surprise that Robert should be wandering around at this late hour.

'Got a stamp?' he asked easily.

The night porter disappeared into the small office behind the desk and reappeared with a stamp.

'Thanks,' said Robert. 'Put it on the bill, will you? Room seventy-four.'

He turned away, licking the stamp and affixing it to the corner of the card which he read once again, smiling to himself before he dropped it into the postbox by the front doors.

Chapter Thirty

The weekend passed much too quickly for Frances and Stephen. Frances's overwhelming relief at finding her fears were unfounded, her guilt at having been so ready to misjudge Stephen when he'd been doing his best to help Hugh, a very genuine sympathy for Cass's grief: all these sensations enabled her to throw her reservations to one side and to be as happy and loving as she had ever been with him. Stephen who, despite her telephone call, was expecting to have a battle on his hands regarding Hugh's future, was taken aback to find that she had completely capitulated. Sending up a prayer of gratitude, he determined to make the weekend a special one.

As it happened, Rowley rather added to the fun. Stephen and Frances had been the sort of parents who were at their happiest when the children were small. They enjoyed the bath-time and bed-time routines, picnics, birthday parties and Christmas. Frances especially had loved the early years when the children cuddled up for stories, mispronounced words and each new discovery was seen through the fresh eyes of childhood.

The fact that Rowley adored Frances naturally helped a

great deal. He was disposed to be shy at first, when Stephen arrived, but Stephen, well versed in the ways of children, had stopped off to buy some chocolate buttons and a large red fire engine. Rowley was quickly won over. He and Stephen played an exciting game with the fire engine and the train, using the little figures as passengers and firemen, whilst Frances watched, smiling at Rowley's shrieks of excitement. Stephen arrived moments before Pippa left to meet Robert at the Bedford and she was able to slip away without any fuss whilst Frances and Stephen settled down to keeping Rowley happy.

Since their marriage had rarely been free of the presence of children, neither of them found it too difficult to renew the strong bonds of their love with Rowley at hand. He was too young to understand their private conversation and the occasional displays of their affection merely added to his feeling of security. After lunch they drove to Bellever Bridge where he paddled in the river and played Poohsticks with Stephen, Frances holding on to him tightly from behind lest he should tumble over the parapet into the water below. Whilst he dozed on the rug, exhausted by his activities, Frances and Stephen talked in quiet voices, listening to the chuckle of the water and to the skylarks, singing high above them.

Not a word did Frances say of her suspicions or the rumours she had heard. She had always been quite unable to admit her jealousy, hating the humiliation of it, fearing that it might give him a weapon, but now, as they sat on the sun-warmed rug with Rowley tucked between them, Frances looked at Stephen and knew herself for a fool. His profile, so like Hugh's, was serious as he stared at the sparkling water, hoping for the sight of a dipper, and she felt a surge of love for him. She sat up properly and reached for his hand.

'I've missed you,' she said.

He looked at her quickly. 'If only the wretched house would sell,' he said, 'and we could be together. You know, I've been hoping that Laura Jackson may decide to stay in New Zealand with her daughter. The house would be just perfect for us.'

Frances squeezed his hand tightly. 'That last couple were really interested,' she told him. 'They're coming back for another look on Tuesday.'

Stephen sighed. 'I wish you could be with me but I suppose it would be madness to leave the house empty. Or even with Pippa there.'

'I think so.' Frances released his hand and leaned back on her elbows. 'Not fair to Pippa. I'm sure it won't be long now before it sells.'

They were both silent, both thinking about Hugh, both cautious of raising the subject again. Stephen was unwilling to divulge Cass's part in Hugh's recovery; Frances was not ready to admit that she knew about it. Stephen hoped Frances would assume that Hugh's new-found happiness was due to the fact that he was being allowed to stay at Trendlebere. Stephen had stopped on his way home to see Hugh and talk to Max, and had told Frances about his own feelings over lunch. He'd been impressed with Max, delighted at Hugh's happiness and wellbeing, and was confident regarding the future of the school. Calmly, Frances had agreed with him and Stephen – his arguments and reasoning alike unneeded – relapsed into relieved silence and the moment had passed.

Now, they were reluctant to raise the subject again, fearing to spoil the tranquillity of the day. Frances would have liked to go over the whole thing again, discussing Hugh's prospects and the likelihood of the scheme succeeding, and her hope that Lucinda would return to complete his happiness, but for once she decided that Stephen's contentment should be put before her worries about Hugh and they were saved from the possibility of any further discussion by Rowley waking and demanding his tea. In the opening of the hamper all awkwardness fled and presently they walked together by the Walla Brook, Rowley riding on Stephen's shoulders.

A quiet evening in front of the television completed the day and, when they went to bed, their lovemaking was simply an extension of their happiness, warm, satisfying, familiar, and infinitely healing.

Annie drifted back to wakefulness reluctantly. She had been dreaming of Max and Hugh but this time Perry was with them and they were all trying to find Pippa, who was in some kind of danger. As Annie awoke, she could still hear Perry's voice speaking urgently in her ear.

'Get hold of Terry Cooper,' he was saying. 'He's the chap we need. Terry Cooper . . .'

Annie woke right up and stared at the ceiling. For once, the grief which accompanied such wakefulness was lost in rising excitement. Terry Cooper; that was the name Pippa had mentioned: the man who had told her of Robert's affair, the man with whom Robert was in competition. Annie sat up, clutching the quilt to her breast. Terry Cooper would know why Robert had suddenly appeared again in Pippa's life.

She sat for some moments, amazed at this revelation, and instinctively thought about Max. She knew exactly how he would translate such a happening. He would say that, whilst she slept, her subconscious had come up with the name, remembered from those earlier conversations, and the brain's need for rational explanation had put the words into Perry's mouth in a dream.

Annie knew better. Leaping from bed she hurried to her bag on a nearby chair and scrabbled for her diary. She wrote the name down at the back, fearful that she might forget it, and hurried into her clothes. She was halfway through her muesli when she remembered that she had no idea of the name of the agency for which Robert and Terry worked. Spoon suspended, she stared fiercely ahead, brain working overtime. It was no use. She was quite certain that she had never heard the name. She could almost hear Max saying, 'Just goes to show that it's the subconscious, or Perry would have told you that, too!'

'Come on,' she said grimly to Perry. 'Do your stuff. You've taken me so far but what the hell do I do now? I can hardly ask Pippa!'

She washed up the breakfast things slowly and took her coffee out to the courtyard. The martins were still busy with their second brood and she was fearful, as always, that they might have left it too late and would perish in the storms as they flew across the wintry seas. How Perry would had loved to see them! 'Look at that fat chap at the front,' he'd said, in previous summers. 'Bagging all the best bits. I don't think that animals have favourites like we do. He's getting the lot because he's the pushiest: no conscience about his brothers and sisters. And the parents just go along with it.' She watched the parent birds feeding the babies, who sat largely and squarely at the mouth of the nest, peering out, demanding more food. How relentless babies were! How time-consuming. She knew she would never have had the patience for it.

She thought of Frances, worrying over Hugh, and Pippa, coping with Rowley, and knew that motherhood was not for her. Pippa, now, was a born mother. How excited she'd been when she knew she was pregnant, how delighted with Rowley! Annie remembered Pippa's grief for a friend who, at the same time, had lost her baby with a miscarriage. Pippa had been quite distraught; hurrying round to be with her, trying to cheer her up, terrified that she was rubbing it in by having to take the baby Rowley with her. The woman's husband had worked with Robert . . .

Annie sat bolt upright. The woman had been Terry Cooper's wife – she had the connection now – and she had lived near enough to Pippa for regular daily visits. This was the answer she'd asked for! Once again Annie knew that Perry had come up trumps; by direct communication earlier this morning and now, by a subtle guiding of her thoughts – a method he so often used – he had passed her test with flying colours. He was there, helping and encouraging her. She knew it!

Annie swallowed her coffee and hurried inside to the telephone. Settling herself with a pad, she resigned herself to a long task. With the help of Directory Enquiries, she painstakingly made a list of all the T. Coopers in the Farnham area and began to dial. She was lucky within a few minutes of beginning. A woman answered the telephone sounding preoccupied.

'Is that Mrs Cooper?' asked Annie for the sixth time.

'It is.'

'You don't know me at all,' began Annie, feeling a fool, 'but could you just tell me – do you know Pippa March?'

'Yes. Yes I do.' The voice sharpened a little. 'Why? Is she OK?'

'Your husband is Terry Cooper who works with Robert March?'

'Yes he is.' She was sounding impatient now. 'But why—'

'I'll explain everything,' said Annie rapidly, 'if you'll just give me a moment. Please?'

By the time she'd finished she had a friend at the end of the telephone. Mary was only too ready to believe the worst.

'I was terribly upset when Pippa moved away,' she said. 'I miss her a lot. We've spoken once or twice on the telephone but this is the first I've heard of any reconciliation. Look, I won't telephone Terry at the office. You can't be certain who's listening on the exchange. I'll talk to him the minute he comes home. I know the agency is being taken over by an American company but everything's under wraps at the moment. How is Pippa?'

'She's OK,' said Annie. 'Recovering. But this will have

set her back, of course. The trouble is, she's still in love with Robert and I fear it may already be too late.'

'Oh, no it won't be!' promised Mary. 'Not if I have anything to do with it. Look, give me your number and Terry can phone you tonight when he gets in.'

'Bless you,' said Annie. 'I'm so worried. Thank God you take me seriously.'

'I wouldn't trust that man for five minutes,' said Mary. 'If he's reappeared then there's an ulterior motive. Perhaps Louisa has chucked him, but that still wouldn't explain why he's trying to get Pippa back. In my opinion, he's never loved her.'

'That was her father's opinion,' agreed Annie, 'and my husband's too. I'll look forward to hearing from you later.'

With a huge sigh of relief, she went back out into the sunshine, giving thanks that Terry's surname had not been Smith. Slowly her excitement gave way to anxiety. What right had she to interfere in Pippa's life? How could she be sure that Pippa wouldn't rather take the risks involved in living with Robert than be without him? Annie sat wrapped in thought, the twitterings of the martins ignored. Supposing, through some action of hers, Pippa refused to go back to Robert and regretted it for the rest of her life? Annie rubbed her forehead with her fingers and tucked her hair back behind her ears. Surely the best thing was to give Pippa the opportunity to decide for herself? If she decided she'd rather have Robert on any terms then at least she knew where she was with him. No one could *want* to be deceived or tricked into a relationship.

Annie remembered the saying 'Where ignorance is bliss,

'Tis folly to be wise.' Could it be true? She imagined herself with the proofs of Robert's deception in her hands; showing them to Pippa; destroying her happiness; undermining her confidence in the process. Would she be able to do it?

'If you can't do it, I can,' said Terry Cooper later that evening. 'I've done it once already, so I've got nothing to lose. Perhaps it's better that an outsider deals the blow.'

'It's really good of you,' said Annie. 'It sounds so sort of melodramatic, doesn't it?'

'No,' said Terry flatly. 'It sounds only too possible. I know that he and Louisa are still seeing each other so I can't imagine why he should start pursuing Pippa again. Look, I'm going to have to delve about a bit. I might not come up with anything for a day or two so you'll have to be patient.'

'I'm just so afraid that Pippa might do something silly in the meantime,' said Annie anxiously.

'I can understand that and I'll be as quick as I can. Keep your fingers crossed.'

'I will,' said Annie fervently. 'Good luck!'

She replaced the receiver and sat for some moments in thought. As she sat brooding, the telephone rang. It was Hugh.

'We were just sitting here,' he said, 'thinking about Pippa. Did you remember the man's name?'

'I did,' said Annie triumphantly. 'I've just been talking to him. He agrees with me that something's up. He's going to scout round tomorrow and see if he can find out what's going on. Tell Max it was a brilliant idea of his.'

'Hang on.'

She could hear Hugh talking volubly and Max's deeper voice answering.

'He says,' said Hugh's voice in her ear, 'how did you remember the name? Did it come in a blinding flash of inspiration?'

'Tell him,' said Annie with a great deal of satisfaction, 'that Perry told me when I woke up this morning,' and put down the receiver on Hugh's shout of delight.

Chapter Thirty-one

From over the street Terry Cooper watched Louisa arrive at her flat. Crossing the road, he ran swiftly up the steps and pushed the door open before she had time to shut it properly behind her. She frowned at him in the gloomy light of the hall, her letters still in her hand.

'What on earth are you doing here?'

'Just visiting,' he answered lightly. 'I'd like to have a chat with you if I may.'

She stared at him measuringly and then shrugged. 'I can spare you a few minutes.' She jerked her head towards the stairs. 'I'm on the first floor.'

'After you,' he said, following her upstairs and into the flat.

She dropped her bag on a chair in the hall and idly flipped through her post. He saw her stiffen at the sight of a postcard, reading it swiftly and then tucking it behind the other letters before she turned to him.

'Go on into the sitting room,' she said, indicating the door. 'I'll . . . just . . .' She hesitated.

'Just what?' asked Terry. 'Slip into something more comfortable?'

She looked at him with dislike, still holding the letters. 'I suppose it's too much to ask that I read my post in privacy?' she suggested.

'Not too much at all,' he answered cheerfully, 'but can't you do it when I've gone? Or is it a love letter you've got there?'

'Mind your own business,' she said coldly. 'D'you want a drink?'

'Not particularly.' He refused to precede her into the sitting room. 'I just want a chat.'

With an exaggerated sigh she went before him, putting the letters beside the chair in which she sat, gesturing that he should sit on the sofa.

'So what d'you want to talk about?' she asked.

'About you and Robert.' He smiled at her. 'I've been ferreting about today and found out one or two interesting things. D'you want to know what they are?'

'Not specially.' She looked bored. 'But I have the feeling that you're going to tell me anyway.'

'I am,' he admitted. 'I found out that we're being taken over by Pawley and Straker and Harrison Pawley is to be our new senior partner. He and Hannah are moving over here and Miss Louisa Beaumont is on her way to the good old US of A.'

'I suppose you got it all out of Alison.' She sounded indifferent – but her eyes were wary.

'Well, I did,' he said. 'I took her to lunch and wheedled it out of her. She swore me to secrecy, of course, although the new order is to be announced any day now.'

'You needn't have bought her lunch.' Louisa yawned and

crossed her legs. 'You can buy Alison with a packet of pork scratchings. How she got to be an executive secretary I'll never know.'

'She also told me that Robert's in line for Head of Sales.'

Louisa raised her eyebrows. 'So?'

Terry sat back in his chair and stretched out his legs. 'So,' he said, 'after her third glass of wine she admitted that, Harrison and Hannah being such a family-loving couple, it would be very sensible if Robert and Pippa got together again. She said that she'd heard that they'd split up but that Robert was denying it and saying that Pippa's been ill and is recuperating with friends in the West Country.'

'It's none of my business,' said Louisa coolly. 'As you said, I'm on my way to the States. What Robert does is his business.'

'But you admit that it's in his interest to get Pippa back pronto?'

Louisa was silent and he saw her swallow. The telephone in the hall rang and he moved quickly. 'I'll get it, shall I?'

She was on her feet, hurrying past him, glaring as she disappeared. In a flash, Terry was by her chair, picking up her letters, extracting the postcard. When she returned he was sitting on the sofa and his face was dark with anger.

'You cow!' he said quietly. 'You've really set her up between you, haven't you?'

Louisa's glance flew to the table and back again to his face.

'"The citadel has just fallen",' he quoted. '"I've marked our bedroom on the front. She was a pushover but I couldn't have done it without all your advice. Missing you. All love,

Robert." You absolute cow. How could you do that to another woman?'

'Oh, for God's sake don't be so bloody high-minded,' she said contemptuously. 'Men do each other down every day of the week. Why should women be different?'

'No reason,' said Terry sadly. 'I suppose I just hope they will be.'

'So what do you read now that you can't get the *Boy's Own Paper*?' she sneered. 'What do you do for fairy tales in your neck of the woods? Grow up, Terry. Robert wants Pippa back so I gave him some advice on how to handle it. It's none of your business.'

'Oh, I think it is,' he said thoughtfully. 'I think Harrison and Hannah will be interested to know the real truth. It might even affect your job in the States.'

She stared at him, calculating. 'They wouldn't believe you,' she said.

'Who's living in fairyland now?' he asked. 'Of course they'll believe me. I'll show them the card and they can confront Robert with it. Pippa's view should be interesting, too, once she knows everything.'

Louisa bent quickly to pick up her letters and then turned on him furiously. 'Give me my property,' she said. 'How dare you! It was despicable enough of you to read it but to steal it as well . . .'

He got to his feet, pushing her away. 'Don't try to moralise. You're in a very poor position. But I'll do a deal with you.'

'What is it?' she asked at last, her face sullen.

'I won't tell the Pawleys anything,' he said. 'Robert can

keep his promotion and you can go to the States, as long as you swear that you won't warn Robert that I know or that I've seen the card.'

She hesitated, studying the proposition from all sides. 'What are you going to do?' she asked at last.

'I'm going to make certain that Pippa knows the truth about both of you,' he said. 'If she refuses to take Robert back once she knows, then it's up to him how he tries to con Harrison and keep his promotion. But I won't lift a finger against him or you, as long as you promise. I want to get in first with Pippa without Robert queering my pitch.'

'I haven't got much choice, have I?' she said, and snorted derisively. 'He asked if he could telephone and I told him not to. I thought that might be him just now, actually. I didn't want him droning down the phone, wanting sympathy and advice. So I told him to drop me a card when the citadel had fallen.' She shook her head. 'Christ! Who would have thought that the bloody fool would take me seriously?'

He stared at her for a long moment. 'What an absolute sweetie you are, Louisa,' he said disgustedly. 'I know that your word means nothing but I promise you, if you warn Robert of what I plan to do, the whole story and this card goes before Harrison immediately.'

'Oh, for God's sake,' she said, 'I don't give a damn about either of them. Why should I? I wanted him off my back. I shall be gone in a couple of weeks so I don't care.'

'Does he think you might come back to him eventually?' he asked curiously. 'This card sounds very affectionate.'

'Probably.' She shrugged. 'He's conceited enough. I've let him think so just to keep him quiet.'

'And what happens to Pippa at that point?'

'It's irrelevant. I'm not coming back. Will you go now?'

'Gladly,' said Terry. 'Just remember what I've said.'

'Oh, get out,' she said impatiently. 'You've got what you wanted. Bugger off!'

He went, slamming the door behind him, and she stood for some moments staring after him. Presently she took a deep breath and shook her head. She had no intention of risking her new position in the New York office just to save Robert's skin. She was bored by the whole business and she longed to put the affair behind her and be free of him for good. It would be a relief now to get right away; to start her new exciting life in New York. An idea occurred to her and, with a little nod of satisfaction, she went to the table in the corner and poured herself a large drink.

At the same moment, Robert was deciding that it was time he returned to London. Officially he had until the weekend but, having achieved his object, he was becoming restless. It was clear that Pippa had no intention of inviting him to stay at the farmhouse and he really had no desire to go. Having met Frances briefly, he had the impression that she might be the kind of woman to ask questions and he felt safer at the Bedford. The truth was, he was weary with playing the lover, maintaining the role of the erring but repentant husband, and it was even more tiresome if they went out as a family and he had to act the devoted father too.

Fortunately, he'd never disclosed how much time was at his disposal and now he made it clear that he must be on his way back. He knew that Louisa would be leaving for the States very soon and he wanted to see her before she left. He had accepted the fact that he must be reconciled with Pippa but he was still hoping that, at some future date, Louisa would come back to him. Another problem was exercising his mind. It was important that Pippa never disclosed the story of their separation to the Pawleys and he was wondering how he should broach this with her. He decided, after a great deal of thought, that he would wait until she was safely under his roof before he worried too much about it. The fact that they were together again should effectively scotch any rumours that might reach Harrison's ears and he could always put them down to jealousy if pressed.

He was pleased with himself. The only remaining loose end was the date on which Pippa and Rowley should return. He couldn't fit them both into his tiny flat, and he didn't want them on the scene until Louisa had gone, but it couldn't be left in the air. Pippa was needing continual persuasion to agree that she would return to him – she was still suffering from a kind of shyness – and it was obvious that there must be a home to which they could both come. He'd tentatively offered his idea of a country cottage which had found favour in her eyes. Hoping to keep her safely tethered for a few more weeks, he suggested that he should contact some agents and ask them to send relevant details of cottages to her; or she might like to make a few enquiries herself? He made it clear that he would be prepared to live anywhere – within reasonable commuting distance – if she would only forgive and forget.

She promised to think about where she might like to settle down with Rowley, obviously relieved to have a little more breathing space. Robert spoke warmly of the joys of village life and how wonderful it would be for Rowley to be in the real country, and wondered how he could get her into bed one last time. In the first place it would increase the chance of her becoming pregnant; and in the second it would bind her more closely to him. He telephoned her and asked if she would come and have dinner at the hotel. He'd decided, he told her, to leave very early the following morning and he had yet to pack; would she object to a quiet dinner with him? She agreed, much to his relief, and he knew that it would be fairly simple to get her up to his bedroom afterwards.

He made it clear to the staff that it was his wife who was coming to dine with him – just to be on the safe side – and, when he suggested that she might like to chat to him whilst he packed, she made no objection. She sat rather awkwardly in the armchair, watching him fold clothes and put them into his suitcase. He talked easily and presently he kneeled beside her and put his arm around her.

'I wish you were coming with me. I suppose there's no chance of Frances looking after Rowley?'

His heart was in his mouth until she answered.

'Oh, I couldn't do that. It wouldn't be fair. Just for one night was OK but I wouldn't want to leave him.'

'I suppose not.' He ran his hand along her thigh and pressed his lips against her hair. 'If only you know how I hate myself for all this.'

He turned her chin and kissed her and her arms went

round him as he pressed her back into the chair. She clung to him and he began to fumble with her clothes.

'Oh my darling,' he muttered. 'How can I bear to leave you? Oh Pippa . . .' He pulled her up and half carried her across to the bed.

Afterwards, he helped her to tidy herself, made her some coffee and then escorted her down to the car park.

'You won't forget to contact the estate agents, will you?' he asked with pretended anxiety, holding her closely before allowing her to slide into the driver's seat. She promised, still shaken from his passionate lovemaking, and he watched her drive out, his hand raised in farewell until she'd turned on to the road.

He went back into the bar and ordered a brandy which he carried upstairs with him. He shut the bedroom door behind him, sank down on the bed and downed half the brandy in one gulp. It was over and he had won. He raised the glass to himself before swallowing the other half. Twenty minutes later he was fast asleep.

Chapter Thirty-two

When Terry telephoned to tell Annie what he had discovered, her overwhelming anxiety was how Robert's treachery should be conveyed to Pippa. She tried to put herself in Pippa's place, imagining how she would have felt if Perry had behaved in such a manner. A cold dark horror possessed her and, for a brief moment, she felt the pain and humiliation as though this terrible betrayal had actually occurred. She imagined, too, how she would have felt if a close friend had told her such news and she involuntarily reacted against it. Surely it must be better to hear such a thing from an acquaintance?

She slept badly and woke early, unrefreshed and undecided. Taking her stick she went out and up the lane. It was a pearly soft white morning, the farther fields and hills obscured by a thin shining mist which was diffused by a brighter golden light. Soon the sun would break through, transforming the finely spun webs which stretched from twig to twig and draped themselves about the fluffy heads of the willow herb. The heavy dew soaked her shoes and the air was chilly. She walked slowly, still immersed in thought. What remained of Pippa's pride must be kept intact if it were at all possible. If Terry broke the bad news to her, she would have the choice. If *she* chose to tell her friends, that was her business; otherwise only she, Annie, would know the truth.

Annie strolled along beside the hedge, brooding. The sheep huddled in the middle of the field, their breath steaming, their yellow eyes watching her progress. They were the Dartmoor Whitefaces, prettiest of all the sheep in Annie's opinion, but this morning she barely noticed them. Her thoughts were all with Pippa; what would be the kindest – or least brutal – method of destroying her newly found happiness?

That Pippa *was* happy Annie did not doubt. The previous evening, after Terry's telephone call, she had spoken, in turn, to Frances and Pippa. They had both had wonderful weekends, she gathered. Pippa, somewhat reticently, described her weekend in Salcombe and Annie had cursed beneath her breath. Pippa sounded rather like a young girl after a first date; still dazed by the precarious happiness of its promise. Robert, she told Annie, was going back to London early next morning and she and Rowley were remaining at the farmhouse for a while. Annie drew a breath of relief, thanking heaven that Terry had bought them time and that Pippa had not returned with Robert. Frances was more prosaic but just as happy. She was going to Wales next weekend and – here she lowered her voice lest Pippa should hear and feel anxious – she would be only too pleased, now, to sell the farmhouse and be gone.

Relieved though Annie was to hear that all was well between Frances and Stephen, her real concern was for

Pippa. If Terry were to be designated informer, where should the deed take place? If only it could be done so that no one else need know; but he could hardly break such shattering news in a café or any public place. And how would the arrangement take place? If Terry telephoned, Pippa would immediately suspect that something was wrong unless he could convince her that he was just passing; down on holiday, perhaps?

Annie gave an exclamation of frustration and turned homeward, calling upon Perry for guidance. The sun penetrated the thinning cloud and its brightness and warmth poured down so that each web with its sparkling drops shone, jewel-like, in the hedgerow; small miracles of design and delicacy. Even Annie was distracted from her thoughts and stood for some moments in silent contemplation. Blackberries hung in plump and glossy clusters and the scent of some late-flowering honeysuckle drifted gently on the soft air.

A memory slid into her mind; she and Perry on an autumn holiday in Wales. He had wakened her, dragging her out on another such early morning walk, and they had marvelled at the treasures they had discovered. It had been so happy a holiday that they had returned to the hotel many times. They'd both loved Wales . . . Annie resolutely pushed away the pain of remembering and deliberately concentrated on Frances, wondering whether she would be happy in Wales. Thank God all was well there, again, and that Frances had agreed to go to stay with Stephen for the weekend. It would be good for them to be alone together without Pippa and Rowley . . .

Annie straightened up sharply, her hand clenching on her stick as she saw the solution. Pippa would be alone at the farmhouse for the whole weekend. If Terry could contrive to see her there, the deed could be done without an audience; without anyone else suspecting the truth. He could turn up without any prior warning which had two benefits. The first was that Pippa would not have to spend hours in suspense, wondering what he might have to tell her; the second was that she wouldn't have the opportunity to telephone Robert and hear his story first. Although how he could ever explain away the postcard . . . !

Shaking her head in disbelief, Annie continued on her way home. She couldn't let Pippa go back to such a man, unaware of his base nature, believing his lies, which had been concocted with the connivance of his mistress. No. Terry must come down to the farmhouse and tell her the truth. She, Annie, would be standing by, to be summoned should it prove necessary. It was the right thing to do; she was sure of it. In this case ignorance could not possibly be bliss. She walked faster now, her mind made up; determined to speak to Terry as soon as possible, calmer now that the decision had been made.

Max laid down his knife and fork with a sigh of contentment whilst the Mutt watched from his blanket, anxious lest his master should have forgotten himself so far as to leave no scraps on his plate.

'I always say there's no one to beat your steak and kidney pie, Mother,' he said appreciatively.

Mrs Driver patted her curls thoughtfully. 'Pity that Hugh

isn't here,' she observed, unwilling to show her pleasure at his praise. 'Looks like he could do with feeding up.'

'Hugh's OK,' said Max easily. 'He's one of those thin wiry types.'

'He's looking better,' she acknowledged cautiously. 'Got over his problems, hasn't he?'

'What do you know about his problems?' Max glanced at her sharply.

'He's told me things.' Mrs Driver looked bland.

'I bet he has!' Max snorted. 'Poor Hugh! Did he know he was getting the third degree? Must have been like taking candy from a baby. So what did he tell you?'

'Oh, this and that,' she said evasively, getting up to clear the dishes. 'He's a nice lad, I'll say that for him. Misses that girlfriend of his.'

'Yes, well,' said Max, after a pause. 'Probably just as well. We don't want girlfriends complicating matters.'

Mrs Driver put the leftovers into the Mutt's bowl. '*You* might not,' she said pointedly. 'What about this Pippa, then?'

The silence, this time, went on for so long that Mrs Driver turned to look at her son.

'What about her?' he asked with an attempt at indifference. 'She's got problems with her husband.' He shrugged. 'She's Hugh's friend, not mine.'

'Nice girl, though.' Her nonchalance was masterly.

'Have you met her?' He was startled out of his studied detachment.

'Hugh introduced me one day,' she told him with ill-concealed satisfaction. 'I just popped by for a minute but you were out. Very nice girl.'

'Well, Hugh won't get far with her,' said Max, deliberately choosing to misunderstand her. 'She's in love with her husband.'

Mrs Driver gave one of her sniffs. 'That's as may be.'

'Mother,' said Max warningly. 'Pack it in! What about that apple pie?'

She bustled about, getting the pie from the Aga, stooping to pat the Mutt, putting the clotted cream into a small bowl; perfectly at home in his kitchen.

'Good job you've got that dog,' she said, sitting down again and preparing to serve the pie. 'Came up here one day when you were both out and he barked the place down. Anyone could break in easy, stuck out here, but they'd think twice the racket he was making. I always say that a dog's better than a burglar alarm.'

'Oh, we sleep much easier in our beds knowing that the Mutt's dead to the world in front of the Aga,' said Max with immense irony. 'I can't think how we managed without him. But I promise you that we can do very well without women. So if you find any of those round the dustbins, Mother, I suggest you get that manager of yours to put 'em out of their misery!'

To Frances's great relief, the couple who came to view the farmhouse for the second time made an offer. They had already exchanged contracts on the sale of their own house so there should be no impediment this time. Knowing that Pippa had decided to go back to Robert, Frances felt that she could rejoice with a clear conscience. Everything, it seemed, was going to end well: Stephen, happy in his new position; Hugh, sane and cheerful; a new life for herself with Stephen in Wales. What other blessings could life shower upon her? She discovered the answer to this question when Caroline telephoned.

'Mum?'

'Hello, darling.' Frances detected some kind of tension in her daughter's voice and her stomach tightened. 'Is everything all right?'

'Oh Mum, you'll never guess.'

Frances experienced a wave of panic. 'Caroline! Whatever is it? Are you both OK?'

'Oh, yes!' Was Caroline laughing or crying? 'We're having a baby, Mum! Isn't it fantastic? It was confirmed this morning. I didn't want to tell you in case I was wrong. Are you pleased?'

Now it was Frances who didn't know whether she was laughing or crying. 'Oh darling! It's wonderful. Oh, I can't tell you . . . You clever, clever girl. And James, of course. How is he? He must be so thrilled. Oh, wait till I tell Daddy . . .'

By the time they'd finished, Frances wondered whether it might be possible to expire from so much happiness. Pippa entered thoroughly into her joy, insisting on celebrating the news with a toast to Caroline and James and the baby, and, by the time she telephoned the news to Stephen, Frances was almost incoherent with bliss and wine.

Now, as she hung the last garment on the line in the orchard, she remembered the terrors that had beset her a year before. Sitting again on the dry-stone wall, listening to a buzzard mewing as it circled above her, feeling the sunshine on her back, she recalled her anxieties and fears and her furious antipathy for Cass Wivenhoe. Frances picked idly at the dry powdery lichen and stared out across the fields to the high shoulders of the moor. Hugh had told her of Cass's generous offer – her memorial to Charlotte – and she remembered certain passages of Cass's letter. Frances's eyes filled with tears. She saw the child, Charlotte; rubbing down her pony with a wisp of straw, the shy brief smile, the adoration in her brown eyes as she looked at Hugh. How swift she, Frances, had been to berate her for her jealousy at Caroline's party! She remembered her own jealousy of Cass, and her own method of dealing with it, and felt ashamed. How should a shy fifteen year old be expected to cope better than she had with those agonising pangs? She thought of her hatred and bitterness for Cass – her refusal to allow that she might be grieving – and her shame increased. An idea occurred to her and she slipped from the wall and went indoors.

A little later she was driving up The Rectory drive. She braked on the gravel sweep before the front door just as Cass appeared, walking round from the stables where she kept her car. She peered into the car, frowning, and then raised a hand to Frances.

'Hello there,' she said, as Frances climbed out. 'How are you? This is a nice surprise.'

She looked a little wary and it occurred to Frances that she was wondering whether this visit might not be a purely friendly one. Frances smiled at her.

'I wanted to come and see you. We're hoping to move

soon, you know, and I wanted to make certain of saying goodbye.'

'I heard you were off,' said Cass cautiously as they went up the steps together. 'Wales, isn't it?'

'This is silly,' said Frances, as she followed her into the kitchen. 'Let's be honest. Can we be? I know that you've been seeing Stephen . . .'

Cass swung round from the Aga, her hands up, as if warding off an accusation. 'Now don't get the wrong idea,' she begged. 'Honestly . . .'

Frances was shaking her head. 'Don't worry,' she interrupted. 'I know why you were seeing Stephen.'

'Has he . . .? Did he . . .?' Cass fell silent, afraid of saying too much.

'Felicity told Pat.' Frances grinned at Cass's expression. 'Yes. It would be her, wouldn't it? And Pat told me. And then a friend of Stephen mentioned that he'd seen you together. I must admit I was very worried.'

'Stephen didn't want you to get the wrong idea,' explained Cass. 'He thought that you might . . .' She hesitated, seeing the pitfalls.

'That I might be jealous.' Frances completed the sentence for her. 'And he was right.'

'Oh Frances,' said Cass sadly. 'There's never been anything of that sort between me and Stephen. He's the most married man I know.'

Remembering Cass's remorse for her past actions, Frances realised that any light-hearted teasing would be out of place. 'I know that too,' she admitted. 'I've always been a bit . . . well, silly like that. I'm afraid Stephen's been on the end of a certain amount of flak from time to time.'

'I'm so glad he told you,' said Cass sincerely. 'Secrets can be very dangerous.'

Frances saw her expression darken as she remembered the result of keeping secrets. 'It wasn't Stephen who told me,' she said quickly. 'It was Hugh.'

'Aah,' said Cass slowly. 'Hugh. I see.'

'The thing was,' explained Frances, 'that I got the wrong end of the stick. I thought that you and Stephen were . . . you know. I couldn't decide what to do. In the end I spoke to Hugh. He was so horrified that things might go wrong that he told me the truth.'

'I see.' Cass was watching her thoughtfully.

Frances took a deep breath. 'How can I thank you?' she asked. 'You've taken away all his guilt and he's so happy.'

'There shouldn't have been any guilt,' said Cass swiftly. 'The guilt was mine. He was sweet to her. It was frightful to think of him in that state.'

'Nevertheless, only you could have pulled him out of it. It was very generous of you.'

'He showed you the letter,' said Cass. 'Didn't he?'

'Yes,' said Frances at last. 'Yes, he did. But please don't blame him too much. I was in a bad way. I was refusing to see or talk to Stephen and it was the only way he could prove that what he was telling me was the truth. I thought it was just a cover for an affair.'

'Oh God!' cried Cass. 'I'm so sorry, Frances. Oh hell! There's no end to it, is there?'

'Yes. Yes, there is.' Frances went to her and put an arm

about her shoulders. 'I've been taught a very valuable lesson. Hugh is like a new man. And you,' she looked at Cass's unhappy face, 'you've been given the chance to grieve. None too soon, either.'

'It was such a relief.' Cass tried to smile. 'You can't possibly imagine what a difference it's made. I'm so grateful to Stephen. Poor fellow.' She shook her head. 'I wept all over him. It must have been frightful and he was so kind.'

'And been more than repaid by what you've done for Hugh,' said Frances gently. 'He was very near the edge, you know. And even though he loves this new job, without you it would always have been tainted with guilt and remorse.'

'Yes. Well, I know all about those two,' said Cass grimly. 'But I deserve them, he didn't.'

'I didn't mean to upset you, I just wanted to say thank you. And he's so thrilled about the stable block.'

'The stable block?' Cass stared at her, surprised out of her unhappiness. 'He told you about that, too?'

'He certainly did. They both told me, solo and chorus. They think it's wonderful of you both.' Frances gave her a hug and then went back to sit at the table. 'They're planning a plaque. "In loving memory of Charlotte Wivenhoe". And Hugh wants to add "*Semper fidelis*". But he's going to ask you first.'

'What does it mean?' asked Cass, after a moment.

'"Always faithful",' translated Frances quietly. 'He says it sums her up so exactly. I agree with him.'

Cass bent her head and the tears poured down her cheeks. 'It does,' she sobbed. 'Oh, he is so exactly right. From the beginning she was always so faithful in her love. For Tom and the little ones and my father and Hammy. For Giles and then for Hugh . . .'

She broke down in a storm of weeping and Frances, who noticed that Cass had not mentioned herself in the catalogue of Charlotte's loves, went back to her and put her arms around her.

'Cry then,' she said, rocking her as though she were a child. 'Why not?'

'I'm sorry,' said Cass presently, recovering herself. 'This is becoming a habit. You took me by surprise.'

'It's not fair, is it?' Frances smiled. 'Did you think I'd come to accuse you?'

'To tell the truth,' admitted Cass, blowing her nose. 'Just for one moment, I did. Once before a wife came to accuse me and when I saw it was you I had a terrible sense of *déjà vu*. Rather horrid.'

'Poor Cass. Are you OK?'

'Of course I am,' said Cass, looking more like her usual self. 'But I think we'll skip the coffee and go for the hard stuff. I think we both need it.'

'Good idea,' agreed Frances cheerfully. 'And then we'll catch up on all each other's news. I've got a very exciting bit to tell you.' She thought about Caroline and the coming baby and began to smile.

'I can't wait!' said Cass. 'Hang on while I pour out. By the look on your face it's something we're going to need to toast.'

Frances watched her collecting glasses and bottles and felt a tremendous sense of release. It was, after all, so much more satisfying to love than to hate and she wished that –

especially where Cass was concerned – she hadn't taken so long to discover it.

Chapter Thirty-three

Once Frances had left for Wales, driving away on Friday afternoon, an unnatural silence descended on the farmhouse. Even Rowley seemed exhausted by the excitement that had persisted until her departure. Her visit to Cass had set the seal on Frances's happiness and there had been a constant procession of telephone calls and visitors from friends who wanted to congratulate her on her imminent grannyhood and to chat about the move to Wales.

Pippa had been moved by the excitement, the happy sharing of all these friends, and spent willing hours discussing possible names for the coming baby and shopping for knitting patterns. Nevertheless, she heaved a sigh of relief as the car disappeared down the lane. She was looking forward to having some moments to think about her own future. Having studied the area which fell within the radius Robert had marked out on the map, she had given a great deal of thought as to where she might like to live. There was still an air of unreality about the whole thing, however, and she wished she had the courage to invite Robert down for the weekend.

As she sat watching the television, with Rowley tucked

in for the night, she wondered why she needed courage to ask her own husband to spend a weekend with her. The truth was that, foolish though it might be, she still felt shy; their relationship was not that of a couple who had been married for several years. The coolness which had existed before the final rupture, and the months of separation since, had put a distance between them which could not be bridged in one short week. Perhaps if he should telephone, she might be courageous enough to offer an invitation but it was not until Saturday afternoon that she heard from him.

'How are you both?' he asked tenderly. 'I'm missing you so much. I wish this little box of a flat was bigger. Never mind. I've got some rather interesting properties to look at. Have you done anything on the house-hunting front?'

Despite the fact that there was no one to overhear her, Pippa still felt rather tongue-tied and, although they talked for several minutes, she was unable to feel at ease with him or to suggest that he should drive down to see them. It was much too late in the weekend anyway, she told herself afterwards but she had the feeling that, had he known she and Rowley were alone, he would have driven down very readily.

Cross with herself, she strapped Rowley into his seat and went for a little drive in the car but her restlessness persisted and she half wished that she'd made some arrangement with Annie. She'd forgotten what it was like to be alone – that is, without adult company – and, on Sunday morning, she telephoned Annie and invited herself to tea. Annie sounded rather odd, distracted and nervy, and said that she had friends coming so that Pippa was obliged to contemplate another day with only Rowley for company. She wondered at herself as they ate breakfast together. She'd never felt quite like this before; dissatisfied, restless, uneasy. It was as if she had some premonition of disaster . . . Pippa put such fantastical imaginings down to the fact that her period had just started – which had caused other confused feelings of disappointment and relief – and took Rowley out to play in the garden.

During the drive from London, Terry's thoughts were busy. He felt nervous and had to make a great effort to concentrate on his driving, glad that it was Sunday and the roads were less busy than usual. He reviewed the conversation he had held with Annie, committing to memory certain vital facts. She had warned him to say nothing of her involvement. It was essential, she'd insisted, that Pippa believed that he was the only person who knew of the collusion between Robert and Louisa. This immediately raised the problem of how Terry had discovered Pippa's whereabouts. Unfortunately, though she and Mary had spoken on the telephone, Pippa had never bothered to explain where the farmhouse was situated. He and Annie both agreed that Robert must have no idea that Terry was about to pay a visit. This had caused them a considerable amount of anxiety. Even if they could stretch credibility so far as to say that Robert had mentioned it in idle conversation – unaware of Terry's intentions – he would hardly describe the location minutely or tell him Frances's surname, even if Robert should know this detail.

It was Annie who conceived the idea that he should say that he'd wormed it out of Louisa. After all, the interview with Louisa would have to be reported if only to disclose how he had come by the postcard. Terry, who was praying that Pippa may be convinced without his having to produce the card, demurred at this. Surely, he protested, Pippa's very first question would be, 'How on earth did you know I was here?'

Mary, with her practical grasp on the situation, had said firmly that he'd have to muff it. He must be vague, she said, and immediately seize on a different topic of conversation; like how glorious the countryside was or how much Rowley had grown. He'd think of something, she promised him, when the moment came. Terry, turning off the A38, his mouth dry, prayed that she was right. He followed Annie's instructions carefully and, at last, drew up beside the gate in the narrow lane. Swallowing nervously, he glanced at his watch. Annie had told him that Rowley had a sleep every afternoon after lunch and that this was the most sensible time to arrive; the most likely time to find Pippa at the farmhouse.

Pippa, who heard the car and had wondered for one heady moment if Robert had suddenly driven down to see her, came hurrying out. Her delight at seeing Terry was so great that he managed to bluff his way through, just as Mary had foretold.

'How are you?' he asked, hugging her. 'What a lovely house. And how's Rowley? Asleep? Oh well, perhaps I'll see him before I go. No, Mary's not with me but she's fine. She sends her love . . .'

By this time they were in the kitchen.

'Well, this *is* a surprise,' said Pippa, able to get a word in at last. 'But what on earth are you doing down here if you're not on holiday?'

There was a silence. Terry knew that it was impossible to keep up a barrage of small talk but also that there was no slow lead-up to what he had to say. He rubbed his face with his fingers and folded his arms across his chest.

'This is terrible,' he said.

Pippa turned quite white. 'Oh my God!' she cried. 'Has something happened to Robert?'

The question and her look made him feel like an executioner. 'No,' he said quietly. 'Robert's fine. Look, Pippa, I have to say at once that this visit is for the same reason as my last one. I must tell you some unpleasant facts. Please try to forgive me for this but . . . well, I've just got to tell you before it's too late.'

Pippa leaned against the Aga, holding the rail behind her. 'Robert's been down,' she told him. 'He's explained about his affair with Louisa. You were absolutely right but it's all over now. He said it was like a kind of madness and I . . . I believe him. It's very sweet of you to be concerned . . .'

'No, love,' he said heavily. 'It's not all over. Just listen for a moment, if you will. The thing is that there's been a takeover. Remember Harrison and Hannah Pawley? Yes, well, Harrison's bought us out. John Spencer is a sick man and is about to retire. Robert's been offered Head of Sales, which is wonderful for him, but it's on the condition that he's still a happily married man. The Pawleys don't like divorce and he knows that if they suspect that he's left you they won't be so anxious to consider him for the post.'

He paused. He'd been determined to get in as much as

possible before she questioned him but he could see that she was still trying to take it all in.

'I don't quite understand,' she began slowly, and his heart sank. 'They must realise by now that we've separated . . .'

Terry was shaking his head. 'Robert's told them that you're ill and recuperating with friends down here,' he said. 'It's a question of persuading you back before they discover the truth.'

She stared at him, trying to fumble her way to some understanding. 'D'you mean . . .?' She gave it up. 'What are you saying?'

'When Robert discovered, through Louisa, that the Pawleys were taking over, he knew he'd have to get you back. Louisa had wangled the position for him and between them they worked out a strategy to bring you back to him.' Terry closed his eyes for a moment on the effect of his brutality upon her. 'I don't know what he's told you but it's a lie. He needs you so as to get that promotion.'

'No.' Pippa shook her head.

'Yes, love,' said Terry wearily. 'I'm afraid so. Louisa's been offered a post in the New York office which she's accepted so he had nothing to lose. They cooked up a plan between them.'

'I can't believe it.' She remembered Robert's expressions, his voice as he pleaded with her; the weekend at Salcombe. Her face crumpled. 'Oh, it can't be true.' She stared at Terry with sudden suspicion. 'So how d'you know all this? You've always been jealous of him. How do I know that this isn't some . . . some trick?'

Terry leaned his elbows on the table and put his head in

his hands. 'Do you honestly believe I'd do this? Even if Robert and I were in the running for the same job, d'you really believe I'd come all this way on purpose to say such things?'

'I *can't* believe it,' she said desperately. 'Not after all the things he said and . . . and . . . ' She clasped her hands together, twisting them, squeezing them. 'Oh God. There must be another explanation. How can you know about it, anyway? Robert wouldn't have told you.'

'Louisa told me,' he said at last. 'I heard through the grapevine that Robert had come down to the West Country to see you and, in light of the takeover and knowing the Pawleys, I was suspicious.' He passed quickly over this lie but she had no reason to suspect him. 'I decided to confront Louisa. Whilst I was with her I saw a postcard.' He hesitated. 'It was from Robert.'

'A postcard?' Pippa frowned at him. 'What d'you mean? What postcard? When was this?'

'It was on Tuesday.' He knew that nothing could prevent it all coming out now. 'I went to see her after work. The postcard had arrived that morning from . . . from Salcombe. It said certain things . . .'

Pippa was shaking her head again. 'It's not true.'

'I read it, Pippa. I took it away with me . . .' Too late he realised his stupidity.

'Have you got it?' she asked. 'I want to see it.'

'No,' he said. 'No, don't do that. Honestly . . .'

'I want to see it.' Her face was stony. 'I simply can't believe you otherwise.'

With great reluctance he took the postcard from his jacket

pocket and pushed it across the table to her. She stared at it for some moments and then moved forward to pick it up. She stared at the picture – at the biro cross against one of the hotel windows – and then turned it over. She was so long reading it, rereading it, that Terry got to his feet and went round the table to her. She stared up at him.

'I'm sorry,' he said inadequately. 'I'm so sorry. But how could I let him . . . get away with it?'

'So go on.' She held on to the card and faced him squarely. He thought that she looked like a complete stranger; her face stiff with shock, her eyes alive with pain. 'What did Louisa say?'

'She told me everything I've just told you. I took the card because I was afraid that you might not believe me without it. She doesn't care any more. She's going out to the States. I shall do nothing else. It's up to you now. I gather that you'd . . . decided to go back to him?'

He saw her swallow, gain control of herself, and he put out a hand to her. She moved a little away from him, turning the card in her hands.

'Yes,' she said at last. 'I believed him, you see. That he'd been bewitched but that the spell was broken and he deeply regretted it. He wanted to make a new start. And . . . I wanted it, too.'

He was frightened by this iron calm. 'This is terrible!' he burst out. 'Oh God! I shouldn't have done this. I had no right.'

He sat down at the table and, after a moment, she laid a hand lightly on his shoulder.

'Poor Terry,' she said, as though it should be *her*

comforting *him*. 'This is the second time you've come to my rescue. Please don't regret it. Imagine if I'd discovered this after I'd gone back to him!'

He twisted round so as to stare up at her. 'Are you sure? You'd rather . . . know?'

She looked at him but he had the feeling that she wasn't seeing him. 'Yes,' she said, as though coming back from some great distance. 'Of course I would. It's bad enough finding out now.' She stared down at the card in her hand and then looked at him. Her smile didn't touch her eyes. 'Will you go now, Terry? Please just go. I'm not even going to offer you a cup of tea. I can't speak of my gratitude for your friendship . . . I can't . . . talk at all. Please could you leave me alone?'

He was frightened by her appearance. 'You won't do anything . . . you know? Anything silly?'

She smiled more genuinely then, shaking her head reassuringly. 'There's Rowley,' she said simply. 'How could I?'

'Shall I come back? Just in case?' he pleaded, hating to leave her.

'No,' she said, quite definitely. 'Please. I shall be quite all right. I'll telephone you, I promise, and I'm truly grateful, only, just at the moment, I can't bear the sight of you.'

He stepped back at the flare of hatred in her eyes and with a quick nod, he turned away from her and went out to the car. When the sound of the engine had quite died away, Pippa looked again at the postcard. 'The citadel has just fallen. I've marked our bedroom on the front. She was a pushover but I couldn't have done it without all your advice.

Missing you. All love, Robert.' She squeezed her eyes closed, to shut out the humiliation and pain, and, sitting down at the table, she buried her head in her arms.

Chapter Thirty-four

Although she sat up waiting into the early hours, worried and beside herself with frustration, Annie received no telephone call from Pippa. Terry had called in, as arranged, on his way home and Annie felt her heart jolt anxiously as she saw his face.

'Bad?' she asked, leading him out into the sitting room and indicating an armchair.

'Awful,' he said, sitting down. He cast about for an adequate phrase to describe the scene but shook his head.

'Oh God!' Annie looked visibly distressed. 'Poor, poor Pippa. She believed you, though?'

'Oh, yes. She believed me – but not until I'd shown her the postcard.'

'Oh hell!' said Annie feelingly.

Terry nodded his agreement. 'I gave her the full works. I had to. It was . . . bloody. She . . . she asked me to go. She said she was grateful but that she wanted me to leave. She said . . . she said that she couldn't bear the sight of me.'

'Oh, my dear.' Annie laid a hand on his shoulder. 'I'm so very sorry. But it was bound to be her reaction. I'm sure you can understand that.'

'But it wasn't like that last time,' protested Terry. 'She was very upset then, too, but she didn't look at me like she did this afternoon.'

Annie could see that he was genuinely hurt and upset and she sat down opposite, leaning forward so that she could see his down-turned face.

'It was different last time,' she said gently. 'Oh yes, it was. Last time your visit came at the end of a long, unhappy period when Robert had already declared his intention of leaving her. Your explanation confirmed that he was in love with another woman, which Pippa suspected. It was a kind of relief to her because it explained his behaviour. This time she's in quite a different state. Robert has talked her into believing that it was just a mad moment and that he loves her and wants her back. They've spent a romantic few days together and she's allowed herself to believe in a happy future with him. Then you come on the scene and smash it all to bits. Not only has Robert lied in his teeth and deceived her all round but he's planned it all with his mistress. You've dealt her a terrible blow, Terry. Nobody ever loves the bringer of bad news. In the old days they put such messengers to death.'

'Thanks,' said Terry bitterly, after a moment. 'I feel really great now!'

'I'm so sorry,' she said again. 'It will pass and she'll bless you. This is only temporary. But you can see why I chickened out.'

'Too bloody right, I can!' said Terry crossly, forgetting that it was he who had suggested that it would be better that an outsider dealt the blow.

Annie smiled a little. 'It wasn't pure selfishness,' she said. 'The thing is that, apart from Frances, I'm all she's got at the moment. Frances might decide to go to Wales at any moment which leaves me. I couldn't afford to be in your position.'

'I suppose not,' he said unwillingly.

'The second thing is that Pippa believes that no one knows what's happened except you. This means she can hold on to her pride. She doesn't have to tell anyone if she doesn't want to. If she thought I knew, she might suspect that I'd tell Frances and Frances might tell Hugh and so on. You've been a very good friend to her, Terry, and she'll be eternally grateful to you.'

'But not just yet,' said Terry wrily although he looked a little happier.

'Not just yet,' agreed Annie. 'Were you with her long?'

He shook his head. 'Just as long as it took to tell her. Half an hour? I don't know. She even refused to make me a cup of tea.'

'Poor girl. And poor Terry. You've had more than enough for one day,' said Annie sympathetically. 'And now you've got a long drive back. I'll make you some tea and give you something to eat before you start your journey. Try to relax for a moment.'

After he'd gone, she'd sat waiting, worrying, but there was no telephone call. She dithered between driving over to check on Pippa, telephoning her, or leaving her to lick her wounds in private and without interruption. By Monday lunchtime she could bear it no longer. Guessing that Frances would be back from Wales, she dialled her number. It was Frances who answered the telephone.

'I'm fine,' she said in answer to Annie's question. 'We had a lovely weekend. Really, that house is just what we want. Yes. Pippa's OK. Looks very tired, actually. I haven't been in long. Did you want to speak to her?'

Annie assured her that she was just checking she was back safely, replaced the receiver and wandered out into the courtyard. She roamed about, unable to relax, and presently she fetched the car and drove out to Trendlebere.

Max and Hugh were in the middle of lunch but they made her welcome although she refused their offer of food.

Max studied her drawn face. 'Any progress?' he asked casually. 'Any more messages?'

She laughed and then, to her horror, found herself blurting out the whole story: the takeover, Robert's deception and collusion with Louisa, the postcard and, finally, Terry's visit. They stared at her, shocked. At the end, she dropped her face into her hands.

'I should never have told you,' she said. 'It's unforgivable of me. It was just . . . Oh, I don't know. It's just that I don't know what she'll *do*? How do you recover from a blow like that?'

'We knew some of it anyway,' said Hugh comfortingly. 'We were bound to want to know how it worked out. We'd have given you no rest until you'd told us.'

'Speak for yourself,' said Max blightingly, watching Annie. 'So Pippa knows the whole lot, does she?'

Annie nodded. 'He'd been so persuasive, you see. Terry had to show her the card to convince her.'

They both winced away from the brutality of it and Max remembered the look in Pippa's eyes when she'd thought, for one brief moment, that he was Robert.

'Poor Pippa,' said Hugh. 'What a bastard!'

'She had to know,' said Annie, as though convincing herself that her interference was justified. 'Imagine what he might have done if she'd gone back to him? I just wish I thought she had somewhere to go. Frances will be off in a month or so and then what? Poor girl . . .'

'She can come here,' said Hugh suddenly. 'She can come and live here. In one of the conversions.'

'Have you gone mad, boy?' Max was staring at him in disbelief. 'What d'you think I'm running here, for God's sake? A refuge for widows and orphans? I'm not a philanthropic society, you know. I'm trying to run a business.'

'I don't mean like that,' said Hugh impatiently. 'I meant that she can be our cook. She'd be perfect for it. She can live in and she'd be busy and have lots of people around. Just what she needs and it solves our problem, too.'

Annie and Max stared at him in silence and then looked at each other. Annie raised her eyebrows questioningly.

'I . . . I don't know.' Max frowned. 'Would it work?'

'Of *course* it would work!' cried Hugh enthusiastically. 'Why not?'

'She'd be lovely with the children,' admitted Annie. 'But I don't think she's a great cook.'

'Well, then,' began Max, almost relieved.

'She doesn't need to be a cook,' said Hugh contemptuously. 'It's not cordon bleu stuff. These are kids.

They'll want mountains of sausages and beefburgers and we can get those great big cans of soup like they supply to hotels. I've applied for our cash-and-carry card. It'll be simple. Anyone can do that sort of cooking.'

'Hang on,' said Max. 'Just hang on a minute. What about Rowley? He'll be running about. Getting in everyone's way.'

'Not necessarily,' said Hugh. 'The level outside the top floor of the barn can be paved and fenced. He'd be quite safe and out of the way when we're busy.'

Max looked at Annie, feeling himself outmanoeuvred. 'What do you think?'

'I think,' said Annie slowly, 'that she'd be just as good as anyone else who might apply for the job. If you get a young single girl, she'll want time off and there will be boyfriends or she'll leave to get married. Of course you might get a divorcee but then she might have children, too.' She shook her head. 'I just don't know.'

'I think she'd be great,' said Hugh stubbornly. 'And we've got no one else. It's fate. Go on, Max. Phone her up and ask her.'

'What, *now*?' asked Max. 'We need time to think about it.'

'No, we don't,' said Hugh. 'We need someone as a housekeeper. We know Pippa and we like her, she'd be great with the kids and she needs a home. Everyone's problems solved at one stroke.'

Max stared at their hopeful faces and, sighing heavily, got to his feet and went into the office.

'Brilliant!' Hugh's eyes gleamed. 'Just perfect!'

Annie remained silent. Things were moving a little too quickly for her liking. They looked up when Max returned, both trying to read his face. He looked cheerful.

'What did she say?' asked Hugh.

Max shook his head. 'Nothing doing,' he said, unable to totally conceal his relief. 'She says she doesn't think she's cut out for it.'

Hugh looked ludicrously disappointed. 'But why on earth not?'

Max shrugged. 'She didn't go into details. I told her to think about it.'

'Perhaps it was a bit quick,' suggested Annie. 'After yesterday, I mean. But bless you for thinking about it. It must be a comfort to her to know that someone wants her.'

'I'll go and see her,' announced Hugh. 'Talk her into it.'

'You'll do no such thing,' said Max roundly.

'No, you mustn't,' said Annie quickly. 'And for heaven's sake, remember to keep what I've told you a secret. Pippa would die if she thought I was telling everyone. I feel very ashamed of myself. I'm just so worried about her.'

'Give her time to think it over,' advised Max, looking at Hugh's frustrated face. 'Give us all time. Cup of tea, Annie?'

'No,' said Annie hastily and with some alarm. 'No, thanks. I must let you get on with your work.'

Max grinned maliciously, perfectly aware of her opinion of his tea. 'You'll have to get on to Perry,' he said, following her out. 'Tell him to pop round to Pippa and have a word in her ear.'

'"Oh, ye of little faith",' murmured Annie sententiously and he burst out laughing.

'Ask her to supper,' he said, becoming serious, 'and ask us, too. We'll sound it out better that way than going bull-headed at it. If she's had her confidence knocked she might not be ready to think about a job.'

Annie looked at him, surprised. 'I thought you didn't want her,' she said, touched by his concern.

'I want what's right for everybody,' he said irritably, disliking being forced into admitting that he cared about Pippa. 'I deal in facts. I like reality. Perhaps that's because I don't get my old dad chatting to me from beyond the veil.'

'Perhaps that's because he knows he'd be wasting his time,' retorted Annie. 'I don't suppose you ever listened to him while he was alive. Why should he bother now he's free of you?'

He was chuckling as he opened the car door for her and she drove away feeling much happier. She would take Max at his word and arrange a supper party – and the sooner the better.

'So what did Max want?' asked Frances curiously.

Pippa lifted Rowley into his highchair. 'He's offered me a job,' she said carelessly. 'As cook-cum-housekeeper-cum-just-about-everything.'

'Goodness!' Frances looked thoughtful. 'It wouldn't have been a bad idea, actually. If you hadn't been going back to Robert, that is.'

'I'm not going back,' said Pippa quietly, giving Rowley his spoon. 'I've changed my mind.'

'Not . . .?' Frances looked thunderstruck.

'No. I've given it careful thought over the weekend and . . . I don't truly feel that I can trust him. I'm not prepared to risk myself again.'

Frances tried to think of some suitable remark and simply shook her head. 'I'm so sorry you feel like that,' she said at last. 'Are you certain?'

'Absolutely certain.' Pippa bent over Rowley, terrified that she might break down into tears. 'Come on,' she whispered to him. 'Eat up.'

He smiled blindingly at her and obligingly swallowed his mince. 'Woglet eat,' he commanded. She held the spoon to Woglet's knitted lips, glad to keep her face turned away from Frances.

Frances decided that she'd better leave well alone. She'd vowed to stop interfering and knowing best but she wondered what Pippa would do once the farmhouse was sold. No wonder the poor girl looked washed out. No doubt she'd been brooding on it all weekend. Frances felt quite selfish, being so happy whilst Pippa was obviously having difficulty in coming to terms with her own situation. Frances wondered what had made her change her mind. Questions trembled on her lips but she resisted them.

'If that's the case,' she said cheerfully, 'perhaps you ought to think about Max's offer. Those flats he's building over the dormitories are really nice.'

'Can you see me being a cook, Frances?' asked Pippa despairingly. 'I'd be hopeless. I thought I'd look at properties over Ashburton way.'

'Near Annie,' said Frances with relief. 'What a good idea.'

Pippa tucked Rowley up for his rest and went downstairs to wash up. She felt as though she were functioning on autopilot, although her heart was heavy with anguish. Silently she went over and over the scene with Terry; agonised by the pain of Robert's duplicity; shuddering when she thought of how she had made love with him and how readily she'd been duped. She burned with humiliation when she thought of him, laughing about it with Louisa. 'She was a pushover . . .'

Pippa gave a low cry. She was hurting so much she could barely stand upright. How could she have been so taken in? To begin with it had seemed like a miracle: as though her fantasies had become realities. He had been so plausible, so tender . . . The tears poured down her cheeks and she prayed that Frances would not suddenly appear. Pippa buried her face in the tea cloth, trying to control herself. Soon she must tell Robert and then she must make plans. The money from the sale of the house in Farnham was sitting in their joint deposit account, gathering interest, and she must arrange with him to have her half paid into her own account. She had no compunction in taking her share. The legacy from her father had gone towards the purchasing and upkeep of the house in Farnham.

Drying her cheeks, she wondered how she would tell Robert; how she could bear to speak to him at all. She had already decided not to betray Terry's part in it. If only it could be over, finished – and yet some part of her wanted to talk to him, to hear how he explained himself and his actions. Did she hope that, even now, there might be some explanation? Pippa shook her head. The postcard destroyed any hope of that. 'Missing you. All love, Robert.'

Throwing down the tea cloth, Pippa ran upstairs, shut herself in her bedroom and gave way to a storm of weeping.

[illegible]

[illegible] conscience
[illegible] telephone [illegible] need to keep
[illegible]

Chapter Thirty-five

When Robert arrived back in London to find that Louisa, according to the woman in the flat below, had gone away quite suddenly on leave he was very put out. He'd managed to convince himself that her move to New York was simply to give him the time to gain his promotion and settle Pippa somewhere in the country. Once his wife was lulled into a false sense of security, and he'd proved himself in his new position, then Louisa would return and things would go on – not quite as before, perhaps – but they would be together. He was certain that she would be longing to hear how their plan had succeeded and he was puzzled and disappointed. He had hoped for praise and rewards and she hadn't even left a forwarding address.

Robert wandered about London and eased his conscience with spasmodic telephone calls to Pippa. He had to keep her warm; up to the mark. He looked into the housing question, selecting the details of several cottages in Hampshire and Surrey to send to her, and continued to wonder where Louisa had gone.

On Wednesday evening he telephoned to Devon. Frances was having supper with a friend and Pippa was alone. To begin with, he noticed nothing odd about her voice. He spoke tenderly to her and asked her if she'd come to any decisions as to where they should live.

'Yes,' she replied quietly. 'I'm going to live down here in Devon. I don't care much where you live, Robert.'

He was silent with shock. 'But, darling,' he said at last. 'What's all this about?'

'This is about you being a contemptible bastard,' she replied, still sounding quite calm. 'You deceived me and lied to me and I never want to see you again.'

'Wait a minute!' he cried, anxious lest she should hang up on him. 'What are you talking about? I love you . . .'

'Don't you dare say those words to me!' At last her voice was vibrant: alive with anger and pain. '*You* dare to say that after the unspeakable things you've done?'

'What have I done?' He tried to inject a note of humorous ignorance. 'Please, Pippa. Tell me.'

'"The citadel has just fallen",' she quoted. '"I've marked our bedroom on the front. She was a pushover but I couldn't have done it without your advice. Missing you. All love, Robert."'

Robert was dumbfounded. How on earth could she have seen the postcard? He tried to remember his actions. He'd posted it straight into the postbox. She couldn't possibly have seen it. For one crazy moment he wondered if Louisa had sent it to her. But why? His brain rocked.

'Wait,' he said, licking dry lips. 'Wait . . .'

'What for?' Her voice was scornful. 'More lies, more excuses, more deceits? How could you possibly explain away this postcard with a picture of the hotel in Salcombe, sent to Louisa Monday of last week?'

'Listen,' he said rapidly. 'You've got it all wrong. That's not about us. It's about a difficult client I've been dealing with. She decided to give me the account and I was letting Louisa know. She's been working on the case with me.'

He held his breath. Would she buy it? The silence seemed endless.

'Why did you mark our bedroom?'

He exhaled silently. She was going to fall for it. 'I can't remember, my darling,' he said caressingly. 'It's just a silly thing you do on postcards, isn't it? And you must remember I had other things on my mind. I was just obsessed with being with you again.'

'Is that why you said you were missing *her*? Why you sent her *all* your love?'

He swallowed. 'I . . . A complete aberration. This account is so important . . .'

'Don't you usually send that kind of communication by memo in the office? You'd been away a few days by then. You say the citadel has *just* fallen.'

'A figure of speech. And I was working on it while I was away. The client phoned me at the hotel . . .' He was sweating, the receiver slippery in his hand.

'Why didn't you tell me about the takeover by Harrison Pawley? Or your promotion?'

He was silenced. How could she know these things? he asked himself. Could it be possible that Louisa had betrayed him? But why?

'It didn't seem relevant,' he said. 'In light of us getting together again nothing seemed that important. Honestly,

Pippa, I don't know who you've been speaking to . . .' *Could* it be Louisa? Perhaps she had been taken with a fit of jealousy and had rushed down to Devon with the card. He had to know. 'Has Louisa been there?'

It was Pippa's turn to think rapidly. 'What if she has?'

'Then you mustn't believe a word she says,' he said quickly. 'She's terribly jealous of you and furious that we're getting back together.'

'That's not the way I heard it,' said Pippa slowly.

'Darling, please!' cried Robert. 'Please! Tell me what she said.'

'I've heard many, many things, Robert, which I believe are true.' Pippa's voice was serious. 'I'm giving you one last chance. I want the absolute truth. Only then can we go forward together. No more lies, Robert. Did you plan all this with Louisa when you heard about the takeover?'

Robert stood in anguished undecided thought. Was it best to tell the truth? She loved him, no doubt about that, and she was giving him a chance. Best, then, to tell the truth – up to a point – and explain the rest away as soon as he could. He'd say that he wanted them to get back together anyway; that the takeover had merely been the excuse that had given him the courage to approach her again; that he'd applied to Louisa for advice because he was so desperate to get her, Pippa, back that he didn't want to take any chances of getting it wrong; that the postcard had been written out of massive relief and joy . . . All these thoughts chased round in his brain. He'd *make* her believe him. He'd drive down tonight, dammit . . .

'Yes,' he said quickly. 'But . . .'

'No buts. And the postcard was about me?'

'Yes, but honestly, darling . . .'

'There. That wasn't too painful, was it?'

'Oh, darling.' He was glossy with relief. 'Oh, thank God. You see . . .'

'Yes, I see.' Her voice was low and hard. 'I see you're a double-dealing bastard. You're contemptible. An absolute swine. I never want to see you again and for two pins I'd phone Harrison and tell him just what kind of slime you are!'

The line went dead and, trembling, he replaced the receiver on its rest. Cursing his stupidity he paced to and fro, seeking a way out. Finally he was obliged to accept the fact that there was none. He'd shot his bolt. There was no point in phoning again or driving down to see her. He'd been fooled into telling the truth and it was over. But how, he asked himself as he paced, how had she known? Only Louisa could have betrayed him. But why? An idea slid into his mind. It was quite simple, after all. Louisa wanted him back. She'd regretted her impulse and was trying to drive a wedge between him and Pippa. Surely, though, Louisa must have realised that he'd have dropped Pippa flat if only he thought that he and Louisa could be together? Of course there was the problem of his promotion which would certainly go by the board if any of this got to Harrison's ears.

Robert flung himself into a chair and tried to think it through. Pippa's last threat had frightened him and, for most of the night, he sat slumped in his armchair, seeking a solution. By the morning he knew what he must do.

* * *

He managed to see Harrison first thing. The tall, gaunt, commanding figure surveyed him with easy friendliness.

'So what's the problem, Robert?'

Robert looked ill. Drawn and tired, he stared at his hands. 'Something rather awful has happened, sir,' he said shakily. 'I've been in Devon, as you know, with Pippa. She's . . . she's met someone else and she wants a divorce.'

'Dear God!' Harrison rose to his feet.

Robert managed a trembling smile. 'Sorry, sir. It's just . . .' He passed a hand across his brow. 'I . . . can't quite take it in. I've been trying and trying to persuade her to change her mind but she was absolutely brutal. And then there's Rowley.' He swallowed hard, wondering if he could manage a few tears to convince Harrison, who was known for his sentimentality in all matters related to the family.

Harrison pressed the intercom. 'Jean? Bring some coffee.' He looked compassionately at Robert. 'I just don't know what to say here.'

'No. no. There's nothing. It's just like she really wanted to hurt me. To make it as painful as possible.'

'And there's no chance she might be . . . ?'

'None,' said Robert quickly. Speed was of the essence and it was his weak point. He couldn't risk suggestions of time being given to reconciliation. 'She's . . . she's having his child.'

'Jesus!' muttered Harrison. 'And she seemed such a sweet kid. Hannah just adores her.'

'Yes, well.' Robert allowed himself a mirthless chuckle. 'She's always known how to act up to those around her. I've had rather a lot of trouble . . . Still, you don't want to hear my problems. It's just . . .'

He paused and they were both silent whilst Jean came into the office and put the tray of coffee on a low table. Harrison jerked his head towards the door and she went out. He began to pour the coffee.

'Just what?' he asked, passing Robert a cup.

'Thank you.' Robert sipped the hot fragrant liquid. 'I've given this a lot of thought since I got back,' he said, 'and I think that the best thing for me would be to go abroad for a while.'

'Abroad?' Harrison looked shocked. 'You mean you want to leave us?'

'No, no. Good grief, no!' There must be no doubt about that. 'It's just . . . I feel I want to get right away. Try to forget. You know?'

'Well, of course I can understand that.' Harrison looked thoughtful. 'But you don't want to burn any boats, my boy.'

'No, I realise that. And I wouldn't want to leave the company. It's been my whole life. Even more so now, of course. But . . . I really need a change of scene. I was wondering.' He stared up at Harrison with just the right amount of anxious desperation. 'Might you have any vacancies in your New York office?'

'I see what's in your mind.' Harrison nodded slowly, approvingly even. 'Well, several of your colleagues have gone out, of course, and one or two of our people back home are coming over here. I think it's an excellent plan, to integrate. I've brought Jean over with me and Louisa Beaumont's already left for New York.'

'Already . . .?' Robert gaped at him but luckily Harrison

was turning to refill his cup. He pulled himself together quickly. 'I didn't realise that Louisa was going. I'd heard the odd rumour, of course . . .'

'She said she'd got her reasons for wanting to get off,' said Harrison, 'and there was nothing to keep her here. At least there would be one friendly face to welcome you.'

'I don't know Louisa too well.' Robert appeared indifferent to Louisa's reasons for leaving, quite sure in his mind, however, that he was right and that jealousy had made her run away, having first tried to destroy his future with Pippa. 'Does this mean that you think that there might be a position for me, sir? Naturally, I wouldn't expect anything like the promotion I was in line for here.'

'There's always a place for a bright young man in my organisation, Robert,' said Harrison weightily. 'It needs thinking about and I can't promise you Head of Sales. It wouldn't do, to put you straight in over the heads of my staff there.'

'No, no. I quite see that,' said Robert hastily. 'I'd be so grateful . . .'

'Leave it with me and take things easy, you hear? Extend your leave and get your affairs sorted out. I'll be in touch.'

'Thank you, sir.' Robert appeared much moved and Harrison gripped his hand warmly.

'Come on over tonight for a drink,' he said, touched by Robert's plight. 'I may have news for you.'

Robert passed down the corridor, trying to keep himself from grinning. The sentimental old sod had fallen for it just as he'd hoped and, with luck, he'd be out in New York with Louisa by the end of the month; earlier if he had anything to do with it. As he went down in the lift and passed through the reception hall, he wondered why on earth Louisa had cut and run. His smile widened as he thought of her; suddenly jealous and angry with herself for pushing him back into Pippa's arms. The postcard must have been the last straw. Well, it would do no harm at all for her to suffer a few pangs of jealousy.

He stood on the pavement amongst the bustle and roar of traffic and wondered if he should telephone her. On the whole he thought not. Let her suffer a little; as she had made him suffer! It would all add to the welcome she'd give him when he arrived in New York, although she'd probably hear through the grapevine that he was on his way. He was surprised at how little he minded losing his promotion. He knew that he'd get there in the end. With Louisa beside him all things were possible. Robert dodged across the road, between the buses, and dived into the underground.

Chapter Thirty-six

Several weeks after her conversation with Robert, Pippa stood ironing in the kitchen whilst Rowley rode round and round on his tricycle, Woglet perched before him on the seat. Frances was upstairs, in the last throes of packing; outside, the rain poured down relentlessly. Pippa was trying to make up her mind to put in an offer on a small house in Haytor Vale. Annie had agreed that she and Rowley could move back to the cottage whilst the sale went through because in a fortnight Frances would be gone and the farmhouse occupied by its new owners.

Pippa smoothed the iron thoughtfully over a denim skirt. Everyone was being so sweet to her. They respected her decision to divorce Robert and no one had tried to talk her out of it or discuss it in any way. She was deeply grateful for this, being quite unequal to the task of explaining. Annie had invited her to supper with Max and Hugh and it had been a very light-hearted evening. Pippa had got through it quite adequately, laughing at their descriptions of life at Trendlebere as the opening of the school came closer and parrying their request that she should reconsider their offer. They didn't press her and she was amazed, though relieved, that they were unaware of the person inside her who was still shocked into a kind of numbness which was interspersed with bouts of anguished misery.

'Woglet needs ironing.' Rowley sat before her, astride his little tricycle, Woglet extended in one hand whilst the other twiddled up his hair.

'Poor Woglet!' Pippa brought her mind to bear on her son. 'It's much too hot. It would burn him.'

Rowley brooded on this, clutching Woglet to his chest so as to put his thumb in his mouth. Presently he shot off again at enormous speed, negotiating the table leg with accuracy and skill. The familiar plop of letters falling on the doormat carried him out into the hall where he collected up the post and brought it back to her. Pippa glanced idly at the envelopes and then peered more closely at a formal-looking letter from the bank. She was waiting to hear from her lawyer, regarding the removal of her share of the house funds into her private account. Maybe this was the long-awaited letter telling her that they had been paid in at last. Although why the bank should inform her . . . Pippa switched off the iron, pushed the ironing board well out of Rowley's way and slit open the letter. She frowned over the contents and then read it again more carefully.

'. . . we regret to inform you that, until funds are paid in to cover your overdraft, no more cheques will be honoured . . .'

She scrabbled quickly to look at the enclosed statement and caught her breath. No money had been paid in at the end of the last month and now, well into October, she was overdrawn. Obviously Robert must have forgotten to make his end-of-month payment, but with all that money sitting in their deposit account she felt that the bank might have been less official about it. Feeling cross, she took the letter out to the hall and telephoned the branch in Surrey. At length she spoke to the manager.

'But there *is* no money in your deposit account, Mrs March,' he explained rather coolly. 'Mr March withdrew it before he left for America. He told us that you were seeking a divorce and that you'd be making your own arrangements from now on.'

'*America*?' gasped Pippa. 'But what's he doing in America?'

'I understand he's been offered a position in the New York branch.' The manager, a friend of Robert's, had heard his version of the story and was on Robert's side.

'But how could he take the money? Half of it is mine.'

'It was in a joint account,' said the manager patiently. 'It only requires one of either of your signatures to withdraw it. I'm sorry.'

'I don't understand,' said Pippa with terror in her heart. 'Do you mean that there is no money at all?'

'No money at *all*,' confirmed the manager emphatically, 'and you have an overdraft.'

'Please,' Pippa said, 'please give me a moment. This has come as the most terrible shock. I had no idea that Robert was going to America. He didn't tell me.'

'When he spoke to me he said that you were seeking a divorce.' The voice was unsympathetic. 'That he had attempted a reconciliation which you had refused.'

Pippa opened her mouth to ask why Robert had confided in him and suddenly remembered that he and Robert were old squash partners. She took a deep breath.

'Please give me a few days,' she said as coldly as she dared. 'I promise to sort it out as soon as I can.'

Trembling she went back into the kitchen and sat down at the table. Rowley watched her for a moment and then, abandoning his tricycle, came to lean against her leg.

'Mummy read,' he requested anxiously.

'Oh Rowley.' She looked at him impatiently and then swallowed back her fear and made herself smile. 'In a minute. Go and tell Frances it's time for a coffee break.'

She heard him climbing the stairs laboriously, one step at a time, his childish treble uplifted. Presently Frances came pattering down, Rowley astride her hip. Her hair stuck out untidily and her face was damp with perspiration.

'I've finished the airing cupboard,' she announced triumphantly. 'Thank goodness I had that clear-out when Caroline got married.' She stared at Pippa's pale face. 'What's the matter?'

Pippa glanced meaningly at Rowley and Frances raised her eyebrows. '*Play school*!' she said promptly. 'Now what's big Ted up to today, I wonder?'

She carried Rowley off to the sitting room and Pippa heard the sound of the television. Frances returned and sat down opposite.

'What's up?'

Pippa shook her head in despair. 'You won't believe this.

Robert's gone off to America and he's taken all our money with him. Drawn out the lot from the deposit account.'

'*What*? D'you mean he's gone for good?'

'It seems so.' Pippa shrugged. 'My guess is that he's gone out to be with Louisa now he knows I'm not going back to him.'

'Has Louisa gone to America?'

Pippa remembered that Frances had no idea why she had changed her mind about going back to Robert. 'There's been a takeover by an American company,' she said briefly, 'and Louisa has taken up a post in their New York office.'

'I see.' Frances frowned. 'But are you saying that there's been an administrative mistake or that Robert's run out on you?'

'He paid no money in last month,' Pippa told her. 'I had all that expense with the car plus the bill from the storage company, so I was a bit low. I've just had a letter saying I'm overdrawn and the manager tells me that Robert has gone to America taking all the money in the deposit account and telling the bank that from now on I'm on my own.'

'But can he do that?' Frances was trying to take it in. 'Can he just draw your money out without any questions?'

'It's a joint account,' Pippa said wearily. 'It only needs one signature. It explains why my lawyer has found it so difficult to get a reply from Robert's lot. They probably can't trace him.'

'But you must *do* something!' cried Frances. 'Telephone

the office and ask for his address. He can't just disappear. What about Rowley?'

'He won't give a damn if he never sees either of us again,' said Pippa bitterly. 'This is to pay me out for turning him down.'

'You can't let him get away with it,' said Frances strongly. 'You must fight.'

'What with?' Pippa rubbed her eyes and began to laugh. 'It's almost funny, isn't it?'

Her voice was high and only just under control and Frances detected a note of hysteria.

'No!' she said sharply. 'It's not funny at all. Come on, Pippa. *Think*! Who could you talk to who will know the facts?'

Pippa gulped down a rising tide of uncontrollable mirth and stared at her across the table.

'There's Terry,' she said at last. 'Terry Cooper. He works with Robert. His wife and I are great friends.'

'Then phone him,' said Frances firmly. 'Go and do it now. You must have the office number somewhere?'

Pippa got up obediently, rummaged in her bag which lay on the dresser and went out into the hall. Frances sat perfectly still, listening to the rise and fall of her voice as her mind darted hither and thither.

'Oh Terry,' she heard Pippa say, 'oh no. Don't apologise. It was very brave of you to tell me. I'm sorry I was so beastly to you. It was just such a shock . . . I know but for you to come all this way and for me to be so horrid . . . He's gone, has he? But why? . . . He said that, did he? . . . No, don't say anything. Let them think it's the truth. It really doesn't matter any more . . . I hope you're right and she kicks him in the teeth . . . The thing is, he's drawn out all the money from the house and left us destitute. Hang on! . . .'

Frances heard her talking to Rowley who now appeared in the doorway. She got up quickly and held out her hand to him. Pippa's voice resumed the conversation, lowered now, and when she finally came into the kitchen Frances was playing with Rowley.

'So that's that,' she said, resigned.

Frances, who had been busily putting two and two together, looked up innocently. Pippa nodded to her above Rowley's blond head. 'Exactly as we suspected. Terry says it'll be a miracle if we can ever get anything back from him.'

Frances drew down the corners of her mouth. 'Blackmail?' she suggested. 'Would he want his employers to know that he's . . .' she glanced at Rowley, 'taken all the loot,' she said succinctly.

Pippa shook her head. 'I can't think,' she said dully. 'It's too much of a shock.'

Frances climbed to her feet and went to her, putting an arm about her. 'Sit down,' she said. 'It needs thinking about. Meanwhile you've got us. And Annie. Between us you'll be OK till we can sort things out.'

Pippa allowed herself to be pushed into a chair and ministered to. She had neither the will nor the energy left to think for herself.

Annie sat in the warm October sunshine, sipping a cup of coffee and waiting for Pippa. The house martin babies had flown at last: the cheeping and chirruping had ceased and there was an unfamiliar silence in the courtyard.

'Until next year,' murmured Annie. 'They'll be back in the spring.'

She ruminated over the past year and all that had happened in it. Frances was off to Wales any day now; Hugh was settled at Trendlebere. Only Pippa was still adrift, too shocked and hurt to take decisions and organise her life. Frances had come over for a farewell supper and Annie, seeing that she'd guessed most of the truth, told her the whole story.

'Poor Pippa,' Frances had repeated over and over. 'Poor, poor child. Whatever will she do? How do you find the confidence and self-esteem to pick yourself up after a blow like that?'

'She simply must,' said Annie. 'She mustn't waste her life. Especially not because of a shit like Robert!'

They'd embraced, promising trips to see each other, and Annie had gone back to her brooding.

'*Do* something!' she ordered Perry. '*You* said she mustn't go back to Robert. You made me get hold of Terry Cooper. So *do* something!'

Now, as she sat sipping her coffee, she remembered how unwilling she'd been to house Pippa and Rowley after their flight from Surrey. How long ago it seemed; how long since she'd enjoyed the absolute privacy she'd sought. How long, too, since she'd known that emptiness of heart or the weight of surplus, unrequired love.

'The only thing to do with love,' Perry had said, 'is to

give it away. No other use for it. Give it away. You get it back a hundredfold.'

Well, she'd done it – up to a point – and it was true that the terrible loneliness had passed; the feelings of futility and emptiness were sensations of the past. She still longed for him dreadfully, of course – nothing would change that – but she no longer felt alone. Surely there was nothing more for her to give? She'd agreed that Pippa and Rowley should come back to her until Pippa was sorted out and she intended to do everything she could to help her.

'Don't stint it!' Perry's voice seemed to echo from somewhere in the hall, as though he were passing up the stairs. 'The Lord loves a cheerful giver . . .'

The front door opened.

'Hi!' said Pippa. 'It's me.'

Annie hugged her, giving a quick glance up the stairs. Max was right: she was potty. She smiled quickly at Pippa and took her into the sitting room. The weather had been uncertain – dull mornings of rain, followed by mellow golden afternoons – and Annie had lit the woodburner, just in case.

When she brought the coffee, Pippa was sitting in Perry's chair. She smiled up at Annie.

'It's odd,' she said. 'I woke up this morning feeling more positive. Still undecided and frightened, but I had just a fleeting feeling that I would be able to cope after all.'

'Of course you will,' said Annie stoutly, kneeling on the rug beside her. 'I'm looking forward to having you both back again . . .'

'We're not coming,' Pippa said.

Annie gazed at her in consternation. 'Not coming?'

Pippa shook her head. 'I was almost decided. And then sitting here I knew. It was as if someone was telling me . . .' She looked puzzled.

Annie glanced round instinctively. 'Someone . . . ?'

'I'm going to take the job at Trendlebere,' said Pippa. 'I'm terrified but I'm going to do it.'

'Oh!' Annie kneeled up, the better to register her delight. 'That's wonderful. It's absolutely right, of course, I always knew that. Oh, thank God . . . !'

'But you'll have to help me.'

Annie sank back on to her heels, her joy subsiding a little. 'Help . . . ?'

'You've got to,' pleaded Pippa. 'Just until I know the ropes. I feel so frightened and so useless. My confidence has deserted me. Please?'

'But what can I do?' cried Annie. 'How can I help you?'

'You could come in part time,' said Pippa, seizing one of Annie's hands and holding it tightly. 'Just at mealtimes. Till I know I can do it. You remember what Robert used to say about my cooking?'

'Hugh said he'd help you,' said Annie feebly. 'Just tinned soup and sausages and things.'

'Please,' insisted Pippa, her eyes huge in her pale face. 'Just till I know I can?'

'Don't stint!' cried Perry encouragingly, passing the door, and going out into the garden. 'The Lord loves a cheerful giver . . .'

Annie's eyes filled with tears. 'Of course I will!' she said warmly. 'If you want me, of course I'll come. It'll be the most tremendous fun. You'll see!'

'Oh, Annie.' Pippa slipped to her knees, beside her on the rug, and they hugged and hugged. 'Bless you. I don't think I could do it without you.'

'You haven't got to,' said Annie cheerfully. 'Now drink up that coffee and I'll get us a drink. I need one, if you don't.'

Pippa gulped back her coffee and stood up. 'Not for me,' she said. 'I'm going straight up there now before I lose my nerve. Frances says that they haven't got anyone yet, but I don't want to miss the boat now I've decided.' She gave Annie another hug. 'Thanks. I feel so much better.' She hesitated by the front door. 'It's odd,' she said, puzzled, 'but I could have sworn that when I was waiting for you . . .' She shook her head. 'No. Forget it.'

Annie waved her off, went back into the kitchen and poured herself a large Scotch.

'You old bugger!' she muttered. 'Now see what you've done?'

She swallowed deeply, put her glass down on the terracotta tiles of the plinth and began to laugh with sheer happiness at the thought of the chaos and excitement ahead.

Hugh stood outside in the yard in the warm spring sunshine and surveyed the scene with satisfaction. It was just as he imagined it. The mini-bus was parked at the entrance to the open-fronted barn, the canoes were stacked against the wall whilst his horse, with two of the ponies in attendance, jostled at the gate of the nearest paddock. Soon the children would be here. There was another reason for his happiness. Hidden in his pocket, his fingers caressed a crisp envelope. A few weeks before, he'd received a letter from Lucinda. She was home from Geneva and had telephoned Frances to find out how things were with Hugh. Her feelings were unchanged and, with Frances's blessing, she had written to Hugh suggesting a meeting. Hugh's heart bounded upward with joy and he waved to Rowley, whose blond head could be seen bobbing in the fenced yard behind Pippa's flat.

Max came out of the house, the Mutt at his heels, and his eyes crinkled a little as he watched Hugh, accurately reading his thoughts. He leaned against the door jamb and gave himself up to a deep secret contentment. His dream had become a reality and, along with it, he seemed to have found himself a family. This hadn't figured in his plans. He'd always been more concerned with the building of the school, the planning of its itineraries, the prospect of offering children the opportunity to have fun, than with the personal aspect of the business. Now, along with a dog and some horses, he had staff: Hugh, who seemed a born organiser with a continual fund of ideas, endless energy and enthusiasm; Annie had taken over the administrative side of the business, demonstrating the practical efficiency she'd practised all her working life. Even Pippa was becoming a very creditable cook . . . Max gave an inward chuckle, remembering how the three of them had sat at the kitchen table, whilst Pippa, flushed and nervous, had cooked twelve breakfasts all at once – the maximum she'd ever be called upon to cope with – insisting that they ate four each. Rowley had accompanied the party with a rendering of 'Baa, Baa, Black Sheep' from his highchair whilst trying to force a sausage between Woglet's woolly lips. Afterwards, they'd revived an exhausted but triumphant Pippa with a large brandy . . .

Hugh turned and saw him. 'It's just as I imagined it,' he declared. 'The mini-bus, the canoes, the horses. Our cook is in residence and we've even got a part-time secretary. It's exactly right. Is this how you saw it from the beginning?'

'I could see the buildings,' Max admitted, 'and I could imagine the activities. But the staff and so on . . .' He shook his head. 'I never thought about that very much. It was just me and the school.'

'And now you've got us,' said Hugh blithely, as though it were a matter for congratulation and rejoicing.

Max bit back a smile. 'So I have,' he said sardonically. 'I was hoping for a quiet, obedient second-in-command and a nymphomaniac cordon bleu cook who could type. What do I get? I get a bossy, know-it-all partner, a neurotic cook with a monster of a child and a potty part-time assistant who chats to the dead. Not to mention a scruffy mongrel. Terrific!' He sighed heavily and with a great deal of self-pity.

Hugh pursed his lips and shook his head in mock sympathy. '*Sic biscuitus disintigrat*,' he murmured, with a resigned shrug.

Max looked at him suspiciously, eyes narrowed. 'OK,' he said reluctantly. 'I asked for it. So what does it mean?'

Hugh grinned. 'That's the way the cookie crumbles,' he said.

Looking Forward

Marcia Willett

Life at The Keep changes forever when Fliss, Mole and Susannah arrive in the summer of 1957. Their parents and elder brother have been killed in Kenya so the children are sent to their grandmother, Freddy, in Devon.

Freddy is no stranger to grief, but she would be lost without her devoted helpers, Ellen and Fox, who enable her to cope with this latest tragedy. And, above all, she looks to her brother-in-law, Theo, to guide her while the children heal their wounds and embark on the treacherous journey to adulthood.

Looking Forward is a magnificent novel, introducing us to the unforgettable Chadwick family.

'A genuine voice of our times' *The Times*

'A fascinating study of character' *Publishing News*

'Very readable' *Prima*

'Rich characterisation here, and not a little humour, too' *Manchester Evening News*

0 7472 5996 8

HEADLINE

Thea's Parrot

Marcia Willett

As soon as George Lampeter, a submarine commander, sets eyes on Thea, twenty years his junior, he's found his partner for life.

Just about everyone knows of George's long-standing affair with the intimidating Felicity Mainwaring. Her husband's death had prompted many to speculate that George would end up marrying his formidable mistress. No one expected this outcome more than Felicity herself and as her phone calls to George go unanswered she becomes increasingly anxious.

George somehow manages to duck Felicity's attempts to contact him long enough to marry Thea, and the couple embark on a harmonious life together in the heart of rural Devon. Then, in Thea's opinion, George begins acting strangely. If she had been more aware of her husband's past, she might have noticed his behaviour changing from the day that she told him an old friend of his had dropped in for a chat while he was in London – Felicity Mainwaring . . .

0 7472 4904 0

HEADLINE